the child between us

BOOKS BY ALISON RAGSDALE

ALISON RAGSDALE

the child between us

bookouture

Published by Bookouture in 2022

An imprint of Storyfire Ltd.
Carmelite House
50 Victoria Embankment
London EC4Y 0DZ

www.bookouture.com

ISBN: 978-1-80314-690-4
eBook ISBN: 978-1-80314-689-8

For my sisters. There are none better or more precious.

You know full well as I do the value of sisters' affections:
There is nothing like it in this world.

— CHARLOTTE BRONTË

PROLOGUE

It is the sweat that wakes me. The unnerving, clammy trickle between my breasts as I begin to pant, the air in the room seeming to pulse around me. My hair sticks cloyingly to the back of my neck as I throw the covers off.

Isla. My twin. The other half of my heart.

Your name floods my mind, along with images of us together as children, giggling as we kicked each other under the dining table, making indoor tents out of old sheets and riding our bikes along the river at Dunkeld. Next, I picture us, huddled together, freezing on the shore at Loch Lomond, as Mum and Dad – with ruddy cheeks and matching bright smiles – coaxed us into the icy water.

Born only minutes apart – we were inseparable – and yet I felt like a protector, a parent rather than a sister, for much of our lives. Even though I was a child, too, I felt responsible for you.

Then, I see you curled up at the end of my bed, on our seventeenth birthday, after I found you trying to take those pills. You were crying, hugging your knees to your chest, your painfully thin arms wrapped around your shins as you rocked yourself.

I never knew what to do when you got like that. When the heavy blanket of depression that hovered behind you took you over. Sometimes I resented the way Mum and Dad wrapped you in cotton wool, the constant allowances they made for you, when I was expected to just understand. Then, overtaken by guilt for my lack of compassion, I would lavish you with love and try to make you believe how special you were, to us all.

When your face would turn pale and you'd cry, for no apparent reason, I thought if I tried to make you laugh, held you close and sang to you, it would take away the hurt of that darkness buried deep inside, that tortured you so profoundly.

I was naïve, and too easily persuaded by you to paper over the cracks that those episodes would leave on your heart, for a lifetime. I even agreed to keep your secret from that awful night, not telling Mum and Dad, despite knowing I should.

Now, still trembling, I sit up in bed, my heart rattling in my chest, then I whisper your name. '*Isla. Where are you?*'

It has been almost six years since I've seen your face – an exact copy of my own. We have the same, deeply waved, mop of red hair that hangs below our shoulder blades, matching moss-coloured eyes, full lips, and high cheekbones dusted with freckles. We are identical in every way – on the outside.

It seems like yesterday when you left me that cryptic note at my studio, saying that you were sorry, but that this was the only way you could survive, before you disappeared.

Suddenly, my breathing becomes laboured, and I shove the duvet away and stand up, stumbling blindly towards the window.

Stuart is asleep, his left arm and leg dangling over the edge of the bed, and his mouth agape. His messy blonde curls obscure the chocolatey eyes that initially pulled me in to his nocturnal, musical world, as he snores softly into the pillow. He even sleeps messily, and I tut loudly as I trip over yet another abandoned shoe.

As I reach the window, I turn to face the bed, the windowsill hard against my hip. *Isla.* I scoop my hair up into my hands and hold it away from my clammy neck, and suddenly, with a choking certainty, I know that you need me, even more than you did on that night when we were teenagers. I have to find you.

I close my eyes, willing you to send me a signal, for our thoughts to meld as they did when we were children.

Just hold on, Isla. I'm coming.

1

Cassie Hunter pushed her front door open, careful to avoid the stray shoes that she knew her boyfriend Stuart would inevitably have left just inside the entrance. Her high-ceilinged, top-floor loft, in a block of converted nineteenth-century sailors' homes, overlooking Edinburgh's Leith harbour, had been taken over by Stuart's presence – and by his mess. It had been a gradual but pervasive invasion of her space over the past three months since he'd moved in – something she'd thought long and hard about before agreeing to. Her personal space was her sanctuary and trusting him enough to share it with him was not something she'd taken lightly – considering her past experiences.

Six years earlier, Cassie had had her heart broken by her first love and had struggled for months to regain her shattered confidence and begin to believe that she could rebuild her life. The experience had left her wary of fully trusting people and determined never to allow herself to be so vulnerable again.

After almost a year of throwing herself into work, and focusing on healing, she had taken a leap of faith and moved her growing jewellery business to trendy Leith – Edinburgh's former port district. She had set up a studio in a converted tobacco warehouse on Commercial Street – blowing her life savings, and taking a hefty mortgage on the loft, on nearby Shore.

She had met Stuart almost a year ago at a concert, and their relationship had moved fast – much faster than would have made Cassie comfortable in the past. His folk trio was going from strength to strength, booking many of the best venues in the city. He was a typical creative, with big dreams that drove him, and little time for, or understanding of, the effect that his tumultuous, nocturnal lifestyle had on those around him. But he had a lust for life that was contagious, and he was handsome, which didn't hurt. He could make Cassie laugh, too. A major factor in what drew her to him.

However, Stuart was also a slob. His clothes, shoes, slew of guitars and wads of music were habitually strewn across the floor, dumped on the coffee table, or left in corners, cluttering up the place. Cassie couldn't get used to seeing her orderly home in this unkempt state, and while she was happy that Stuart had moved in, his untidiness was a bugbear that was beginning to cause tension between them. Tonight, after a disturbed night's sleep, followed by a long day at the studio, her patience was at a particularly low ebb.

She had been working on the final designs for a new bracelet collection, long after the rest of her team had left to enjoy the remains of the weekend. When a launch was approaching, there were few days off to be had, for any of them. She had eventually walked home, in the pounding rain, watching the Saturday-night lights of the buildings surrounding the Water of Leith shimmering on the rippling surface to her left, like clusters of floating stars.

Now, as Cassie's eyes adjusted to the darkness of the room, the wall of windows at the far side of the living area framed the moody night sky. Sighing, she kicked a rumpled trainer that sat squarely between her and the fridge, where the last of a bottle of buttery Chardonnay was calling her name.

A few moments earlier, startled by the screech of a police siren, she'd twisted her ankle on the cobbled street outside her building, and now it was throbbing as she hobbled over to the kitchen area. She flicked on the light, slipped off her shoes, dumped her wet coat and bag on one of the high stools at the long, marble-topped island and opened the fridge.

Grabbing the wine bottle, a glass, a bag of frozen peas and a tea towel, she hopped over to the sofa. Sinking into the soft leather, she wrapped the peas in the towel, then put her foot up on the coffee table, knocking some sheets of music onto the floor. As she moulded the cold parcel around her ankle, the shock of the chill on her skin made her gasp.

As she poured the remainder of the wine into the glass and took a long swallow, her mind went back to the previous night, and to her sister, Isla. Waking like that had really thrown Cassie, the sense that Isla was in trouble so overwhelming that Cassie had been unable to go back to sleep. Having no means of contacting her sister, at 5 a.m. Cassie had showered and dressed, quietly tiptoeing out of the flat without waking Stuart, so that she could work for a couple of hours at the studio alone, before the team arrived.

Her day had fast become so hectic that she hadn't had a chance to try to trace Isla, but Cassie had been unable to get her sister out of her mind. Now, with Stuart playing at a gig in the Edinburgh Festival until the wee hours, his absence, and the associated silence, provided the perfect time to try again.

Cassie wasn't sure why she'd never told him about her twin, but what she did know was that – despite her initial efforts to find Isla after she disappeared – Cassie was ashamed about the amount of time that had gone by since she had seen Isla, as if it was Cassie's fault in some way. Another part of her was still hurt, and angry, that Isla had simply walked away without providing a clue about where she was going, or why she was leaving Edinburgh so suddenly. It was typically Isla – an inward-looking decision that had left her family both confused and devastated.

Shifting her foot, Cassie adjusted the ice pack, then pulled her phone from her pocket. Across the living area, her grandmother's carriage clock was ticking on the floating shelf above the wood stove, and a faint woody smell lingered in the room from the last time they'd lit the pot-bellied heater some weeks ago – during a summer storm, not unusual for August in Edinburgh.

As she stroked the screen of her phone, the display glowing in the dimly lit room, Cassie frowned. The last number she had for Isla was no longer in service and, other than that, she had nothing to go on. Over five years ago, Isla had walked out of her job at an art gallery on Rose Street, with no explanation. She had left the note for Cassie, and a similar one for their parents, Russ and Sadie. Heartbroken, they had tried for years to locate their daughter, with no success, even with the help of an investigator. Isla had disappeared without a trace.

When Russ had died suddenly two years ago, Sadie, wanting to be closer to Cassie, had sold the family home in Dunkeld, and now lived in a pretty, light-filled flat near Leith Public Library. Thinking about it, another wave of frustration swept through Cassie. Isla had an artful way of avoiding things that she didn't want to deal with, and often, especially in their teen years, Cassie had had to step in. Unable to bear seeing their parents worrying, yet again, about their moody daughter, Cassie would compensate for Isla's withdrawal by being overly bright, cracking silly jokes and playing the fool. Her antics generally worked, cheering her parents while allowing Isla to take herself away somewhere to brood, until she could rally, and re-join the family.

Cassie had often wondered if her parents had deliberately

called Isla after a remote island, sensing that this daughter would want to isolate herself from them at times. While the notion was somewhat far-fetched, it had become a self-fulfilling prophecy.

When Russ had passed away, Sadie had fallen apart, so Cassie had taken over – managing all the legalities, arranging the funeral and reception afterwards. Then she had juggled the demands of her business while spending a month living with her mother, helping her work through all the heartbreaking bureaucracy of death.

As she remembered that time now, not for the first time, Cassie wondered if Isla even knew that their father was gone. Cassie had imagined Isla, in a long dark raincoat, hovering behind the small crowd of friends gathered at Russ's graveside. Cassie had even turned around several times, in the hope of catching a glimpse of her sister's outline, but Isla had not been there.

A familiar flicker of hurt made Cassie close her eyes for a second, then she focused on the phone again. Tapping the search engine icon, she frowned. How did you even start to find someone who so obviously didn't want to be found?

Stuart slammed the front door, bringing Cassie bolt upright in bed, her heart racing. As she squinted at the clock on the bedside table, the display saying 5.59 a.m., she shoved the curtain of hair away from her face and blew out a long breath.

As she listened to him bumping around in the kitchen, dumping his guitar cases, and yanking open the fridge door, she threw off the duvet and sat up, spreading her toes wide on the cool, wooden floor. Picturing him grabbing the orange juice and drinking it straight from the carton, she grimaced, and circled her head until her neck popped.

'Stuart, you bugger. Do you have to make such a racket?' she called out. 'You're worse than a herd of elephants.'

'Sorry, gorgeous. I was dying of thirst.' He threw the door open and crossed the bedroom, his lean frame outlined in black jeans and a graphic T-shirt, his denim jacket dangling from his hand. The chocolatey eyes took her in, scanning her features, as she stood and slipped her robe on and eased the curtain of hair out from behind the collar. 'Don't get up yet.' He tossed his jacket towards the low, tartan-covered bench that sat under the window, then he sucked in his cheeks and took up a GQ model pose that always made her laugh. As the coat missed the target and landed in a pile on the floor, Cassie closed her eyes rather than say something. 'I was hoping for a cuddle,' he whispered, employing, as Cassie called it, his best bedroom voice.

'Now I'm awake, I might as well get moving. I've got to get to work early.'

'But it's Sunday,' he whined, pouting theatrically.

'The new collection is almost finished, and I promised Syd the final drawings today if he's going to get them rendered and into production in time for Christmas.' She smiled fondly at Stuart as she padded over to the window and began to draw the long, linen curtains. 'You know what it's like around a launch.'

Outside, the morning was already surprisingly bright. The pinkish light bounced off the amber-coloured stone fascia of the warehouse across the body of water that flowed in from the North Sea. Below the window, the row of familiar houseboats was lined up, stem to stern, now serving as offices for various businesses – their reflections bleeding into the water beneath them like a fiery Turner painting.

Cassie loved this view, and would often stand and soak it in, her mind finding a place of rest that little else could provide in her hectic life. Each time she stood here, her somewhat risky investment in the loft made increasing sense, and she'd smile to herself, feeling beyond fortunate.

As she scanned the boats below, Stuart's arms circled her waist from behind. He pressed his body in close to hers, pushed his chin into the soft muscle of her shoulder, as she caught a waft of his musty breath. His lips brushed her cheek, and the tiny hairs on her arms stood to attention, as always happened when he touched her.

'I really have to get ready for work, Stu.'

'But I'm irresistible.' He laughed softly. 'You know it's true.'

She reached around and squeezed the back of his neck. 'Not *that* irresistible.'

He sighed, dropped a kiss on her jaw and moved away. 'I'm pretty shattered after last night, anyway.' He yanked his T-shirt out of the waistband of his jeans. 'The crowd was insane. We did four encores, and they were still stomping their feet when we finally walked off stage.' He beamed, his eyes creasing at the edges as the childlike dimples at either side of his wide mouth puckered his shadowy, unshaven cheeks.

'That's great, love.' She smiled, pulling the belt on her robe tighter. 'You'll need to get some sleep before tonight.' She nodded at the bed as he tossed his T-shirt onto the floor and walked towards the bathroom, wiggling his backside comically. 'Stuart Macpherson, you are such a messy sod.' She lifted the shirt and stuffed it into the laundry basket behind the door.

'All part of my charm,' he called from the bathroom as the overhead shower began to thunder water into the old, cast-iron bath.

'Yeah, I don't think so.' She laughed, catching her reflection in the mirror above the long, narrow dressing table that sat on the opposite wall to the bed. Running a finger under each mossy eye, as always happened when she looked at herself, an image of Isla's face flashed brightly, the slight frown that permanently resided above her sister's brow, the nervous way she'd suck in her bottom lip and cover her mouth with her fingertips when she spoke.

Cassie took a deep breath. As soon as the world was fully awake, she needed to find a way to locate her twin.

By 7.30 a.m., Cassie was walking into the bright studio on Commercial Street, a covered coffee cup in one hand and her bulky canvas holdall in the other. She didn't subscribe to handbags, finding them pretty but utterly useless in terms of space, and as a good part of her world was carried on her shoulder, day-to-day, it seemed only fitting to give it room to breathe.

As she crossed the open-plan studio, passing the two high drawing tables she and her team would work at, collaboratively, discussing designs and materials, she caught a waft of the stale coffee sitting in the machine that she'd forgotten to throw away when she'd left the previous night. Making a mental note to do so now, she took a sip of her hot latte.

At the opposite side of the room, next to the glass partition that separated Cassie's tiny, private workspace from the rest of the studio, was the bank of sophisticated computers where her business partner, Syd, a South African transplant from Johannesburg, worked.

Cassie and Syd had gone to Edinburgh College of Art together and had soon become friends, after discovering their mutual love of working with metals, crystals, and semi-precious stones. When she'd decided to start her small, bespoke jewellery company seven years earlier, at just twenty-two, she'd asked Syd to join her, and they'd been best friends and business partners ever since.

He was an avid gardener and kept her supplied with soft fruit and tomatoes almost year-round, and when he wasn't at work, or in his greenhouse, he was dancing at a local salsa club. She admired and rather envied his zest for life, his ability to laugh at himself and his huge heart, that had been broken more than once in the time they'd known each other. Syd loved large, and hard, and consequently he threw himself into relationships like, as he aptly put it, a bungee jumper leaping off a bridge.

Hector, their twenty-four-year-old marketing executive, a keen surfer, and novice bagpipe player from Fife, used the other workstation. He had joined the company two years earlier after a year wandering around Australia, where he'd acquired several Aboriginal tattoos and a slight Aussie twang to his accent.

It was a small but close-knit team, and they'd taken the company from strength to strength. They now supplied distinctive, handmade pieces online, to Edinburgh's Jenners – the landmark department store – and several small jewellery shops in Edinburgh, Glasgow, Birmingham and, most recently, Liberty of London.

Cassie pulled the chair out from behind her desk and dumped the holdall on the ground. Shrugging off her jacket, she draped it over the back of the chair and turned towards the small kitchen area, intending to make some fresh coffee before Syd arrived. As she made to cross the studio, she heard her phone ringing in her bag. Turning back, she fished around in the holdall until she found it. Pulling it out, she saw a number she didn't recognise from an unfamiliar area code. On the point of ignoring the call, which she suspected was another telemarketing attempt, an image of Isla's face materialised again – the eyes wide and beseeching, and the mouth pinched into a narrow line.

Her heart skipping, Cassie answered. 'Hello?'

'Hello. Is this Miss Cassandra Hunter?' The voice was mellow and unfamiliar.

'Yes, this is Cassie. Who's speaking?' She frowned, holding the phone away from her and switching to speaker mode.

'My name is Ian Bannister. I'm calling from Brock and MacNair, we're solicitors on the Isle of Lewis.' His accent was unusual, the a's sounding flat and the r's guttural.

Surprised that a solicitor would be working on a Sunday,

Cassie frowned, letting the information sink in for a second or two, curious and yet suddenly afraid of what was coming next – certain that she did not want to hear it.

'Miss Hunter?'

Cassie nodded. 'Um, yes. What can I do for you?'

The man cleared his throat. 'I have some news...' He hesitated. 'I'm afraid I have some distressing news for you.'

The gathering knot of anxiety under Cassie's breastbone tightened as she held the phone closer to her mouth. 'What news?'

'Miss Hunter, I wonder, are you alone?'

'Yes, I am, but what does that matter?' she snapped, immediately regretting her tone. 'Look, I'm sorry. Please just tell me what's happened.' She began to pant softly, her tongue feeling spongy, and the walls seeming to lean in towards her as she racked her brain, searching for a clue as to what this man might have to say.

'Could you perhaps call someone to be with you?' He coughed. 'I'm afraid it's not—'

'Just tell me, Mr Bannister. Whatever it is, just say it.' Her breathing was ragged now as she dragged the chair out and slumped into it, her elbows thumping onto the top of the desk.

'It's about your sister.'

As the sound of crashing waves flooded Cassie's head, she closed her eyes and waited, her breath held hostage by the lump in her throat. *Isla*.

2

Cassie opened her eyes, scanning the room, looking for something to anchor herself to before the tidal wave hit. Isla's face was now etching itself on the window across the studio, hovering like a ghostly backdrop to Cassie's view, wherever she looked.

As she forced a dry swallow, the sense of foreboding she'd had, ever since waking in a panic the previous night, twisted dangerously in her core.

'What's happened to her?' she croaked.

Ian Bannister cleared his throat awkwardly. 'I'm afraid there was an accident. Miss Hunter, I'm sorry to tell you that your sister has passed away.'

Cassie's free hand clamped over her mouth as she felt the air being sucked from her. *Isla.* This couldn't be right. It had to be a mistake. As she panted into her palm, suddenly swirling through her mind were images of a crumpled car, smoke spiralling up from its bonnet, then, a bicycle, its wheels twisted, and its frame bent as it lay by the side of a misty, one-lane road. She shook her head, trying to clear the gruesome snapshots she'd conjured as she stared out of the window, the sky tinged with pink as the sun hovered behind a veil of frothy cloud. It was paradoxically and cruelly beautiful when nothing should ever look that perfect again.

'Miss Hunter?'

Her insides quivering, Cassie sat up straighter. 'Yes, I'm here,' she whispered. 'How did it happen? When?' Her voice failed her.

'Yesterday, here on the island.' He paused. 'Miss Hunter, it appears that she drowned at the beach near her home. I'm terribly sorry.'

As Cassie blinked repeatedly, the information filtered through her addled brain. *Yesterday*. When she'd woken, knowing that Isla needed her. Of course. *At her home on the island*. What was Isla doing on Lewis? *Drowned*. Of everything this faceless man had just said, this was the only part that felt credible, Isla having always been a nervous swimmer, and that fact brought Cassie's eyes closed once more.

Now, the images she was seeing became uglier, and as tears began to course down her cheeks, Cassie grappled with the onerous thought that was pressing in. Was it possible that Isla had finally finished what she'd started twelve years earlier, before Cassie had knocked the pills from her hand, wrapped Isla in a blanket and rocked her as she'd cried herself to sleep? A sleep she would wake from, profoundly damaged and changed, forever. As Cassie relived that dreadful night, memories of their teen years came cascading back, transporting her through time as she pressed her eyes tighter, and willed them away.

Since their early teens, Isla had developed a crippling lack of self-esteem that had taken on weight and depth the older she got. Rather than grow out of it, she had seemed to grow beneath it, like grass spreading under a plastic film, desperately seeking the light but unable to break through the invisible barrier above. This pattern had followed Isla into her twenties, often keeping her at home in front of the TV while Cassie was out partying –

something that Cassie had only occasionally felt guilty about back then. Then, a few months after their twenty-third birthday, Isla had disappeared from her life, without a trace – until now.

'Miss Hunter? Are you all right?' Bannister sounded anxious.

'I'm here.' Cassie gulped, her throat constricting, and her chest aching as if she'd been thumped. 'Who found...?' The question just wouldn't form itself. She needed to know what had happened, but, at the same time, she couldn't bear to know – the details already taking on a hard-edged form that she would carry in her heart forever more.

'I think it would be better to discuss everything in person. Are you able to come to Lewis, to settle Isla's affairs?'

Hearing him say her sister's name was a jolt, a reminder of a sound that, unless she or her mother uttered it, from now on, would cease to exist in the world outside their hearts.

As she fought to control her breathing, she swiped her wet cheeks and shoved a long twist of hair behind her shoulder. 'Come to Lewis?' She tried to picture the remote island, with its white sandy beaches and mysterious standing stone circles, that she'd only seen photos of.

'Yes, there are a number of things we need to address.' He paused. 'But it'll have to be done in person.' He stopped. 'You are her executor.'

Surprised that Isla had named her rather than their mother, Cassie tried to picture Sadie, the narrow shoulders hunched under the ubiquitous camel-coloured cardigan. Cassie saw her mother's crisp, strawberry-blonde curls lank and separating, and the wide-set, sky-blue eyes full of agony and confusion. She pictured her mother, heartbroken and adrift, standing in some drab bedsit, amidst Isla's mess of clothes, and the piles of magazines that, once read, Isla could never part with, and the image was blinding.

Sadie had never recovered from her husband's death, becoming reed-thin and watery-eyed and withdrawing from the various social activities that she'd once enjoyed. But despite her heartbreak, and Isla's mysterious disappearance, Sadie's two girls had remained her world. With Isla's absence a painful burden they had shared, Cassie had become more of a caretaker than daughter to Sadie, and when Cassie let herself be honest, she missed the time when her mother had been her rock.

Sadie was the only person who was able to tell Cassie and Isla apart, an ability that their mother treasured, but that, tragically, she'd never be tasked with again, and accepting that cut deep into Cassie's centre. With everything she didn't know, Cassie was certain that she needed to find a way to protect her already fragile mother from as much of this pain as she could. Snapping her back to the present, Bannister spoke carefully. 'So, when do you think you might be able to come, Miss Hunter?'

Cassie wiped her nose on the back of her hand, scanning her desk for a tissue. Her world had grown increasingly hectic over the past few months, with Stuart moving in and then her preparing for the launch of the new jewellery line, and the thought of going away now, at the worst possible time, was inconceivable, but even as she had the thought, she was racked with guilt. How had she and Isla grown so distanced, so estranged, that Cassie hadn't known where Isla was or how she'd been living her life? The very least that Cassie owed Isla was to go to where she had lived for the last five plus years, perhaps see where she had worked, the streets she had walked along, and maybe made new friends – take in the place where her sister had spent her last moments. Picturing it, Cassie could not stop the forces that had been building inside her. The sob, a harsh, gulping hiccup, seemed to float across the studio, like a cloud of toxic vapour.

'Miss Hunter, I'm so sorry.' Ian Bannister's voice was full of concern.

Cassie shook her head, sniffing loudly. 'I'll look at my schedule and make arrangements to come as soon as I can.' She nodded to herself, standing up, then clamping her icy fingers around the edge of the desk. 'Can you please text me your contact information, address, et cetera?'

She walked unsteadily to the window and, leaning against the sill, looked down at the glittering water below. Several people were already walking along the waterside path, some carrying paper coffee cups much like her own, and others talking into their phones, or to the person next to them, all such normal images of a morning – like any other morning that she'd observed from this window. But as she blinked her vision clear, Cassie knew that nothing would ever look normal to her again. The universe was dented, Isla's absence leaving a void inside her that nothing, and no one else, could ever fill.

Stuart had been asleep when Cassie had blundered back into the loft. She'd left a brief note for Syd at the studio, saying she'd had an emergency and would call him later, locked up and rushed back along Commercial Street, oblivious to the stares of the people she'd passed as tears had rolled unchecked down her cheeks.

As she'd crossed the bridge to Shore, she'd looked over at her loft windows, seeing the curtains drawn once again, and pictured Stuart in bed with the covers pulled up over his head, snoring loudly into the feathers.

Upstairs, she'd dumped her coat and bag inside the front door, walked straight into the bedroom and flipped on the light, and now, Stuart was groaning under the quilt. 'Turn it off. I just got to sleep.'

'Stuart, please get up. I need to talk to you.' Her voice was ragged, her breathing shallow. 'Stuart?'

He flicked the duvet away from his face and shielded his eyes from the overhead light. 'What is it? I'm knackered.' He yawned, taking a few moments to register that she had not moved or said anything more. As his eyes opened fully and he took her in, realisation dawned. 'What's up? Is something wrong?' He sat up, running a hand through the mop of curls that hung around his face in a little-boy-lost kind of way. 'Cassie?'

She forced her legs to work, putting one foot carefully in front of the other, feeling the slight rise in the floorboards on her side of the bed and keeping her eyes glued to the ground. Reaching the bed, she crawled on top of the covers, fresh tears blinding her to Stuart's open arms.

'Cassie, what's going on? You're scaring me.' He leaned forward, his arms going around her and then drawing her into his bare chest. 'Talk to me, gorgeous.'

Curled into him, she began to talk, at first haltingly between gasps, then more slowly and calmly, as the whole story of Isla unfolded. As she told him about their childhood, Isla's moods, her sadness that had seeped into the whole family at times, Stuart began to shift under her arm, his body tensing as she told him how much guilt she felt now, over everything that had happened in the past to distance her from her twin.

'I feel so empty, as if my innards have been scooped out.' She hiccupped, pressing a palm to her stomach. 'I should have tried harder to find her.' She shook her head. 'She and I were connected in a way that I can't describe. Twins is more than siblings, Stuart. We were two faces of the same person.' She heaved herself up to sit next to him, scraping her hair away from her tacky cheek as he turned to her. 'Does that make sense?'

She looked over at his face, the dark brown eyes hooded as

he frowned slightly, as if unsuccessfully trying to decipher what he was hearing.

'All this time and you never told me you had a twin.' His frown deepened. 'Why did you hide that?'

She met his eyes, seeing a wash of confusion. She didn't blame him. It had been stupid to pretend that her life was simple – a case of what you see is what you get. It had never really been that way, with Isla in the mix, and now never would be again. 'I don't know. Perhaps I wanted you to think my life was straightforward. No skeletons, so to speak.' She shrugged miserably.

He tipped his head to the side, the trademark dimples framing his mouth. 'None of us have straightforward lives, Cassie. If we think we do, we're either lying to ourselves or have lived small.' He laid his palm on her thigh. 'So, what now?' He crossed his legs under him, the duvet draped across his knees like a tent.

'I have to go to Lewis, see her solicitor and settle her affairs.' She gave a juddering sigh. 'I'm not sure exactly what that involves, but I need to go and get it done, and I can't let Mum come with me. It'll be too distressing for her.' She swallowed over the lump in her throat.

'Are you sure that's wise?' he frowned.

'Yes. I need to figure out what happened, then find a way to tell her that won't send her tumbling back to where she was after Dad died.' She shook her head miserably. 'It's going to break her.'

'So, when will you go?' He slid to the edge of the bed and stood up, his boxers hanging low around his narrow waist.

'As soon as I can get it organised.' She shifted backwards and leaned her head against the headboard. Everything ached – her neck, her back, the tight rope of muscles across the tops of her shoulders, even her eyeballs were throbbing. 'Maybe even tomorrow.' She eyed him as he kicked a T-shirt across the room and dragged a drawer open, looking for a clean one.

'Right.' He turned his back on her and pulled on the T-shirt. 'The sooner you go, the sooner you'll be home, I suppose.' He turned to face her, his mouth dipping at the edges in an exaggerated, clown-like way.

For a moment, Cassie was unsure whether he was genuinely upset, or was pulling a face to try to cheer her, then just as she decided that it didn't matter either way, her phone rang in her bag, out in the hall. Instantly, she knew that it was her mother, as Sadie always called her on a Sunday morning, around this time, to confirm that Cassie was still coming for lunch. Cassie's determination to protect her mother from something that she knew she couldn't, for long, raised her heart rate to a clatter as she scrambled off the bed and darted along the hall.

As she pulled the phone out of her bag, Sadie's photo pulsed on the screen, a broad smile splitting her oval face as she sipped on a drink, with two colourful straws in it. Cassie had snapped the shot the previous summer when she'd taken her mother to Loch Lomond for a long weekend, at a posh, spa hotel.

How on earth could Cassie find a way to tell her what had happened, without crushing any remaining spirit left in Sadie? And what would losing one of her precious daughters do to her poor mother's brittle state of mind?

3

The following morning, the flight to Stornoway had taken less time than Cassie had expected but had been a bumpy ride that had left her queasy and desperate to leave the small plane. She'd been filled with a mixture of dread at what was to come on the island and self-doubt at having hidden the truth from her mother the previous day on the phone, less than convinced that she'd done the right thing, coming to Lewis alone. But it was too late to go back. Once she'd handled all the legalities, and arranged to have Isla's body brought home, she would tell her mother in as gentle a way as possible, but for now, Cassie needed to concentrate on the task at hand.

Now, walking across the car park at the small airport, the morning was crisp and cool, and as she squinted into the sun, she was annoyed that she had not thought to bring her sunglasses. The light here seemed to have a different quality to that of Edinburgh. There was a clarity to the sky that made her stop for a few moments next to the small Ford she'd rented, her chin lifting as she took it in. Beneath the slightly acrid airport smells, the air was laced with something floral that reminded her of her mother's perfume, and as Cassie tried to identify its source, Isla's image came to her again. This time, Isla was smiling, her hair lifting behind her in a thick red curtain as she stared out at the ocean, her profile serene and her cheeks smooth and dry.

Even as Cassie tried to focus on the practicalities that lay ahead, her heart was breaking, and a sense of bone-deep loneliness – of being cast adrift – that she'd never felt before had taken up residence in her chest, seeping up into her throat until she could almost taste it.

Her eyes filled again as she tossed her holdall onto the back seat, then got into the car and closed the door, just as the thrum of another plane, preparing to land, hummed above her head.

Twisting the rear-view mirror towards her, she ran a finger under each swollen eye and tucked a stray twist of hair back into the high bun she'd secured with two mother-of-pearl inlaid chopsticks that had been Isla's. As she let her fingers linger on the smooth sticks, she swallowed back the insistent press of tears and pulled out her phone.

Ian Bannister's assistant, Heather, had sent her their address in Stornoway, and the plan was for Cassie to go to the office first, to meet with Ian, go through the necessary paperwork and pick up the keys to Isla's place. Cassie intended on going on to her hotel to check in, then go to Isla's home that evening. While Cassie had no idea how Isla had been living, her guess was it would be in a minimalist flat of some kind, small and simple to keep, with easy access to the shops for all the junk food Isla loved so much.

Cassie's map app showed Bannister's office as nine minutes away and, checking the time, she calculated that she should be fine to seek out some coffee on the way and still be there by 10 a.m., as arranged. She had hardly eaten since receiving the news about Isla, unable to force anything past the lump in her throat, and today was no exception, but a hot drink and a shot of caffeine now felt essential.

The short drive through Stornoway was relatively easy. Having left the slightly more stark, industrial area around the airport, the roads became pleasantly quiet, and tree lined. The houses Cassie passed were a variety of styles, but many of them were either of pale grey stone, or brick, most with stepped gables, enclosed front porches and peaked, dormer windows on the upper levels. Most of them had colourful, well-tended gardens behind low stone walls topped by wrought-iron fencing, and as Cassie passed, she tried to imagine Isla living in any one of these cosy-looking homes. Could Isla have found a home here? Cassie found it hard to see her somewhat bohemian sister feeling comfortable in this sleepy, island neighbourhood.

Finding herself on James Street, Cassie soon spotted a parking space near the solicitor's office, close to the Stornoway Ferry terminal. As she turned off the engine and gave her puffy face one last glance in the mirror – the pink nose, her green eyes red-rimmed and darkly shadowed – she sighed. Even her usually crisp white shirt was unironed, and her tan linen jacket badly rumpled from the journey. She was a wreck and, what's more, she couldn't care less.

Spotting a café opposite where she had parked, she dragged her bag across her and got out of the car, her legs feeling heavy and cumbersome.

Heather was impressively tall, at least six feet. A slender, Amazonian type with kind brown eyes, a mop of dark-blonde curls streaked with grey at her temples and a criss-cross of – what Sadie referred to as – gin-drinker wrinkles around her mouth and cheeks. Cassie guessed that Heather was in her late fifties as she welcomed Cassie, and then ushered her into an overly warm office, just off reception.

'Would you like something to drink?' Heather's accent had the same flat a's and rounded r's as Ian Bannister's.

Cassie shook her head. 'Thanks, but I got myself a coffee across the street. Had a caffeine emergency.' She tried to smile.

'Right. Totally get it.' Heather rolled her eyes. 'Daily occurrence, here.' She swept a hand around the low-ceilinged office. There was a long window overlooking the road, floor-to-ceiling shelves jammed with leather-bound books, a row of battered metal filing cabinets along the wall behind them and a well-worn leather-topped desk, stacked with several piles of manila folders. Some had their contents fanning out from between the flaps, threatening to escape the pile at any moment, and flutter down onto the floor. Cassie could smell the traces of cigar smoke, but from long ago, perhaps trapped in the heavy tartan curtains that bracketed the window.

There were two wood-backed chairs in front of the desk and Heather gestured to one of them. Suddenly exhausted, Cassie sat down as Heather circled the desk, her back now to the window.

'I'm afraid Ian's been called away to a family emergency. He asked me to apologise for him.' She looked embarrassed, her cheeks colouring as she lifted a file from a pile on the desk, then took a brown envelope from inside it. 'He suggested that, in the meantime, you take these and perhaps pop out to your sister's house.' She pulled a metal ring out of the envelope with two keys on it, one that appeared to be antique with a long shaft and a classic gap-tooth arrangement at the end. 'It's about an hour from here, but it's a lovely drive.' She smiled at Cassie, then her eyes clouded over. 'I'm very sorry for your loss, Miss Hunter.'

Cassie accepted the keys, frowning as she processed what she was being told, her brain still operating through a veil of disbelief. 'Thank you.' She paused. 'An hour? She doesn't live...' She paused, her use of the present tense instantly jarring. 'She didn't live here, in Stornoway?' She corrected herself.

'No. At Beach Bay, in Carnish, on the west coast.' Heather

pointed to her left, then hugged the file to her middle. 'Are you sure I can't get you anything before you go?'

Cassie shook her head. 'No. I'm fine, thanks.' It was a banal statement, and wholly untrue, but it was the best she could do.

'Ian hopes to be back around four-ish, if you'd care to come back then. But he says he'll phone or text you if anything changes.'

Cassie stood up, slung her heavy bag over her shoulder and turned towards the door. Realisation dawning, she halted and swung back to face Heather. 'Um, I need the address.' Her cheeks began to warm, once again; the admission that she had no idea where her sister had lived for over five years utterly humiliating, particularly in the face of this well-meaning stranger.

'Oh, sorry.' Heather's eyebrows jumped slightly as she opened the file. Taking out a lined index card, she handed it to Cassie. 'Here we are.' She smiled again, then a glint of something behind her eyes made Cassie pause. Seeming to notice Cassie's questioning gaze, Heather cleared her throat awkwardly. 'I'm sorry, but it's quite uncanny.' She nodded to herself. 'You really are identical.'

In so many ways, she and Isla were completely identical, and yet, they were also nothing alike. A strange phenomenon that existed with many twins, and yet something that was still hard to wrap one's head around. 'Did you know my sister well?' Cassie tried to keep her voice steady, still unable to believe that she was talking about Isla in the past tense.

'I met her only the once.' Heather smiled sadly. 'Such a gentle soul.' She stopped herself, her eyelids flickering as if she were recalling more than she was prepared to share.

Sensing her discomfort, Cassie nodded. 'Yes, she was.'

· · ·

Heather had not lied. The drive across the island was scenic, the road meandering through mile after mile of moorland and a patchwork of green fields dotted with low shrubs and drystone walls. Some sections of wall were tidy and well maintained and others less ordered, even crumbling into piles here and there, making them all the more beautiful, in Cassie's mind. The homes and farms she passed were mostly whitewashed with dark, slate roofs, the properties bounded by long stretches of white fencing, in stark contrast to the outline of the sweeping, moss-green hills softening the horizon.

Heather had told her to be sure to stop, approximately half-way, at Callanish and take the short walk up to the five-thou-sand-year-old standing stones. Both Cassie and Isla had always been fascinated by the Neolithic stone circles that were scat-tered throughout the Highlands, but Cassie was far too distracted to stop. This was hardly the time for sightseeing, regardless of her fascination with these mysterious, ritual sights.

As she reached Loch Rog Beag, the land began to rise gently on her left, and the glistening water was so close, on the right of the car, that it felt as if she could have reached out of her open window and trailed her fingers in it as she passed. Breathing in the cool, aromatic air, she focused ahead, still trying to imagine what kind of place Isla had been hiding in, all these years, and the more remote the country that the narrow road wound through, the more puzzled Cassie became.

The road eventually began to veer inland, winding through a series of small, vivid green hills, all melding into each other like a tie-dyed blanket, until Cassie saw a sign for Miavaig.

The water had trailed away to a strip that she now crossed by driving over a narrow stone bridge. Then, as the road cut deeper through the land, the lower slopes of the hills on either side of her were scattered with fallen rock, and lively streams trickled alongside the road.

The GPS showed that she would reach her destination in

twelve minutes, and frowning at the open, seemingly empty country around her, Cassie drove on.

The land began to lower again on her right until suddenly the view opened up across Ardroil Beach, towards the half-moon curve of Uig Bay. It was as if a curtain had been drawn, revealing a painting so incandescent, so utterly breathtaking, that Cassie gasped, immediately pulling over and stopping the car.

As she stepped out, and stretched her lower back, tears suddenly pricked her eyes as she took in the pristine white sand of the beach below, not a single dark spot or footprint to mar it, and the North Atlantic water – a crystal-clear turquoise, reminiscent of the Caribbean, rather than western Scotland. The water seeped away from the shore, darkening as it went, and far out in the distance melted into the horizon – turquoise and sky-blue meeting across a harmonic line, as they would on an artist's palette.

Letting the light breeze cool her cheeks, she stared ahead, taking it all in. 'I think I understand now, Isla.' She tugged the prongs out of her bun and let her hair fall loose down her back. 'Stunning,' she whispered, as a massive seagull circled above her head, its calls carried away on the breeze, as Cassie turned back to the car.

The signs for Beach Bay were old and faded, and Cassie almost missed the last of them, standing crookedly at the junction of four narrow lanes, with a pretty farmhouse sitting up on a hill to her right. Spotting the sign, she turned left and followed the road as it narrowed even more, until she was faced with nothing but a grassy hillside with a broad gravel strip which she presumed was for parking, just as the GPS announced that she had reached her destination.

Frowning, Cassie switched off the engine and got out of the

car, scanning her surroundings, ready to reach for her phone and call Heather for further directions. Then, just as she turned back towards the car, she spotted a footpath leading away from the gravel, disappearing around the side of the hill.

Her curiosity piqued, and following her instincts, Cassie grabbed the heavy keyring from her bag, locked the car, then turned and followed the path, letting her fingers brush over the blanket of short grass that covered the side of the hill she was circling.

After a few moments, the path tracing the natural curve of the land and Cassie letting it guide her, a sight materialised in front of her that she knew she would never forget. Stopping in her tracks, she held her breath, as there, on the edge of the unspoiled sands of Uig Bay, was a stunning, natural-stone and turf-roofed cottage, built into the hillside. It was in the style of the Neolithic homes that were dug out of these hills centuries before.

The front of the cottage was a gentle convex curve that echoed the shape of the land above and behind it, and there was a wall of windows with French doors at the centre, wrapping around the hillside. They reflected the stunning view behind her – the white sand looking ghostly as the sky took on an almost greenish tinge on the glass.

There were three broad sections of stone wall, each sweeping down from the roofline to around knee height, with more windows either side of them, and a thin metal chimney speared up towards the sky, seeming to sprout from the grassy bank above the house. On the right of one of the sections of wall was a single, glass-paned door, its dark-wood frame seeming to melt into the stone around it.

To her left, artfully set amongst a series of large rocks, was a slate patio with three wooden loungers, several terracotta pots with ferny plants in them and a giant slice of natural wood serving as a low table.

Turning back around, Cassie scanned the horizon, imagining Isla standing in this very spot, her eyes, and heart filled with this incredible natural beauty, and her soul at peace. As Cassie's eyes filled again, a flock of noisy seabirds circled above her, calling into the wind, the familiar sound transporting her back to childhood summers at Loch Lomond.

'I'm so glad you found this place, Isla.' Her voice caught. 'I just wish I'd known where you were.'

As she stood still, reluctant to move, to use the smaller of the keys to open the French doors, or the bigger one to open the single door, Cassie's inner voice was howling at her. As twins, it was often expected that their existences were permanently intertwined, that their hearts and minds matched so identically that they were incapable of independent thoughts, choices, or even desires. For years, Cassie had felt that to be true, until Isla's depression had caused her to pull away from Cassie. As they'd moved into their early twenties, it was as if Isla was slowly becoming a stranger, at times even an adversary, but underneath all that, Cassie had held onto the knowledge that, when it came down to it, she would always know what Isla needed, what would help and soothe her.

But here, standing in this isolated spot, this little slice of heaven that Isla had called home, Cassie realised that there had been so much about her sister that she had not known, and if this was the case, what else was she about to discover, beyond those doors?

4

The house was surprisingly light inside, the curved wall of windows channelling the sun across the open-plan living room and into the kitchen behind it. Cleverly placed metal surfaces, like a collage of mirrors, stainless-steel appliances and intricately stamped tin tiles covering the ceiling allowed the light to bounce around inside the room, and a pale-coloured stone floor added to the distinctly Mediterranean feel, all of which held Cassie to the spot.

How many times had Isla stood in this same position, and taken in the stunning room? Cassie tried to conjure an image of her sister, hugging a cup of tea to her chest as she scanned the newspaper, or stirring a pot at the cooker, humming something tuneless as she used to when she thought no one could hear her. The images evoked a mixture of comfort and pain, so blinking her vision clear, Cassie slid the keys into her pocket, noting the weight of them against her thigh.

Standing in the open door, to her right, a cream-coloured sofa and two barrel-shaped chairs sat facing a tiled fireplace, their backs to the kitchen, and next to them, on the left, was a rustic dining table, with four hand-carved chairs pushed in close to it. In the centre of the table was a bronze sculpture, an elegant female form with a long skirt and a smaller, childlike figure at her side, with one narrow arm slung around the woman's hips. The lines were elegant, and perfectly proportioned, but what drew Cassie in was the hair. Each of the two figures had long, deeply waved hair that reached below their shoulder blades, reminiscent of both hers and Isla's. But the most startling thing was that there seemed to be actual movement in the long locks, as if the two figures were standing on the shore, their chins lifted as they let the sea breeze brush their skin.

Cassie closed the door behind her, catching a waft of jasmine – Isla's favourite scent – and made her way over to the table. As she stood behind the sculpture, she could see the detail more clearly, the finely formed fingers, the tilt of their heads – just like Isla when she was lost in thought – the curve of the shoulders and length of the necks, all coming together to form a picture of her sister, seemingly represented at two different stages of her life. The gentle intimacy of the figures was so poignant that it tugged at Cassie's throat. Where had Isla found this work of art, such a beautiful and symbolic piece?

Cassie gently turned the sculpture around, feeling the surface rough under her fingertips, as she took in the greenish patina that gave it an aged appearance. As she looked at the faces, she was disappointed to see them featureless, blank ovals that were almost eerie – the lack of eyes particularly sad, given the view they'd been facing. Frowning, she returned the sculpture to its original position just as her phone rang. Pulling it from her back pocket, she saw Ian Bannister's name on the screen.

She walked over to the window and pressed her palm to the glass, feeling its surprising warmth under her fingertips. 'Hello, Mr Bannister.' She surveyed the pure white sand of the beach, the arc of the shore and the rows of white-topped ridges that the wind was plucking from the surface of the water.

'Hello, Miss Hunter?' He sounded breathless. 'I'm so sorry. I had a wee bit of a personal emergency today.' He paused. 'My son crashed the car. No injuries, thank goodness, but as my wife is away visiting her mother in Glasgow, I'll need to stay here and sort things out.'

'It's all right. I understand.' Cassie watched a group of long-legged birds wading along the shore, their beaks bobbing into the water every few seconds. 'I'm glad he's OK.' She turned back to face the room. 'So, you won't be available at all today?' She sucked in her bottom lip, suddenly hoping that she could spend more time here in Isla's sanctuary before having to face the reality of reading a will – if Isla had even left one – of picking through her sister's life like a scavenger searching for any last morsel of sustenance before the bones were clean.

'That's right. I'm terribly sorry.' A harsh cough truncated his words.

Cassie had no intention of prodding for any more details. She of all people understood the need to keep certain things to oneself. 'It's fine, really. I'd booked into a hotel for tonight, anyway, so shall we get together in the morning?' She turned back to face the window and watched as the wading birds now rushed away from the incoming tide like a group of children playing in the shallows.

'Yes, let's say ten?' He sounded more focused now. 'I have everything prepared, so it shouldn't take us too long.' He paused. 'Um, did you go to the house?' His question was somehow guarded.

Cassie nodded. 'Yes, I'm here now.' She turned back to face the room. 'It's lovely.'

There were a few moments of silence, and then he spoke quietly. 'I never saw it in person, but knowing your sister...' He hesitated, and unable to absorb anything else that might be painful, Cassie cut him off before he could finish his thought.

'Ten o'clock is fine. I'll see you then,' she said.

'Oh, right. Good. See you then.'

Slipping her phone back into her pocket, she crossed the room and walked down the narrow hallway leading away from the living area, where a series of art-deco-style wall sconces lit the way. At the end of the corridor, there were two doors, side by side. Opening the first, she walked into another bright room, with a queen-size bed at one end, and a broad window, once again framing the stunning view of the beach below. The bedding was a soft, mushroom-coloured linen, and the blue-grey and red tartan blanket neatly draped over the end of the bed took her back to Nana Mary's home in Dunkeld, where touches of the MacPherson hunting tartan were dotted throughout the old Victorian house. A series of cushion covers, curtain tiebacks, placemats and even guest towels in the little downstairs bathroom, had all been set out as reminders of who they were and where they'd come from – or so their nana had always said. Seeing the familiar colours here, in this remote hideaway, was comforting, as if Isla had wanted a touch of her past around her, perhaps as a reminder that she was not truly alone despite her solitude.

There was a mirror-fronted wardrobe against the side wall, and a tall chest of drawers in the corner of the room, with a collection of framed photographs on top. Cassie walked over and scanned the mismatched silver frames. There were a couple of shots of the view outside the window at different times of year, one of a snow-topped mountain range that Cassie couldn't identify and one of Sadie, looking fuller in the face than she was now and wearing big square sunglasses. Seeing it, Cassie's fingers went to her mouth. She'd have to face her mother within the next day or so, to tell her this soul-crushing news, and the prospect was enough to make Cassie feel nauseous.

As she was about to turn away, something caught her eye, and she lifted a small frame from behind a larger one. Staring back at her was her own face and Isla's, their cheeks flushed as they each bit into the same, massive cloud of candy floss, their identical eyes alight and their noses only inches apart. Cassie instantly remembered that night, when they'd been eight, and they'd all gone to the funfair that had set up in a field just outside Dunkeld. Isla had wandered off at some point, sending their parents into a blind panic, until they'd finally found her sitting in the shadows inside the psychic's tent, mesmerised and absently drinking a Coke as the woman in a shimmering kaftan and crimson turban told fortunes.

Smiling sadly at the memory, Cassie leant forward to replace the photo when another drew her eye. It was of a young girl, perhaps four or five, with stunning blue eyes, the irises rimmed with dark circles, making the blue seem almost surreal. Her hair was long and deeply waved, a rich brown colour with hints of gold at the temples. Frowning, Cassie lifted the frame and studied the picture, something familiar about the distinct young face making her squint. The child's face was a perfect heart shape, with a narrow, pointed chin, full cheeks and a high forehead. She was smiling, her little pearly teeth showing only slightly as she tipped her head to one side.

As Cassie's pulse began to quicken, she wiped her thumb over the glass, feeling no dust or residue – so it had been recently cleaned. As she stared at the child, there was a seismic shift inside her, as if a rock that had been in front of an opening she hadn't seen before had rolled away, revealing something she was unprepared for. She'd never considered herself particularly maternal, being so consumed with her work and business, but seeing this angelic little face seemed to release dozens of fluttering wings in her chest, and beneath that new sensation lay a raw longing that made Cassie take a long, slow breath.

Unnerved at the strength of what she was feeling, Cassie

carefully put the photo back, adjusting it to stand exactly where it had been, all the while the child's eyes seeming to follow her, like those in a portrait did when you walked away from it. As she stood still, shaking her head at the unlikely notions that were suddenly flooding her mind, the inner voice that seldom guided Cassie wrong whispered to her, and her hand shot to her mouth.

What was Isla's connection to this child?

Swinging around, Cassie scanned the room, looking for further clues, but seeing nothing other than a robe hanging behind the door, and a stack of *National Geographics* on the single bedside table, she walked back out into the hall.

Opposite the bedroom was a bathroom with a deep tub, half-shielded behind a shower curtain covered in shimmering gold and silver mermaids. It was a whimsical choice for her sister, but somehow seemed to fit the otherwise spartan bathroom. Just as Cassie was about to leave, she spotted a row of little yellow ducks on the edge of the bath, and her mouth instantly went dry. What was Isla doing with toys in her bathroom? Trying to keep a lid on the anxiety that was now pressing up inside her, Cassie forced a swallow and roughly gathered her hair into a loose bun, which she secured with the pearly tongs from her pocket.

Next, she walked across the hall and pushed open the second door, immediately struck by the scent of baby powder, and the rush of warmth that coated her face as she walked inside. The walls were a shell-pink colour, and on the opposite side of the room was a single bed, the duvet cover dotted with fairies of various sizes, with gossamer wings and rosy cheeks. Soft toys were stacked in rows across the pillow, a donkey with its tongue sticking out, a semi-bald teddy bear, an elephant with one ear missing, a family of well-loved friends that each belonged precisely where they lay.

As Cassie blinked repeatedly, the truth of what she was

seeing now undeniable and almost blinding, her eyes were drawn to the wall behind the bed. It was decorated with a mural of a magical forest, complete with a winding avenue of tall, shiny-leaved trees. Rows of brightly coloured flowers lined a stone path that led to a waterfall in the distance, where a tiny fawn had dipped its head to drink. The whole scene was like a page taken straight from a fairy tale, and as she let her eyes linger on the fawn, Cassie's heart began clattering under her shirt.

At the end of the bed was a small chest of drawers, also decorated with a trail of fairies that appeared to be climbing up the front, the one at the top having disappeared inside the drawer, except for her little green shoes left sticking out. An unnerving rushing sound flooded Cassie's ears as she walked to the chest of drawers and pulled the top one open. It was full of tiny vests, numerous pairs of socks with cartoon characters on them and a stack of T-shirts in various shades of pink and purple. The baby powder smell was stronger now, and as Cassie pulled out a T-shirt with a unicorn on the front and held it up to her nose, her heart felt as if it was collapsing in on itself.

Isla, were you a mother? The idea was as unfathomable as it was devastating and, unwilling to accept that her sister would have chosen to hide something as momentous as this from her, Cassie whispered hoarsely, 'No way. It's just not possible.' And if Isla *had* been a mother, where was the child now? Had something happened to the little girl that had sent Isla into the depths of despair, and then, ultimately, to her death?

5

As the questions multiplied, taking on a life of their own, Cassie replaced the T-shirt and closed the drawer. Directly above the chest of drawers, at eye level, was a long wooden shelf, crammed with books of various shapes and sizes – stories about ponies and fairies and a battered picture book about an undersea kingdom ruled by a giant octopus. As she ran her eye along the shelf, she stopped at a copy of *Green Eggs and Ham*, sandwiched between *Alice in Wonderland* and a series of Winnie the Pooh books with badly cracked spines.

She and Isla had always argued over the copy of *Green Eggs and Ham*, after Nana Mary had given it to them one Christmas, without a label. Their mother had said wisely that they both owned it, but Cassie had read it more often than Isla and so had kept it on the table next to her bed, with the other Dr Seuss books she'd been collecting. One night, in a fit of rage, Isla had taken the book up to the attic and scribbled all over the cover with a red pen.

Cassie's hand was shaking as she pulled the book off the shelf and looked down at the damaged cover, then ran her fingers over the deep grooves. There it was, red pen and all, and

even before she could open it, another set of images filled her
head. She saw Isla's eyes, one minute bright with mischief and
laughter, then the next, shadowed, her bottom lip trembling,
right before she cried.

Cassie had loved Isla deeply, and it had often felt like the
two of them against the world, but there had been other times
when Cassie had no idea what went on in her sister's mind.
Remembering that confusing mixture of feelings Isla had
provoked in her, Cassie was suddenly overcome by such a surge
of regret, over her absence and disconnection from Isla over the
past few years, that she felt light-headed. She may not always
have sufficiently protected Isla, or made enough allowances for
her delicate nature, but Cassie had tried her best and had been
deeply hurt and mystified as to what had caused her sister to
disappear from her life without a trace.

The sculpture on the table, the book in Cassie's hand and
the little T-shirt she had just replaced in the drawer all drew a
map to something so precious to Isla that she had spent years
keeping it to herself, unwilling to share it with her family. As
Cassie slid the battered book back onto the shelf, her sister's
recent decisions cripplingly sad, Cassie once more succumbed
to a new wave of tears that had been building up ever since
she'd arrived at this place, less than an hour before.

Out on the patio, the midday sunlight was pallid. The pastel-
blue sky was streaked with wispy clouds and a brisk wind
carried the tang of the sea up the gentle slope to where Cassie
stood. She breathed deeply, tasting salt at the back of her
tongue, as the heavy keyring hung from her index finger.

Behind her, the single door seemed to pulse its presence
into the hillside, so Cassie turned to face it, her hair working
loose from the bun and sliding down over her left shoulder.
Grabbing it up and resecuring it with the tongs, she crossed the

patio and stood at the door. Hesitating for a moment, she held the larger key out, her hands trembling slightly at the prospect of what else she might find here, then she slid the key into the lock and opened the door.

As her eyes adjusted to the relative dimness inside, Cassie stroked the wall to her left, searching for a light switch. Finding one, she flipped it on and as the room came into focus, she gasped. She was in some kind of artist's studio, a long room wrapping around the right side of the hill, with two large windows overlooking a stone path that echoed the outline of the land. It was cool inside and smelled of damp clay and something slightly musty that Cassie couldn't place.

Opposite her was a long workbench covered with a pile of twisted wire, and next to that were two huge lumps of amber-coloured wax, three blocks of modelling clay and a long narrow tray filled with tools, the like of which Cassie had never seen before. As she walked over to the bench, she stared down at a selection of palette and paring knives, paintbrushes and four slender chisels with varying-sized heads.

Next to the bench, on her left, was another long wooden table, slightly higher than the bench, and tucked under it were a series of boxes, some with dusty moulds in them. There was also a shoebox filled with candles, some half melted and others with pristine white wicks, and a large bag of plaster covered with a coating of white powder so thick it almost obscured the lettering on the side. Frowning, Cassie bent down and dragged a finger through the white dust, rubbing it between her finger and thumb, a chalky smell floating up to her as she wiped the particles off on her jeans.

Over by the window was a kiln, a cylindrical oven encapsulated inside a series of curved stone blocks, that sat on a plinth of thick wooden planks. Next to it was an array of ladles and deep spoons hanging from a rack on the wall and a pair of thick wooden paddles criss-crossed with scorch marks.

Beside the kiln, mounted on the wall, was a giant white-board, plastered with layer upon layer of pencil sketches on sheets of thin white paper, all held in place by magnets. There was a series of drawings in the centre of the board, simply of hands, each one beautifully captured, either at rest, with the fingers gently curled towards the palm, or held open expec-tantly, as if another hand would soon slip into it. Around the edges of the board there were numerous outlines of human faces, arms, and feet, some more detailed than others, and there were some studies of animals, too.

As she scanned the crowded board, one sketch in particular caught Cassie's eye. It was of a man, with a wide jaw, a long, Roman nose and heavy eyelids, that instantly made her think of her father. He would often make fun of his big nose, then sniff their necks noisily when he hugged them, making them giggle. The poignant memory made Cassie smile sadly as she stepped slowly backwards towards the centre of the room.

The floor was a rough-cast concrete, the colour of a winter sky, and the light from the windows on her right shone in in two thick shafts of gold that cut across the room, each heavy with dust motes. As Cassie took it all in, another of the sketches caught her eye, half obscured by one of an aquiline horse's head that hung in front of it.

Walking back to the board, she gently moved the horse away to reveal a pencil outline of the stunning sculpture she'd just seen on the dining room table. As she slid the sketch out from under a large magnet, Cassie's pulse quickened, and her eyes filled again. There, on the paper, with a level of detail that snatched at her heart, was her own and Isla's face, the wide-set eyes, the slim nose, the high forehead, and next to that, the image of the little girl in the photograph.

Cassie blinked, more pieces coming together to form a picture of her sister's secret life – a life that Cassie could never have imagined for her. Isla had become a gifted artist. A sculptor. And a mother. As these mysterious fragments circled her heart, Cassie whispered hoarsely, 'Isla, why couldn't you tell me?'

Back inside the cottage, Cassie sat cross-legged on the floor, with her back pressed against the French doors. Her hips had grown numb from the cold stone underneath her and her back ached, but she'd barely moved for over an hour since coming back inside. She had slid down the door and let the tears come, washing her face as she'd hugged her knees to her chest, losing track of time, and now, the room was beginning to darken around her.

As her stomach grumbled audibly, she pressed her hand into her middle and checked her watch. It was close to 1.30 p.m. and registering the time, she realised that she hadn't eaten since the previous afternoon, so rising stiffly, rubbing her sore eyes, she stood still for a moment, feeling the blood rushing back into her feet.

As she walked over to the kitchen, she glanced out of the windows to her right. The sky had dimmed to a dangerous grey, tinged with purple, and the tall gorse bushes that ran along the hillside beyond the beach were bending like a row of lithe dancers, the wind forcing their limbs away from the shoreline. Cassie shivered and hugged herself as she made her way to the fridge and pulled open the door, scanning the sparse contents. There were two unopened bags of lettuce, a tray of baby tomatoes that looked slightly sad, some eggs and a carton of milk. On the bottom shelf, there was a row of juice boxes, a few individually wrapped cheese sticks and some tiny yogurt pots, all strawberry flavoured. Cassie eyed the unappealing contents and sighed.

Isla had loved junk food when they were growing up, often skipping the wholesome meals their mother cooked in favour of packets of crisps, sweet popcorn, and French bread pizzas she'd heat in the microwave. By the time the twins turned thirteen, Sadie had given up trying to encourage Isla to eat healthily, or join them at the table more – yet another battle that their mother had decided wasn't worth the fight, if it kept Isla happy.

Cassie had sometimes resented having to sit at the kitchen table with her parents, eating salads and grilled fish, while her sister lay upstairs on her bed with a bag of pretzels, but, as ever, Cassie had felt the need to compensate for Isla's absences. She would fill the silence with stories about her day at school, the latest horrors of the neighbour's one-eyed cat that used all their gardens as its personal litter tray, or what their grumpy French teacher had said that day.

Miss Trudeau, who had a head of wild grey hair, and consistently smelled of garlic, caused great amusement in the classroom. She would bring her spaniel to school and the little dog would lie under the teacher's desk and pass wind so putrid that the children would be gagging, opening the windows whenever Miss Trudeau turned her back on them. To amuse her parents, Cassie would impersonate her teacher, sometimes getting up and acting out the dramatic way the Parisian woman gesticulated as she talked. Sadie and Russ would laugh heartily as Cassie eyed the door, wondering if the joyful noise might coax her sister back downstairs. Occasionally it worked, and Isla would appear in the doorway, smiling as she watched her sister's antics, but, more often than not, Cassie would help her mother clean up, then climb the stairs to find Isla asleep on top of the covers, in the twin room they shared, or with her nose in a book and her earphones on, indicating that she wasn't in the mood for talking.

Now, Cassie grabbed a yogurt and shut the door of the fridge, just as a clap of thunder overhead made her jump. As she opened three drawers, searching for a spoon, then walked over to the window, the sky darkened even more and fat raindrops began to patter onto the patio, then, blown against the window, they ran in thick rivulets down the glass – blurring the view.

Cassie ate the yogurt in four spoonfuls, the tartness of the strawberry pleasantly refreshing – reminding her of the delicious fresh fruit that Syd would ply her with at home.

As she stared out at the quickening storm, her decision to stay here rather than drive back to Stornoway settled in more, and the relief that she felt surprised her. The universe had made it easy for her to spend a little more time in her sister's retreat, and the prospect, rather than difficult, was comforting.

With a cup of hot tea and a bag of Twiglets Cassie had found in a cupboard full of crisps and crackers, she sat at the dining table, her laptop open, in front of her. She had been putting off calling Stuart, not feeling ready to talk about what she was experiencing – share all the shocking truths she was discovering. As she stared at the screen, skimming through the list of emails in her inbox, seeing several from Syd about the new collection, a stab of pain in her stomach made her wince. How would she get through these next few weeks?

Looming large, obliterating all the hard tasks that would inevitably come after Cassie's meeting with Ian Bannister and everything she must do to close out Isla's tragically truncated life, Cassie tried to imagine how she could possibly tell her mother something that would shatter what little peace was left to her, forever. The weight of the responsibilities that faced Cassie, that she had no choice but to take on, suddenly felt like more than she could bear, so she slapped the laptop closed and let her head droop onto her forearms. How had this happened? How had she lost her sister?

Cassie pressed her eyes closed, trying to picture Isla in the last moments of her life, floundering in choppy seawater – perhaps shouting for help where no one could hear her, as her lungs filled with water, but the vision was so searingly sad that Cassie sat bolt upright, her eyes landing once again on the sculpture.

Pulling it towards her, she carefully lifted it, noting the surprising weight of the piece, then, on an impulse, tipped it over so that she could see the underside. There, etched in the bronze, was the name I. J. Hunt. The two initials were clearly for Isla Jane, but the truncation of the surname made Cassie frown. Perhaps the 'er' of Hunter had worn off, over time?

She held the sculpture up closer, squinting at the lettering, then noticed a tiny stamp underneath her sister's name. It was of a bird, with elegant wings and a long V-shaped tail, and above it the words *Swallowtail Arts*.

Cassie's frown deepened as she placed the sculpture gently back in its spot on the table. Then, opening her laptop, she typed in the search bar: *Swallowtail Arts Isla Hunter*. Within moments, a web page loaded for a gallery in Glasgow, the home page a subtle collage of watercolour and oil paintings, wood carvings and bronzes. Spotting the tab 'Our Artists', Cassie clicked on the drop-down menu, scanning the list of names, until she stopped at I. J. Hunt. Her heart thumping wildly, she clicked on the name.

There was no photo, which, given everything she was learning, didn't surprise her, but there was a brief bio saying that I. J. Hunt was an artist of great repute, with pieces of her work housed in many prestigious galleries, stately homes, and gardens through Scotland. As Cassie read the few lines again, trying to allow what she was seeing to sink in, below the bio she noticed a series of thumbnail images. It was a collection of stunning sculptures that made her eyes widen as she shook her head – marvelling at the beauty before her.

There were several variations on the mother-and-daughter, that stood on the table in front of her, some sitting together on large sea rocks, or kneeling in grassy pastures. There was one with the two figures lying in an ingeniously created hammock, the material bulging in a way that showed the long-limbed bone structure of the mother perfectly through the cloth.

One in particular stood out to Cassie, drawing her eye like a magnet, of the mother carrying the child on her hip, their heads inclined towards each other and their cheeks touching. The body language was more eloquent than any explanation might have been, the love that connected the two figures almost palpable, and as she stared at it, Cassie struggled to focus.

Flabbergasted by all she was seeing, she scrolled through the various images several times, each one representing another sliver of Isla's life, her time, her days, her incredible artistry, all of which Cassie had been shut out of, and the realisation plucked painfully at her heart.

Cassie waited for Stuart to answer, her phone thrumming against her warm cheek. Just as she was preparing to leave a voicemail, she heard his voice, thick with sleep. 'Hey, gorgeous. How's it going?'

Taking a second to compose herself, as she always did before she was less than completely honest, Cassie said, 'Oh, it's going OK.' She sucked in her bottom lip. 'Were you still asleep, you lazy toad?'

Stuart gave a strangled laugh. 'Aye, you caught me. I was working on a new song and nodded off on the couch.' He laughed again. 'So, how's Lewis?'

Cassie turned to look out of the window just as a flash of lightning speared down through the moody sky, disappearing into the water in the distance. 'Stormy, now.'

'You can count on the west for that.' He snorted. 'So, how did it go with the solicitor?'

'I haven't actually seen him yet.' She paused, the thought of explaining everything once again exhausting. 'We're meeting in the morning instead.'

'Why? What happened?' He sounded more alert now.

'He had an emergency.' She paused. 'It's fine, Stu. I'm going to stay at Isla's place tonight instead of the hotel. It's better actually. It gives me some time to get myself together before I see him.' She nodded to herself, wanting to be done with this conversation, the sound of her own voice somehow contaminating the peace of her sister's sanctuary. 'Stu?' She jumped in before she'd have to go into any more detail, then she heard him yawn.

'Yeah.'

'I'll be back around seven tomorrow night. Can we go out for a meal, as I won't want to be arsed with cooking.' A shiver trailed across the back of her shoulders, making her shove her free hand into her armpit. 'How about Gianni's, for some souvlaki?'

'Good idea. We haven't been there in donkey's.' He paused. 'Cassie?'

'Yes?' She walked to the dining table and lifted her sweater from the back of a chair and draped it around her shoulders, hunching forward as she hugged herself.

'You doing OK?'

Hearing the concern in his voice, she consciously straightened up. 'I'm fine. Just tired.' She nodded to herself. 'Look, I'd better go. I'll see you tomorrow.'

'All right. See you then.' He waited for a second or two before adding, 'Bye, gorgeous.'

In the main bedroom, Cassie skirted the bed. The covers were smooth and crisp, probably unslept in, and the pillowcases had obviously been ironed. As she eyed them, every last drop of energy drained from her.

A few minutes earlier, she had found the thermostat in the kitchen and cranked up the heat, the midsummer storm having dragged the temperature down rapidly. Having called to cancel her hotel room, she had brought her bag in from the car and set it in the corner of the bedroom, the rain still clinging to the outside like fat drops of glycerine.

The thought of a warm bath was tempting, but now, despite the early hour, Cassie craved sleep more than oxygen. Her body was as riddled with pain as was her heart, and as she opened her bag and found her toothbrush, she stumbled towards the bathroom, her stomach gripping her like a vice. The pain was high up, under her diaphragm, and as she pushed her fingers into the soft flesh, she gasped. That stress and emotional pain could manifest in this way, never failed to amaze her – the mind and body a fascinating machine – humbling in its complexity.

She quickly washed her face with the bar of soap on the sink and scrubbed her teeth, avoiding her reflection in the mirror, her own face too painful a reminder of what she'd lost. Then, back out in the hallway, she turned and looked at the second bedroom door, a slice of early moonlight sliding under the frame as she stared at the handle. Without thinking, Cassie opened the door, walked in, and stood at the end of the single bed. Before she could reason her way out of it, she moved the collection of toys onto the floor, pulled back the fairy-covered duvet and crawled in, the smell of talc and innocence filling her head.

As she pulled the covers up under her chin, pushing her aching back into the soft mattress, she whispered hoarsely, 'I'm sorry I never got to meet you, little one. I'm your Aunt Cassie.'

6

The following morning, the sun was high in a crystal-clear sky as Cassie opened the curtains in the small bedroom. Despite a restless first hour or so, she had eventually fallen into a deep sleep wrapped in the fairy-covered duvet, deeper even than when she was at home, next to Stuart. He flatly denied snoring like a freight train was rolling through the bedroom, which drove her crazy, but she'd grown accustomed to his noise, and had even learned to sleep through it, at least for part of the night.

Now, as she rolled her stiff shoulders and looked out at the turquoise water below, and the strip of pristine sand lining the curve of the bay, the stark reality of why she was here came back to her in a rush, splintering her moment of serenity. Today she must face the most painful task she hoped she would ever have to face, and as she pictured herself back in the solicitor's office in Stornoway, Cassie turned and carefully remade the bed. She reverently returned all the soft toys to their rightful positions, then walked out of the room and headed for the bathroom, suddenly desperate for a hot shower.

· · ·

She'd found teabags the day before, half a carton of milk that was still fresh and a box of Weetabix, so with a bowl of a cereal that she had not eaten since she was a teenager, Cassie sat at the table and sifted through her emails.

The earthy taste of the cereal brought new memories flooding back, so she set her phone down, fixed her eyes on the scenic view, and let them come. Isla and her lying toe to toe on the sofa, when they had both got measles, their mother warming the milk for their Weetabix and letting them add a little sugar, coaxing them to eat when they had no appetite. Her and Isla jostling to stir the scrambled eggs that their dad made each Sunday morning, as he whistled 'Flower of Scotland' behind them. Her pointing at the ceiling to distract her sister, then snatching Isla's toast from her plate and taking a giant bite out of it.

As Cassie chewed slowly, her heart contracting at the sweet and yet painful images, she pushed the half-eaten bowl of cereal away and sat back, her spine finding the wooden ribs of the chair. Pressing back harder against the wood, she tried to channel her sister, hear her voice, slip inside Isla's troubled heart to understand what she'd been feeling for all the lost years, but all Cassie felt was hollow. Losing Isla was like Cassie's very being having been brutally cut in two, leaving her not knowing which half of her remained, and which would be missing, forever.

The silence that surrounded her was distressing now, rather than comforting, and as she rose, dumped the remains of her breakfast into the sink and drained the mug of tepid tea, another pain in her stomach made her gasp. This time it felt as if a knife was slicing through her, reaching all the way into her back, and she began to pant as tiny beads of sweat bloomed on her upper lip.

A year earlier, around the launch of a new line of necklaces, the stress had caused Cassie to develop a stomach ulcer. It had taken months on a restricted diet and medication to get it under control and now, as she recalled how much pain she had been in, she made a mental note to call her doctor as soon as she got home – before it got out of hand again.

As the pain began to ease, she checked the time. It was 8.26 a.m. and, allowing an hour and a half to get to her meeting, she calculated that she still had time to walk down to the beach, feel the sand between her toes and breathe in the sea air. Grabbing a light, waxed jacket that was hanging on the coat stand by the door, Cassie suddenly froze at the faint smell of jasmine she caught. She tentatively lifted the coat to her nose, one of Isla's favourite scents lingering on the corduroy collar, and as numerous memories flickered to life, Cassie pressed her eyes closed for a second – the pain of her sister's loss like a fresh wound being inflicted.

Taking a moment to collect herself, Cassie slid the coat on, the weight of it somehow connecting her to Isla, then she shoved her phone into the pocket, lifted the keys from the dining table and let herself out onto the patio.

It was a crisp morning, and the metallic scent of seaweed filled her head as she took a deep breath. The short walk to the beach was easy, the well-trodden path leading her through a channel of soft grasses, dotted with patches of gold-tipped gorse lining the way, and within a few minutes she was standing at the edge of the scenic Uig Bay. The sand between her and the water formed a crescent of undisturbed creaminess that called out to her, the need to make her mark upon it suddenly over-whelming.

She slipped off her shoes and socks and rolled her jeans up several times, then paced towards the water's edge. The cool sand was damp against her insoles, and she felt the pull in her calves as her feet sank slightly under her with each step. Seabirds circled noisily above as she used her palm as a visor, staring into the distance, the soft lapping of the water drawing her towards the shoreline.

Suddenly gripped by the realisation that this was likely the spot where Isla had died, Cassie stopped still, her heart beginning to race as she tried to banish the painful images that were flooding her mind.

As her rapid heartbeats gradually began to slow, she braced herself, then dipped a toe into the water, instantly relaxing at the surprising warmth against her skin. It wasn't exactly bath-warm, but it certainly wasn't the frigid temperature she'd expected. She'd read that Uig had a warm, temperate climate, but being a Scot, who'd sat, frozen to the bone, on various blustery beaches in the middle of summer, this was still a surprise.

Stepping further into the water, she let the gentle lapping lull her into a dreamlike state, her eyelids growing heavy and the pain of her memories easing a little with each surge and ebb of the sparkling sea.

A few moments later, the loud screech of a seagull bringing her eyes wide open, she turned and began walking along the shoreline, her back to the cottage and her focus on the horizon.

Deciding she should check the time again, she slipped her hand into the pocket of the jacket, but rather than her phone, she felt something smooth and papery under her fingertips. Pulling it out, she saw that it was a clipping from a glossy magazine that had been folded over several times into a tight square. As she opened it up, another crumpled slip of paper fluttered to the ground, which she picked up, but her eye was pulled to the page from the magazine.

It was an article in *Jewellery Arts Journal*, dated more than a year before, when they had interviewed her about her new collection. There was a photo of her, in the studio, standing next to Syd, who was showing her something on his design board. Cassie's hair was in a loose bun, fiery red tendrils curling at her temples, her trademark white cotton shirt tucked into her black jeans and one of her wide-linked, long silver chains around her neck, with a delicate filigree medallion hanging just above her waistband. She was smiling, the light from the row of windows behind her and Syd highlighting her pale complexion, the freckles that she hated forming a dusting of strawberry dots across the bridge of her nose and cheekbones. Seeing herself that way, so immersed, and yet looking so carefree, brought Cassie's free hand across her mouth. That Isla had got hold of a copy of the magazine, never mind kept the article for so long, touched Cassie deeply. Isla had still cared. She had not cut Cassie out of her heart when she'd disappeared. She had followed Cassie's career, watched her from afar, and somehow that knowledge took the edge off the pain that was rippling inside her.

Turning her attention to the other piece of paper, Cassie opened it up and instantly recognised Isla's handwriting. Cassie's heart flip-flopping, she squinted as she read the handful of words.

Dear Cassie

I've tried to write this a thousand times, but I can never find a way to explain

That was all there was, and as Cassie read it again, and then again, she frowned. What could Isla have wanted her to know that was so hard to communicate?

She shook her head as her stomach gave a painful squeeze. *No, not now.* She pressed her fist into her middle.

As she stared down at the magazine article, and the half-written note, what Cassie still couldn't understand was why Isla had left in the first place. Moreover, how the little girl in the photo had come into Isla's life, and what had happened to the child? Until she could figure all that out, Cassie knew she would have no peace of mind, so, for now, all her hopes were pinned on Ian Bannister and whatever he could tell her.

The drive back to Stornoway went quickly, and soon Cassie was parking opposite Bannister's office once more. She'd been reluctant to leave the peace of the cottage, but now she was back in town, she must ready herself for what lay ahead. As she twisted the rear-view mirror around and checked her reflection, her phone rang. Noting that she still had ten minutes until her meeting, she pulled it out of her bag. Syd's face flashed up on the screen and, taking a moment, she answered it.

'Hiya, my lovely.' He sounded overly bright, but she could picture his concerned frown, the huge, amber-coloured eyes, and the way he pressed his lips together when he was contemplating something troubling. 'Just checking that everything's OK.'

Despite the length of their friendship, Syd rarely quizzed her about her personal life, unless she opened up to him first, and she was hoping that today would be no exception. She'd left him a somewhat cryptic voicemail the night before, saying that everything was fine, but she'd be out for a day or so. She'd said he was not to worry and that she would keep in touch via email. Her being away from the studio right before a launch was totally uncharacteristic, and Syd calling her now clearly indicated that he wasn't buying the half-baked explanation.

'Hi, Syd.' She swiped her thumb under each red-rimmed eye and shifted the mirror back into place. 'I'm OK.' She fought the lump of emotion that was forming around the lie, then, unexpectedly, she wanted to talk, to tell her best friend what had happened in just twenty-four hours – that her universe had been altered, knocked off its axis in a way that would never be righted. Just as she started to talk, Syd spoke again. Quietly, this time.

'Look, I don't want to bullshit you, Cass. That's not how you and I operate. I called Stuart this morning and he told me what's going on.' He paused. 'I'm so sorry, my sweet friend.' His voice cracked around the last word. 'What can I do?'

Cassie pressed her eyes closed, the need to share swamped by the fear of not being able to stem the tears that were pressing in. If she started crying again, she may never stop.

Syd had met Isla several times before she'd vanished into thin air, and he'd said that he thought she was a softer version of Cassie. At the time, it had upset Cassie, the implication that there was a hard edge to her, but Syd had further qualified the statement by saying that Isla seemed so much younger than Cassie, and lost somehow, and that he could see how much Cassie cared for and protected her sister.

As a few weighted moments passed, Cassie blinked furiously. 'There's nothing you can do, but thanks. I love you for asking, and I'll tell you everything when I get home.' She glanced at the dashboard clock. 'I've got to go, Syd, but I promise to call you later, or tomorrow. OK?' She dragged her bag across from the passenger seat, seeing the edge of the magazine article poking out.

'OK.' He sounded dubious. 'I'm here, for whatever you need. And don't worry about the launch. It's all under control.' He paused. 'I'm really sorry, Cass. She was a sweet if troubled soul.'

Cassie nodded as she opened the door and got out of the car. 'Thanks, Syd.'

Ian Bannister was not at all what Cassie had imagined. In his late thirties, he was reed-thin and tall, well over six feet, and his sand-coloured hair was thinning on top. He had a ruddy complexion and big blue eyes that radiated kindness, and when he smiled, his cheeks puffed up, giving him a childlike appearance. He had greeted her warmly and shown her into his office, while the Amazonian Heather had gone to make them some coffee. Now, Cassie sat opposite him, her heart pattering alarmingly as he opened a manila folder and took out a sheaf of papers.

'So, Isla's will and advance directives are both here.' He kept his eyes lowered as he shuffled the top sheets of paper. 'We'll go through the will, which is pretty straightforward, then we can get the formalities done before child services get here.'

At this, the breath went out of Cassie. She'd been on the point of asking him about the little girl that she'd seen evidence of, and whose face was now etched on her mind, so him beating her to it was jarring. 'Child services?' she croaked.

'Yes, the social worker in charge of the case.' He looked at her quizzically. 'They took Marina into care.' He halted for a second or two, then continued. 'It was...'

He talked on, but all Cassie could hear was the name. The gorgeous little girl with the mesmeric eyes had been called Marina. As images of mermaids and fairies and soft sand beaches filled her head, Cassie waited for the bomb to drop – the devastating truth of what terrible event had occurred – something awful enough to keep her sister from coming home. As Cassie panted softly, trying to focus on his eyes, Ian Bannister stopped talking and sat back, his palm resting on the pile of papers.

'Miss Hunter, Cassie. May I call you Cassie?' He smiled gently as she nodded. 'Marina is safe, you've no need to worry. She's been well cared for.'

Cassie's heart felt as if it might implode as she pushed herself abruptly up from the chair. She steadied herself against the desk, her mind racing as his words played on a loop inside her head. *Marina is safe.*

'Cassie, are you all right?' He was up and rounding the desk, then his hand was under her elbow as he eased her back into the chair. 'I know this is a lot to deal with, but Isla was very specific about her wishes, and there's no one to contest the will, so you're fine.' He returned to his seat just as Heather opened the door carrying a tray with two coffee cups on it. She took one look at Cassie and paled.

'Is everything OK, Ian?' She set the tray down on top of a filing cabinet, put a cup in front of each of them, then stood next to Cassie, her hand resting on the back of the chair.

'Yes, thanks Heather.' He nodded. 'This process is never easy, as you know.' His voice was full of compassion as Cassie desperately tried to focus on his face.

He seemed to understand that she needed him to wait for her to collect herself, as he quietly thanked Heather and nodded at the door. The willowy woman picked up on his signal and left the room, pulling the door closed behind her.

'Do you need a minute or two?' He tipped his head to the side. 'We have a wee bit of time until they get here.' He glanced at the clock that hung above the row of filing cabinets.

Cassie's mouth was bone dry, her tongue feeling thick and useless as she lifted the cup in front of her and shakily sipped some coffee. The mouthful of warm bitterness sent a spark through her, as she consciously dragged herself back to the moment. 'So, the little girl...' She cleared her throat. 'Marina, is...' She could not bring herself to say the word alive, instead she just stared at him, the coffee cup rattling slightly in the saucer.

'She's well and will be here in around half an hour. She's been through the mill, obviously, but your niece is a remarkable little girl, Cassie. I only met her a couple of times when Isla brought her in, but she's a bright wee thing, and pretty determined for a five-year-old.' He dropped his gaze to the desk, then, when she stayed silent, he looked back up at her.

As Cassie tried to find the right words, her face must have

told him everything he needed to know, and a light seemed to go on behind his eyes.

'You didn't know?' He frowned, his head shaking almost imperceptibly as Cassie set the coffee cup down, careful not to spill any.

She shook her head, a single tear breaking free and rolling down her cheek. 'Not until yesterday.' She gulped. 'I saw her photo at the house, but I assumed...' She couldn't go on, her throat clenching as she swiped at her damp face.

Bannister's face softened as he pulled a cotton handkerchief from his pocket and offered it to her. 'I'm so sorry. I had no idea.' He lifted the hanky higher, but Cassie shook her head, dragging out a tissue she'd shoved into her pocket earlier and wiping her nose.

'How would you know?' She sniffed, shoving the tissue away. 'It would be natural to assume that Isla's sister, her twin, would know that she had a daughter. That I was an aunt.' The words *daughter* and *aunt* felt foreign, and yet there was a naturalness to them too that took Cassie by surprise. 'I'm an aunt.' She stared at him. 'Oh, my God. I have a niece.' Her fingers fluttered over her mouth and then, she was struck by something so obvious she frowned. 'But what about the father?'

She watched him shrug.

'Not on the scene, and apparently never was.'

As the statement penetrated her reeling mind, its far-reaching implications began to materialise. She was presumably now responsible for a child, an extension of her sister, a living breathing human being who had no parents to care for her. As Cassie tried to picture her hectic life, with Marina in it, images of birthday parties, bath times, car seats, stuffed toys and fairy-covered duvets all melted into one another. The painting that was forming in her mind's eye was colourful, joyful, and yet heartbreakingly sad, a scene underwritten, paradoxically, both by her unadulterated fear of taking on parenthood this way and

a sense of what she could only acknowledge as excited anticipation.

    Suddenly, she bit her lip, and looked Ian Bannister square
in the eye. What if Isla had other plans? What if she didn't want
Cassie to take care of Marina? Afraid that there might be yet
another form of loss coming her way, Cassie closed her eyes
briefly, then looked past him, out of the window. Surely Isla
wouldn't keep her daughter away from her only remaining
family, the way she had removed herself? Surely her sister
couldn't be that cruel?

7

Ian Bannister was staring at her, his mouth slightly open. 'Cassie?'

Cassie licked her lips, her chest burning with the effort of simply breathing. 'She did want me to take Marina, didn't she?'

He nodded, lifting a document from the top of the folder. 'Yes, she did. She was very specific.'

The relief made Cassie feel as if she were falling, the room beginning to spin around her as his voice faded, then came back to full volume.

'There's a note here.' He sifted through the papers and pulled out a slim white envelope. 'It's addressed to you.'

The idea that Isla had left her some explanation for leaving, or maybe even instructions to help Cassie navigate what was to come, was a colossal relief. 'Do you know what is says?' She accepted the envelope, noting that it was not sealed. 'When did she give this to you?'

'No, I don't.' His eyebrows jumped. 'She brought it in a few weeks ago and asked me to file it.' He paused. 'Cassie, you haven't asked about what happened, exactly.' He paused. 'Do you want me to tell you?'

A weight settled on Cassie's chest, another layer piling on top of what she was already carrying. Could she bear to hear the details of Isla's death? Could she live with not knowing? What if Marina asked her one day? Would Cassie be remiss in not having answers? As she let the questions breed, gradually emerging was the realisation that she *must* know, even if it was agonising. There could be no moving on for her unless she understood Isla's last moments – so close had been their connection. So, she met his eyes, and nodded. 'Please.'

Bannister began to talk, his voice low and controlled. Marina had been at a birthday party while Isla had apparently taken an afternoon swim. There had been music playing in the house and all the windows had been open. The wind had been high that day, making the water rough, and no one else had been on the beach at the time.

Why on earth had Isla gone swimming in rough water when she could barely stay afloat in a pool? Cassie absorbed the details, them forming a puzzling picture of such melancholy that she could hardly bear to listen anymore. Then an image of Isla walking out into the sea, staring straight ahead, leaving all that pained her behind, began to materialise. Cassie couldn't bring herself to believe it, so, allowing herself to go there for only seconds, she shook her head as Ian Bannister's voice came back to her.

'Cassie, are you OK?'

She nodded, needing to know it all – every, last, minute detail. 'Who found her?' Her voice shook. 'What music was playing? How long had she been there?'

'It was a young man who was delivering some of her sculpting supplies. He knocked the door and heard the loud music. When he kept knocking and she didn't answer, he waited a while, then got worried, so he walked across the patio and spotted her lying face-down on the sand, then he called the police.'

Cassie closed her eyes briefly, imagining the scene as police officers hauled her sweet sister up the slope to the house, in a body bag, perhaps having to break down the door to get inside. Then, Cassie frowned. 'But there was no damage to the door, or the lock?'

'No. The door was open. Islanders seldom lock their houses, Cassie.' He gave a half-smile. 'This is a safe place to live.' Seeing her confusion, he continued, 'Once he saw her, the lad waited down on the beach until the police arrived.'

She held his gaze, seeing the sympathy brimming there as he began to answer her other questions. Apparently, the young man had reported that the song, 'Don't Be So Hard on Yourself', by Jess Glynne, had been blaring inside the house, and as Ian said the title, the first line of one of Cassie's favourite songs instantly came back to her – 'I came here with a broken heart'. The aptness was agonising, so she mustered all her remaining strength to stay focused while Ian told her that the coroner had estimated that Isla had been dead for two hours when she'd been found. As the bare facts, feeling surreal and not attached to her life, or Isla's, filtered through the wall of pain surrounding Cassie's heart, she licked her parched lips, the slight tang of coffee still on her tongue.

'So, if you're ready, we should go through the will.' He glanced at the clock. 'OK?' He lifted a document from the folder.

'Yes, of course.' She shifted in the chair, her legs beginning to tingle. 'Mr Bannister? Ian.'

'Yes?'

'Thank you,' she whispered.

'For what?' He looked puzzled.

'For your sensitivity. For being there for Isla. For helping her manage all these things.' She swept her hand above the folder on the desk.

His cheeks coloured slightly as he shook his head. 'Your

sister was extremely well organised – and quite savvy. She knew how to handle her own affairs, manage her assets and make provision for the future – for Marina,' he said. 'She'd established herself as a successful sculptor, and businesswoman, and she left her daughter well provided for. She'd paid off the mortgage on the cottage, and there's a substantial amount of money in a trust fund.' He paused. 'Let's just say that Marina won't ever need a student loan, if she decides to go to university.'

This glowing description of Isla's life skills was surprising. She'd never been organised. Always late, reliably the last to arrive at family gatherings, often forgetting what she was supposed to bring, and sometimes not showing up at all. She had also never been good with money, blowing all her pocket money, or salary, as soon as she received it, then begging Cassie for a loan before the end of the month. Cassie would roll her eyes, lend Isla money and tell her that next time she'd charge her interest. Isla would smile and tell Cassie that she was the best sister in the world, and Cassie would know that she'd never see that money again.

As Cassie tried to picture Isla planning for the future, one that she wouldn't have the chance to enjoy, she caught Ian Bannister staring at her, his mouth pinching as if unasked questions were battling to get out. 'I don't want to be insensitive, but may I ask you something?'

'Of course.' A flutter of nerves plucked at her middle.

'How long had it been since you'd seen each other?'

Cassie swallowed over a lump of sadness, the admission once again feeling like a personal failure. 'Isla left Edinburgh almost six years ago, without any real explanation, and no hint of where she was going.' She met his questioning eyes. 'We tried to find her, for years, but she did a good job of hiding herself.'

He frowned. 'Right. I didn't realise.'

Cassie nodded. 'It was a total mystery to my parents and

me, and we've never come to terms with her choosing to just go like that.' She caught herself, the present tense still a natural default. 'We never understood what happened, and we had absolutely no clue about Marina.' She shook her head. 'I just can't understand why...' Her voice gave way.

'Things happen. People battle demons we don't know about or understand. Even family.' He shrugged. 'One thing you should know, though, was that she seemed happy here on Lewis.' He nodded sadly. 'I mean, she kept herself to herself mostly, but when she did come into town, there was a contentedness in her that was almost tangible.'

Cassie raked the hair away from her face and looked down at the envelope in her hand, then folded it and shoved it into her pocket. Whatever was inside deserved the respect of being read in private. 'That helps to know.' She smiled at the kindness he'd just shown her in sharing his impression of her sister, thriving on her remote island home. 'I'll hold on to that.'

The will was brief, and simple. Isla had left the cottage and all her assets to Cassie, and a large amount of money to be held in trust for Marina, for when she reached twenty-one. There was a power of attorney and other documents naming Cassie as her executor, Marina's next of kin and legal guardian. Ian had prepared the guardianship order for Cassie to sign, and she read the document twice, the words seeming to skip about on the paper. Then she accepted the pen Ian Bannister held out to her and, without hesitating, signed in triplicate, each signature taking her closer to her niece, and an entire portion of Isla's life that had been hidden from her.

With the paperwork complete, Heather had come back into the room with copies for Cassie and was just about to leave again when the doorbell buzzed. 'That'll be them.' Heather looked over at Ian. 'Are we ready?' Her eyes flicked between Ian and Cassie, her slender hands sliding into her trouser pockets.

'Ready?' Ian asked Cassie.

Cassie took a second, sitting up straighter, then tugging her shirt down at the back, suddenly self-conscious about her slightly dishevelled appearance. 'Yes, I'm ready,' she whispered, then another thought crowded her aching heart. 'Wait. How much does she know?'

He frowned. 'She knows that Isla has passed away. That you are her mother's sister, and that you'd be coming to get her.'

The fact that Isla hadn't even considered that Cassie might not take Marina was comforting.

'OK'. Cassie exhaled slowly.

Ian stood up and walked towards the door as Cassie, unsure of what to do, rose and hovered awkwardly at the desk.

'Shall I come with you?'

Ian shook his head. 'No. I'll bring her in to you. Just wait here for a minute.' He smiled kindly. 'It's going to be OK, Cassie.'

She smoothed her hair again and nodded, her stomach doing flips as she stared beyond him at the door. She watched him leave the room, his movements seeming deathly slow, then a few agonising minutes later, he walked back in.

Behind him was a short, rotund woman in her fifties, with gentle brown eyes and a head of wild, collar-length silver hair. Close to her left hip, holding her hand, stood the little girl, the heart-shaped face even more pronounced in person than it had been in her photo. Her skin was the colour of milky alabaster, and her hair was a mass of long brown waves held back by a bright, bumblebee clip. Her eyes, those magnetic blue pools, rimmed with black, seemed gigantic as she stared across the room at Cassie, and something oddly familiar about them made Cassie frown, momentarily. Seeing the fear and confusion in them filled Cassie with the desire to bolt across the room and scoop this fragile little person up in her arms, hold her close and reassure her that nothing else bad would ever happen to her again. Cassie shifted her weight from foot to foot as this wave of newfound, protective instinct circled her heart.

Marina held a stuffed giraffe to her chest, its long neck kinked as its head dangled over her forearm.

'This is Marina.' Ian turned towards the little girl. 'And Frances Macleod, the social worker who's been taking care of everything for us.'

The woman smiled at Cassie, her cheeks folding into deep creases. 'Nice to meet you.'

Cassie nodded. 'And you.'

'Marina, this is your Aunt Cassie.' Ian swept his hand towards Cassie.

The little girl hesitated momentarily, then released Frances's hand and lurched forward. 'Mummy?'

Cassie dropped to one knee, the hopeful expression on Marina's face enough to bring Cassie's heart to a stop. 'Hello, Marina.' She held her arms out. 'I'm your aunty.'

Marina stopped short, her mouth hanging open, then her eyes instantly filled. She put her free hand up and began sucking her thumb, her chin quivering around it. 'I want my mummy,' she hiccuped, as Frances walked forward and put her hands on Marina's shoulders.

'It's OK, Marina love. This is your aunt. Remember we talked about this?' Frances crooned.

Letting her instincts guide her, Cassie spoke quietly. 'I know you want your mummy, little one.' She stayed still, her arms extended. 'I do, too.' Despite the renewed surge of loss inside her at the sight of her sister's child, Marina's obvious pain and confusion magically shifted Cassie's focus away from her own suffering. Wanting to comfort Marina in the simplest way she knew how, Cassie wiggled her fingers. 'Would you please give me a wee hug?' She gave a half-smile as Marina's cheeks pulsed, her eyes boring into Cassie's. 'I'd love it if you would.' Cassie's voice grew a little stronger. 'Marina?'

Cassie waited, the seconds ticking past as Ian and Frances remained motionless, until eventually, Marina took a tentative step forward. She let the giraffe dangle at her side as she took another step, then stopped. Cassie felt her knee begin to tingle, but afraid to move in case she startled the child, she wiggled her fingers again. Marina took a moment to consider, then walked slowly into Cassie's arms.

The powerful slew of new sensations that flooded through Cassie was overwhelming. The way her niece felt in her arms, the vulnerable little frame dwarfed by her own, the faint smell of honeysuckle and talc, the sound of Marina's shallow breathing, all sent another wave of such protectiveness through Cassie that, before she could stop them, new tears filled her eyes. Not wanting Marina to see her cry, she held the child against her, lightly but firmly, until she could focus clearly, then she leant back and took in the flushed little face. 'Thank you. I really needed that.'

Marina blinked, her dark lashes impossibly long and clumped together by unshed tears. 'Uh-huh.' Her voice was barely audible.

Cassie released her and stood up, careful to move slowly, as she might if a tiny bird were perched on a branch in front of her. 'Will you come and sit with me?' She pointed at the chair she'd been sitting in. 'So we can have a little chat.'

Marina's gaze tracked the line of Cassie's finger, and with one tentative look back at Frances, who simply nodded, Marina followed Cassie to the chair. Cassie sat and gently drew Marina onto her knee, seeing the bony knees inside black and white polka dot tights, protruding from under the little denim skirt Marina wore. She had a matching jean-style jacket, over a pale pink T-shirt, and Cassie had noticed that her trainers had lights that flashed inside the heels when she walked.

Marina shifted until she was comfortable and then twisted around to look at Cassie again, as if still not convinced that this carbon copy of her mother was, in fact, not her mother. Marina's eyes were bright, and Cassie could see the tears hovering behind them as, suddenly, she knew exactly what she must do.

'So, you know that I'm here to take care of you now, right?' She let a hand settle lightly on Marina's knee as the child gave a single nod. 'You and I are going to stick together, and I'll do everything I can to be a good...' Cassie swallowed the word that was balanced on the tip of her tongue. 'We will both miss your mummy, so much, but she wanted us to be together.' Cassie worked to keep her voice level. 'So, we'll make her proud. We'll be best friends, and you'll like Edinburgh. There's lots to do.' She found a smile, as Marina suddenly stiffened in her arms.

'I don't want to go to Edinburgh.' Marina leaned away, then eased herself off Cassie's knee, the giraffe once again clasped to her chest. 'I want to go home.'

Cassie took a second to process what was happening and was instantly mortified that she had been so thoughtless. All Marina knew was Lewis, her pretty home overlooking the sea, her life with her mother, and with Isla torn from her this way, anything outside of that sphere had to seem utterly terrifying. Adjusting her plans in her head, Cassie continued.

'We'll go back to your house today, and get your things, then maybe in a day or so, we'll go to Edinburgh so you can see it. How does that sound?' Cassie tipped her head to the side. 'We'll get your room all set up there, and you can bring anything you want with you. All your toys and books and stuff.' Cassie watched as Marina's face darkened and a fat tear oozed over her bottom lid.

'No. I want to go home.' She shook her head, at first slowly, then faster and more frantically, until, panicked, Cassie stood and moved towards her. In an instant, Marina darted away from her, ran back to Frances, and buried her head in the woman's middle. 'I'm not going with you,' she sobbed, her voice muffled against Frances's sweater. 'I hate you,' she sobbed again. 'I want my mummy. I want to go home.'

8

Frances had kindly lent Cassie the car seat she'd been using so that Cassie could secure Marina in the back of the Ford, next to her little bag of belongings. Then, with no idea of how she was going to persuade her young niece that she must leave her home, never mind move to a city she knew nothing of, Cassie had driven back to the cottage.

Marina had stayed silent for the majority of the trip, mumbling a yes, each time Cassie asked if she was OK, and then staring back out of the window, her giraffe under her chin and her narrow shoulders hunched towards her ears. Eventually, Cassie had turned on the radio and let the music fill the yawning silence separating her from her sister's child.

As she kept her eyes on the road, once again Cassie wondered why Isla had done this. Why she had hidden Marina not only from her sister, but from their mother, depriving Sadie of the joy of being a grandparent? While Isla could be selfish sometimes, seemingly unaware of the effect her behaviour had on her family, she was not a spiteful or cruel person, so the mystery surrounding this decision only seemed to deepen, the more Cassie thought about it.

Now, back in the house, as the clock on the cooker read 2.10 p.m., the temperature having dropped quite a bit, Cassie cranked up the heat a little. They had stopped at the local shop on the way, so she emptied the contents of the shopping bags onto the kitchen counter.

Marina had scuttled off to her room as soon as they'd arrived, so having put the food away, Cassie made her way down the hall, then stopped outside the half-open door of the room she'd spent the previous night in. As she hovered outside the door, she heard Marina talking, her voice little more than a whisper, but clear enough to make out. 'You sit there, Raffy. I'll get you a drink, like my mummy does.'

Cassie heard the gentle lapping sound that Marina was making and instantly chided herself for not asking Marina if she was hungry or thirsty as soon as they'd arrived. Isla wouldn't have made that mistake, Cassie was sure. Feeling newly inadequate, she took a moment or two, then pushed the door all the way open.

'Marina, would you like a drink, or a snack? It'll be a little while before I make dinner.' She leaned against the door frame, trying to look relaxed. 'I can make you a sandwich, or there's some yogurt.' She waited for Marina to turn around.

Marina flicked a glance over her shoulder, then considered for a moment, before saying, 'Is there rice pudding?'

'Oh, I don't know. I'll have a look.' She smiled at the little girl whose rosy tongue was sticking out as she held a tiny plastic cup under the nose of the giraffe. 'Who's this? Is that Raffy?' Cassie took a step inside the room, careful not to get too close, too soon.

'Uh-huh.' Marina nodded. 'He's thirsty.'

Cassie eased closer. 'I can see that.' She stood next to the bed where Marina was sitting, surrounded by her stuffed toys. 'Is he your favourite friend?'

Marina nodded. 'Mummy says he is the cleverest giraffe in

the world.' She set the little cup down on the bedside table, her referring to Isla in this way sending a shard of sadness straight through Cassie, as sharp as any blade.

'Well, I'm sure he is, if your mummy said so.' Cassie moved to the end of the bed and perched on the edge of the mattress. 'How about you come into the kitchen, and we look for some rice pudding?' She waited for Marina to meet her eyes, then nodded encouragingly.

'OK.' Marina shifted and carefully tucked Raffy in next to a threadbare rabbit with a blue felt coat. 'Raffy is sleepy now.' She shunted herself off the bed and stood up, then yawned widely. 'He needs a nap.'

Cassie followed suit and stood up, wondering if this was Marina's way of saying that she was tired. There was so much Cassie didn't know, and would have to learn, and fast. The prospect of instant motherhood seemed like a sheer mountain face she'd have to climb, with no map at hand, its slopes slick with ice. Even so, Cassie found that she was not as afraid as she probably should be.

'Let's leave him to snooze and then maybe, after lunch, we can have a nap, too?' She held a hand out to Marina, expecting to be rejected, but the little girl surveyed her for a moment, then slid her fingers into Cassie's. This small act of acceptance from the child brought a lump to Cassie's throat as she led her niece out into the hall, Cassie careful not to bump her way past the door as her eyes filled once again.

They hadn't found any rice pudding, but Marina had seemed content with a yogurt and some banana sliced into it. She'd eaten silently as Cassie made herself a sandwich, then they'd sat opposite one another at the table. The silence between them had felt less cumbersome than in the car, until Cassie noted that Marina's eyes were full of tears.

'Oh, sweetheart, what's wrong?' She jumped up and rounded the table, desperate to scoop Marina up into her arms, but still unsure how that would be received.

Marina sniffed and wiped her nose with the back of her hand. 'That's Mummy's chair.' She gestured to where Cassie had been sitting. 'She always sits there.'

Cassie gasped. 'I'm sorry. I didn't mean to...' She hesitated at the side of Marina's chair. 'I'll sit over here instead.' She pointed at the chair to her left. 'Is that OK?'

Marina sniffed again, then nodded. 'I want Mummy.' Her face crumpled, and unable to stop herself, Cassie folded her arms around her niece and lifted her up, feeling the tension in the little girl as she held her against her chest. Then, Marina's legs wrapped around her waist and her arms went around Cassie's neck, and Cassie felt the warm puffs of breath between the child's ragged sobs, brushing her neck.

'Oh, Marina. I know you want her. I wish she was here, too. But we have each other, and I'll always be here to take care of you. I promise.' Cassie gulped. 'Just like your mummy wanted.'

Marina buried her head in Cassie's neck, her breathing gradually levelling off as her crying began to subside.

'How about we go and see if Raffy is awake? Perhaps he'd like a wee snuggle from you?' Cassie shifted Marina onto her hip and walked towards the hall.

Marina stayed quiet, her thumb now back in her mouth and her eyes red-rimmed and watery.

In the bedroom, Cassie gently lay Marina on the bed, slipped off her trainers and covered her with the duvet. 'You snuggle up and I'll be right here.' She patted the mattress, watching as Marina turned to face the wall, dragging the giraffe up under her chin. Cassie moved a long twist of hair away from Marina's cheek and tucked it behind her ear as the child once again stuck her thumb into her mouth. 'Would you like me to read to you?' Cassie gathered a handful of long, wavy hair and moved it away from the child's neck, draping it across the pillow.

Marina nodded, her eyes looking heavy.

Relieved, Cassie whispered, 'What story would you like?' She eyed the shelf across from the bed. 'Do you have a favourite one?'

Marina nodded against the pillow and said, 'Green Eggs.' Cassie felt the bed shift beneath her, the mattress seeming to suck her exhausted body in. Of course, it would be the Dr Seuss book.

As soon as Cassie was sure that Marina had fallen asleep, she tiptoed out of the room and went back into the kitchen. It was almost 3 p.m. and she still needed to change her flight, then call Stuart and fill him in on everything that had happened. So much of the foundation of her life had shifted in the last few hours that having to explain that to him seemed surreal, and now the magnitude of what she'd just done, signing those papers, had begun to sink in. But as she recalled the way she'd felt when she'd first seen Marina's photo, and that over-whelming sense of longing that had caught her off guard – her gut reaction of fierce protectiveness when she'd met her in Ian Bannister's office – the decision felt undeniably right.

Next, she tried to imagine the conversation, and what Stuart would say about everything that had happened, but when it came to Marina, she found she was unable to picture his reaction. They had talked briefly about wanting a family, but Stuart was almost two years younger than her, and at just twenty-seven, he had said he'd like children sometime in the future, when his music career was more established. Now, she was about to present him with a five-year-old, as a permanent part of their life together, without consulting him first, and despite feeling sure of her decision, she felt a flicker of concern about how she'd handled things. All she could do now, however, was focus on the practicalities of what came next, and part of that was arranging for Isla's body to be taken home to Edinburgh.

Ian Bannister had given her the name of a funeral home that would help her arrange everything, but they'd told her it would take a couple of days to organise, so grabbing her phone, she called the airline and moved her flight out by three days, buying an additional seat for Marina. Then, rather than call Stuart and face the reality of what she was about to do to him, to expect of him, she threw herself into preparing the chicken she'd bought, eventually figuring out Isla's oven. As she raked around in the drawers and cupboards, locating all the pans and utensils she needed, Cassie remembered the unopened letter in her pocket.

A few minutes later, with the chicken in the oven, she pulled the letter out and sat at the table, with her back to the window, in the seat she'd told Marina she would use from now on. As Cassie held the envelope in her hand, she began to tremble, her fingers tingling as she flipped it over and opened it. It contained a single sheet of heavy paper, the writing unmistakably Isla's, with the long, curled tails on the y's and the s's in loops, like tiny fish.

Cassie focused on the six lines, her heart clattering wildly as she read them, then read them again.

Dear Cassie,

I'm sorry for everything. Please take care of my darling Marina and love her as she deserves. None of this was her fault. I tried to be what she needed. She should have been yours.

Isla x

Cassie slowly shook her head, the words on the page blurring and then coming into focus again. Much as with the half-written note she'd found in the jacket, the day before, Isla's words made little sense. Why on earth would Cassie think any of this was Marina's fault? And what did '*she should have been yours*' mean?

9

Cassie lay in Isla's bed, the room rapidly growing chilly, and now almost pitch black, aside from a tiny strip of moonlight seeping through the gap in the curtains. Her stomach beginning to ache again, Cassie turned onto her side and dragged the duvet up, over her head, trying to focus away from the pain and get her mind around how she was going to tackle things the next day. It wasn't going to be easy to persuade Marina that they couldn't stay here.

Marina had eaten a little dinner, let Cassie bath her and then the child had pulled on her own pyjamas, with heart-breaking determination, as Cassie had hovered in the doorway of the bedroom, wanting to help her but electing to let Marina do it herself. She had fallen asleep soon after Cassie had read *Green Eggs and Ham*, again, Marina's breathing becoming slow and rhythmic, her eyelids fluttering slightly, then eventually becoming still.

As Marina had lain on her side, Cassie had lingered on the edge of the bed, taking in the curve of the child's cheek, the high forehead, the thick dark eyelashes and the sharp slope of her nose, when suddenly Cassie had been filled with a deep sense of déjà vu. As she'd stared at the little girl, whose features were becoming more familiar by the second, Cassie had struggled with the sensation that she knew this face, this profile, but from before she'd first met her niece. Of course, there was the genetic connection, and that some of Marina's mannerisms reminded Cassie of her sister, but there was something more than that – a deeper sense of recognition that was curious. As she'd tried to analyse the odd feeling of familiarity, unable to put her finger on what was making her feel this way, she'd heard her phone ringing out in the kitchen. Anxious not to wake Marina, she'd slipped out of the room as quietly as she could, closed the door behind her and dashed along the hall.

Stuart had sounded disappointed. 'So, you're not coming home tonight?' He'd sighed. 'What's going on, Cass?' He was responding to the two-line, somewhat cryptic text she'd sent him before putting Marina to bed, and she hadn't been surprised he'd been upset.

'Sorry.' She'd kept her voice low. 'So much has happened, I just couldn't get everything done today.' She'd stood at the window, watching the dimming disc of sun slipping below the scattering of clouds that had laced the sky ever since they'd arrived back that afternoon.

'Why? What's happened?'

Cassie had taken a second to compose herself, then told him everything, a low buzz of adrenaline keeping her pacing in front of the darkening window as she'd talked.

'Shit. She had a kid?' He'd been understandably shocked. 'That's awful. I mean for the wee girl.'

'Yes, it's utterly heartbreaking.' Cassie had swallowed hard. 'She is so sweet, Stu. Sort of timid but incredibly brave, too. I don't have any idea how she's dealing with all this. So much loss, at such a young age.' She'd swallowed. 'It's bad enough for me, as an adult, but I wonder if she'll ever get over it?'

'Children are pretty resilient though, aren't they? She'll

probably bounce back faster than you think.' His somewhat flippant tone had irritated Cassie.

'Wow. Nice. Full marks for empathy, Stu.' She'd shaken her
head. 'She can take as long as she needs to, as far as I'm
concerned.' She'd sighed. 'Look, I'm absolutely whacked. I need
to get some sleep.' She'd checked the clock, surprised to see that
it was only 8.40 p.m. 'It's been a long day.'

'Aye. Of course.' He'd sounded contrite. 'Get a good night's
sleep then, and I'll see you Friday. Just text me your flight info.'

As she'd been about to hang up, she'd suddenly remembered something else. 'Oh, Stu, can you please tidy up the spare
room. It looks like a rock band threw up in there.' She'd given a
half-smile as she heard him huff. 'Seriously, it's a tip. Can you
please put your guitars and stuff away in the cupboard in the
hall, and maybe make up that bed with clean sheets?'

A few seconds had passed before he'd answered.

'Um, sure. So, you're bringing her here?'

Cassie had taken a moment, frowning as she'd tried to
formulate her reply, then she'd spoken quietly. 'Yes, of course.
Where else would she go?'

He'd laughed, a short, forced kind of laugh, then said something about having just been joking, but the conversation had
then ended rather abruptly.

An hour later, after Cassie had showered, answered several
emails and then fallen into bed, their conversation had
continued to circle her mind, and it had left her with a dull
sense of foreboding – a weight at her centre.

Now, as she breathed through another shot of pain in her
stomach, she thought about the future. A future with her
mother, Marina and Stuart – her family – around her. As she
smiled at the image of something that she hadn't known she'd
wanted, so badly, she opened her eyes and sat up again, tugging
the duvet around her shoulders. What would she do with the
cottage? If Marina moved to Edinburgh with them, there would

be no need to keep this place. It would sit here, empty, deteriorating and potentially costing a good deal of money to maintain. While she mulled over the practicality of keeping it, versus selling it and putting the money into Marina's trust fund, Cassie's eyes began to feel heavy. Finally, she slid back down in the bed, willing sleep to come quickly, before another pain grabbed at her stomach.

The following morning, Cassie woke with a start. She was buried under the covers but heard a scuffling sound that brought her upright in the bed, as she shoved the duvet away from her face.

Marina was standing at the bottom of the bed, her eyes wide and her bottom lip trembling. Raffy was tucked under her arm and her pyjama bottoms were twisted awkwardly around her tiny waist.

'Good morning, little one.' Cassie's voice was rough. 'Are you OK?'

Marina skirted the bed and, taking Cassie by surprise, tugged the duvet back and crept in beside her. 'I had a bad dream.' She shifted over and curled into Cassie's side.

'What did you dream about, love?' Cassie pulled her closer, savouring the new sensation of the warm little body next to hers.

'Mummy was floating in the water.' She sniffed. 'She was crying.'

Cassie closed her eyes momentarily, rationalising that there was absolutely no way Marina had seen her mother in the sea – the prospect unimaginable. Cassie took a second to compose herself, then, when her heart stopped thumping, she gently combed her fingers through Marina's hair, the softness of the waves another new sensation. 'That does sound scary, sweetheart. But you know it was just a dream, right?'

Marina nodded, her nose pinking up as she swiped at a tear on her cheek. 'Why did Mummy leave me?'

Cassie shifted, to see Marina's face. The huge, dark-rimmed, blue eyes held Cassie's, Marina's so full of pain, and unanswered questions, that Cassie instantly felt adrift and angry, all at once. *How could this have happened, Isla?*

'Marina, it's really hard to explain, and when someone dies, it's the saddest thing in the world. But your mummy loved you so much, and she didn't want to leave you.' Cassie fought to keep her voice level and block the ever-present tears from clogging her throat again. 'We have lots of lovely memories of your mummy, so she'll always be with us.' She pressed her palm to her chest. 'We can talk about her whenever you want, and we'll tell her what we're up to.' She found a smile. 'You can tell me whenever you feel sad, or need a cuddle, OK?' She held Marina's gaze. 'Your mummy will always be here with us, Marina. Always.' Cassie patted her chest again.

Marina settled herself against Cassie's side, then, after a few moments, she sat up and swung around to face Cassie. 'Is Mummy here, in the house?' Her eyes were wide, the sky-blue irises seeming to glow.

Cassie bit down on her bottom lip, realising that she'd confused the little girl, but as she was about to speak, Marina jumped from the bed.

'Mummy is here.' She gave a tiny smile, her cheeks puckering in such an endearing way that Cassie was lost for words. Marina looked around the room as if expecting to see Isla standing at the window or sitting on the low chair in the corner. 'Can she hear me?'

Cassie pushed the covers away and sat on the edge of the bed. This was uncharted territory and the deeper she waded into it, the more she felt completely out of her depth. All she could do was follow her instincts, and at this moment, Marina needed to feel connected to her mother, in any small way;

Cassie wasn't about to destroy that. 'I think she can, little one.' She stood up and stretched her arms above her head. 'And she's probably thinking it's about time we got dressed and had some breakfast.' She went to the chair and tugged on her sweater, over the old T-shirt of Stuart's she'd slept in.

Marina's cheeks were flushed and her expression full of a light that had been absent since Cassie had first laid eyes on her. 'Can I have Cocoa Puffs?'

Cassie laughed softly, Cocoa Puffs being Stuart's favourite cereal, that she teased him about, saying that he was well beyond kindergarten now, and should be eating something healthier for his breakfast. 'If there are any, you may have some.' She nodded, wondering if there would come a time when she would be able to resist that angelic face, those incredible eyes, and perhaps even say no to something. At this moment, it was the last thing she could think about.

The late morning sun was watery, gentle fingers of light stroking the surface of the water. As Cassie and Marina sat with their backs to the cottage, across the bay, the pristine sands of Ardroil and Uig Bay stretched into the distance.

There was not a soul in sight as the breeze lifted a thin cloud of sand from the dunes on their right, smudging the clean lines of their tops against the sky. It had been cool, but not cold enough for coats when they'd left the house ten minutes earlier, and now Marina had shed her shoes and socks and was digging her toes into the sand. 'I forgot my bucket and spade.' She spoke to her feet as Cassie shifted on the clammy sand and slipped her own shoes off.

'We're not staying too long, love. We need to make some lunch, soon.' She set her shoes neatly next to her and pulled off her socks. 'Shall we paddle?' She heaved herself up and extended a hand to Marina.

'OK.' Marina let herself be helped up and together they walked to the water's edge.

Cassie had been practising her speech while in the shower, and this seemed like the right moment to tackle the subject of them leaving Lewis for Edinburgh. Pulling her shoulders back, Cassie stepped into the lapping water. It was now or never. 'Marina, you know yesterday, how we talked about going to Edinburgh?' She looked straight ahead, rather than at the little girl, whose head had snapped around and was now staring at her. 'Well, we need to start to pack up some of your things, and then we're going on a plane ride on Friday.' She looked down at her niece and smiled encouragingly. 'Have you ever been on a plane?'

Marina's eyes became hooded. 'No.' She pouted.

'It's fun. We'll be up above the clouds.' Cassie pointed to the expanse of blue above them. 'We'll be able to look down and see the island. Maybe even see this beach.' She swept her hand in an arc.

'I don't want to.' Marina dropped Cassie's hand and took a step away from her, Marina's hands closing into tight fists.

'Sweetheart, we need to go to Edinburgh for a while. I have to work, and you'll like it there, I promise.' As Marina's face darkened, Cassie nervously saw the situation slipping away from her. 'You can come in and see my studio, where I work, if you like?' She grappled for something that might appeal to the little girl, who was now staring straight ahead, her chin set in a familiar way that once again made Cassie pause. 'I make jewellery. Bracelets, earrings and necklaces, and lots of pretty rings.' Cassie edged closer to Marina and gently lifted one fist, easing the rigid fingers open. 'I could make something, just for you.' She felt the tension coursing through the chilly little hand. 'What would you like? A bangle, maybe? Or a necklace?' Cassie heard the desperation in her voice. 'Marina?'

The child seemed to be chewing on something, her rosy lips

pursing and releasing as she finally looked up at Cassie. Her eyes were swimming with tears as she choked out the words, 'If we go away, Mummy will miss me. I want to stay here, with Mummy.' She gulped. 'Don't take me away.'

Cassie's chest ached as she took in the combination of fear and pleading in the dark-rimmed eyes. She desperately tried to find the words she needed, to reassure her niece that, at some point, all would be well. That, one day, their lives would move on. That they'd be able to function without missing Isla every second of every day, but the words just wouldn't form themselves. Instead, Cassie knelt on the sand and drew Marina to her, as Marina wrapped her arms around Cassie's neck. The tightness of the grip once again ignited something inside Cassie, a glow of maternal instinct that she'd had no idea she possessed, and she spoke softly.

'Wherever *we* are, Marina, that's where your mummy will be. It's not the house she's in, it's inside us, in our hearts. Which is better because, that way, she'll stay a part of us both, forever, wherever we are.' Marina's tears were warm against Cassie's neck, then were instantly cooled by the breeze that was picking up. 'Do you understand, sweetheart?' Cassie eased back, and wiped Marina's tears away with her thumb.

Marina blinked several times, then nodded slowly.

'Good girl. I will always do what's best for you, little one.' Cassie smiled. 'That I can promise you.' As she said the words, she knew she meant them, more profoundly than any promise she had ever made before. The only question was, would Stuart embrace her little niece, and would he choose to be part of the family Cassie so desperately wanted to give Marina?

10

Three days later, Cassie had packed up as many of Marina's belongings as they could carry, with the promise that they would come back soon for the rest. Cassie had cleaned and tidied the house, emptied the fridge of anything that would spoil and redirected the mail to her loft in Edinburgh. For now, the cottage would remain closed until she could decide what to do with it, and until Marina began to adjust to her new life in the city. Cassie knew that it would take quite a while, and as she carefully folded tiny pairs of pyjamas and strawberry-covered socks, tucking them into a huge holdall she'd found in a cupboard, the outline of her life continued to shift in a way that left her riddled with angst.

She was going to become a parent, a mother to this sweet little girl, and in doing so honour her sister's wishes. The prospect, while daunting, also brought a deep sense of rightness with it – as if a long-missing puzzle piece had suddenly materialised.

In stark contrast, Cassie had arranged for Isla's body to be transported back to Edinburgh, something that felt as wrong and jarring as anything ever could. Isla had requested cremation in her will, but as there were no crematoriums on the island, taking her home to Edinburgh had been the only option. It had been surprisingly simple to put the logistics in place, which, for Cassie, somehow added to the deeply disturbing face of what was happening.

With everything organised, having spoken briefly to Stuart, bringing Syd up to speed on what was happening, then putting Marina to bed, unable to sleep, Cassie had stayed up all night, checking on the little girl every couple of hours. The sight of her niece sleeping soundly comforted Cassie, knowing that at least while Marina was asleep, she wasn't hurting. As Cassie let that comfort fill her up, it served as another reminder of how surprisingly easy it was to put Marina's needs first.

Despite that tiny light in the darkness of the situation, Cassie had paced around the living room, wrapped in a soft blanket she'd dragged from the back of the sofa, newly tortured by how she would soon have to face her mother and, with that meeting, the unavoidable task of telling her about Isla.

Now, as the rising sun bled into a crimson sky, the fiery tapestry reflected perfectly on the surface of the calm water below, an exhausted Cassie stood at the dining table, staring at the sculpture of the mother and child. The irony of the imagery, the tacit connectedness of the two figures and the cruelty of the separation that had happened here, under this turf-topped roof, all collided in a way that made Cassie sway. As she steadied herself against the table, she knew, without a doubt, that she had to take this seminal piece of art with them. It belonged with Marina, *to* Marina, and Cassie would make sure it was never far from her niece's view.

As Cassie lifted the sculpture and wrapped it carefully in an Arran sweater of Isla's that she'd pulled from a drawer, Marina silently slipped into the living room. Her thumb was in her mouth, Raffy dangling from her other hand, and her faded jeans and rose-coloured sweatshirt were both dotted with tiny crystals that caught the light when she moved.

Seeing her, Cassie tucked the bulky bundle under her arm and smiled. 'Hello, little one. Are you nearly ready to go?' She crossed the room and began stuffing the sculpture into another holdall she'd found in Isla's wardrobe.

'Are we taking Mummy?' Marina eyed the bag, a section of the sculpture protruding from the bottom of the sweater, the lettering on the base clearly visible.

'Yes, we'll stay together, the three of us.' Cassie nodded, then, tucking the end of the wool-covered figure into the bag, tugged the zip closed. 'She'll stay snug in there until we get home.'

Marina's eyes were wide as she spoke around her thumb. 'Can she sit with us on the plane?'

'We'll keep her close, sweetheart. Don't you worry.' Cassie tried to banish the image of a coffin, sliding into the hold of a ferry, the shiny casket juddering as it moved into the cold, dark space. A chill trickled down her back, and she shivered. 'Summer or not, we'll need our coats today, Marina.' She stood up straight and rubbed her upper arms briskly. 'Shall we do one last check before we go?' She extended a hand to Marina, who slid her fingers into Cassie's. Seeing the clouds gathering behind Marina's eyes again, Cassie squeezed the little fingers. 'It won't be long before we come back here. I promise.'

As Cassie circled the room, scanning its contents, and the morning light seeped in the wide windows casting long, finger-like shadows across the floor, Marina stuck close to her side. Moving together, their steps in synch, Cassie mentally ran through everything that awaited her in Edinburgh – everything that she'd necessarily blocked out over the past few days. There was Stuart, and what his welcome would look like, this time. The business, and the upcoming launch of the new line that she'd been badly neglecting but was looking forward to getting back to. Introducing Marina to Syd, her best friend, and saving grace on the work front. She knew he'd be a big hit with Marina, his kindness surrounding him like a shiny aura. And, of course, her mother, the wide-set blue eyes twinkling behind smudged bifocals, the network of tiny spider veins that had begun to appear on her high cheekbones, her face, injured and yet trusting, and totally unaware of the next blow that was coming. As a shadow of Sadie's face lingered before her eyes, Cassie blinked several times to banish it. *Oh, Mum. How am I ever going to tell you this?*

The one light in the whole sad tale was, of course, Marina. Cassie knew that Sadie would be overcome with joy to have a grandchild, a little person to shower her love and wisdom on, and as Cassie tried to picture her mother and Marina together, she felt a bubble of happiness at the prospect of that introduction, and the potential it had for healing – for them all.

Four hours later, Stuart opened the door to the studio and stepped back, his cheeks flushed, and his fair curls still wet from the shower. Even though he was wearing a smile, Cassie noticed that it hadn't quite reached his eyes. He had on a clean University of Glasgow sweatshirt over the ubiquitous torn jeans he lived in, and his bare feet stuck out from beneath each frayed trouser leg. 'Welcome home, gorgeous.' He moved back as Cassie stepped inside and dumped the two heavy holdalls in the hall, before he passed her and dragged her small suitcase inside.

Marina was lingering in the doorway, so rather than force her to come inside, Cassie shrugged off her jacket, hung it on the hook by the door, then gave Stuart a tight hug. 'She's very fragile. Be kind,' she whispered.

He leaned back and met her eyes. 'Of course.' He gave a gentle smile.

Cassie cupped his cheek, smiled warmly and then surveyed the room behind him, expecting to see the usual mess of shoes, guitars, abandoned clothing and piles of sheet music littered about. Instead, the place looked immaculate, the kitchen counters were clear, the coffee table empty of clutter, the cushions neatly placed on the sofa and the tartan blankets they wrapped themselves in when they watched TV folded and draped across the back. As she took it all in, out of the corner of her eye, she caught Marina taking a tentative step forward.

'Thank you for this.' Cassie linked her fingers through Stuart's, feeling the familiar, calloused, guitar-player roughness. 'The place looks great.'

'It took me a fair while, but I got there in the end.' He grinned, this time the light sparking behind his eyes. 'So, where's...' He swung around to see Marina standing in the centre of the hall, her thumb in her mouth, her cheeks flushed, and Raffy tucked under her arm. Her green anorak was tied around her waist, and much of her lustrous hair had escaped the Alice band Cassie had pushed it back with, long dark spirals falling over her shoulders and curling around her face. The effect was breathtaking, causing images of Isla and pink-cheeked Botticelli angels to flutter to life behind her niece.

Going to Marina's side, Cassie gently circled the narrow shoulders with her arm. 'Marina, this is your Uncle Stuart. Remember I told you about him?' Before they'd left the cottage, Cassie had taken time to explain to Marina who Stuart was, and how he would fit into her life, and the little girl had seemed unfazed, but now she seemed nervous – her wide-eyed expression faun-like. Seeing this, Cassie pulled her a little closer to her side and waited, then looked over at Stuart, her eyes saying everything. As she willed him to say something kind, he finally took a step forward.

'Nice to meet you, Marina.' He held out his hand. 'Welcome to... Well, welcome.' After a few moments, seeing that she wasn't going to take his hand, he let his arms drop to his sides and looked over at Cassie, his shoulders rising slightly.

'Shall we show you where your room is?' Cassie leant down and untied the jacket from around Marina's waist. 'It's not very big, but we'll make it nice and cosy for you, and you can pick a new colour of paint, if you like.' Cassie pictured the pretty mural behind the single bed at the cottage, the stunning view across the bay, the smell of the sea and the feel of the sand between her toes and sucked in her bottom lip. 'We'll make it nicer, anyway.'

Marina let Cassie lead her through the kitchen, along the hall and into the spare room. Cassie was pleased to see that while not totally empty of Stuart's mess, he had tidied much of it away, leaving only one guitar propped on a stand in the corner, and a large plastic box filled with sheets of handwritten music, pages of his time tossed in at random as he wrote and discarded another half-written song. The single bed was made up with a striped duvet cover and the bedside light was on, giving the room a warm glow.

'Let's leave your bags in here and we'll unpack later.' Cassie dumped one of the holdalls on the floor under the window. 'We'll have something to eat, and then maybe we can go for a walk along the water.' She pulled up the Venetian blind so that Marina could see the Water of Leith, below her window, the houseboats bright slashes against the murky water they floated in, and the sand and grey stone backdrop of warehouses. 'Do you want me to put Raffy on the bed?'

Marina shook her head, crossing the room and standing on tiptoe to see the view. She took her time to take it in, her head turning almost imperceptibly from side to side as she frowned and pursed her lips.

'What is it, sweetheart?' Cassie moved in closer to her side, seeing Stuart hovering behind them in the doorway.

Marina leaned in, her shoulder pressing into Cassie's thigh.

'Where the sand?' Marina sighed. 'It's dirty water.'

Disappointed, Cassie took a second to compose herself, an image of the crystal-clear water of Uig Bay flashing brightly behind her eyes. 'Yes, it's not like Lewis, love. That place is truly special.' She turned to see Stuart's back disappear as he walked away towards the kitchen. 'This is called Leith Harbour. It's a nice place to live, too. There's lots to do here.'

Marina turned and walked to the bed, sank down onto the edge of the mattress and hugged Raffy to her chest. 'I want Mummy.' Her chin began to wobble as Cassie quickly closed the distance between them and sat next to her niece.

'I know you do, sweetheart.' She drew Marina into her side, smelling the lemongrass shampoo she'd used to wash her hair that morning. 'How about this. We'll put the statue of you and your mummy right here.' She patted the bedside table. 'So you can keep her close.'

Marina sniffed, swiped her nose with the back of her hand and nodded. 'OK.'

Cassie stood up, walked to the window and unzipped the holdall. Pulling out the sculpture, she unwrapped it and then set it on the bedside table, turning it round so that the figures were facing the bed. 'There you are.' She smiled down at her niece, who was staring at the sculpture. 'Is that OK?'

Marina nodded again, then put her hand out and gently touched the face of the mother figure. Cassie's insides folded over at the poignant gesture, as, determined to stay strong for her niece, she swallowed hard.

'Right, lunchtime.'

.   .   .

Cassie lay curled into Stuart's side. He hadn't been playing that night, for a change, so had been around while Cassie got Marina settled. He'd gone for a walk with them along the water, over the bridge to Commercial Street and back. Then they'd each got an ice cream cone from a little Italian parlour below the loft, overlooking the houseboats. They'd sat outside at a small wrought-iron table and watched the world go by for a while, and Cassie had let herself relax into the easy dynamic between them, the sense that this was a snapshot of the future, as welcome as the creamy ice cream had been, on her tongue.

Once they'd got home, Cassie had suggested she cook dinner, but Stuart had persuaded her to call for a pizza instead. While it was hardly the healthy meal Cassie had had in mind, Marina had seemed keen, and had eaten almost two slices, sitting at the tall island in the kitchen, before her eyes had begun to look heavy.

Cassie had bathed her, got her into her pyjamas, this time Marina seeming happy to allow Cassie to help her, then Cassie had read her *Green Eggs and Ham* and tucked her in. Cassie had left the bedside light on and the door cracked open in case Marina woke in the night, afraid, in her new surroundings. Cassie had then lingered at the door, battling with the compulsion to tiptoe back in, lie next to her niece and hold her gently in her arms. The wish to ease Marina's suffering was once again blocking out Cassie's own pain and the need to turn her attention to Stuart, and the new dynamic she'd created in their lives.

Now, Stuart was stroking Cassie's back while she listened to the low hum of music playing in the distance, as often happened in Leith, when she felt a stab to her stomach. Gasping, she sat up and pressed her palm into her middle.

'What's wrong, love?' Stuart sat up beside her, his breath still carrying the tang of the beer he had drunk at dinner.

'My damn stomach is on the warpath again,' Cassie panted softly. 'I must call Doctor Carnegie tomorrow. I'm just so busy,

I've no idea when I'll find time to go.' She focused on the shadowy outline of the window, a sliver of amber light seeping in around the curtains, from the street lights that were dotted along the footpath below.

'Want some water or something?' Stuart put his hand on her back, the presence of his fingers a welcome anchor to keep her from floating away with the pain.

'Yes, please.' She nodded in the darkness. 'There are some antacids in the bathroom cabinet. You wouldn't grab me a couple, would you?' She shifted backwards and leaned against the padded headboard, willing the pain to subside.

Stuart slid from the bed and shuffled out into the hall. As Cassie counted her breaths, the pain easing with each exhale, he came back in with a glass. 'Here you go.' He leaned over to hand her the glass, then, misjudging where her hand was in the dark, he sloshed some water onto the duvet. 'Oh, shit. Sorry.'

'God, Stuart,' Cassie yelped, jumping up from the bed and flicking on her bedside light. She looked around and grabbed the T-shirt he'd dropped on the floor when they'd gone to bed and began dabbing at the covers. 'You're such a bulldozer,' she hissed, then, despite her exhaustion and irritation, she laughed. It had been the first time since receiving the news of Isla's death that she had laughed, and the sensation was freeing.

'It's good to hear that.' He gave a goofy grin. 'You have a sexy laugh.'

Smiling at him, she dropped the damp T-shirt on the floor and crawled back under the covers. 'Just get in and give me a hug, you big eejit.' She reached over and switched off the light as Stuart flopped back onto the bed and burrowed under the covers.

As she rolled over to face him, accepting the malty kiss that he gave her, she heard a strange sound. It was high-pitched and filled with panic. Cassie sat bolt upright, her sluggish mind talking a moment or two to focus. Marina was crying and shouting something, her young voice ragged between gasps and sobs.

Cassie threw off the covers and ran out into the hall, her heart thumping under her nightshirt. As she crossed the room and reached the bed, Marina turned over to face her. Her eyes were huge and her mouth agape. 'Mummy?' She gasped, her hand reaching out to Cassie. 'Mummy, you came back.'

Cassie took a second to assess what was happening, unsure whether Marina was awake or dreaming, but as her niece grabbed at her hand and pulled her down onto the edge of the mattress, Cassie knew that it didn't matter, either way. Marina needed her mother, cripplingly badly, and for now, there was nothing to be gained from adding to her hurt by reminding her that Isla was gone. 'It's all right, sweetheart. I'm right here.' Cassie pulled Marina into her arms, then dragged the duvet around them both, feeling the heat pulsing from the little girl's back. 'I'm here, Marina. I'll always be here.'

11

Cassie had spent the entire night with Marina, stretched out next to the little girl as she slept, initially fitfully, then deeply, her breathing becoming slow and steady. Afraid to leave her alone again, Cassie eventually found the cadence of her own breaths were matching Marina's, until Cassie also fell into a deep sleep.

When she woke, with Marina's right arm draped across her chest, Stuart was standing in the doorway watching them. Startled, Cassie glanced at the bedside clock and for a moment forgot it was Saturday, briefly panicked at it being 9.35 a.m. As her foggy brain began to clear, the flash of relief that she needn't rush into the studio right away made her sigh.

'Is she OK? I missed you last night.' Stuart stretched, a broad strip of pale skin appearing where his T-shirt rose above his pyjama bottoms.

'Yes, sorry,' she whispered, shifting the duvet, and moving gingerly away from the still sleeping child. 'She had a bad night.' She slid out from under Marina's arm and sat on the edge of the bed.

'So did I.' Stuart yawned. 'Hardly slept at all.' He ground

his fist into his eye as Cassie hid a smile. As she'd lain in the semi-darkness next to Marina, waiting for sleep to come, she'd heard him snoring through the wall. The rumble had been soothing initially, then, as ever, had begun to set her teeth on edge.

'Yeah, I heard you not sleeping.' She grimaced. 'Poor you.'

Stuart's eyebrows lifted as he leant against the door frame. 'What? I was awake for hours.' His bottom lip protruded in a childlike pout as he forced his flat stomach out to form a pot belly. Something he always did to make her laugh.

Amused, as ever, by the babyish gesture, and losing the will to argue the point, Cassie rolled her eyes at him. Standing up, she raked her hair into a rough twist, which she then released over her shoulder. Her back was tight and aching from lying awkwardly in the narrow bed, so she bent forwards and let her upper body hang, as her mother had taught her to when she'd had a painful growth spurt at fourteen and reached her full height of five feet seven. It was the only time that she and Isla had been different heights, Isla taking another few months to catch up with Cassie. As she let the weight of her body do the work, she felt the satisfying release – the separation between her vertebrae relieving the tension that had built up.

When she straightened up, Stuart had gone, and turning around, she caught sight of the sculpture, the figures seeming to be leaning in towards Marina as she slept. Her hair was partially covering her face and her one arm extended beyond the edge of the bed, the unicorn-covered pyjamas twisted around her narrow elbow. She looked peaceful, so entirely empty of angst, and pain, that something shifted inside Cassie's heart. Even in the short time that this little girl had been in her life, Cassie felt a deep bond forming, a connection of such strength that it shocked her. She leaned down and gently moved the hank of hair away from Marina's face, revealing one rosy cheek, the high forehead and the profile that once again felt strangely familiar.

Cassie gathered her own unruly hair into her fist, leaned in and dropped a light kiss on Marina's jaw, catching a waft of jasmine soap and something she couldn't place. It was warm and slightly powdery, perhaps simply the smell of childhood. Then Marina stirred, her eyes slowly opening as she rolled onto her back.

As Cassie watched, the peaceful expression slipped from her niece's face and, when she turned her head to look at the window, then back at Cassie, realising where she was, Marina's face crumpled.

As a heart-stopping ache rippled through Cassie, she sat down and gathered Marina into her arms. 'It's OK, sweetheart. You are safe here.' She began to rock the child, who was whimpering now. 'You are safe with me.'

Despite trying to stay focused on Marina, and what she needed to feel comfortable, anxiety about the new jewellery line had been playing havoc with Cassie's nerves, so with Marina finally settled in front of the TV with one of the *Frozen* films, and Stuart working on a new song at the kitchen island, she'd asked him to watch the child for an hour or so, to let her run over to the studio and get caught up with what she had to do the coming week.

Aside from all her work demands, Cassie had already researched primary schools in the area and knew she'd have to register Marina immediately if she wanted to get her into the closest one, with the best reputation, in time for the new term starting in a few weeks. She'd mentally added this to her to-do list – that was growing exponentially, spanning everything from learning and anticipating all of Marina's needs and being the rock she needed, to shopping and cooking, while being careful to keep Stuart on an even keel – a litany of tasks that overwhelmed her each time she thought about it.

The following day was Sunday, so she would be going to see her mother. Not having spoken to Sadie in several days, it was the longest Cassie had ever left it, and as she struggled with the words she would use, how she would try to cushion the devastating truth she had to share, her mouth grew dry. There was no way to protect her fragile mother from the pain of Isla's death, and that knowledge was harder than anything else Cassie had to bear.

Now, dressed, and ready to go to the studio, she stared at her reflection in the mirror, her fiery hair tamed by a soft, grey bandana, her mossy eyes still darkly shadowed. The sight of her slim, freckled nose and high forehead tugged her thoughts back to her sister, as always happened when Cassie caught sight of her reflection anywhere. But this time, as she stared at herself, there was a new quality to her face that made her frown. There had been a subtle change. Perhaps a shift in the way she held her head, the appearance of some tiny lines at the edges of her eyes, or the recent, more taut line of her mouth? As she stood still, scrutinising her reflection, it came to her. The change was not in her features, it was inside her – lurking behind her eyes. For her entire life, whether they'd been close to one another or with distance separating them, she'd always had Isla. Known that Isla was out there. But within a handful of days that had changed, irrevocably. The other half of her soul was gone, and by leaving Cassie, Isla had taken that tacit security away.

As Cassie swallowed down tears, a wave of loneliness threatened to choke her. With her father gone, and her mother barely functioning, still hovering on the edge of grief, Cassie suddenly felt entirely alone.

Closing her eyes, she directed her thoughts to Stuart. Her future. He was right here, the man she could potentially spend the rest of her life with, so why was she feeling so isolated?

. . .

Twenty minutes later, having kissed the top of Marina's head
and Stuart's cheek, and leaving a plate of sandwiches for them
in the fridge, Cassie left the loft and walked briskly across the
bridge spanning the Water of Leith. The late August sun was
peeking from behind a veil of lacy cloud as a breeze curled
across the water and lifted Cassie's hair from the back of her
neck, making her shiver. Her sandals were clicking noisily on
the pavement as around her the life of this, her favourite part of
the city, buzzed.

She'd called Syd just moments ago to tell him she was
going into work, unsurprised to find that he was already at the
studio, and now, knowing that she was only a few minutes
away from seeing her best friend, she picked up her pace. She
pictured Syd's face, the wide smile, the intense amber eyes,
and the way he slapped his lean thighs with both hands when
he laughed hard. She wondered what he'd say about her
bringing Marina here, about her playing mother, but Cassie
knew that Syd would support her and tell her she'd done the
right thing, the only thing she could. Marina deserved better
than life had given her and the more that sank in, the more
determined Cassie became to right the little girl's listing
world.

Cassie skipped into the street momentarily, dodging a
young woman with a double stroller, then crossed Commercial
Street to the two-storey warehouse that housed her studio.
Before she could put her key in the big metal lock, the door was
buzzed open from upstairs and, smiling up at the paned
window, she pushed the door open and ran up the stairs, two at
a time.

Syd was sitting at his computer, his back to the door. 'Hi,
Cass. I saw you across the road.' He swung around in his chair,
then, seeing her face, he stood up and opened his arms wide.

'Come here, my beautiful friend.' His mouth dipped at the corners. 'How are you?'

Cassie walked into his arms and buried her head in his shoulder, catching the scent of coffee and the cinnamon he always dusted his lattes with. Her eyes filled, and her throat knotted itself as she stepped back. 'I'm OK, Syd. I mean, I'm not, but...' She shrugged, digging into her giant bag for a tissue. 'It's been a shitty few days, to be honest.' She found a packet of tissues and pulled one out. 'I had no idea I could cry this much.' She exhaled, mortified when a tiny bubble formed at her left nostril. 'Or produce this much snot.' She gave a choked laugh as she wiped her nose.

'Sit yourself down and I'll make some tea.' Syd's large hands were on her upper arms as he eased her back into the swivel chair across from his desk. 'For the record, I've always known you were a snotty cow.' His face was blank for a moment, then it folded into his trademark grin, the large space between his two front teeth filled with the tip of his rosy tongue.

'Oh, shut it.' Cassie gave a shaky laugh, then blew her nose loudly. 'Can you lace that with something please?' She spoke to his back as he stood at the long counter where the sink and kettle were.

Filling the kettle, Syd shook his head, the shine on his shaved head making it look like a big, ebony egg. 'No more day boozing for you, man. You're a mother now. You have responsibilities.' He turned and caught sight of her slack jaw. 'No more late-night wine-and-design sessions. No more spontaneous buying trips to London, or Brussels.' He wagged a long finger at her. 'So, talk. I want a minute-by-minute account of everything that's happened. How is it going at home? How are you coping? What did Stuart say about everything? And how is the little girl?' He paused. 'I'm sorry but I don't remember her name.' He grimaced, holding his hands out, palms up.

'Marina.' Cassie swallowed hard, his questions making her

situation feel startlingly real. A few days ago, she had taken about three seconds to make a decision that would alter the course of her life, forever, and this was perhaps the first opportunity she'd had to fully consider what that meant. 'God, Syd, what have I done?' Her hand shot to her mouth, and her face felt suddenly hot, so she shrugged her suede jacket off and draped it over the back of the chair. 'I don't even know if I can *do* this. Be a mother, I mean.' She accepted the steaming mug he held out to her, lowering it to her thigh and feeling the heat instantly permeate her jeans. 'I haven't a clue what I'm doing.'

Syd eyed her as he sat back in his chair. 'Darling girl. You already *are* a mother. You've been mothering for almost a year.' He gave an exaggerated smile. 'You have a six-foot tall, bouncing baby boy, called Stuart.'

Despite herself, Cassie laughed, as a last tear trickled down her cheek. She swiped it away and nodded. 'You're right, but that daft, boyish charm is part of what I like about him.' She took a sip of the hot tea. 'I think Marina might actually be more mature than him.' She laughed again and wiped her nose once more. Syd had a magical way of helping her put things in perspective.

Syd set his mug on the desk and linked his fingers between his knees. 'Seriously though, Cassie. If anyone can do this, it's you. You're strong enough. You have enough love.' He leaned back and grinned again. 'And you have me – so you're all good.'

'I know I do, but I can't lean on you the way I have been this past week. I basically abandoned you, and right before a launch.' She dropped her eyes to her mug. 'I need to get my life in order.'

'And you will.' He shook his head. 'Give yourself a break, honey. It's only been a week. You lost your only sister and gained a five-year-old child. No one on earth would be taking that on without some fear, and a bucketload of self-doubt.' He lifted his mug and took a sip. 'You're not super-friggin'-woman, even though you think you are.'

She smiled at her friend. 'Thanks, Syd. I'm just scared. I want to do whatever I can to give Marina the life she was meant to have. I just wish there was an instruction manual for heart-broken five-year-old girls, because I've probably done so much wrong, already. Like, first, don't drag her away from the only home she's ever known. Second, don't install her in your bland spare room and tell her it's all going to be fine. And third, never leave her with your slobby but lovable boyfriend who probably wouldn't notice if she goes out and buys herself a beer and some cigarettes.' She gave a soft laugh.

Syd shrugged. 'Best advice?'

She nodded. 'Please.'

'Follow your gut. Your instincts are rock solid. They never let you down, Cass.' He lowered his chin. 'I've been around you long enough to see that's true. Whatever you think is best for Marina, I guarantee you, is what is best. Let things unfold on their own. It will take time for her to adjust. And for you to learn all the ins and out of parenting. You're bound to make some mistakes here and there, but I have every faith in you.'

She let his words settle on her, the calm certainty of what he'd said clinging to her flushed face like a refreshing dew. To have this balm poured onto her raw nerves was exactly what she needed, and typical of Syd's sensitivity. The fact that she had not heard this same endorsement, or felt this level of interest, or concern, from Stuart suddenly hit home, and disappointment pushed up inside her.

Looking at her closest friend, the man she'd gone into busi-ness with straight out of university, who'd been there for her when she'd had her heart shattered by her first love, six years earlier, and then when her dad had passed away, and who was firmly here to support her again, she was overcome with grati-tude for his presence in her life. As close as they were, it had been wholly natural that she'd seen Syd through the devastating loss of his parents, in a bus accident in Johannesburg, just nine months earlier. Now, seeing his kind face, his soulful eyes, she thanked the universe for him, yet again.

Cassie stood up and crossed the studio, stopping at the row of windows overlooking Commercial Street. Hearing the mournful wail of a foghorn, floating in from the sea, she watched the cars slipping past and the collection of people dotted along the pavements below. Some were walking alone, others holding hands, going about their day as if everything was normal in the world, blissfully ignorant of the tidal wave of change that she was navigating.

They'd spent an hour talking through the logistics of the launch of the new collection. Thankfully, Cassie's main involvement was in the design phase of a new range of jewellery, which had been completed months ago, and in her absence, Syd had managed the final stages with his usual flair. The first samples had come out of production with virtually no alterations required.

The Infinity line was a collection of silver bracelets made up of alternating extended oval loops and concentric circles, each linked to the other by a small silver fist. Each bracelet was slightly different in the number of ovals or circles it comprised and the configuration of the links. The clasp was customisable with a circular indentation where the customer could insert either their birthstone, a sliver of mother-of-pearl or an enamel disc that came in several colours. Cassie had enjoyed designing them, working with the pure simplicity of the shapes, and Syd had come up with the clasp idea, as a way of individualising each piece.

As with all their products, they had named each one, and in this case, they'd used traditional Gaelic women's names. On

Cassie's insistence, each display box would contain a small card giving both the name's meaning and the correct phonetic pronunciation. The collection of six designs consisted of the Moire, Caitlin, Labhra, Edina, Fiona and finally the Isla – a particularly delicate bracelet with multiple pairs of identically sized, connected circles. It had made Cassie think about the eternal link between her and Isla and naming it for her had been a small but deeply personal tribute to her beloved sister. That Cassie had taken that decision before knowing of Isla's death now made the gesture even more significant.

Now, as they studied the samples, Cassie held one up to the light, the mother-of-pearl glimmering. 'They look great, Syd. I'm so pleased with them.' She set the bracelet back on the black velvet tray that lay on the design table.

'Yeah, me too.' He lifted the tray and slid it into the long cabinet that sat along the back wall. 'Hey, why don't you take one of the Isla samples and make it fit Marina?' He smiled. 'I bet she'd love it, man.'

Cassie smiled. 'That's a lovely idea.' She walked to the kitchen area and put the empty mugs in the sink.

'You could put her birthstone in it.' Syd was next to her, gently nudging her out of the way as he lifted the scourer and began washing up. 'Move. You wash up like my half-blind grandma.' He huffed.

Cassie playfully thumped his solid bicep, picturing Marina's narrow wrist with one of their designs around it, then she frowned. She didn't know Marina's birthday, never mind the size of her wrist. There was so much she didn't know about this little person who had already taken up so much room in her heart, but despite that, what Cassie *was* sure of was that she would learn. She would figure out how to do this – all of this – and do it right.

12

Marina had had a better night, waking only once, and asking for a drink of milk. Cassie had heated some up and then read to her, until Marina had fallen back to sleep. Marina's hand had been clasped around Cassie's wrist and, reluctant to break the precious connection, Cassie had lain next to her for an hour until Cassie's hip went numb, before easing herself out of the bed, then tiptoeing back to her own room.

Having had her conversation with Syd, Cassie felt a little less adrift, but earlier that evening, when she'd asked Stuart to watch Marina for a couple of hours the next day, to let her visit her mother, he'd seemed reluctant. 'I suppose so, but don't be too long.' His brown eyes had been filled with what looked like panic. 'I've got to work on the new song, and Charlie and the guys are getting together at the Fiddler's Arms at two, and I said I'd meet them.' He'd reeled off a couple more band members who'd be at the pub at the Grassmarket, by the castle, where they often met for a late Sunday lunch, while Cassie was with her mother.

Tempted to ask him to change his plans, just this once, to help her out, Cassie had instead bitten her tongue. She had, after all, sprung this drastic change on him by bringing Marina into his life, with no notice or chance to discuss how he felt about it, so the least she could do was allow him this time to himself – and to adjust.

Later that night, Stuart had quickly passed out after a large plate of spaghetti Bolognaise, and telling a series of corny knock-knock jokes that had made Marina giggle – a sweet, musical sound that had warmed Cassie's insides. She had lain next to him in bed and taken in his slender wrists and angular shoulders, the tangle of fair curls on the pillow, and the way he slept with one arm draped across his eyes, as if he was sheltering from the sun. Once again, she'd pictured the three of them, functioning as a family, something that even to imagine left her feeling full of hope, until she'd eventually drifted off herself.

This morning, Cassie had scrambled to get breakfast out of the way before telling Marina that she was going out for a while, again. Marina had looked as if she might cry until Cassie had promised to bring her an ice lolly on her way home. 'I won't be more than a couple of hours, my love, and you can watch the other *Frozen* film while I'm gone.' She'd pointed at the clock on the cooker that read 11.46 a.m. 'See when that clock says this?' She'd written 1.45 on a piece of paper and put it in front of Marina. 'That's when I'll be back.' She'd hugged Marina, who had insisted on choosing her own clothes that morning and was sporting a pair of leggings covered in butterflies and a long T-shirt with a faded unicorn on the front. Her feet were in a pair of yellow, duck slippers, each complete with a bright orange bill and two dark beads for eyes, and Marina's hair was loose, flowing down her back in a sea of chocolatey waves. 'You look lovely, today.'

Cassie had tucked the hair behind Marina's ears and cupped her chin, the urge to change her plans and stay at home suddenly overwhelming. The thought of leaving the little girl again had left Cassie feeling edgy, and not only because she was slightly anxious about Stuart's ability to remain focused enough to watch Marina closely, but also because Cassie found that being apart from her niece was becoming more of a wrench each time. But until Cassie had seen her mother, had the chance to explain what had happened to Isla, and gently introduce the concept of her having a granddaughter she'd never met, there was no alternative.

Sadie's first-floor flat was on North Junction Street, a ten-minute walk from the loft across the Water of Leith, in a three-storey converted warehouse building. Its facia was dashed with rows of sash windows, and a set of well-worn stone steps led up to each of the four, glossy green front doors. Cassie liked the way the building seemed to watch her, like a line of friendly faces looking down on her, the windows the eyes and the sandstone lintels above them the eyebrows. She'd always look up and give them a nod as she went through the front door, using the key that her mother had given her.

At one end, the building housed a small pub called The Dolphin, with a friendly local clientele, and next to it was one of the best fish and chip shops in Edinburgh. Sometimes, if her mother was tired, or if Cassie was popping over midweek for a visit after work, they'd treat themselves to a fish supper, the crisp haddock always piping hot, and the gloriously thick chips soaked in malt vinegar.

Aside from the proximity to Cassie's home, one of the main reasons Sadie had bought the flat was its location opposite a pretty park where she liked to walk each day, and they'd often go over there after their Sunday meal. There was a particular bench that Sadie liked to stop at, where they'd sit shoulder to shoulder, and watch the swans gliding across the pond that the park encompassed.

Cassie had called her mother that morning to remind her

that she'd be coming over at noon and now, as she climbed the steps, saying her customary hello to the faces above, Cassie's stomach was twisting angrily. She'd made a note to call Doctor Carnegie first thing on Monday and now, all she could do was will the pain not to build to something she couldn't hide from her mother.

Rather than let herself in, Cassie rang her mother's door-bell, somehow wanting to delay the inevitable, even if only for a few more seconds.

A few moments later, Sadie opened the door to the flat and smiled broadly. 'Hello, love. Come in, come in.' Her face was pale, her half-lensed glasses summarily smudged, and her camel-coloured cardigan buttoned up over her favourite Black Watch tartan trousers.

Cassie took a second to compose herself, once again second-guessing her decision to have gone to Lewis alone and drip-feed her mother with the shocking truths Cassie had been absorbing since learning of Isla's death. But regret, at this stage, was point-less, so she dropped her bag near the door and hugged her mother tight to her chest.

As Sadie began to gently pat Cassie's back, as she had done ever since Cassie was a child, Sadie's soft curls tickled Cassie's chin, and her eyes filled. All her strength and resolve to handle this in a calm, collected way evaporated as she melted into her mother's embrace.

'Gosh, that's quite a hug.' Sadie eased herself back from Cassie's arms and, seeing her face, instantly frowned. 'What's wrong, love?' She shoved the murky glasses further up her nose. 'Come and sit down. I've got the kettle on.'

Torn between relief that her mother seemed a little stronger than usual today and dread at what she had to share, Cassie followed Sadie along the narrow hall and into the bright kitchen. The small drop-leaf table that sat under the window was laid for two, and Cassie could smell something fragrant and spicy – like a curry – in the oven.

Sadie made tea, talking animatedly about her friend Jean, who lived next door, and the ginger kitten that had shown up on her doorstep the previous morning. Meanwhile, Cassie sat at the table, her heart pattering wildly as she mentally re-rehearsed her script. Then, Sadie set a mug in front of Cassie and sat down opposite her daughter.

'It's lovely to see you.' Sadie gave a single nod, then looked at her daughter quizzically.

There was no way to put this off any longer, so, Cassie's heart threatening to explode through her white linen shirt, she reached across the table and took her mother's free hand in hers, feeling a slight tremor in the bony fingers. 'Mum, I have some-thing very sad, and difficult, to tell you. It's about Isla.'

At the mention of Isla's name, Sadie lifted her chin abruptly. 'What do you mean?'

Cassie took a steadying breath, then spoke softly. 'Isla's gone, Mum.'

Sadie shook her head. 'Och, I know. But she'll be back. You know what she's like. Always was a bit of a flibbertigibbet.'

'No, Mum. I mean she's gone.' Cassie's heart contracted as she willed her voice not to give out. 'There was an accident, and she's passed away.' She heard herself say the words, but she still felt removed from them, like they were a line from a tragic play, and not related to her, or her mother.

Sadie's hand shot up to cover her mouth, leaving Cassie's hand achingly empty, Sadie's face turning ashen. 'You can't mean that.' She spoke through her fingers as she pushed her mug away. Then, seeing Cassie's expression, Sadie closed her eyes. 'How do you know?' she sputtered. 'What happened?'

Cassie steeled herself, mustering every molecule of strength that was left to her, and then spoke as fluidly as she could. 'She drowned, just over a week ago. She'd been living over on Lewis for the past few years.' Cassie paused, picturing the cottage and the stunning seascape that had captivated both her sister, and her. 'It happened at the beach right by her home.' Cassie's voice finally cracked, and she gulped down a sob as Sadie's face contorted, her mouth gaping and her tongue curling towards the back of her throat, the agonised expression more than Cassie could bear.

A single fat tear oozed over Sadie's bottom lid, and her whole body began to tremble, as she reached over and enclosed Cassie's hand with hers. 'Oh, my Isla,' Sadie croaked, gasping between sobs. 'My poor, sweet girl.'

'Mum. I'm so, so sorry.' Cassie stood up, circled the table, knelt in front of her mother and wrapped her in her arms, tears tracking freely down Cassie's face. 'I'm here. I'll always be here.'

13

Cassie had stayed with her mother for two more hours, making her some sweet tea, and calling Jean to tell her what had happened and asking her to come and stay with Sadie for a while.

Torn between desperately wanting to comfort her mother and being anxious that Marina was at home with Stuart, who would be wanting to leave for the pub, Cassie eventually told Sadie that she had to go to the studio, but that she'd call that evening and be back the next day.

Cassie had held her quivering mother tightly, breathing in the soft scent of lily-of-the-valley and wishing that she could take on all the heartbreak herself. Then she'd tugged on her jacket, waited for Jean to arrive, and cried the entire walk home. The cool breeze had cut right through her clothes, as she avoided the curious and concerned gazes of the numerous people she passed, her chin dipped as she focused on the pavement.

Fifteen minutes later than she said she'd be home, she let herself into the loft and instantly heard Marina crying in the spare room. Having just had possibly the most shattering experience of her life with her mother, this was far from what Cassie had hoped to come home to.

She had left Sadie with Jean, who'd said she would stay with Sadie until she went to bed. Not able to explain why she needed to leave, and not stay the night as she would have had it not been for Marina, Cassie was grateful when Jean didn't question her about it.

Cassie had not said anything about Marina, as Sadie had been inconsolable, and afraid to overload her with too much shocking information to process, Cassie had decided to take the little girl with her the following day, in the hope that seeing her, meeting Isla's daughter, might help Sadie feel a little less destroyed.

Now, Cassie dumped her bag, kicked off her sandals and rushed along the hall and into the spare room. Marina was lying on the bed, her back to the door. Raffy was jammed up under her chin and she was sobbing into his twisted neck. The doleful sound sparked a painful tugging in Cassie's chest, as she gently rolled Marina over and scooped her up into her arms. 'What is it, little one?' she crooned. 'What's happened?'

Marina wrapped her arms and legs around Cassie's frame and buried her face in Cassie's hair. She felt the intense pressure of the hug, a sensation that brought with it a wave of such overwhelming, protective love that Cassie blinked several times to clear her vision. Instinctively, she began to slowly rock from one foot to the other, as if she knew that gentle motion would help distract Marina from whatever it was that had driven her to such heart-rending misery.

'Marina, sweetheart, can you tell me what's wrong?' Cassie tried again.

Marina lifted her head a little and sniffed loudly in Cassie's ear. 'I didn't mean to.' Her breath was raspy. 'I didn't mean it.'

Just as Cassie was about to ask what she didn't mean, Stuart appeared in the door. His shoulders had rolled forward with the force of him jamming his hands into his pockets and his mouth was set in a miserable line.

'What's going on?' she mouthed, still moving from foot to foot as Marina's sobs began to subside.

Stuart pulled his hands out of his pockets and raked one through his tangle of curls. 'I'm afraid I got a bit angry with her.' He grimaced. 'But Marina touched something I told her not to, and now it's ruined.'

Cassie frowned, supporting Marina's weight beginning to make her arms ache. 'What on earth?'

Stuart pointed behind her to where the guitar had been propped up on the stand. It was an expensive Martin, acoustic electric model, that he had bought after touring the factory in Pennsylvania the year before. As Cassie turned around, she saw it leaning against the wall, the honey-coloured face scarred with a network of dark blue and green scribbles.

Her heart sank as she walked over and saw a packet of Sharpie pens scattered across the rug, and a few sheets of Stuart's music lying there, with similar scribbles on them. Taking a moment to process it all, Cassie closed her eyes briefly, then turned to face him. 'I'm really sorry, Stu. I'll replace it.' She saw his eyebrows lift.

'It cost over two thousand dollars, Cassie.' He shook his head. 'I told her not to touch it.' He held his palms up as Marina hiccupped.

'I know, and I said I'll replace it.' Cassie eyed him, then mouthed, 'She's only five,' a mixture of guilt and frustration making her suck in her bottom lip. She shouldn't have left them alone together again. It was too soon.

Marina leaned back in Cassie's arms and looked into her eyes, heavy tears clinging to the little girl's mass of eyelashes. 'He said I was a bad girl, but I was making it pretty.' Her lower lip quivered as she swiped her runny nose with the back of her hand. 'My mummy said I was a good girl.' She gulped. 'I want to go home.'

Cassie's heart ached as she pressed her cheek against Marina's, a salty tear leaking into Cassie's mouth. 'It's all right, sweetheart.' She felt Marina shudder. 'It's going to be all right. I'll fix everything.'

Once Stuart left for the pub, after dropping a perfunctory kiss on her forehead, it had taken Cassie a while to calm Marina down. Cassie had taken her for a walk along the water, bought them an ice cream cone, which they'd then eaten sitting next to one another on the sofa. As they'd watched cartoons, Marina had eventually lain down, with her head on Cassie's knee, as Cassie combed her fingers gently through the river of long dark waves. The movement had been meditative and calming for them both and soon Marina had nodded off with her arms looped around Raffy's neck.

Now, careful not to wake her niece, Cassie eased herself up from the sofa, took her phone into her bedroom and called Syd. As she paced, chewing on the skin around her thumb, she heard his voicemail kick in, so she left him a whispered SOS message, asking him to please call her back whenever he could. Just hearing his voice would help ease her nerves.

Back in the kitchen, she eyed the half-bottle of Sauvignon in the fridge, but wanting to keep a clear head, she closed the door and made herself a coffee instead. Then she checked her emails, put in a load of laundry and hovered in the living room, waiting for Marina to wake up.

As she watched the child sleep, Marina moved her arm above her head and stretched, her legs extending fully and her toes spreading wide, and another wave of déjà vu struck Cassie. What was it about this little girl, who only vaguely resembled Isla, that felt so familiar?

Just as Cassie was about to try Syd again, Marina opened her eyes and sat up. She looked around the room, and Cassie waited for comprehension to cloud the dark-rimmed eyes again, but instead Marina smiled, leaned to her left, laughed and then snorted softly.

Relieved, but unsure what was happening, Cassie moved over and sat next to her. 'Hello, sleepyhead. Were you dreaming?'

Marina took a second to register the question, then she nodded. 'Uh-huh.'

Cassie smiled at her. 'What about?'

Marina met her eyes, then gave the little snort-like laugh again – another tiny gift that Cassie willingly accepted. 'Raffy was chasing me.' She smiled, then stuck her thumb into her mouth and spoke around it. 'We had bananas for tea.'

Caught off guard, Cassie pulled a funny face. 'Well, you can have some banana now, if you like?' She gestured towards the kitchen, where the fruit bowl stood on the island.

'OK.' Marina nodded, stood up and adjusted her leggings. 'Can Raffy have some, too?'

Cassie nodded. 'Of course. We can't have him going hungry.' She made her way to the kitchen, Marina trailing her, then Cassie helped Marina onto one of the stools at the island and sliced a banana into some yogurt, placing the bowl in front of the little girl. 'Eat up.'

Just as Marina was going to take a bite, she held the spoon in front of her mouth, and paused.

'What is it?' Cassie scanned the spoonful, wondering if she'd missed something – forgotten some magic element to the perfect bite.

Marina blinked, then lowered her spoon. 'My mummy said I was a good girl.' She lifted her gaze to Cassie's. 'Why is Uncle Stuart angry?'

Cassie felt the sharp edge of the question and it sent a chill down her back. How could she explain his behaviour and not let her own disappointment show? 'He's not angry anymore, sweetheart. He just gets grumpy when he's tired. But if he tells you not to do something, next time try to listen to him. OK?' She smiled at the earnest little face. 'Now eat up.'

Stuart crept into bed beside her, and Cassie lay still, feigning sleep. It was after 11 p.m. and she was exhausted. The last thing she wanted was a drunken, fumbled attempt at lovemaking or, worse, an argument. She'd left his bedside light on for him, as she always did when he was out late, and as she kept her eyes closed, expecting the smell of beer to accompany him into the bed, she was surprised to smell the tang of toothpaste instead, and then feel his fingers gently moving a long hank of hair away from her cheek.

'Are you awake, gorgeous?' He leaned in and kissed her jaw, his cheek prickling hers as his lips then moved down to the curve of her neck. 'Cassie?' His cool breath made her shiver, involuntarily, and despite her exhaustion, hope of them finding common ground made her turn onto her back and look up at him.

'I am now.' She widened her eyes. 'What is it, eejit?'

Stuart shifted up and leant back against the headboard, his face unusually taut and his eyes intense. 'Can we talk?'

Cassie knew that tone. It was something she'd heard perhaps twice in their entire relationship, and it usually accompanied him telling her something he knew she wouldn't like. Her body heavy with fatigue, and a sense of foreboding creeping back into her momentary hopefulness, she pulled herself up and sat next to him. 'OK.'

Stuart lifted her hand from the duvet and linked his fingers through hers. 'Look, I'm sorry I got angry with her.' He paused, as Cassie bristled at him not using Marina's name. 'But this is a lot. You know.' He absently massaged her palm with his thumb. 'I'm just not sure what to do, or how to be with her.' He pressed a little harder, his thumb finding a tiny knot of tension that ordinarily Cassie would have let him knead out of her hand, but now she slid it away.

'What do you mean?' She looked at his profile, an angular silhouette, outlined against the pool of light beside him.

'I don't know how to deal with Marina.' He turned to look at her. 'Cassie, I don't know if I'm ready to be a dad.' He locked on her eyes for a few silent and yet eloquent seconds, then dropped his gaze to his lap.

Cassie pushed the covers away and shifted to the edge of the bed, the need to put some distance between them overwhelming. If this was going in the direction she thought it was, she needed to protect herself, if not with words, then at least with some personal space. 'Stu, she's only been here a couple of days. We all need to find our feet.' She grabbed her robe from the end of the bed and shrugged it on, pulling the belt tight around her waist. 'I know I sprang this on you, and that wasn't fair. I'm sorry for that. But there really was no other choice to be made. It'll just take us all some time.' She turned to face him, seeing his frown and the slight shake of his head. 'I'm sure we'll get there.'

He avoided her eyes, turning to look at the golden strip of light outlining the curtains.

Disappointed at his silence, she continued, 'I'm all she's got in the world, Stu.' She patted her tightening chest. 'We are all she's got.' She drew a line in the air between them, hoping that he'd turn to face her, a new smile behind his chocolatey eyes.

Stuart moved the duvet away and got up, his pyjama bottoms trailing on the floor as he walked to the window, then he leaned his hips against the sill. 'Cassie, what I'm saying is that I want to be with you, so I'm going to try to make this work, but I don't know if I'm cut out to be a father.'

'You mean so soon?' She held her breath, each second painfully elongated as she waited for his answer.

'I mean, maybe ever.' He frowned, his hooded gaze sliding back to the floor.

Suddenly, unable to absorb one more emotionally charged element into her life, Cassie took a deep breath. Tears had no place in this conversation, and she must keep them from seeping in and diluting her message, so she controlled her voice as best she could. 'Perhaps we both need time to think, Stuart? I can see that. But I'm afraid there's no question of Marina going anywhere, and whatever that means as far as our relationship goes, we need to figure it out soon.' She paused. 'I can't have her feeling any more unsettled than she already does, so you and I need to make some decisions.'

'Right. I get it.' He eyed her. 'But I don't know if time will change how I'm feeling. I'm sorry, Cassie.' His mouth dipped at the corners, but this time there was no mischievous sparkle behind his eyes. No musical laugh waiting to burst forth and lighten the moment.

Cassie felt as if the walls were closing in, the air growing thick and her ears beginning to ring. Was this real? Was he going to make her choose between them – because if so, her choice had already been made when she'd laid eyes on Marina.

14

Monday morning was a classic, dreich day in Auld Reekie – the nickname that Edinburgh had been given, centuries earlier. It had been coined in the seventeen hundreds, when the city had been enclosed on three sides by a high wall, and the Nor' Loch water along the fourth side, to protect it from invaders. As the population had grown inside the enclosed space, and it had become overcrowded, the smoke rising from all the chimneys and coal fires, combined with the stench of the Nor' Loch – that had stood where Princes Street Gardens now was – had all created a foul-smelling fog that had become unbearable for the residents. Three centuries later, the city had been lauded as the Athens of the north and was renowned for its beauty, and architectural splendour, but the nickname still lingered – as the smell once had.

Edinburgh's August weather was often a mixture of the warmth of the tail end of summer and damp glimpses of the autumn to come. This had never bothered Cassie before, but today she didn't have time for rain. She was already late getting into the studio, couldn't find Marina's jeans or wellington boots, and Stuart had been in the bathroom for forty-five minutes, despite her tapping on the door repeatedly and telling him that Marina needed the toilet. He'd eventually come out and gone straight back to bed, leaving Cassie dashing around, still in her underwear, and Marina half-dressed and glued to the TV, with her thumb in her mouth.

Cassie had made an appointment with Parkview Primary School, nearby in Leith, for later that morning, and as she finally found Marina's jeans and boots stuffed under the spare bed and passed the master bedroom, where Stuart was already snoring again, she knew there was no way she could ask him to watch Marina, while she went to the meeting.

As she helped Marina into her trousers, and then threw on a pair of jeans, and a creamy silk sweater, Cassie sifted through ideas of what to do with the little girl for the hour Cassie would be at the school. Inevitably, Syd came to mind, and she crossed her fingers and hoped that he wouldn't mind helping her out.

'You're going to come into work with me today, sweetheart. And see my office. That'll be fun, won't it?' Cassie brushed Marina's hair and pushed it back from her face with a tartan-covered Alice band, the thought of having Marina with her brightening the prospect of the day.

Marina shrugged, her lips pursing. 'Mummy's work was at home.' She tipped her head to the side. 'I went with her every day.'

Picturing the glass-paned door, set in the hillside, leading to Isla's workshop, Cassie nodded. 'Yes, and I bet that was fun. Being with Mummy when she was making her beautiful statues?'

Marina nodded, a glaze seeming to sweep across her eyes, dulling the life in them.

'Right, let's get this show on the road.' Cassie chivvied her niece along, before any more memories, or perhaps tears, could waylay them further.

Ten minutes later, they put on their waterproof jackets,

closed the door behind them and walked down the stairs and out onto Shore. The wind instantly buffeted them, bringing with it the metallic smell of the water, and the sounds of the harbour coming to life. A radio thumped from inside a passing car as Cassie drew Marina close to her side, sheltering her under a giant golf umbrella.

As they headed for the bridge, Marina happily stamping in many of the network of puddles that had gathered on the pavement in front of the loft building, Cassie laughed at her antics, then found herself replaying Stuart's startling statement about parenthood over and over on a loop in her mind. She knew that he was genuinely struggling with the drastic change she'd foisted upon him, and part of her wanted to take the time to help him work through his fears, discover a way to find peace with this new dynamic in their lives. But for now, she was necessarily focused on Marina. On getting her into the right school, and more importantly, on taking her to meet Sadie. From there, Cassie had no idea how the day, and now, her future with Stuart, would play out. All she knew was that Marina was quickly becoming her priority, and with that, Cassie realised that she was growing excited at what lay ahead.

Syd had, predictably, been an angel, welcoming Marina with a huge hug. 'I'm your Uncle Syd.' He'd grinned as Marina had smiled shyly up at him. 'I'm the most fun one of this lot, so whenever you need cheering up, I'm your man.' He'd winked and patted his broad chest. He'd then set up a special drawing board for Marina and laid out a pile of coloured pencils next to a bowl of strawberries he'd brought in from his greenhouse. 'Sit here, my little darling. Have a strawberry. They taste like sunshine.' He'd pulled the swivel chair out and laughed. 'Uncle Syd will feed you up, and then we'll draw a lovely picture.' He'd nodded at the drawing board as a grateful Cassie had mouthed, 'Thank you.'

Hector had been in the office, too, working on the marketing campaign for the Infinity line, and had offered to help keep Marina amused – maybe even play the bagpipes for her, if she liked. He kept a small set of indoor pipes at the studio and would play whenever they contracted a new distributor, or received a huge order, and Cassie and Syd would laugh as he marched around the studio, his blue eyes twinkling, his long, brown ponytail bouncing between his shoulders, and a bony elbow pumping the tartan bag as the mournful wail of 'Flower of Scotland', or 'Scotland the Brave', filled the airy space.

Cassie had been so grateful at their willingness to help her that she'd hugged them both tightly. 'You two are the best. I honestly don't know what I'd do without you.'

When the time had come to head out, she'd kissed Marina and told her she'd be back soon, then, once again feeling torn at having to leave her little niece, dashed off to the school.

Cassie had already filled out the official application for Marina online, but was relieved that, twenty minutes later, the meeting with the head teacher was going well. The head was a soft-spoken woman called Mhairi Sommerfield. Perhaps in her late thirties, she had kind, hazel eyes, and a shiny cap of blonde hair.

'Your application is all in order, Miss Hunter, and so, on the first day of the autumn term, next week, please bring Marina to the main office first, to meet me. Then I'll introduce her to her class teacher, Miss Stanley. She will take you and Marina to see her classroom for the first time and will introduce her to the children in her form.' She nodded. 'I'm sure your daughter will do well, here.' She smiled warmly.

Cassie let the word spin for a few seconds, enjoying its implication, then she shook her head. 'I meant to tell you, Miss

Sommerfield. Marina is my niece. My sister...' Her voice caught, so she softly cleared her throat. 'My sister has passed away, and Marina lives with me, now.'

'Oh, I didn't realise.' The head teacher's cheeks began to colour. 'I'm so sorry about your sister, but Marina is very lucky to have you.' She smiled, almost shyly. 'We'll take care of her, Miss Hunter. We'll make sure she settles in OK.'

'Thanks. I have a good feeling about this place.' Cassie nodded. 'And you.' She found a smile. 'So, we'll see you next Monday?'

'Lovely.' Miss Sommerfield nodded, handed Cassie a list of everything that Marina would need and then showed Cassie out, wishing her a good week. Her to-do list was already at the point of exploding, and now she had only six days to get Marina ready for her first proper school experience, and all that entailed. The responsibility of managing this major landmark in her niece's life, the first of many such special moments that Isla would not be there to witness, was overwhelming. But now, as Cassie thought about taking Marina in to meet her teachers and classmates, and seeing where she would sit, play during breaks, and wait for her to come and pick her up, it all sent a sparkle of excited anticipation through Cassie that made her eyes prickle.

Parkview was an excellent school, and only a short walk from the loft, which added not only to its appeal, but also to the convenience factor of getting Marina there each day and collecting her afterwards. Cassie had hoped that she'd be able to rely, at least to some extent, on Stuart to help with picking Marina up, filling the gap between the end of school and Cassie getting home from work, but based on the scene she'd come home to the previous night, all evidence pointed to the contrary. Cassie also needed to make sure that she could manage without asking for too much help from her mother, and while that tugged sorely at her heart, she'd simply have to find a way to make it happen. If Stuart came around, which she still hoped he would, then, in time, he might step up and become more involved. For now, however disappointing it was, she would count him out of the care equation.

When she'd got back to the studio, she'd hugged Marina, and admired her lovely drawing. Grateful that the little girl was so happily occupied, Cassie had gone through her emails, returned some calls from suppliers, and spoken with the local, artisan manufacturer they used. With her checklist complete, Cassie now swung her chair around to see Marina, sitting at Hector's desk, her cheeks flushed and her little wellington boots swinging back and forth under his chair. She was eating a cheese and cucumber sandwich that Cassie knew Hector had intended for his lunch.

Cassie smiled fondly at the young man. 'Oh, Hector. That's so sweet of you. Can I go and grab something else for you?'

He waved his hand, dismissively. 'Och, it's no bother. I need to lose a few, anyway.' He patted his washboard stomach. 'Marina is doing me a favour.' He winked at the little girl whose cheeks were pulsing as she chewed.

Syd was smiling from across the studio, his head down as he focused on his design board, but Cassie had seen the tell-tale lift to his cheek, the way his dazzling grin almost leaked around the sides of his face. He was fond of Hector, and although Syd was only four years older, he treated the younger man like his little brother – scolding him like a mother hen if he felt Hector deserved it and praising him liberally for every small victory.

As Cassie took a moment to take in the scene and enjoy it, surrounded by her chosen family, her heart felt lighter. Then, her mother's face materialised, floating like a gauzy veil across the happy scene. It was time to take Marina to see Sadie and navigate that as best she could, and all Cassie could hope for was that Sadie would find some joy in the child – find Marina as much of a comfort as Cassie did. Marina was a welcome, bright light in the dark that they all badly needed, and as Cassie looked across the studio at her niece, another rush of profound love pushed up inside her.

15

Marina stood next to Cassie at the front door of Sadie's flat, Marina's hand twitching inside Cassie's, and Marina's little boots shuffling on the rough doormat. Cassie had explained to Marina that she would be meeting her mummy's mummy, and Marina had asked, with heartbreaking earnestness, what her mummy's mummy's name was, where she lived and would she have any biscuits. Cassie had told her that her gran, Sadie, would definitely have Jammie Dodgers, as those were her favourites, which Marina had nodded sagely at, as if Sadie had earned her stamp of approval already.

As Cassie waited for the door to open, her stomach knotted painfully and she gasped, just as her mother appeared. Sadie's fair hair was wildly fluffy, as if she'd just had a fierce wind at her back, and her sheepskin slippers looked oversized and thread-bare. She wore a long, purple, collarless shirt that Cassie didn't recognise, over a pair of dark blue trousers. 'Hello, love.' Sadie's eyes were crimson and puffy as she nodded, then her gaze dropped to Marina and her eyebrows lifted.

'Hi, Mum.' Cassie eased herself half in the door. 'Can we come in?'

'Of course. And who's this bonnie wee thing?' Sadie's voice was hoarse as she stepped back and beckoned to them.

'Let's go inside, and I'll explain.' Cassie said.

Frowning slightly, Sadie closed the door behind them and then, rather than head for the kitchen as she usually did when Cassie arrived, led them into the sunny living room. The two wide windows overlooked the street, and in the distance, the green of the park was visible behind a long, wrought-iron fence.

Sadie sat down in her wing-backed chair, next to the window, and pointed at the two-seater sofa that faced the fire-place – above it, the new smart TV Cassie had installed for her, the year before. 'Do you want something to drink?' She addressed Cassie, but her eyes kept settling on Marina, who, rather than sit down, had wandered over to Sadie's bookshelf and was now staring intently at a framed photo of Cassie and Isla, when they'd been eleven years old, sitting between their parents at the beach. Cassie had forgotten about the photo, and seeing the way Marina seemed mesmerised by it, she knew she must speak quickly before the child said something that might upset Sadie. This was it.

'Mum, I want you to meet Marina.' She beckoned to the little girl, who, hearing her name, turned around.

'Pleased to meet you, Marina.' Sadie found a smile. 'And how do you know my Cassie?'

Cassie stood up, positioning herself behind Marina, letting her hands linger on the child's shoulders. 'Marina is Isla's daughter. This is your granddaughter, Mum.' She spoke slowly and softly.

Sadie blanched, her hand flying to her mouth, and her eyes instantly filling with tears. Her brow was repeatedly knitting, then smoothing again, as if she was party to some internal dialogue that was at first confusing, but then made sense.

After a few moments, she gathered herself, clearing her throat. 'My goodness. Well, come and say hello to your old granny, Marina. I'm so happy that you're here.' She stared over at Cassie and shook her head, Sadie's eyes full of questions, but then, a second later, she extended a hand to Marina, who momentarily leaned back against Cassie's legs.

Just as Cassie was about to say something to reassure Marina, to Cassie's surprise, Marina walked forwards, her eyes lighting up and her face opening into a sweet smile, as she slipped her fingers willingly into Sadie's.

'Hello.' Marina smiled shyly up at Sadie, her eyes scanning her grandmother's features as if seeing someone familiar.

Sadie stared at her granddaughter, Sadie's face awash with a gentle light that Cassie had not seen in a while, then Sadie smiled. A genuine smile, filled with recognition and warmth. 'Oh, you're a gorgeous wee thing.' Her eyes filled again, then she sat up straighter, her shoulders going back. 'She's like Isla...' She frowned slightly at Cassie, then shook her head, returning her gaze to Marina, who was still watching Sadie's every movement – as if mesmerised.

'Do you have Jammie Dodgers?' Marina's eyes were bright, her rosy mouth pursed in anticipation.

Sadie laughed, the sweet sound making Cassie exhale as the tension of the moment disintegrated. 'Yes, it so happens I do. And how did you know that, young lady?' Sadie gently poked Marina's tummy.

Marina giggled. 'Aunty Cassie told me.' She dipped her chin coyly. 'Can I have one?'

'May I *please* have one?' Cassie wiggled her eyebrows at Marina, who smiled broadly, then parroted Cassie's words.

'Yes, you may.' Sadie stood up, still holding Marina's hand. 'Come with me and we'll get you one, and maybe a glass of milk, too. Do you like milk?' Sadie walked towards the kitchen and Marina happily followed her. 'Your mummy loved milk when she was a little girl, Marina.'

Cassie watched them go into the hall, choosing to hang back

and let them have their time together. It was clear that Marina recognised something in Sadie, and that Sadie saw her lost daughter in her granddaughter's face, both responses being exactly what Cassie had hoped for.

Seeing them disappear down the hall, still talking to each other, Cassie smiled. While Isla's tragic death was so painful, and hard to comprehend, Marina was a gift that Isla had left them, to help them heal, and as the truth of that became clearer with every day that passed, Cassie tipped her head back and said a silent thank you to her sister, that felt overdue.

Marina had taken a book about the meaning of flowers from Sadie's shelf and was lying on her bed as Cassie tucked a light blanket over her legs and kissed her flushed cheek. 'I'll be in the lounge with Granny. You have a wee rest and then we'll all go for a walk. OK?'

Marina nodded sleepily as she turned the page. 'OK.'

Cassie smiled down at her and made to leave.

'Aunty Cassie?' Marina's voice was soft.

'Yes, sweetheart?' Cassie hovered in the open door.

'I like it here.' She patted the bedcover. 'It's cosy at Granny's.'

Cassie's heart bloomed, relief and happiness coursing through her. 'I'm so glad, Marina. Granny is very happy you're here, too.' She nodded. 'Now, try to have a nap.'

Marina turned to face the wall, the book falling closed beside her as she yawned widely.

In the lounge, Sadie had made them coffee and was sitting in her chair by the fireplace. She was staring at the window, a slight frown tugging at her forehead.

'I'm sorry I kept this from you yesterday, Mum. I just felt it would've been too much to dump everything on you at once. You're not angry with me, are you?' Spotting the coffee cup on the table next to the sofa, Cassie crossed the room, as Sadie's frown melted into a sad smile.

'No. I understand, Cassie.' She paused, her eyes taking on a dreamy sheen. 'She's a dear little thing. So gentle-natured, and obviously bright as a button, too.' She nodded to herself. 'I can see Isla in her, that's for sure. And the way Marina hesitates before she speaks, like she's making sure that what she's about to say is right – it's Isla all over.' She sipped some coffee, then balanced the cup on the arm of the chair. 'Why would Isla hide her from us, do you think?' Her eyes were full of pain again as Cassie shook her head, sadly.

'I've no idea, Mum. You know what she could be like, sometimes.' An image of Isla's notes flickered behind her eyes as Cassie swallowed hard. Not sharing her sister's words with her mother felt wrong, but there was already so much that Sadie was having to absorb that Cassie held her tongue. Just as she sat down and lifted her coffee cup from the table, Sadie continued.

'I have to say though...' She eyed her daughter. 'Is it just me or does she look a bit like Grant? She has those remarkable eyes, just like his.' Sadie circled her own eye with her finger.

Cassie felt jolted, blindsided by the mention of her ex, whom her mother had adored. Sadie had openly lamented his departure from her daughter's life, despite him ultimately wrecking Cassie's heart. This shocking tangent to the conversation made Cassie's breath hitch. 'What do you mean, Mum?' She set her cup back down.

'She has those same dark rings around the iris as he does.' Sadie traced her eye again. 'I think they call them limbal rings.' She met Cassie's startled gaze.

Cassie felt as if the ground was shifting underneath her, and she cleared her tight throat as her mother's words replayed themselves inside her head, each time growing a little louder until Cassie could sit still no longer.

Getting up, she walked over and leant against the

windowsill. Her heart clattering wildly now, she took a few moments to think about Marina's features, the streamlined nose, the heart-shaped face, the prominent jaw, and yes, those distinctive black rings around the sky-blue irises, and suddenly she saw it. She saw Grant there, and instantly felt the air leaving her in a rush. All those tiny moments of déjà vu came rushing back, the way Marina scrubbed at her eyes when she was tired and stretched all the way down to her toes. How she tipped her head to the side when watching TV, and the little snort that would follow a laugh – all came together to form a picture that Cassie had been blind to, and that sent her tumbling back in time.

Seven years earlier, before the twins had turned twenty-three, Isla had met Grant Henderson, a medical student, at a Christmas party. The following week she had brought him home and introduced him to Cassie. As fate would have it, Grant had immediately fallen hard for Cassie, and despite Isla being visibly hurt, unable to stop the momentum, instantly knowing that Grant was the person she was destined to spend her life with, Cassie had dived into a whirlwind relationship with the tall, blue-eyed, student doctor. She'd been young, and deeply in love, and all else had fallen victim to that – even her sister's feelings.

Grant had proposed within a matter of weeks, and they had planned to marry that April. While Isla had appeared to come to terms with what felt to them all as inevitable, this was something Cassie believed that Isla had never forgiven her for, and Cassie still couldn't think about how she'd handled it all, without regret.

In mid-June, while Cassie was still reeling, devastated that Grant had shockingly called off the wedding less than a month before the date, with little to no explanation, and just when she'd needed her sister the most, Isla had disappeared. The loss of her sister had been crushing, and inexplicable. Cassie's hurt over that had been compounded by the fact that having left her, Grant had never been in contact again – something she had been unable to understand, or process.

Now, her mind spinning out of control, Cassie asked herself if what Sadie had said was possible. Could Marina be Grant's child? And if so, how on earth had she ended up on Lewis, with Isla? As Cassie's cascading thoughts began to gather momentum, forming a hard lump of hurt and disbelief under her ribcage, she shook her head. No. It simply wasn't possible that the two people she had loved the most, in all the world, had done that to her. Was it?

16

They walked to the studio, mostly in silence, Marina happy to observe the passers-by, stopping only to pet a large, shaggy dog that approached them with its owner and when Cassie ducked into a chemist to buy some more antacids. She had an appointment the following day with her doctor, but in the meantime, her stomach pain was hovering at a distracting five-out-of-ten, and she had no time for that, not right now.

Cassie tried to focus on what she had planned for the rest of the day, but all she could think of were her mother's words and the more she played with the sickening idea that her ex-fiancé and her sister had slept together, the less believable it became. Grant had been the most honest and principled person she'd ever known, and the thought that he had cheated on her, and moreover, with her sister, was too fantastical to give credence to. It simply couldn't be true. But, when she started to look at the timing of her cancelled wedding, and of Isla leaving, those factors undeniably lined up, making it hard to discount as a possibility.

Back at the studio, Cassie settled Marina at the drawing

board once again and then beckoned to Syd, who was talking to Hector.

Seeing her expression, Syd patted Hector's shoulder and joined Cassie in the kitchen area. 'What's up?' He leaned against her, his firm shoulder level with her cheekbone. 'You look like you've seen a ghost.' He frowned.

'I kind of have.' Cassie's throat was bone dry. 'I think...' She paused. 'No. I *believe* that...' She couldn't go on, as, frustratingly, tears began to fill her eyes. 'Bloody hell.' She swiped at her face with her palm.

'Let's go for a walk.' Syd hooked his arm through hers and led her to the door. 'Hector, we're going out for a bit. Keep an eye on things, OK, my friend?' As they put their coats on, Syd gestured towards Marina, who was engrossed in colouring in a rainbow that he had outlined for her.

Hector nodded, then gave them a thumbs up as they walked out and headed for the stairs.

Outside, the rain had eased off and the wind had dropped a little. The Water of Leith was topped with frothy white peaks and a small boat, moored at the opposite side, was moving slightly, mimicking the motion beneath it. Cassie made a beeline for the bench that sat at the water's edge, on the cobble pavement across from the studio, and although it was soaking wet, she wrapped her coat tightly around her and sank onto the wooden seat.

Syd watched her sit and shook his head. 'Not me. That thing's saturated.' He stood in front of her and shoved his hand into the pockets of his jacket. 'So, what's going on? How did it go at your mum's?' His molten eyes held hers as Cassie forced a swallow and squared her shoulders.

'It's a long story, but the gist of it is that I think there's a chance that Marina could be Grant's daughter.' She shook her head as Syd's mouth fell open.

'What?' He turned and sat down next to her.

'Yes, I know. It's freaking unbelievable, but it all makes sense somehow.' She sniffed miserably and dug into her pocket for a tissue. Saying it out loud made it feel more plausible, and the thought of Isla and Grant's betrayal tore into Cassie's heart with such force that she pressed her palm to her chest.

'What makes sense?' Syd frowned.

'I kept feeling as if I already knew Marina. There were a few little things that seemed familiar, and yet didn't bring Isla to mind. It was certain mannerisms, and even the way Marina snorts after she laughs.' She gulped over a sob. 'I know it sounds crazy, but there were her eyes, too. There was something about them... and then the minute Mum saw her, she just came right out with it. She said, "oh, she has eyes just like Grant's."' Cassie took a breath, her heart thumping under her jacket as her hurt began to gather force. 'Then I started to think about Isla, her just disappearing that summer,' she paused. 'And not long after Grant backed out of our wedding.' She turned to face Syd, whose mouth was now pressed into a firm line. 'Think about it, Syd. Marina is five. Isla left just over six years ago. Grant dumped me around the same time, too.' She held her palms up. It's not rocket science.' She shook her head sadly. 'And then there were her notes.' The more she thought about it, all the pieces were fitting together more solidly, forming a sickening picture that Cassie could hardly bear to acknowledge.

Syd grabbed her hand and wrapped it between his cool palms. 'What notes? You never told me about any notes.' He waited for her to go on.

'I found a half-written one in an old jacket of Isla's, at the cottage. It was like she wanted to apologise for something, but she never finished it, or sent it to me. Then, she left another for me with her solicitor. It said how sorry she was for everything, and that Marina should have been mine.' She kept her eyes on Syd's, hoping that he'd say something that would explode this theory – prove her wrong. Tears continued to slide down her cheeks, the breeze instantly chilling them on her skin.

'Oh, Cassie.' Syd shook his head. 'When you put it like that, the pieces do seem to fit.' He grimaced. 'But how can you be sure? And this is Grant we're talking about. Mr up front and honest.' He dipped his chin.

Syd was an intuitive and yet supremely grounded person, and Cassie respected his opinion. He was one of the only people she would defer to, if she doubted herself, and she'd been relieved that he had liked Grant when she had introduced them. Syd had embraced Grant as her partner, but he had told her, in no uncertain terms, to slow things down. Displaying his characteristic wisdom, well beyond his years, he'd said that he was worried that they were rushing into marriage and might regret it. Now, as Cassie surveyed her friend's face, she felt a surge of regret at having summarily dismissed his concerns, all those years ago.

'It could still just be a coincidence.' Syd's eyebrows danced as he seemed to play with the idea of Grant's infidelity, then he shook his head again. 'Yeah, I'm still not convinced he'd do that to you.'

Cassie withdrew her hand and gathered the hair that was now blowing across her face, as a chill slid down her clammy back. 'There's only one way to find out.' She blinked into the breeze, the strong smell of coffee from the nearby café mixed with the brine of the water, making her shudder. 'I have to ask him. Outright.' She shook her head. 'Grant won't lie to me. He could never lie to me.' Her throat began to knot itself again as she blew her nose noisily into the tissue. 'I have to find out, Syd.'

Syd was standing now and pacing in front of the bench. 'Well, where do we start? Have you had any contact over the past few years?' As always, he'd immediately put himself on her team and his unwavering support felt like a lifeline.

'No. But I still have his old mobile number, and if that

doesn't work, I can call the hospital where he worked, they'll probably know where he is now.' She stood up, feeling her legs unsteady, a rush of blood towards her feet, making her shins tingle.

Syd held his hand out to her, and she gripped it. 'OK, my friend.' He smiled. 'Let's do this.'

'Thanks, Syd.' Grateful for his predictable solidarity, she leaned her head against his upper arm as they walked across the cobblestones and headed back to the studio.

'He better not have done this, Cassie.' Syd's voice was suddenly menacing. 'I mean it. Nice guy or not, I will make him sorry.'

That evening, as soon as a rather quiet Stuart had left for his gig, Cassie had tidied up the kitchen, tucked Marina into bed and read her a story. They'd talked about her starting school the next week, and Marina had not been keen. 'My mummy said I could go to school at home if I wanted.' She'd pouted around her thumb.

Cassie had taken this to mean that Isla had intended to home-school Marina, which perhaps made sense when they'd been living on the remote west coast of Lewis. For Cassie, despite the sad prospect of not having Marina with her all the time, it felt critical for Marina to meet other children. It would be an important part of her transition to living in Edinburgh, as from what Cassie could understand, they had lived a very solitary life on the island. The child would need to make some friends, to help her feel less alone, so she could have a full life here, and Cassie would do whatever it took to make that happen. 'School will be lots of fun, Marina, and you'll love being with the other children.'

Marina had eyed her for a few seconds, then said, 'But I don't want to go.'

Cassie had hugged her tightly, kissed her forehead. 'It's going to be OK. I'll be there every day to pick you up, and you can tell me all the interesting things you've done.'

Cassie had seen a shadow of fear cloud the black-rimmed eyes and, for a moment, she'd second-guessed herself. Then, she'd shaken the doubt off, rationalising that this was what being a mother was about: making tough or unpopular decisions, steering the ship when the waters got choppy. Even with everything she still had to learn, Cassie knew, without a doubt, that she was up for the job. She'd get Marina through this next step, and all the others that would inevitably follow.

Now that Marina had finally nodded off, Cassie poured herself a glass of wine, took the slim folder with all the documents Ian Bannister had given her from the drawer in the hall table, went quietly into her bedroom and closed the door. Each time she looked at Marina now, all she saw was Grant's face staring back at her, and she'd been waiting for the chance to pull down the old Tupperware box she kept her mementos in, including photographs, letters that meant something to her, and the engagement ring Grant had given her, that he'd refused to take back when he broke her heart.

She lay the folder on the bed, then as she shoved some sweaters to the side and lifted the box down from the shelf in the wardrobe, her stomach grabbed her with such a stab that she gasped and folded forward, the box landing at her feet with a thud. Pressing her hands into her middle, she walked backwards and sat on the edge of the bed, panting through the pain until finally it began to ease. A thin layer of sweat had coated her face, and she tasted salt as she licked her lips. She was thankful that she was seeing Doctor Carnegie tomorrow, as the pains, when they came, were growing in intensity.

Shaken, Cassie picked up the box, settled herself on the bed, set it next to her and opened the folder. On top was the guardianship document and, under it, Marina's birth certificate.

With everything that had happened that day in Ian's office, she
hadn't paid close attention to what was written on the certificate
and now, as she scanned it, her heart began to race.

Child's name: Marina Cassandra Hunter. Mother: Isla Jane
Hunter. Father: Unknown. Date of birth: 19 December.

Father: Unknown. The words seemed to float up from the
page, and as Cassie stared at Marina's full name, her eyes filled.
Isla had given Marina Cassie's name, which meant the world to
Cassie to see. Marina would be six in four months' time and
now at least Cassie knew that. Each new thing she learned
about her little niece was helping tighten the bond between
them, and this was another link in that chain.

She closed the folder and let her palm linger on the smooth
cover, then set it aside and took the lid off the plastic box. On
top was a selection of letters, some from Isla when she'd been in
France for a month, with a boyfriend, a couple from her father
while Cassie had been at university and three from Grant,
who'd written to her from his parents' place on Skye, when
they'd been apart for a while before they'd got engaged.

Under the letters was the brown envelope she was looking
for, so she tugged it out and opened the flap. As she tipped it up,
several photos fluttered out onto her thighs, and she riffled
through them until she found the one she wanted. She slid it
out from the rest and held it up, her hand shaking slightly. It
had been taken at their engagement party. She and Grant were
standing side by side, her head on his shoulder. They were both
beaming as Isla stood behind them, pulling a face and making
bunny ears above Cassie's head. It had made Cassie angry, at
the time, but seeing it now, all she felt was overwhelmingly sad.
Sad for the loss of her sister, of a man she had been deeply in
love with, and for the loss of all those moments – those slivers of
time when she had felt as if she had everything she'd ever
wanted.

As she stared at their flushed young faces, Grant's eyes

seemed to pulse from the picture, the dark rims highlighting the incredible blue of the irises that had mesmerised her the first time they had talked. There, right in front of her, was the answer she'd been seeking, and yet dreading. The swoop of the nose, the angular jaw, the outline of the cheek – it was all Marina, and seeing it now as clear as day, Cassie clamped a hand over her mouth to smother the hurt that was oozing from inside her, in the form of a low wail. How could he have done that to her? How had it happened? As pain flooded through her, beneath it, Cassie knew that unless she figured that out, she'd never be able to move forward and build an honest, untainted relationship with the sweet little girl who had already captured her heart.

17

Cassie's visit to the doctor had been mercifully brief. He'd examined her and then told her he wanted to order some blood tests, which had taken her by surprise. 'Why? Can't you just put me back on that magic potion I was on the last time this happened?' She'd tried not to let her frustration show as she'd tucked her shirt back into her trousers.

Doctor Carnegie had frowned at her, his silver moustache dipping as he'd pushed his glasses further up his nose. 'I'll give you a prescription, but I want to make sure we're not missing anything, Cassie. Just trust me.'

'Oh, as in trust me, I'm a doctor?' She'd grinned at him as he'd laughed softly. Then he'd scribbled on a prescription pad and handed her a sheet of paper.

'Take two and call me in the morning.'

She liked this man. He was serious enough to make her feel heard, but also had the gift of being able to put her at ease, and that seemed to be rare, in his profession. Aside from treating her ulcer, he'd seen her through her depression after her torpedoed wedding, and her upset and anxiety over Isla's disappearance. He'd also helped both Cassie and her mother cope when Russ had passed away. Just today Cassie had filled him in on Isla's death, and Marina's appearance in her life, and as she'd been speaking, the tale sounding surreal even to herself, he had listened, offered his deepest condolences on Isla, and when she'd finally dissolved into tears, he'd handed Cassie a tissue without any fuss or commentary.

She trusted him, so if he felt the tests were necessary, she'd get on with it. After all, it was better to understand what was happening before the ulcer got worse, or maybe even burst. Her stress had been building to a dangerous crescendo since she'd looked at the photo of her and Grant, but until now she hadn't had the nerve to try calling him. Resolving to stop being such a wimp and pick up the phone – at least soon – to try to get to the truth and eliminate at least one thing that was weighing on her – she walked briskly back to the loft. Having left Marina with Stuart for under an hour, Cassie hoped she would find a peaceful household when she got home. And, even better, perhaps this time, Stuart would have figured out a way to bond with Marina.

Cassie heard the glass break the instant she walked in the door, and the crash was followed by a gasp from Marina. Tossing her keys onto the hall table, Cassie walked quickly into the kitchen to see Marina stooped over a puddle of milk on the floor, leaning down and reaching for a slice of broken glass. Horrified, as the scene seemed to slip into slow motion, Cassie shouted, 'No, don't touch it, Marina.'

Marina started, drawing her hand back, then whipped her head around. Her eyes were huge, and her bottom lip was trembling. 'I dropped it.' She hiccupped slightly, the mournful sound digging deep into Cassie's core.

'Just stand back, sweetheart. Everything is all right. I'll sort it out.' Seeing Marina's bare feet, dangerously close to a large piece of glass, Cassie gently took her hand and moved her away from the puddle, and the jigsaw of fragments that were scattered throughout the milky mess. 'Why don't you sit here, and I'll get the dustpan.' Cassie helped Marina onto a seat at the island and pushed her in close to the countertop. 'Stay there now, until I clean everything up. Where's Uncle Stuart?'

As Marina shrugged, Cassie scanned the living room, but there was no sign of him.

'Stay there. OK, little one?'

Anger swooped up inside her, warming her cheeks, as she darted along the hall, surprised to see that their bedroom door was closed. Hesitating at the door, her mouth went slack as she heard Stuart playing the guitar, inside the room. As the melody filtered out to her, Cassie was overcome with the need to fling the door open and yell – ask him what the hell he was thinking, leaving Marina alone in the kitchen, but rather than lose control, and scare Marina, Cassie clenched her teeth. After a moment or two, she turned her back on the closed door and returned to the kitchen. She'd deal with Stuart later.

Marina was still in the seat, her eyes red-rimmed and her nose shiny. She'd shoved the sleeves of her rainbow-covered sweatshirt up to her elbows and her hair had coiled into long ringlets, framing her angelic face. 'I dropped it,' she repeated. 'It was slippy.'

Cassie nodded, grabbing the dustpan and brush from under the sink. 'Yes, I know. Those ones can be slippy.' She began picking up the larger pieces of glass and dropping them in the bin. 'We'll stick to the other ones from now on, I think.' She nodded at two polka-dot plastic glasses she'd bought for Marina to use, that were upside down on the draining board. 'Those are prettier, anyway.' She smiled at Marina, who had stuck her thumb into her mouth.

Marina pouted around her thumb. 'Are you angry to me?' Her voice was little more than a whisper.

The guileless question penetrated Cassie's heart like an arrow as she set the dustpan down on the wet floor and circled the island. 'No, sweetheart, I am not angry with you.' She wrapped her arms around Marina's shoulders, feeling the silky head, heavy against her breastbone. 'It wasn't your fault.' Cassie almost gagged on the next words that instantly pressed in behind her statement, held hostage only by sheer willpower. *It was Uncle Stuart's fault.*

Marina watched Cassie clean up the mess, her eyes dull and her breath coming in little hitches that each tugged at Cassie's insides, as if an invisible string was connecting her with her niece's distress. When the floor was clean and dry, Cassie lifted Marina off the chair and onto her hip. Cassie glanced at the clock on the cooker, seeing that she'd already been away from the studio much longer than she'd intended. She had to get back, as Hector wanted her to weigh in on the social media campaign he had planned, that was scheduled to start the next day. She'd been hoping to leave Marina with Stuart for a little while longer, but there was no way she was doing that now. 'Let's get you changed and then you can come and see Syd and Hector, again. Would you like that?'

Marina nodded, her arms clasped tightly around Cassie's neck. 'I like Hector. He smells funny.' She rubbed the end of her nose with her palm. 'He eats smelly sandwiches.'

Despite the tension that was roiling inside her, Cassie laughed, the instant relief lightening her spirit. 'Yes, he does.' She hugged Marina tighter, recalling Hector's habit of bringing in huge rolls, filled with wads of cheese and raw onion. 'You are a very clever girl, Marina.' She laughed again. 'How about we stop on the way there and buy him some mints?' She leaned back and gave Marina a mischievous smile.

To her joy, Marina put her palm over her mouth and giggled, a warm, bubbling sound that filled Cassie's heart to bursting. This little person had the ability to change everything

– Cassie's mood, her reactions to things, her priorities, her whole life – and everything about that felt wonderful.

As she passed her room, the sound of guitar music still filtering from behind the closed door, Cassie felt her residual anger shift, morphing from fury to disappointment.

Having spent three hours at the studio, then picked them up a takeaway on the way home, Cassie waited until Marina was bathed and sound asleep, then she walked slowly back to the living room.

Stuart was packing up his guitar, getting ready to head out to a gig at a local club. His hair was damp from the shower, his dark blue T-shirt clinging to his back, as he hunched over the shiny black case, clicked it shut and stood up. Turning, he caught her staring at him and raked a hand through his hair. 'Hey.' He smiled. 'I'm just off. Meeting the lads for a drink before we start our set.' He lifted his leather jacket from the back of the sofa and slid it on. 'All OK in there?' He jabbed a thumb towards the hall.

Cassie leaned forward, her hips pressing into the back of the sofa. She was suddenly drained of energy, and empty of anger, or expectation. Even her disappointment was fading, leaving only a frightening void inside her, when she looked at him. Seeing him frown, she said, 'Stu, we need to talk.'

He propped the guitar case up against the armchair, tucking the front of his T-shirt into his jeans. 'What about?' He met her gaze, his brown eyes questioning.

'This whole situation, with Marina.' She circled the sofa and sank down onto the seat, her head, feeling too heavy to support, dropping back against the cushion. 'You can't ignore her and hope she'll just blow away, Stuart. You left her out here on her own, with a glass, and no shoes on.' She shook her head, imagining what could have happened if she hadn't returned when she did, then sat up straight. 'She's five years old.' His blank expression sent a spark of adrenaline through her, threatening to release the anger she'd swallowed down earlier.

Stuart's jaw was twitching as he shifted his weight from one foot to the other, something he did when he was nervous. 'I don't know how to do this, Cassie.' He swept an arm around the room. 'It's changed everything.' His eyes were flashing now, his narrow chin dipping as he focused on her face.

'It, as in Marina?' Cassie stood up, her hands going to her hips.

'Yes, Marina.' He nodded once. 'We've gone from being us, to being parents, overnight. It's not...' He stopped.

'What?' Cassie knew what was coming, but it would still break her heart to hear it.

'How I thought we'd be.' He blinked, then dropped his gaze to the rug. 'It's too much, Cassie. I'm not ready.'

A knot of hurt gathered in her chest that felt as if it would split her apart. He wanted out, and while she knew that if she asked him that and he said yes, she would survive, this was not what she'd wanted. None of this was what she'd wanted, except that now Cassie knew that she had desperately wanted Marina, even before knowing she existed.

She took several shaky breaths, then spoke softly, battling to keep the tide of emotion coursing through her from clouding what she had to say. 'Stu, you know that Marina is in my life now. That's a given.' She paused. 'All I'm asking is that you at least try, but if that's a deal-breaker for you, then maybe this is as far as we can go.'

Her throat was narrowing as she waited for him to say something. Anything that wouldn't scar her. But the longer the heavy silence hung in the air between them, the more she was afraid that she had her answer.

18

The following week, Doctor Carnegie had kindly kept the last appointment open for her so that she could come at the end of her workday. Not yet comfortable to ask her still fragile mother to step in and watch Marina, Cassie had no choice but to leave her with Stuart again.

A knot of concern had been gathering in Cassie's chest at the doctor's request that she come back in so soon, and she'd only waited a few minutes in the outer office before he'd called her in. Now, she hovered next to the chair across from his desk, as he wafted a sheet of paper at her. 'Have a seat, Cassie.'

Her anxiety rising, she dropped her bag on the floor and did as he'd asked. 'Are you trying to scare me, Doc?' She tried to laugh but, instead, made a strange kind of choking sound.

Not entering into their customary banter, he shook his head and then, rather than sit behind his desk, pulled another chair up opposite her. 'There's something in your blood results that I'm concerned about, Cassie. I'd like to refer you to a gastroenterologist for some further tests.'

Cassie frowned. 'Why? This is just the same as last time... well, maybe a bit more painful, but—'

Doctor Carnegie looked at her intensely. 'I think it might be more than that, this time. I want you to see this chap I know over at the Royal Infirmary, he's great.' He paused. 'He'll order some scans and we'll take it from there.'

Her remaining self-control evaporating, Cassie snapped, 'Quite honestly, I don't have time, Doctor C. I'm just too busy.' She paused as his eyebrows shot up. 'I'm stressed up to my eyeballs with launching the new line, with worrying about Mum coping since Isla's death, and making sure Marina is OK, and with Stuart, well, just being Stuart.' Her voice threatened to give way and she fought to swallow the fresh batch of tears that was pressing in.

Doctor Carnegie leaned back and folded his arms across his chest. 'I know you are dealing with a lot, Cassie, but quite honestly, *I* don't have time for you to become seriously ill.' He gave her a twisted smile. 'It'll be a lot more work for me if you do, and I'm not sure you're worth it.'

Relieved to see a flash of the familiar sarcasm, Cassie laughed, despite the nerves now fluttering inside her chest. 'OK. If you say so. But I'm telling you, it's nothing other than stress, and that I've not been eating properly, and probably had too much wine over the last few weeks.' She grimaced. 'You know, drowning my sorrows.'

He stood up. 'If that's all it is, then we'll be winning.' He smiled warmly, now. 'Go carefully, Cassie, and we'll send your info on to the specialist. Oh, and eat something other than a sandwich, please.'

Cassie thanked him, slung her bag onto her shoulder and left the office. She had ten minutes to get back to the studio before Syd had to leave, and then she needed to stop and get something for Marina to eat. Her own appetite had all but disappeared, but having just had the conversation she had, she planned on eating something healthy herself, too.

· · ·

Cassie kicked the ubiquitous running shoe out of her way as she walked into the entrance hall. She could hear the TV on, and the smell of burnt toast wafted over from the kitchen. She'd stopped at an organic food store and bought a huge, freshly cut salad, some grilled salmon, and a chicken breast for Marina, and three potatoes she intended on baking.

As she dumped the bags on the island, she glanced over at the flickering TV, and frowned. An episode of *Adventure Time* that Cassie had recorded for Marina was playing to an empty room. The little cartoon character Finn, and his magical dog Jake, fascinated Marina, and Cassie had found herself using an episode here and there as a childminding aid when she needed to clean, change the beds, or take a shower, knowing that Marina would not budge from the sofa if the programme was on.

Surprised that neither Stuart nor Marina was anywhere to be seen, and yet relieved that she'd come home to a peaceful house, Cassie crossed the room, kicked off her sandals and made her way down the hall, towards her room.

Just as she approached Marina's open door, Cassie heard voices. 'So, you put these two fingers here and your thumb here, and then you strum with the other hand. That's what it's called when you drag your fingers across the strings, like this.' Stuart was speaking slowly, his voice gentle above the sound of a chord being played on a guitar. 'Now you try.'

Cassie stood still, careful not to let them see her hovering just outside the door, as she smiled widely behind her palm. Since their upsetting conversation the previous week, and her and Stuart dancing awkwardly around each other in the loft, this was a refreshing change.

As she waited, afraid to move in case she gave herself away, she heard another, slightly muffled chord, then a bright laugh, followed by a tiny snort, which brought Cassie's eyes closed. The sound worked its way inside her like warm air, wrapping around her anxiety and dissolving the hard lump that she'd been breathing around since her conversation with Doctor Carnegie.

'That's it.' Stuart sounded pleased. 'Good girl.'

A powerful flash of relief, and gratitude, made Cassie hug herself.

'Try it again and we'll surprise Aunt Cassie when she gets home.'

'Can we play her a tune?' Marina asked.

'We'll practise some more chords first, then we'll see what we can do.' His voice moved closer to the door, so Cassie took a deep breath and stepped into the bedroom.

'Well, hello, you two.' She saw Marina sitting cross-legged on the rug as Stuart carefully placed his scarred guitar back in the stand, by the window. Marina had a small guitar on her lap, its glossy face a soft pink colour, with a handful of sparkles inset along the neck, glittering behind the strings. 'Wow, look at you.' She met Stuart's eyes and held his gaze as he smiled at her. 'What a special guitar.' Cassie walked over and wrapped her arms tightly around Stuart's neck, her lips brushing his cheek as he pulled her closer.

'Uncle Stuart gave it to me.' Marina's eyes were bright as she smiled up at Cassie. 'It's pretty.'

'It's beautiful, and the perfect size for you.' Cassie kissed Stuart again, then moved over and lowered herself onto the rug. 'What have you been learning?'

Marina stuck her tongue out as she wrapped her little hand around the neck of the guitar, carefully placing her fingers on two of the strings. 'This.' She strummed, the chord sounding purer this time.

'Well done.' Cassie looked up at Stuart. That he had done this meant more to Cassie than she could find words for, and her burdens felt a little less cumbersome as she looked at him and mouthed, 'Thank you.' He nodded as she stood up again and took his hand in hers. 'Right, I don't know about you two, but I'm starving. Are you hungry, Marina?'

Marina glanced at Cassie briefly, then back at the guitar. 'Uncle Stuart made toast and peanut butter.' She pointed over her shoulder as Cassie's eyebrows jumped.

While toast wasn't exactly as nutritious a meal as she'd have liked, again, he had tried, and at least there was protein in the peanuts. 'Oh, that was nice.' She leaned down, squeezed Marina's shoulder. 'Would you like something else, or are you all right for now?'

Marina shook her head. 'I'm full.' She patted her tummy and then promptly returned her attention to the guitar.

Smiling, Cassie bent down and kissed Marina's cheek. 'All right then. I'm going to make myself something, and then maybe we can all play a game?'

As she and Stuart walked into the hall, she felt his other hand go to her waist.

'Come on, gorgeous. I'll make you some toast, too.' He laughed softly. 'I can do it gourmet style, of course.'

She leaned her head against his shoulder. 'You do make great toast.' She looked up at him. 'Seriously, thank you for that guitar. Where did you find it?'

He turned her towards him and kissed her, the salty tang of peanuts lingering on his tongue. 'You're welcome.' He leaned back, taking in her face. 'I got it at a wee, second-hand place near Haymarket that one of the guys knows. It was cheap as chips.' He scanned her face and then frowned. 'You look a bit pale.'

As her thoughts bounced back to Doctor Carnegie's office, and the worrying results he'd told her about, Cassie shrugged. 'I'm fine. Just need something to eat.' The thought of food was suddenly nauseating as another pain shot through her middle, like a white-hot needle.

· · ·

Two relatively peaceful days later, Stuart was at the loft when they arrived home after school. Cassie had expected him to be out, either at the pub or rehearsing, as she thought he had a gig that night, but seeing his guitar still propped up by the door made her smile.

Settling Marina in front of the TV, Cassie kissed her cheek. 'I'll be back in a few minutes, OK, little one? I'm just going to speak to Uncle Stuart.'

'Uh-huh.' Marina was already engrossed in a cartoon, her thumb in her mouth.

Cassie made her way to the bedroom, and seeing the door wide open, and Stuart standing in front of his chest of drawers, she smiled. 'Hi.' She walked over to his side and leaned into him. 'Nice surprise to have you still here.'

'Hi, yourself.' He continued raking around in the top drawer and seemed to stiffen at her touch, but deciding to ignore it, Cassie went on.

'What are you looking for?' She rested her head on his shoulder and slid her arm around his waist, breathing in the musk of his cologne.

He pulled out several pairs of socks and turned towards the bed, letting her arm slide from his waist.

As she started to follow him, she spotted the suitcase on the floor by the bed, piles of T-shirts and well-worn jeans spilling out onto the rug. She stared at the clothes, then looked up, catching his expression, realisation beginning to dawn. 'What's going on, Stu?'

Stuart walked to the door and pulled it almost shut. 'This big folk producer came to the gig last night and he wants us to go over to his studio in Denmark, to record a demo.' He shoved his hands into his pockets, his angular shoulders curving forwards as he rocked back and forth on his heels. 'It's a brilliant opportunity, Cassie. The guys are really stoked.' He met her eyes, then bit down on his full bottom lip.

Cassie blew out a long breath, then sat heavily on the edge of the bed. 'So, you're going, right now, without even talking to me about it?' She tugged her shirt out of the waistband of her jeans and opened the top button, feeling suddenly nauseous.

'We had to make a decision on the spot. He wasn't going to wait.' He pulled his hands out of his pockets and held them up, like he was waiting for a tray to land on them. 'And to be fair, Cassie, you didn't exactly ask me what I thought about... well, everything changing here.' He shrugged.

Acknowledging the truth of what he'd said, Cassie's nerves were tingling as she ran a hand over the dark green paisley duvet cover, feeling the sateen cool beneath her fingertips. She'd bought this set when Stuart had moved in and complained that all her bed linen was girly. They'd laughed about it, gone into New Town and found something he'd approved of, then come home and Cassie had shoved it all into the washing machine. They'd drunk a bottle of Chianti while they waited for the bedding to dry, then they'd made up the bed together, before falling into it and making love. As she let her hand linger on the soft cover, she tried to remember the last time they'd laughed like that, made love, and fallen asleep in each other's arms, and when she couldn't place any of those things as having happened in recent weeks, she let her chin drop to her chest. He wasn't going to Denmark to record a demo – he was leaving her.

She looked up at him, words seeming useless, and yet, she needed to hear him say it. 'It's not just about the demo, is it?'

He sat next to her and took her hand in his. 'I just think this is the best decision, for me, and for you.' He blinked several times. 'I think, if we're honest, we both know that we want different things now.'

Cassie shook her head. 'But this past couple of days, you seemed like you were really trying. I thought things were getting better.' She forced a swallow as he dropped his gaze to the floor again. 'So, the guitar was a goodbye present?' Her voice cracked the last word into two syllables.

'She's a sweet wee thing, and I wanted to do something nice for her, and for you, but being her dad?' He squeezed her fingers as she let his words, and everything he had *not* said, permeate her aching heart. 'I'm going to go, and you're going to stay here, and be an ace mum to Marina.' He put his hands on her shoulders and turned her slightly to face him. 'Don't hate me, Cassie.' His eyes were glittering, his jaw rippling. 'I really don't want you to hate me.'

She took in the youthful face, the earnest expression, the deep brown eyes, and long face that had held her heart for almost a year. Here they were, at the end of the road, and while she was not entirely surprised, her heart still felt like it had split in two, again.

As she forced another swallow, willing herself to control the desire she had to grip his arm, tell him please not to do this, she also knew that Marina was not a pawn, or a point of negotiation, and if Stuart could remove himself from Cassie's life so quickly, and completely, then this was the only outcome – for them all. However sad it made her to think of him not being in her life, Cassie felt her determination to be the best parent she could be to Marina, even if she was doing it alone, take on more weight.

19

A week later, with September having crept in, the launch had gone as smoothly as they could have hoped. A steady stream of orders for the Infinity line were coming in from distributors, keeping Syd and Cassie on their toes.

As the initial big push was finally over, an exhausted Syd had decided to go home to Johannesburg for four weeks to visit his sister, Kaya, and he had drawn up a detailed plan of action for Hector to oversee, in his absence.

'Are you sure you'll be OK, Cass?' Wearing one of his brightly coloured, traditional Madiba shirts, Syd had held her hands in his and scanned her face. 'I can postpone the trip if you're worried. I feel like I'm abandoning you.' He'd frowned. 'You and my tomato plants.' He'd chuckled softly.

'Absolutely no postponing. You haven't seen Kaya in almost a year. I'll be fine.' She'd flapped her hand at him. 'Hector and I will cope, won't we, Hec?'

Hector had laughed. 'Aye, Syd. This ship won't go down without you, pal.' He'd pulled a comical face. 'At least we hope so.'

Syd had left the following day and while Cassie was

happy for him, knowing he needed the break after carrying the lion's share of the past month's work, she was anxious that her best friend, wingman, and de facto babysitter would be gone.

While they'd been becoming more at ease with each other, their bond deepening with each meal, bath, and story time, this would be the first time she'd be completely alone with Marina, and the prospect had fanned Cassie's s concern about making some unwitting mistake with the child.

Since Stuart had moved out, it had been a struggle, juggling everything. While he hadn't been much practical help, he had at least been a presence, company, making Cassie feel less marooned in her new life.

Determined to cope with the weekday routine herself, she had begun working from the studio in the mornings, after she had dropped Marina at school, then once she'd picked her up, Cassie would work the rest of the day from home. The days sped past, with barely enough time for her to get through her daily task list, and exhausted, she'd often doze off on Marina's bed while reading to her at night.

The weekend had been a gift that allowed Cassie a little breathing space, and the visit to see her mother was a highlight, as Marina continued to be almost entranced in Sadie's presence, Marina providing a much-needed light in the shade of Sadie's sadness. She had read a Paddington Bear story to the little girl, while Cassie had kicked off her shoes and lain on the sofa, letting her mother's voice soothe her weary soul. She'd closed her eyes and listened to Marina's animated questions about the bear, and his favourite marmalade sandwiches.

'Why does he not have butter, too?' Marina had giggled.

'Well, perhaps he's on a diet?' Sadie had laughed softly.

'He's not a fat bear?' Marina had come to Paddington's defence, making Cassie smile.

'Quite right. I think he's the perfect size. Just right for

cuddling.' Sadie's voice had been full of joy – something that Cassie was hearing more of each time they saw her mother.

Listening to the happy exchange, Cassie had let go of her fatigue – let herself believe that her chaotic life was under control – even normal. She'd even let go of the worry over some of Marina's remaining challenges settling in and had revelled in the peace of the moment, each of Marina's laughs and tiny snorts filling Cassie with contented pleasure.

The most recent challenge Cassie had still to deal with had begun during Marina's second week at school, when the head teacher had called Cassie and told her that she'd like her to come in to talk through some concerns they had about Marina's behaviour. Cassie had gone in the following afternoon, a little before the end of school, and had been saddened to hear what Mhairi Sommerfield had to say.

'Marina isn't participating too well in the classroom. She sits alone, apart from the other children, and she refuses to go outside during breaks. She stays inside and colours, or flips through books from the library shelf, despite all our efforts to encourage her to join the others.' Mrs Sommerfield had spoken softly, her eyes full of compassion.

'I'm sorry. I don't know what to suggest.' Cassie had felt newly inept in this gargantuan role she had taken on, questioning her ability to get things right, for the hundredth time. 'Is there something I should be doing that I'm not?' She'd heard the panic in her own voice as Mrs Sommerfield had shaken her head.

'No. I think you're doing a marvellous job, considering everything that's happened.' She'd smiled at Cassie. 'We were wondering if you'd be comfortable popping in one morning next week, perhaps you could observe the class and see what we're seeing?'

Cassie had felt both relieved and nervous about what she might witness, her biggest fear – not knowing how to help Marina through this current crisis. 'Yes, of course. Just tell me when, and I'll be there.'

The following Monday morning, having dropped Marina off earlier, Cassie was back at the school at 10 a.m., and Mhairi Sommerfield met her at the front door. 'Welcome. Perfect timing. Let's pop over to the classroom now. We can peek in through the door without anyone seeing us.'

The classroom was a high-ceilinged, bright space with a row of tall windows overlooking the long playground. When Cassie had seen it on Marina's first day, she'd immediately felt its cosy sense of welcome. The walls were crammed with the children's paintings, including a series of handprints they'd all made, then turned into various animals by adding thick strokes of coloured crayon. There were several 3D mobiles hanging from the ceiling, and multicoloured chairs and tables set up in small groups, all arranged around a large circular mat with a map of the world on it.

Marina had seemed happy to venture in and had immediately gone to the bookshelf at the back of the room, tipping her head to the side as she walked its length, as if searching for a particular title she couldn't find. When it had come time for Cassie to leave her, Marina's eyes had filled, but she had not cried. She'd held her new class teacher, Miss Stanley's hand, and waved silently as Cassie, her own eyes so full that she had bumped painfully into the door frame, smiled brightly, and said, 'See you later.'

Now, Cassie stood next to the head teacher outside Marina's classroom. The door was closed, but they could peek in at the sides of a glass panel and see the children moving around in the room.

'It's music class,' Mrs Sommerfield whispered, her breath carrying the tang of coffee that made Cassie miss Stuart so much that she closed her eyes for a moment. 'As you can see, they're all sitting in the circle, but Marina is over there.' She pointed to the back of the room where Marina sat at one of the low tables, her arms folded on the desk and her forehead balancing on them.

A shot of sadness splintered through Cassie as she glanced back at the lively group of children, all sitting cross-legged in a circle, holding triangles and tambourines. She then looked over at Marina, who seemed to be oblivious to the buzz of activity going on, just a foot or so away from her, as she rocked herself slightly, her heels bouncing on the floor underneath the table. 'That literally breaks my heart.' Cassie's voice was thick. 'I had no idea it was this bad.' She stepped away and walked unsteadily to the other side of the corridor, pressing her back against the wall until Mrs Sommerfield joined her.

'Cassie, listen. Marina has been through one of the worst traumas a child of her age can ever face. The loss of a parent is devastating, regardless of when it happens, but at five, it's life-altering.' She gestured towards the other end of the hall. 'Let's go and chat for a minute. I have an idea.'

Hopeful that there might be some gem of insight coming her way, anything that would make her feel less inadequate as Marina's parent, Cassie followed the head teacher back to her office.

Having agreed with Mhairi Sommerfield that it would be helpful for both Cassie and Marina to meet with the school counsellor, Cassie was feeling a little less adrift. But the image of Marina, her head on her arms, so isolated from the rest of the children, continued to haunt Cassie. Each day when she dropped Marina off at school, Cassie's heart would race, antici-pating that dreaded moment when she'd let Marina's hand go, the wrench now as physically jarring as it was emotionally.

Despite the two gentle and constructive talks they'd had with the school counsellor, Marina had started having nightmares again, often waking in tears and clasping Cassie's hand saying, 'Mummy, you're back.' Cassie would carry the child into the master bedroom and tuck her up, sing or read to her, and stroke her hair until Marina's sobs would ease and she'd fall back to sleep. Cassie would then lie in the dark, staring at the ceiling – wrestling with waves of crushing self-doubt over the magnitude of what she had taken on. The fact that she was rarely alone anymore but had never felt lonelier in her life was startling.

As she wondered where Stuart was, what he was doing, if he missed or even thought about her and their life together, more than once she questioned her decision to let him go. Each time she thought about him, she would press her eyes closed and see his face, the deep brown eyes, the long chin, the tangled curls, then she'd turn on her side, face Marina and let the little girl's breathing guide her own until sleep would eventually win out.

As the days rolled into one another, each a clone of the one before, and with Marina seeming to struggle more than when they'd first arrived in Edinburgh, Cassie gradually felt herself slipping towards despair. It made her think about Isla, and how she had died, unsure whether her sister had indeed been pulled under by the current or had silently waded in until the water had closed above her head. Then, scared by her own thoughts, Cassie would force herself to go outside, immerse herself in the world, take long walks with Marina and watch the stream of humanity moving along the Royal Mile, or through Princes Street Gardens.

They'd climbed to the top of Arthur's Seat, and she'd shown Marina the different facets of her new home: the scenic face of Old Town, the classic Georgian architecture of New Town, the zoo, the pretty enclosed gardens of Stockport – Cassie's Edinburgh, and beyond its bounds, the beauty of the surrounding Highlands. Marina seemed to relish being outside and each time Cassie saw a light return to her niece's eyes, Cassie questioned herself for having taken the child from her home, the peaceful cottage overlooking the scenic bay of Uig, and the drama of the Outer Hebrides, beyond.

Cassie had decided that they'd go back to Lewis for a few days at half-term, in mid-October, and Marina had been delighted, asking how many sleeps until she could go home. Cassie had helped her make a calendar with a square for each day that Marina could put a giant red cross in as it passed.

Three weeks after Stuart had gone, and ten days after Cassie had had various tests carried out at Edinburgh Royal Infirmary, she had just dropped Marina at school when her phone rang. She answered it as she walked briskly along Commercial Street, heading for the studio, and instantly heard an unfamiliar edge to Doctor Carnegie's voice. Hearing him at all made her realise that she'd had a relatively pain-free couple of weeks, and as her spirits lifted, she imagined the news of her results would set her free from the niggling worry she'd been suppressing.

'Hi, Doc. I'm on the move, as usual.' She laughed. 'No rest for the wicked.'

'Cassie, I'd like you to come in and see me as soon as you can.' His words brought her crashing back down, her stomach instantly tensing as if he'd punched her.

'Oh, God. What now?' She worked to keep her voice light. 'Do I have two ulcers this time?' She stepped into the street to make room for two women, walking arm-in-arm along the pavement. As a van rushed past, sending her hair flying across her face, she shoved it away and turned into the wind, letting the breeze cool her warm cheeks. She could hear the whine of bagpipes in the distance, which was almost a daily occurrence in the city, but on the other end of the phone, Doctor Carnegie's silence was distinctly unnerving. 'Can't you tell me what the results were now?'

'I'd prefer you to come in, Cassie. In think we should talk in person.'

At this, she stopped short, her heart thumping as she caught her reflection in a shop window. Once again, Isla stared back at her, wide-eyed and flushed, her hair floating away from her head in a fiery red cloud. 'Is something wrong?' She choked out the words, edging closer to the shopfront and pressing her palm against the rough, sandstone wall.

'I really think it'd be better if—'

'Just tell me, please,' she sputtered. 'Please.'

He hesitated for a moment, then she heard him sigh. 'Cassie, the initial scans showed a spot on your gall bladder. It's small, and seems to be minimally invasive at this point, but it appears to be malignant.'

Cassie's eyes clamped shut and she began to pant. This could not be real. This was a terrible dream that she'd wake from, coated in sweat, and washed with relief that she was in her own bed.

'Cassie, are you there?' His voice floated through her thoughts, a stark reminder that she was indeed awake. Wide awake.

'Yes,' she whispered.

'We're going to get an MRI set up as soon as possible, so we can see what we're dealing with.' He cleared his throat. 'If we've caught it early, Cassie, the prognosis is good.'

'And if not?' Her eyes were stinging, and her throat was on fire as the very atmosphere around her felt hot – pressing cruelly onto her skull, shoulders and back, squashing the air from her and paralysing her at the same time.

'We'll deal with whatever we find when we know more.' He sounded tired. 'Call the office tomorrow and we'll get everything set up. And, Cassie, please try not to worry.'

White-hot fear surged through her. Try not to worry? Didn't he know that everything was different now? Whatever they found or didn't find, the reach of this situation was so much farther than it would have been just a matter of weeks before. Now, it wasn't just about Cassie. Not only did she have a grieving mother who needed her, but she had a child whom she must raise, protect, love, and see safely into adulthood. If, God forbid, there was something seriously wrong, who would take care of her mum, who had already lost one daughter, and of Marina, who had already lost a mother?

20

Ten days later, Cassie hung up the phone and slid down the wall in the kitchen. She hugged her knees to her chest and dropped her head onto her forearms, her heart thumping dangerously.

The word cancer had the power to change lives, shape futures – even eliminate them – and as she tried to process what Doctor Carnegie had just told her, her head began to shake. This could not be happening. It simply wasn't possible. Other people got cancer, not her, and not at only twenty-nine.

Doctor Carnegie had said that the MRI showed two spots on her gall bladder, and the gastroenterologist was scheduling her for exploratory, endoscopic surgery as soon as they could get it set up. Cassie knew what that entailed, as despite her determination to be positive, to deny a potentially invasive cluster of cells the right to warp her thinking, she had succumbed to the demon internet over the past few days, researching all the potential scenarios she might be facing.

'It looks as if your liver and bile ducts are clear, which is a very good thing, Cassie. But until the exploratory surgery, we can't be certain that the cancer hasn't spread.' His voice had sounded forced, overly upbeat, and she'd pictured him pacing across his office, his eyes fixed on the window as he grimaced.

Now, as she pressed her eyes closed, grateful that Marina was glued to the TV, Cassie pictured her organs, lighting up like beacons as cuckoo-like cells crept in and took up residence in places they had never been invited. Knowing that she must try to stop this negative spiral, to get a grip, she sat up and pressed her head back against the wall, feeling the cold surface unyielding behind her.

She could still smell the shepherd's pie she'd made them for dinner, and the TV was burbling from across the room, a game show host asking questions and a studio audience laughing as directed. This whole situation was bizarre. That life went on, irrespective of the news she'd just been given, was hard to comprehend, and yet, as she heaved herself up from the floor and opened the fridge, it also seemed exactly as it should be. Life did indeed go on, and whatever else happened now, everything was about Marina. She was the future, and as Cassie took out a half-full bottle of Sauvignon and picked up one of the polka dot glasses from the draining board, she gripped the bottle tightly. There was no damn way she was going to miss out on seeing Marina heal from her broken heart, learn to live with Isla's loss and become a happy child, make friends, grow into a grumpy teenager, a wife, a mother.

Cassie filled the glass almost to the top and took several gulps, then set it on the counter, letting the subtle, citrus after-taste linger on her tongue. Screw cancer. That's all there was to it. Cancer hadn't met Cassie Hunter.

After a few restless hours in bed, when Cassie's courage had come in heady surges, then had ebbed away to a trickle, leaving her sweaty and tearful, at 3 a.m., she gave up on sleep. She threw the covers off, shoved her feet into her slippers and crept into the spare room to check that Marina was still sleeping.

Inside the golden halo of the nightlight that she'd started leaving on for the child, Cassie could see the smooth cheeks puffing out slightly as Marina exhaled, and next to her, shrouded by a heap of covers, Raffy was wedged tightly under her chin. Cassie resisted the urge to kiss her little niece, reluctant to risk shattering the peaceful sleep she was enjoying, so Cassie backed away slowly, pulled the door almost to and tiptoed into the hall.

While things were slowly improving, Marina was still sometimes isolating herself at school and waking with nightmares two or three nights a week. Their outdoor excursions and her Sunday visits to her grandmother's flat had become the highlights of her week, and Cassie seldom saw the little girl smile aside from at those times. The reality of that was increasingly hard to take, as Cassie had tried everything the counsellor had suggested to help Marina and was beginning to feel defeated.

What Cassie needed was someone to talk to, to share her burdens with, but even as she knew it to be true, no one she would normally tell could be there for her right now.

Syd, the person she would naturally have confided in, was still away on his well-deserved break and she had no intention of disrupting that with her grim news. While Hector was a sweet guy whom she'd grown fond of, she had never talked to him about her personal life and wasn't going to start now. Her mother, while seeming to gain strength from her time with Marina, was still fragile, and Cassie would not burden her with anything else until she knew precisely what she was dealing with. That simply was not an option.

As she navigated her way across the dark living room, heading for the kitchen, as had been happening more frequently recently, especially since Isla's death, Cassie reflected on her life. When she reached the fridge and poured herself a glass of orange juice, she acknowledged the sad reality that having been a workaholic for the past decade, her support network had become unsurprisingly narrow. Most of her child-hood and university friends had slipped away over the years. She'd been so laser-focused on her goals – her future as a self-sufficient businesswoman – that it had left little time for those people in her life. Now, with Stuart gone, too, she was very much alone, and swallowing her self-pity with another mouthful of juice, she walked back into the living room.

Earlier, as she had lain in the dark for hours, going back and forth about if, when and how to contact Grant, the idea of even hearing his voice again enough to make her nervous, she'd made a tentative plan – such as it was – and phase one started now. Wrapping herself in the blanket from the back of the sofa, she set the glass on the coffee table, lifted her laptop and typed Grant's name into the search field. Even though she was still working on pure assumption, based only on the child's eyes, and certain mannerisms, there was something deep inside Cassie that had acknowledged the likelihood of her suspicions being accurate, and if she didn't man up and contact Grant, it would always be an unanswered question. Besides, if he really was Marina's father, the little girl needed him now, perhaps more than any other human being on the planet.

It took precisely two minutes to find Grant, listed as one of Edinburgh's top-rated paediatric oncologists, located at a prac-tice in Stockbridge. As she hovered over the Meet Our Team tab, the word oncologist seemed to strike her in a tender place, under her ribs. It had been almost six years since she'd seen Grant, or talked to him, and after he'd left, it had taken her two years to be able to say his name, let alone contemplate what he was doing with his life. She'd been deeply in love, and so certain of their future together, that his decision had rocked her to her core. To this day, she didn't fully understand what had happened to make him change his mind about the wedding, but now there could potentially be an entirely new dimension to the connection they'd once had – and it was asleep in the other room.

Cassie scrolled through the list of names, paused a moment, then clicked on Grant Henderson. As soon as his photo popped up, she caught her breath. His face was slightly fuller than she remembered, his jaw more heavily defined, and his hairline had receded slightly. She quickly calculated that he was thirty-four now, and she could see a new maturity reflected in his features. He still had thick, glossy-brown hair, the familiar narrow cleft that split his chin, and then, she saw the eyes. The bright, kind, blue eyes, rimmed with black, duplicates of Marina's, seemed to follow her as she sat back and let the laptop slide down her thighs. This man had been her first, true love, her best friend, and fiancé, and now, despite her nervousness about reopening that painful door, she had procrastinated enough. The moment had come to reach back in time and contact him. Not for her, but for Marina.

The following morning, with Marina safely at school and Hector on a conference call with their public relations agency, Cassie went into her office and closed the door. She had found Grant's direct phone number and after the frightening attack of pain she'd had at dawn, sending her rushing into the bathroom, her determination to contact him was overriding her fear of hearing his voice again.

As she tapped out the number, her hands were shaking so much that she had to put the phone on the desk and switch to speaker mode. Each ring seemed to last for an eternity until suddenly, he answered, 'Hello?'

Cassie swallowed hard, took a shaky breath and leaned in, her mouth close to the phone. 'Hi, Grant?'

There was a pause and she thought she heard him sigh. 'Um, yeah. Who's this?'

Cassie frowned, then realised that he wouldn't recognise her new mobile number. In the same instant, she was slightly hurt that he didn't know her voice. 'It's Cassie.' She sucked in her bottom lip. 'Cassie Hunter.'

'God, Cassie. What a surprise.' He sounded relieved. 'How are you?'

Cassie lifted the phone and switched off speaker mode. As she tried to formulate what she was going to say, she pressed her eyes closed. *So stupid.* She should have made notes, at least practised this before she just dived in. As she opened her eyes and stared out of the window, watching a lean man in a black tracksuit cycling past the building, she exhaled. 'I'm OK, Grant.' She shook her head at the lie, but there was so much to unpack between them that she had no idea where else to start. 'How's life with you?'

'Oh, you know. Busy. Good. All about work, as ever.' He laughed softly, sparking a surprising memory of him lying with his head on her bare stomach, them both laughing as his warm breath tickled her skin.

'Good, good.' She grimaced. 'I see you went into paediatrics. That's great.'

'Yes. I got hooked during my residency and then, well...' He stopped.

'What?' She frowned.

'Working with these wee souls – seeing their courage, I was a goner, so to speak.' She could hear the smile in his voice, picture the way his eyes would cloud over when he was deep in thought. When they'd been together, they'd talked about their future family, even deciding on names for the four children they'd planned on having, in their thirties. That bittersweet memory now brought Cassie's eyes closed as she realised how deeply she'd buried that want, that fundamental need to be a mother – until now.

'I can understand that.' She pictured Marina, her stoic little face as Cassie left her at school each day, the glittering eyes that remained dry despite all the child was feeling. 'Kids are remarkable.'

'Truth.' He paused. 'So, how long has it been?'

Cassie took a second to reply. 'Six years, give or take.' She leaned forward and propped her elbows on the desk, these platitudes becoming somewhat comforting.

'Wow. Six years.'

'Yep.' She nodded.

'So, what made you call? I mean, I'm really glad to hear from you.'

Cassie closed her eyes again, willing the right words to materialise. She'd come this far, so now she must jump in. 'I was wondering if we could meet up. Maybe grab a coffee, or a drink or something?' She hoped she'd sounded casual, non-confrontational. 'We have a lot to catch up on.'

'Um, yeah. That'd be great.' There was genuine if tentative warmth in his voice. 'When were you thinking?'

Cassie immediately went into calendar mode, mentally skimming through her week – the meetings, all the outstanding company paperwork she'd been avoiding, the school runs, shopping, laundry and the cleaning that she crammed in whenever she had a spare moment. 'What's today?'

He laughed, sending a contagious trickle of joy through her. 'It's Tuesday. You never knew what day it was.'

Cassie smiled, recalling the way he'd tease her about her ability to lose herself in designing something to the point where she would forget to eat, miss lectures, or sometimes turn up to them on the wrong day, always caught off guard and embarrassed at her mistake. 'True enough.'

'I'm actually off on Thursday afternoon if that works for you?' He cleared his throat.

'I can make that work.' She hoped that was true, but she wasn't about to hang up without a firm meeting being agreed.

'Great. How about one o'clock, over at the Jolly Judge?'

At the mention of their favourite pub, an ancient drinking hole tucked into an alley off the Royal Mile, in the shadow of the castle, she was overcome by a picture show of happy memories that made her drop her chin to her chest.

'Or we can go somewhere else.' He seemed to have sensed her hesitation.

'No, that's fine. I'll see you there at one.' Relieved that the timing would give her two hours before she needed to pick Marina up, Cassie nodded decisively.

'Good. See you then.' He hesitated. 'And Cass. It's so good to hear your voice.'

Her throat on fire, she croaked, 'You too, Grant.'

Cassie ended the call and leaned back in her chair, feeling the soft leather giving way to the pressure of her spine. She had two days to figure out how she was going to approach this, find a way to present her question without sounding like a raving lunatic. With so little to go on, all she could hope for was that he would be understanding, open, and provide her with the answers she so desperately needed.

21

Two days later, Cassie jumped off the bus at Princes Street and walked across the Mound, the famously pretty route that runs behind the iconic Scottish National Gallery – the path skirting the eastern end of Princes Street Gardens and linking the Old and New Towns. The pub was only a ten-minute walk from the bus stop, but anxious that she was already five minutes late, rather than enjoy the familiar landmarks and soak in the scenery, Cassie hurried along the footpath, head down and heart pattering under her shirt.

Just seeing Grant again would be hard enough, aside from the delicate nature of what she intended to ask him. Typically, having made the call, she had forged on with her mission, not allowing herself to analyse it too much, in case she chickened out of seeing him, but now, the prospect of what she was walking into – seeing the former love of her life after years of absence – was finally beginning to sink in.

Reaching the Royal Mile, she turned right, navigated her way around a lively group of German students, and headed for Lawnmarket. The September sun was doing its best to break through a veil of cloud as a gentle, southerly breeze brought the smell of garlic with it from one of the restaurants she passed. The wall of tall, sandstone buildings on either side of her, each with a history of its own dating back centuries, ran the length of the Royal Mile. Most of them now housed touristy shops below, filled with tartan and cashmere, and they all had high-ceilinged apartments above.

Despite its blatant commercialism, and the crowds that occupied it in the summer, Cassie loved this part of Old Town. She would often wander around, people-watching as she listened to the ubiquitous bagpipers, positioned at the top end of the mile near the castle, and try to identify the myriad languages floating across the cobbled streets. Edinburgh's diversity was one of the reasons she loved living here and that Marina was still struggling to settle in made Cassie sad.

She'd considered the possibility that the little girl may never feel at home here, pining for her island home, every tear she shed piling on top of Cassie's growing doubt at the decision to uproot Marina at such a difficult time. But Cassie had had to put those thoughts away, the implications just too complex to think about now that her own foundation was feeling precarious. If the future was clear to see, she might be able to consider ways to make this easier on Marina, but until Cassie knew what was going on with her health, all she could do was try to hold it all together and focus on the happy times they were having, whenever they came.

Marina had been droopy that morning, saying that she had a tummy ache and didn't want to go to school, a tactic that she had been using more regularly over the past couple of weeks. The school counsellor had advised Cassie on how to handle it and Cassie had been gently telling Marina that if she ate her breakfast and went to school, that when Cassie picked her up, they could go for a walk and get ice cream or sit down on the bench on Shore and feed the swans. So far, offering these types of incentives had been working, until this morning.

'I don't want ice cream,' Marina had pouted, slumped at the kitchen island, still in her pyjamas, her eyes hooded and dull. 'I want to stay here, with you.'

Cassie had paused a moment, grasping for the magical distraction tactics that her own mother had used on them, as children. 'Sweetheart, I am going to work, and you can't stay here on your own, now can you?' She'd smiled at the cross little face. 'Let's get you ready and then this afternoon we'll do something fun. Maybe we can bake some biscuits when we get home. How about that?'

Marina had shaken her head, the long mane of dark curls splitting over her shoulder. 'I want to go to my house.' She'd eyed Cassie. 'My own house.'

Cassie had summoned every last ounce of patience, willing herself to conjure something that would help Marina get past this, but all she could come up with was, 'Well, it's not long now. Only twenty-three more days and we'll be going back to Lewis.' She'd pointed at the calendar. 'It'll be here in a flash.'

Marina had reluctantly let Cassie dress her and they'd walked to the school. As Cassie had waved to Marina, watching her being met by her teacher in the playground, Cassie had swallowed over a nut of loss, as now happened each time they were parted. The stoic little face, the full cheeks, the mass of brown wavy hair held back by an Alice band and the Little Mermaid backpack, slung between the narrow shoulders, all tugged at Cassie's heart with such force that she'd taken a second to compose herself before turning away.

Now, with that image still glowing in her mind, she spotted the familiar wynd, tucked between two shopfronts, their windows packed with colourful tartan scarves, boxes of shortbread, Highland fudge and Harris tweed handbags. The mysterious little alley led her to the stone entrance of the below-ground pub where she and Grant had spent many a happy weekend, playing darts, tasting local ales, and eating piping hot pies and chips, as they'd laughed, and planned their life together.

Seeing the familiar steps, leading down to the cosy bar, Cassie stopped in her tracks. She hadn't been here in years and had in fact avoided the place if Syd had suggested coming here – always nervous that she might bump into Grant. It was mainly locals who drank at the Judge, the hidden entrance being easy to miss – despite its proximity to the heart of Old Town – but that was why she and Grant had liked it. They'd soon got to know the staff, and regulars, and within a few months had felt like regulars themselves.

Lifting her chin, Cassie hefted her bag higher up her shoulder, shoved a wisp of hair away from her face and walked down the steps. Inside, her eyes gradually adjusting to the dim light, she scanned the bar area. The familiar, thick stone walls, the low beamed ceiling and the slightly sour smell of beer all sent a tinge of nostalgia rushing through her as she took in the collection of lunchtime customers, dotted along the bar and sitting at the series of small tables lining the wall by the giant, inglenook fireplace.

There was a table tucked into the corner near the fire that she and Grant had always gravitated to and as she walked the length of the bar, her heart skipped a beat when she saw him sitting there, his back to the wall, a paned-glass window set high up in the thick stone behind his head. He was wearing a smart black shirt, and a tan leather jacket was draped over the chair behind him. His chin was dipped, and he was checking his phone, his thick hair so glossy that Cassie could almost feel it beneath her fingertips and picture his eyes half closing in pleasure as she ran her hands through it, her nails gently grazing his scalp.

Just as she was about to approach the table, he put the phone down and lifted his head, spotting her instantly. As he stood up, he smiled, the cleft in his chin seeming to deepen as his dark-rimmed eyes met hers. Cassie hesitated for a moment, regretting her plain white shirt and well-worn jeans, and the meagre lick of mascara she'd applied, then she stepped forward and returned his smile. 'Hi.'

'Hi yourself. You look great, Cass.' He walked around the table, then held his arms out momentarily before seeming to rethink and dropping them back to his sides. 'It's really good to see you.'

Cassie swallowed, dragging her gaze away from those mesmeric eyes. 'You too.' She pulled a chair out, sat down and dumped her bag on the floor. 'It's been a while.' She instantly regretted the flippant statement, but her heart was now thumping so wildly that she could hear it inside her head.

Grant sat opposite her and gently pushed a half-pint of Guinness towards her. 'I hope this is still your poison of choice.' He smiled shyly, as, across the bar, a bear of a man with a wild white beard and wearing a Utilikilt laughed loudly at something the woman opposite him had said.

Not having drunk Guinness in years, Cassie laughed softly. 'It's fine, thanks.' She pulled the sweaty glass close to her. 'Well, here we are again.' She lifted the beer and waited for him to raise his, then she tapped hers to it. 'Cheers.'

Grant took a sip and set his glass down, assessing her face, taking in each feature as if it was the first time he'd seen it. 'So, what's been going on with you? How's the family, and the business of course?' He leaned back, leaving his palm flat on the table. 'Still producing your beautiful creations?'

Cassie took a sip of beer, the rich, toasted, malty flavour sparking another slew of poignant memories that she sifted through in the seconds it took her to set her glass back down. 'The business is doing well, thanks.' She nodded, suddenly flooded with nerves again. There was so much she needed to tell him, and as she took another second to filter the cascading thoughts that were making her blink, Isla's face flashed behind her eyes. There really was only one place to start.

'Oh, my God, Cassie. I'm so sorry.' Grant reached across the table, his fingers just centimetres from Cassie's. 'How did it happen?' His eyes were full of sympathy.

She held his gaze as he waited for her to continue. 'She drowned.'

Grant thumped back hard against the chair. 'Jesus.'

Cassie nodded, her throat clogging with grief. 'I know. It was a terrible shock.' She blinked through a reel of images of Ian Bannister's office: Heather's kind face, the paperwork she'd signed, the drive to Uig Bay, the grass-roofed cottage tucked into the hillside, the stunning beach, the willow coffin they'd had made for Isla and the beautiful sunny day that they had had her cremated, just outside the city.

'Cass?' He leaned forward again. 'Are you OK?'

Tugged back to the moment, Cassie raked her hair away from her face and looked over at him. The photo of Marina was tucked in her bag, and now, all she could think of was pulling it out and asking him, point blank, if he knew about her. As she stared at him, her internal voice whispered that the Grant she knew would never have hidden from something as important as this, he'd have stepped up, taken on his responsibilities. But maybe he wasn't the man she'd thought he was?

22

Cassie grappled to form the words, and something inside her shifted. As she scanned Grant's face, taking in the sharp jawline, the heavy, dark brows, the slight shadow of growth that made the contours of his face stand out even more, she swallowed hard. 'Grant, I need to ask you something. It's not easy for me, so please let me get it out. OK?'

He frowned. 'OK.'

She lifted her chin, a sudden surge of determination making her bold. 'What really happened six years ago? What made you walk away?'

Grant looked as if she'd slapped him, his eyebrows lifting, and the little tic that she used to see in his jaw jumping, as it always had when he was anxious. 'What?'

'You never really told me the reason.' She felt her throat begin to knot, but determined not to cry, to let him see that she still hurt in the place where he'd wounded her, she shrugged.

Grant took a moment, then he spoke, his voice low and controlled. 'Cassie, I did tell you, you just weren't hearing me.' His mouth dipped, but taking in her expression he continued. 'A couple of months before the wedding, I told you that I was overwhelmed. I was slammed with finals, having to move to a new flat, and trying to keep my head above water with my student loans – and you were so consumed with the business that you could hardly think beyond that. We were both stressed out of our minds, and I told you that I felt we were rushing things, unnecessarily.' He paused. 'I asked you if we could talk about postponing the wedding, but you wouldn't even entertain it.' He eyed her. 'You were determined that we go ahead, regardless of how I felt.'

Cassie let his words hang in the air, their barely concealed barbs hitting their mark. 'That's not fair,' she sputtered. As far as she remembered, he had told her that he thought they should consider postponing, but when she'd refused, he hadn't pressed the point.

'All I needed was some time. I loved you, Cass, but you were always in such a hurry.' He dropped his eyes to the table and flipped over a warped beer mat. 'I don't mean to be hurtful, but it felt like our wedding was just one more thing on your checklist that you needed to get done.'

Cassie caught her breath, his words cutting deep. 'That's so not true. I adored you. I just wanted us to be together.'

'No, Cassie. You wanted marriage, your way, and on your timeline, and the more you pressed me, the more it scared me. Honestly, I started to question whether I wanted everything that came with being married, at all.' His voice thickened. 'Perhaps I didn't make that clear at the time. If so, then I'm sorry.' He nodded sadly. 'Basically, I was scared witless, Cass.'

Was this the real reason he'd walked away, let their future together disappear in a smog of pain and misunderstanding? Cassie blinked her vision clear, letting the new information percolate. 'But all you had to do was be honest. As far as I was concerned, we'd argued briefly about the timing of the wedding, and then just weeks before it, you left me. You broke my heart in two, Grant.' She paused, surprised that the pervasive pain that she'd thought was dead and buried was once again encapsulating her heart. 'I had to clean up the entire, humiliating mess, face my family and friends on my own, and that wasn't fair of you.' A single, traitor of a tear broke free and trickled down her cheek. Angrily swiping it away, she shook her head.

'You're right. I handled it badly.' He nodded. 'I screwed up, but I was young, weak and selfish.' He looked into her eyes. 'I'm so sorry I hurt you.'

Her insides turning somersaults, Cassie met his gaze, the clear blue eyes pinning her to the spot as they always had. 'I just wish I'd understood. I'd still have been gutted, but it would have made it easier to cope with.'

Grant reached across the table and opened his hand, his long fingers inviting hers in. 'I know that now. But it was a long time ago, Cass. We've both grown up since then.' He paused. 'I'm truly sorry.'

Cassie resisted the reflex of sliding her hand into his, feeling his quiet strength soak through her skin. Filled with sadness at every lost moment they'd missed out on, she sighed. 'You know, the saddest part is that if you'd asked me now, I'd have been willing to give you time, but I don't know if I have it to give, anymore.'

Grant frowned again, his eyes questioning. 'What do you mean?

Instantly wanting to snatch back what she'd said, in a moment of self-pitying weakness, she shook her head. 'Oh, nothing.' She needed to stay separate from him, guard her heart, until she'd done what she'd come here to do.

Refocusing on her mission, she leaned down, opened her bag, and pulled out the photograph of Marina. She was sitting astride a wooden horse on the merry-go-round in Princes Street Gardens. Her cheeks were pink, and her eyes shone brightly as she gripped the pole and smiled coyly at the camera. Her sunflower-covered T-shirt glowed against the dull grey of the sky, highlighting the intense blue of her eyes. Her hair flew away from her face, and her chin was slightly lifted, as if she was enjoying the feel of the air on her skin – the entire image one of sweet youth and untethered joy.

Cassie placed the photo on the table and slid it towards him, her heart now threatening to split right through her chest.

Grant looked down at the photo and frowned, then he looked back at her. 'Who's this?'

Cassie moved the photo a little closer to him. 'That is Marina. Isla's daughter.'

At this, Grant made a soft, grunting noise. 'Wow. I didn't know she'd had a child.' He looked back at the photo, then carefully picked it up. 'She's a wee doll. How old is she?'

Cassie leaned back in the chair, her hands dropping into her lap. 'She'll be six in December.' She eyed him, seeing his frown return. 'She's wonderful, Grant. A real chip off the old block.' This was below the belt, but suddenly, Cassie was back in that place of betrayal, of feeling exposed and violated all at once.

'She's very like Isla.' He lifted his eyes to hers, the shadow of a question clouding them.

'I was thinking more of her father.' Cassie hesitated for a second, then continued. 'Grant, don't you see the resemblance?'

He lifted the photo again, scrutinising it before handing it back to her. 'She definitely has your, and Isla's smile, and the family nose.' He hadn't picked up on the cue.

Cassie took another look at the photo, then turned it to face him again. 'Grant, the reason I wanted to meet is...' She forced a swallow. It was now or never. 'I need to know if you slept with Isla.'

Grant's eyebrows jumped and his jaw went slack.

'I'm not sure what I want to hear, but I have to ask you.' She felt fresh tears pressing in so willed them away as she raised the picture up in front of her chest. She would stay strong, even if it choked her. 'Just look at her. She's you, Grant. The eyes, the cheekbones, the mouth, the way she speaks, the way she moves, and even laughs.' Cassie lost the battle as tears began to track down her face. 'Just tell me the truth, please.' She hiccupped. 'I think I deserve that, at least.' She lay the photo back on the table.

His eyes were huge, the frown splitting his forehead framing his obvious anguish as he took a moment, met her gaze, and then slowly nodded.

Cassie felt the movement like a physical blow, and closed her eyes, as the foundation of her fragile world cracked a little more.

_____

23

Cassie swirled the remains of the creamy froth around the glass. The slight bitterness of the Guinness mixed with the tang of betrayal had left her with an acidic taste in her mouth, and her stomach roiling.

Grant had gone outside to take a phone call from work, so she'd made her way to the ladies' room, cleaned up her wrecked face and returned to the table just as she saw him walk back into the pub.

Having him admit to cheating on her was utterly devastating, the reasons for his abandoning her now building into a shocking kind of awakening that made her question everything she thought she'd known, both about him and her sister. But now that she finally knew the truth, buried underneath the hurt, Cassie was angry – so angry that she could hardly see straight. There were more questions she still had to ask, and as he sat down opposite her, she couldn't contain herself any longer.

'Did you leave me because of Isla?' She shoved the glass away from her. 'At least crawling away, filled with crippling guilt over the shitty thing you did would be more plausible than just being scared of marriage.' She heard the bitterness in her voice. Not an attractive quality, and yet, she felt completely entitled to feel this way.

'No. I give you my word, Cassie. I didn't go because of Isla.' His voice was gruff. 'I should have told you what happened, and I am deeply, deeply sorry I didn't.'

Cassie stared at him, seeing the pain in his expression, but sympathy was beyond her. 'Did you and Isla laugh about it? Think I was an idiot who you'd both got one over on?' Her throat was on fire.

'Cass, don't do this.' He shook his head.' You know me better than that.'

Cassie snorted. 'Yeah, well I thought I did.' She dug her thumbnail into the soft wood of the table. 'Seems I'm a crappy judge of character.'

Grant sat back and rubbed his palms down his thighs. 'Isla and I...' He hesitated.

'What?' she snapped.

'It was a one-time thing. A terrible mistake that we both regretted immediately.' He nodded to himself. 'It should never have happened.'

Cassie stared at him, trying to banish the image of him holding Isla close to his chest, running his hands through her hair, down her back, the way he had with Cassie, letting his tongue linger on hers after a kiss. Then she saw Isla's note, the words searing themselves on the backs of her eyes – *I'm sorry for everything... She should have been yours.* The torturous picture show in her mind was ripping new holes in Cassie's tattered heart as Grant reached over and covered her hand with his.

'Cass, stop. Whatever you're imagining, it wasn't like that.'

Startled that after all these years he could still see inside her head, Cassie pulled her hand away. 'Well, how about you tell me how it *was*, Grant? I'm all ears.'

He scanned her face, his own a mask of misery, then he

dropped his hand into his lap and sighed. 'OK. I owe you that much.'

Cassie sat back and crossed her arms. While she knew that what he was about to say would be torturous, if she didn't face it, every murky fact, she might never be able to move on. 'Go ahead.'

Grant dipped his gaze to the tabletop. 'Do you remember that night, the March before the wedding date, when we took Isla to that party at my neighbour's house in Haymarket?'

Cassie stared at him, trying to dredge the night in question out of the depths of her memory.

'You and I had argued – something to do with flowers, I think – and you were in a foul mood. Within about twenty minutes, you told me that you'd had enough of the party and wanted me to take you home.' He paused. 'I said I wanted to stay a little longer, that it would be rude to disappear so soon, but you stormed off anyway.' He lifted his eyes to hers. 'After you left, Isla was having a great time, laughing, dancing, being totally carefree and, for a split second...' He swallowed. 'Just for a moment, I wondered if I'd chosen the right sister.'

At this, Cassie's hand flew up to her mouth. 'Are you bloody serious?'

'Let me finish, Cass.' His palm hovered a little above the tabletop. 'Isla and I had more to drink. A lot more. And then, she followed me out to the garden where I'd gone to get some air. When she asked me if something was wrong, I confided in her that I was having doubts about the wedding, but that you weren't hearing me.' He moved his empty glass to the centre of the table. 'Isla was kind and sympathetic. She just listened to me, then told me that she sometimes felt the same way about you, and that I should listen to my gut.' He shrugged. 'Anyway, one moment we were talking, then the next...'

Cassie's heart was thumping like a drum, and tiny beads of

sweat had bloomed on her upper lip. She couldn't take much more of this. *Isla, did you really feel that way?*

'Cassie, I will never forgive myself for letting it happen, but I need you to understand that it was not intentional or done out of any kind of malice. I never, ever wanted to hurt you, or Isla. I had no idea she was pregnant and knew nothing about Marina. If I had...' His eyes were brimming, and as Cassie tried to find the right words, a way to slap his explanation away and condemn him as the cheating scumbag that he was, something deep inside her held her back.

No matter how hard she tried to block them out, wrapped up in his reasoning there were certain unattractive truths about herself that Cassie hadn't wanted to face and so had buried over the years. She had been brutally single-minded back then, focused on work to the point of becoming myopic, missing cues and signs from the people around her, particularly Isla, and even Grant. As Cassie stared at him, letting the veil slide away from her own behaviour, regret began to surface through the anger. She couldn't hold herself entirely blameless in this, and the knowledge was levelling. But, even so, it wasn't within her power to let him off the hook yet. There was still too much unresolved pain, and anger, to contend with.

'I'm not saying I was perfect, Grant, but what you did was unforgiveable.' Her throat was on fire with the effort of not screaming at him. 'And worse still, both you and Isla kept it from me, which makes it even *more* unforgiveable.' She forced a swallow. 'If you'd just told me the truth.' She swiped at the tears that were tracking down her cheeks.

His eyes were full of misery as he surveyed her face, then he shook his head. 'Would it really have made a difference?'

She sucked in a breath. 'Yes, I think it would.' She nodded decisively.

'Isla obviously didn't think so.' Instantly seeming to want to take back his mumbled words, he pressed his lips together, then lifted his chin and sighed. 'Look, all I can say is I'm truly sorry. I know it's not worth much, and well overdue, but it's no less sincere.'

Cassie scraped the hair away from her forehead, suddenly feeling claustrophobic. She swivelled around in her chair and nodded at the exit. 'I need to get some air, Grant. I can't stay here any longer.'

'Let me help you.' He was up, his hand extended towards her.

'I don't need your help. I just need to get outside.'

Cassie walked close to the buildings, their proximity keeping her grounded, while Grant stayed closer to the kerb. The post-lunch crowds had ebbed away along the Royal Mile, the last few groups of workers heading back to offices to finish their days, as Cassie checked her watch for the umpteenth time. She had just enough time to get to the school to pick up Marina, but only because she'd ordered an Uber rather than take the bus.

'Are you OK, Cass?' Grant moved in next to her.

Unable to risk him touching her, the contact possibly crumbling her last ounce of resolve to keep from crying again, she shoved her hand into her pocket. 'No, but I will be.' She focused ahead, looking for the car that was picking her up.

As she scanned the street, willing the car to arrive and whisk her away from this place, and from him, Grant's revelation was still circling her mind. Reflecting once again on how she had treated people in the past whom she'd cared about, Stuart's face materialised. She had never really let him in, not like she had Grant. Wounds create scar tissue, and sometimes that tissue causes further problems. It can block natural and necessary functions, create a barrier, leave its own mark like a thickening fingerprint, and as Cassie scanned the steady stream of cars sliding past them, she was filled with regret. If she'd handled the situation with Marina more sensitively, not let Stuart feel so utterly railroaded, would he have stayed? Letting the notion fill her mind, beneath all the what ifs was a nugget of truth that her gut wouldn't let her ignore. If she were honest with herself, when she really considered her life with Stuart, Cassie had known they weren't well matched, and now that whole relationship felt like yet another instance of her sheer will and single-mindedness overwhelming her instincts – and the truth.

'Is that it?' Grant pointed at a silver Toyota that was standing across the street, the hazard lights flashing.

Startled back to the moment, Cassie checked her phone and nodded. 'Yes.' She turned to face Grant and instantly knew what she must do next. 'Grant, if you're willing, I'd like to do a DNA test. Just to be sure.' She glanced over and waved at the Uber driver. 'If it comes out as we suspect, then you need to meet Marina.' She locked on his eyes, looking for any sign of fear, or a potential retreat, but all she saw was relief.

'Of course. Makes total sense.' He nodded, his fingers raking through his hair. 'I'll set it up, if that's OK, and I'll text you the clinic info.' He searched her face.

'Sure. Just send it to me.' She hefted her bag higher up on her shoulder. 'Thanks.' She held his gaze, her eyes gritty from the tears she'd shed. She was ready to put some distance between them again.

'Cassie, I'm truly sorry. You know that, right?' He reached for her hand, but she stepped backwards, physical contact too much to contemplate.

'I suppose so.' She nodded at him, a smile a step too far, and still more than he deserved.

24

The following day, determined to lose herself in work, to distract herself from everything she'd learned the previous afternoon, Cassie had had a productive morning at the studio. All had been going well until a series of dagger-like stabs to her stomach had sent her to the bathroom, where she'd bent over double, her palm pressing into her middle as she panted – sweat coating her upper lip.

She'd been careful to conceal what was happening from Hector, who'd been deep in conversation on the phone about a marketing campaign for the new line. Now, with her morning's work done and her pain having mercifully eased, she had collected Marina from school, and they were heading back to the loft.

The mid-afternoon sun was bright, long silvery strands of light glinting across the water as they crossed the bridge. Seeing the row of houseboats ahead, Cassie led Marina to the seawall and pointed at the colourful crafts. 'Have you ever been on a boat, Marina?'

Marina rose onto tiptoe and looked down at the water. 'A little one.' She nodded to herself. 'With Mummy.'

Cassie squeezed Marina's hand a little tighter, Isla's face materialising on the surface of the rippling water below. 'Was it fun?'

Marina nodded. 'We had sticks with string, but no fish came.' She looked up at Cassie. 'Just a welly.'

Cassie laughed at the image. 'Oh, no. That was disappointing.' She smiled at her niece, whose eyes were bright.

'Mummy said never mind, and we had a picnic.' Marina pursed her lips, a tiny crease splitting her forehead. 'Picnics are my favourite. Can we have a picnic?'

This tiny offering was a welcome gift, of such magnitude that Cassie was momentarily overcome. 'Of course we can, sweetheart. How about right now?'

She saw Marina's eyebrows twitch, then a smile crept across her face.

'Now?' Her mouth fell open, revealing the tip of her rosy tongue.

'Yes. We'll go to Lucio's and get some yummy sandwiches, and cakes for pud, then we can go down to the shore and find a special bench I want to show you. We'll eat our lunch and feed the swans.'

Marina was nodding. 'Just us?' Her fingers gripped Cassie's tightly as she scanned her aunt's face.

'Yes, just us girls.' Cassie turned her back on Marina and crouched down. 'Hop on, then.'

Marina seemed unsure what to do, so Cassie beckoned to her.

'Climb on my back and I'll give you a piggyback.' She smiled over her shoulder as Marina tentatively climbed onto her back. 'That's it. Now, hold on tight, and off we go.' Cassie stood up, feeling Marina's arms lock across her throat and her legs tightening around her sides.

As Cassie began trotting towards Shore, Marina started giggling. 'This is funny.' Her voice was jolting with the movement, sounding oddly staccato. 'Go faster, Aunty Cassie.' She squeezed her knees into Cassie's ribs as if she were riding a pony. 'Faster.'

Cassie picked up the pace a little, gripping Marina's calves tightly through her polka dot leggings, a bubble of joy forcing its way up Cassie's throat. 'Giddy-up, horsey,' she called into the quickening breeze, enjoying the amused glances from the people they were passing. Her cotton jacket flapped out from her sides as she avoided a young couple walking hand in hand, turned left and headed for the Italian delicatessen where she often stopped for wafer-thin slices of prosciutto, buttery mozzarella, and cartons of pitch-black olives that tasted of her teenage summers.

Suddenly overcome by hunger, but a kind of hunger that went far beyond the need for food, Cassie lifted her chin and squinted into the sunlight. 'I love you so much, Marina.' The words felt wonderful to say, a simple statement of truth that glowed at Cassie's centre, like a steadfast candle in the dark.

Marina's grip tightened around Cassie's throat. 'You are my favourite.' She pressed her chin into the taut muscles of Cassie's shoulder.

Cassie's vision blurred as she navigated her way towards the green, red and white striped awning, flickering invitingly above the bay window of Lucio's Deli. 'And you are mine, little one.' She forced a swallow. 'Forever and always.'

Marina had chosen an egg mayonnaise sandwich and a cream-filled cannoli, while Cassie had plumped for a mozzarella and sun-dried tomato ciabatta and a sliver of tiramisu. They'd walked along Shore all the way to the Sandy Irvine Robertson bench, dedicated to a famous wine merchant who'd lived in Leith. A bronze sculpture of him lounged on one end of the bench, as he looked out over the water, and Marina had been fascinated by the life-size work. 'My mummy made small ones of these.' She'd pointed at the sculpture. 'She was clever at it.' Marina's eyes had begun to cloud slightly as Cassie, pleased that Marina had made the association with Isla's work, gently took one little hand in hers.

'Yes, she was, sweetheart. Very clever. In fact, I think she was the best artist that I've ever seen.' She'd nodded, seeing Marina's smile return. 'I think you are very clever, too.'

Marina had lifted her chin, the gentle breeze separating the curtain of hair coating her back. 'I'm like my mummy.' She'd nodded to herself. 'She liked picnics, too.'

Determined to keep the mood light, Cassie had pulled Marina onto her knee. 'How about we sing a song to old Sandy here? Just for fun.'

Marina had snorted softly. 'What song?' She'd turned to look at Cassie, her eyes full of light again.

'How about "Michael Finnegan"?' Cassie had shifted, letting Marina slide back onto the bench beside her. 'Do you know it?'

Marina had shaken her head.

'It's a silly song about a man who grew whiskers on his chin, but then the wind blew them in again.' Cassie had made a comical face, causing Marina to giggle.

'That's silly.' Marina had laughed again. 'Tell me it.'

Cassie had smiled, pulling back her shoulders, and had begun to sing the song that she and Isla had sung over and over, in the back of the car, whenever the family had been on road trips. While their mother had laughed, their father would eventually beg them to stop, and as the familiar lyrics floated away on the breeze, Cassie let herself slide back to her childhood, and those precious, innocent moments that now meant so much more than they had at the time.

Half an hour later, as they'd been leaving, Marina had patted Sandy's head and said, 'We'll come and see you again.'

Cassie had laughed softly at the sweet gesture, and then done the same. 'See you soon, Sandy.' She'd then taken Marina's hand and they'd walked back to the loft in contented silence.

As the day had drawn to a gentle close, Marina in the bath playing with a plastic boat, Cassie had stood in the doorway, her heart full of such peace that she'd made a silent vow that she'd dedicate more time to these types of spontaneous outings. Marina's smile and musical laugh echoing back to Cassie were precious gifts that carried so much power – enough to erase pain, loss and fear. Wholly invaluable.

25

A week later, October had brought with it a snap of cold, and incessant rain that had lasted for days. Syd had come home from Johannesburg laden with bags of biltong, the dried springbok meat he knew that Cassie loved. He'd also brought her a book on how to braai, which she had laughed out loud at as she did not possess a barbecue, and a bottle of exquisite Stellenbosch wine that he'd snuck into his suitcase.

His first night back, once Marina was tucked into bed, they'd polished off the wine as Cassie had filled him in on everything that had happened with Grant. Syd had been suitably appalled at the proof of Grant's indiscretion, but had then moderated his usual, hyper-protective impulses. 'Well, who knew he'd prove to be a dog, but at least you know what happened, and can stop torturing yourself, my love.' He'd smiled sadly at her.

'What do you mean?' She'd frowned, irritated to have been so transparent, even to her best friend. Since seeing Grant, she couldn't deny that she'd been thinking about him, and their relationship a lot, but Syd's observation had made her uncomfortable.

'Come on, Cassie, you know you've never really got over him.' Syd had held his giant hands out, palms up. His tie-dyed T-shirt had made his glossy skin glow as he'd wiggled his sculpted eyebrows at her. 'Maybe now you can let it go and move on, once and for all?'

Taken aback, and yet unsure why she was surprised at him going for the jugular like this, she'd laughed, the release feeling welcome, and overdue. 'Damn, Syd. You know I hate it when you're right.'

'Well, Cassandra, you must hate me all the time.' He'd laughed heartily, slapping his thighs. 'Because I'm seldom wrong, and I'm right again.'

With their catch-up almost complete, Cassie had broached the next favour she needed from him. The previous day, she had finally received a date for her exploratory surgery, to take place on the twelfth of the month. She would be in hospital for an overnight, and as Cassie still had not wanted to involve Sadie, until Cassie knew more, Syd had predictably offered to stay at the loft to take care of Marina. 'I'll be a fab interim parent.' He'd pulled a comical face. 'At least I'll try not to do anything stupid that you'll string me up for later. Maybe I can teach her to salsa? Dancing is good for the soul. You know, you could use some of that too, man.'

Cassie had laughed. 'She's five, you idiot.'

Syd had widened his eyes. 'So? Start them early. She'll be on *Strictly* before you know it.' He'd chuckled.

'And as for me, you know I have two left feet.' Cassie had rolled her eyes, then hugged him. 'Marina loves you almost as much as I do.'

Hugging her so tightly her ribs felt as if they might crack, he had nodded approvingly. 'Well, she obviously has impeccable taste.'

They'd talked through the logistics of the surgery, and the

days after, and thankfully the timing had worked out well. Marina's half-term break started on the seventeenth, so Cassie planned on having nine full days off to recuperate, and taking her niece home to Lewis, as promised. Cassie knew that the one-on-one time together would be a gift, but despite her determination to remain positive, she couldn't help but wonder how many more opportunities they might have to do this.

Just this morning, a Saturday, Cassie had opened the DNA results that had been sitting in her bag for two days, her too afraid to open them. Inevitably, they had shown that Grant was Marina's biological father. Seeing the confirmation in black and white had hurt her as deeply and profoundly as if this unimaginable thing had happened that same day. Cassie had rushed into the bathroom and stuffed a flannel in her mouth so that Marina wouldn't hear her heaving breaths, an overwhelming sense of betrayal snatching at Cassie's heart.

When she'd pulled herself together, she'd stared at the single sheet of paper until the lines had blurred, then back at her reflection in the mirror. As she'd focused on her flushed cheeks, and mane of wild red hair – badly needing a brush – Grant's face had eerily laid itself over hers on the glass. He was Marina's father, and fact was fact, but the thought of bringing him into Marina's life – yet another new element for the child to absorb after everything she had been through – made Cassie shake her head. Did he deserve to have this glorious little human as part of his life? Could he be trusted not to bolt when things got tough? Could she share her precious niece now that she was sure that Marina truly belonged with her?

As she sifted through a cascade of emotions, the realisation that regardless of how she felt about him, she could not keep him from his daughter made Cassie blink away the angry tears

that were pressing in. No. This introduction had to happen. It
was just about how, and when.

She'd pulled her phone out of her pocket and called Grant,
her heart pattering as she'd waited to hear his voice. She'd
wanted to shout at him, 'This is not fair. She is mine.' But when
he'd answered, she'd spoken quietly, and steadily. 'The tests are
conclusive, Grant. It's you.'

'OK.' He'd sounded breathless. 'Good. Right. So, what do
we do next?'

Cassie had pressed her eyes closed for a second or two
before refocusing on the closed door. 'We'll take things slowly at
first, but we'll need to figure out when to introduce you to her.'
She'd whispered this time. 'You need to be sure that you're
ready for this, Grant. I won't have her upset, or disappointed...'
Her voice had faded as he'd cut in.

'Cassie, I am ready. I'm more than ready. I will not let her,
or you, down, ever again.'

As she'd let his words linger, she'd nodded slowly. 'All right
then. How about tomorrow afternoon, after we've been to see
my mum?'

'Yes. Great. Whenever works for you.' She'd heard genuine
enthusiasm in his voice, which was both comforting and unsettling. 'Just tell me where and when.'

A few minutes after ending the call, afraid that Marina
might notice her absence and come looking for her, Cassie had
pulled her shoulders back and splashed water on her face,
brushed her hair and met Marina coming down the hall dragging Raffy behind her. 'Can we go to the zoo?'

'Yes, we can.' She'd smiled at her niece and swung her up
onto her hip. 'Gosh, you're a gigantic heffalump.' She'd laughed,
seeing Marina grin, that magical smile banishing all else that
could potentially have darkened the rest of Cassie's day.

Now, Marina was sitting next to Cassie on the bus, Raffy
tucked under Marina's arm, the giraffe wearing a tiny yellow

coat. Marina's blue raincoat was zipped up high under her chin and she'd chosen to wear her yellow wellingtons which her jeans were tucked into. With her hair in a ponytail and a red rain hat pulled down over her ears, the resemblance to Paddington Bear was almost comical. It was the latest book that Cassie had been reading to Marina, so Cassie leaned in and whispered, 'Would you like a marmalade sandwich?'

Marina took a moment to register the joke, then giggled. 'I'm not a bear.' She leaned against Cassie's arm. 'Silly, Mummy.'

Cassie's heart felt as if it might burst. Marina's cheeks were rosy as she turned to look out of the window, seemingly unaware of what she'd said, or its monumental impact on her aunt.

Cassie swallowed hard, then wrapped her arm around Marina's shoulders. 'I wonder if we'll see the tiger today. Maybe he'll not come out in the rain. Cats don't like rain much.' She shifted closer to her niece, as the low buzz of music filtered back from the headphones of the young man sitting in front of them. Cassie couldn't make it out, but the thump of the base reminded her of Stuart, and for a moment, she felt her eyes prickle. Even knowing that this had been the right decision, the right path for them all, she still missed him.

The following day, Cassie and Marina were at Sadie's door, at noon on the dot. The sun had finally come out and the plan was for the three of them to go for a walk in the park after having lunch at Sadie's flat.

As Cassie let herself in, she was surprised to see Jean standing in the hall instead of her mother. 'Oh, Jean. How are you?' Cassie stepped forward as her mother's neighbour moved back into the hall. Jean had a colourful scarf around her neck, and her hazel eyes twinkled behind her tortoiseshell glasses.

'Fine, fine, Cassie. You look well, love.' Jean smiled and wrapped her long, ribbed cardigan tighter around her ample middle. 'And this must be wee Marina?' She leaned down and smiled at Marina, who had moved in behind Cassie's legs, her thumb back in her mouth.

'Say hello to Jean, sweetheart. This is Granny's friend who lives next door.' Cassie eased Marina out from behind her. 'Where's Mum?'

'She's up to her eyes in flour.' Jean nodded towards the kitchen. 'She ran out of butter, so I just brought her some.'

'Really?' Cassie's eyebrows jumped. Her mother had always been a keen baker, but after Russ had died, Sadie had metaphorically hung up her baking trays, as determinedly as she had her interest in much that life had left to offer her.

'She's made a quiche, and now she's baking some treacle scones for the pair of you.' Jean smiled widely, her ruddy cheeks folding into a network of soft wrinkles, then she leaned closer and lowered her voice. 'It's so good to see her like this.'

'Thanks, Jean.' Overwhelmed with relief at this spark of new life in her mother, Cassie drew Jean into a hug, feeling the softness of the kindly woman – a sharp contrast to Sadie's petite frame.

'Och, I've done nothing.' Jean's cheeks coloured. 'I think it's more about this wee one, here.' She nodded at Marina, who was now sitting on the floor tugging at the Velcro strip on her shoe, her hair falling in a glossy curtain around her shoulders.

'Yes, I think you might be right.' Cassie nodded, taking in the determined curve of Marina's shoulders as she eased her shoe off and started on the other one.

'Save me a scone, Sadie,' Jean called over shoulder just as Sadie emerged from the kitchen, her favourite floral apron on and a patch of flour dusting her left cheek. 'Right. I'll be off.' Jean patted Cassie's arm. 'See you soon, Cassie. And you, Marina. You'll need to come next door sometime and meet the

Sergeant Major.' She winked at Marina, whose eyes were wide. The mention of Jean's giant parrot made Cassie smile. The Sergeant Major ruled the roost in Jean's house, and despite being told he was harmless, Cassie was rather nervous of the grumpy old bird – having received more than one nip from the horned beak.

'Bye, Jean. See you later. Thanks for the butter.' Sadie waved a floury hand as her friend closed the door behind her. There was a lighter quality to Sadie's voice, and hearing it made Cassie realise how much she'd missed that over the past few years. As she watched, her mother walked straight to Marina and helped her up from the floor. 'Hello, pet.' She wrapped the child in a hug. 'I've missed you.'

Cassie's heart flip-flopped as Marina looked up at her grandmother eagerly, then slid her arms around Sadie's waist. 'Hello, Granny.'

Sadie looked over at Cassie and smiled. 'I missed you, too, by the way.'

Cassie laughed. 'Oh, good. I was beginning to wonder.'

Sadie laughed too, a genuine, warm sound that moved Cassie deep at her centre. 'Coming to help me finish the scones? I've got a special apron for you.' Sadie cupped Marina's chin in her palm.

Marina nodded. 'Uh-huh. It smells nice.'

'It does smell good in here. Like old times.' Cassie smiled at her mother. 'You two go ahead. I'm going to check my messages.' She patted her pocket.

Sadie held her gaze for a few moments, then led Marina away towards the kitchen, as the little girl quipped, 'I like it at your house, Granny.'

With their lunch over, and Marina snuggled up with a book on Sadie's bed, for a nap, Cassie followed her mother into the living room. Cassie had had a bad night, sitting up in the lounge for a few hours reading, and breathing through the nine-out-of-ten on the scale, gripping pains that had racked her. This morning, the pain was down to a two but now was masked by a flash of anxiety as she thought for the millionth time about her impending surgery, and what they might discover.

As she watched her mother settle into her chair, Cassie made a snap decision that surprised her. With everything that was going on, the information she had been keeping to herself about Grant being Marina's father suddenly felt too cumbersome, and she wanted to share it with Sadie. Cassie wanted her mother's take on what had happened, and more than that, to make sure she agreed with something else that Cassie had decided just the previous day. That it was time that Grant met his daughter.

As Cassie tucked her legs under her on the sofa, she glanced across the room. Sadie was wiping her glasses on a scrap of cotton that she kept on the side table by the fire and staring at her.

'What is it, Mum?' Cassie watched her mother slide her glasses back on.

'Is there something you want to talk about?' Sadie folded her hands in her lap. 'You have that look.' She smiled, her halo of curls pale against her rosy complexion.

'What look?' Cassie lifted her chin, still surprised whenever her mother saw through her this way.

'Cassie, you know you can tell me anything. That's what I'm here for.' Sadie eyed her. 'I know I haven't been too great on that score, for a while, but I'm still your mum.' She paused. 'What is it, love?'

Cassie unfolded her legs and planted her feet on the rug, as a rush of adrenaline made her skin clammy. Sadie's eyes were clear, fully occupied, and she looked stronger somehow, more engaged than Cassie had seen her in ages. Telling her this would be OK. It had to be, as Cassie really needed some support.

'You're right. I do want to tell you something.' She glanced over her shoulder, checking that Marina was still out of earshot. 'It's about Grant.' She paused. 'And there's something else, too, Mum.'

26

As Cassie talked, Sadie's face paled, then took on more colour. She nodded once or twice, laced her fingers together and released them, then shifted to the edge of her chair. All the while, Cassie waited for the slew of reactions she'd expected – shock, disappointment, and maybe even anger, but Sadie's countenance remained calm. Her eyes gave nothing away as she studied Cassie's face, and when Cassie was finished telling her mother all that she'd discovered about Grant, and Isla, she flopped back against the cushion behind her, spent, her voice finally giving way to angry tears. 'How could they, Mum? I just can't take it in.'

Sadie stood up slowly and made her way to the window, her fingers lingering on the latch for a few moments as her engagement ring projected tiny dots of light onto the ceiling. Her hair was floss-like, with the light shining through it as she finally turned, walked over, sat next to Cassie, and took her hand. 'To be honest, love, as soon as I saw Marina, I suspected she was Grant's. It was those eyes.' She shrugged. 'And then, after spending time with her, observing her mannerisms, even the way she reasons things out, well...' She squeezed Cassie's hand.

'I know. I mean, once I knew for sure, I realised that it had been staring me in the face.' Cassie sniffed miserably. 'I just didn't want to believe it.'

Sadie nodded, gently sweeping a length of hair behind Cassie's shoulder. 'I know, my love. It's extremely painful, and I'm sorry you're going through this.' She sighed. 'I am very surprised, and I certainly don't condone what either of them did, but, Cassie, I think after everything that's happened, you need to try to let go of the hurt and find a way to forgive them – especially Isla.'

Cassie sucked in her breath. This was not what she expected or had hoped for. 'How can you say that?' She slid her hand from her mother's, as the simmering sense of betrayal bubbled up inside her again.

'I say it because I know... I *knew* Isla, better than anyone.' Sadie's voice softened. 'She lived in your shadow, Cassie. Always unsure, anxious, and feeling like second cast.'

'I never meant to make her feel that way.' Hurt, Cassie stood up and crossed the room, her back to the window, images of Isla, the fearful eyes, the nervous smile, fluttering behind Cassie's eyes like a poignant film.

'No. I don't believe you ever did. But that was about Isla. Not you, love. She was sweet on Grant from the very start, as you know, and I think more than a bit jealous. Perhaps she saw him turning to her that night as an opportunity to level the playing field.' When Cassie began to protest, Sadie held her palm up flat. 'As I said, I'm not condoning what she did, at all, Cassie. I'm just trying to get inside her skin.' She eyed her daughter. 'I know we often asked a lot of you when it came to Isla. We probably expected too much at times, but you were always the stronger one.' Sadie shook her head sadly. 'She probably wanted what you had, to *be* you for a few minutes, and while I'm hurt for you, Cassie, I truly am, I can't condemn her.'

Sadie pulled a tissue out from the sleeve of her sweater and blew her nose.

A rushing sound flooded Cassie's head as she paced back and forth in front of the window. There was too much hurt to be dismissed so easily. It went too deep. 'But we were engaged, Mum. She knew how much I loved him and yet she did it anyway. And as for Grant, he betrayed me in the worst possible way. What worse hurt is there than choosing to cheat on me, with my own sister? How will I ever be able to get that out of my head, never mind forgive him – or either of them?'

Sadie stood up and joined Cassie at the window, Sadie's warm fingers seeking Cassie's chilled ones. 'I know, love, but one thing I've learned since losing your father is that life leaves no room for regret, or wishing the past were different. The future is all any of us can focus on and now, for both of us, that is Marina. She's a priceless gift that Isla left us both, Cassie. Marina has lost her mother and that's something we can never fully compensate for. We need to treasure and nurture her as best we can, and part of that means moving on – making sure she is safe and cared for and grows up surrounded by a loving family.'

Cassie took a shaky breath, her chest tight with pain. 'I adore her, Mum. She'll have all of that with me.' She gulped.

'I know that, Cassie. But she also has a father.' Sadie halted. 'All I'm saying is that she deserves a family – one that not only loves her but that isn't full of conflict.' Sadie let go of Cassie's hand. 'Do you think you can do that for her, my darling?'

Cassie let her mother's words circle her mind as she grappled for understanding – trying to stand in Isla's shoes, imagine what it was like to feel like an understudy in your own life – and the thought was desperately sad. As she focused on Sadie's gentle eyes, so obviously seeking solace, and reassurance, Cassie held her breath. She could find understanding, but forgiveness still felt beyond her. At least for the moment.

She raked her hair into a twist and blinked her vision clear, her mother's face coming back into focus. 'I can try to get my head around what Isla did, Mum.' Her voice cracked. 'But forgiveness...' She shook her head. 'And as for Grant. Trusting him again.' She paused. 'I can't make any promises.'

Sadie nodded, a soft smile lifting her mouth. 'All I ask is that you try, love.'

'We've arranged for Grant to meet Marina this afternoon, in Princes Gardens.' Cassie sipped the hot coffee her mother had made her. 'I should've told you all this before, Mum, but everything has happened so quickly.' Cassie eyed the door, anxious that Marina was still safely napping in the bedroom.

'It's OK, sweetheart. I understand.' Sadie nodded. 'And I think it's the right thing to do.'

Cassie nodded, relieved and yet slightly taken aback at the grace with which her mother had accepted everything she'd been told. 'I want to see how he is with her, whether he has what it takes to be in her life.' She caught the edge in her voice and locked eyes with her mother. 'And before you say it, yes, I will give him a chance to show me he can be trusted. But I expect full commitment from him, Mum. Not just lip service.'

Sadie was staring at her, nodding almost imperceptibly.

'That sounds reasonable, Cassie.' She paused. 'But I think there was something else you needed to tell me, right?'

Cassie set her cup on the coffee table and ran her hands down her thighs, pinching the sinewy muscles through her jeans. 'Yes, there is.' She nodded. 'I don't want you to worry, but I'm having some exploratory surgery next week. It seems there's something going on with my gall bladder.' The last word caught in her throat as she saw the colour drain from Sadie's face. 'I'm sorry to dump all this on you at once, Mum, but I felt you should know.'

Sadie was up and crossing the room again, her eyes wide. 'What can I do?' She sat next to Cassie, her arm circling Cassie's shoulders.

'Nothing at the moment, but thanks. I'm sure it's nothing to worry about, but you know how thorough Doctor Carnegie is,' she sighed. 'No stone unturned.' Cassie leaned into her mother, the smell of scones and safety threatening to loosen the grip Cassie had on the fear that was gathering in her chest.

Sadie began to rock her so gently that Cassie closed her eyes, wishing to be transported to a time when this was all the comfort she needed, her mother's embrace the cure-all for whatever ailed her. 'Whatever happens, it's going to be OK, Cassie. You can lean on me, sweetheart. I won't break.' She sat forward and placed her palm on Cassie's cheek. 'It's time you let me be the parent again.'

Cassie met her mother's gaze, once again seeing the renewed strength of will behind the kind eyes. 'Thanks, Mum. I love you so much.'

Sadie released her and stood up, extending a hand to Cassie. 'And I love you more than you know.' She tugged Cassie up from the sofa. 'Now, let's get you a cold flannel for your eyes. You can tell me everything, then we'll take Marina for a walk before you go.' She smiled, her head tipping to the side. 'It's going to be OK.'

Cassie nodded, hooking her arm through her mother's as they headed for the bathroom. 'I know it is, Mum.' The words tasted less than true, but Cassie had given her mother enough to deal with for one day – and Sadie had given Cassie exactly what she needed in return. Whatever happened next, they'd deal with it together, and that knowledge was worth everything.

27

Cassie and Grant had agreed that the meeting should take place outside. Somewhere Marina felt happiest. Their semi-truce was new, and fragile, and while Cassie was still smarting about everything that had happened, her talk with her mother had confirmed that she must try to put all that aside so he could finally meet his daughter in an atmosphere of openness and acceptance.

Cassie and Marina had taken the bus from the end of Sadie's road, then jumped off and walked through Princes Street Gardens. Cassie had told Grant to meet them at the merry-go-round at 3 p.m. and as she checked her watch, she saw that they had ten minutes to spare.

'Do you want a doughnut?' She took Marina's hand, feeling the little fingers grabbing hers back.

'Can I have a jammy one?' Marina was looking ahead at the brightly coloured vendor's van.

'You certainly can.' Cassie braced herself for the next hurdle. 'Remember that I told you we're meeting someone special today? Well, his name is Grant, and he likes jammy

doughnuts the best, too.' She recalled his amusing habit of
buying three at a time, two for him and one for Cassie.

Marina nodded, her eyes not leaving the small queue that
had gathered at the van. 'We can get him one, too,' she said,
dreamily. 'But he can't have mine.'

Cassie laughed, the tension in her easing. 'No way, José.'
Just as she was about to join the queue, a movement in her
peripheral vision made her stop. Turning to her left, she saw
Grant, pacing in front of the merry-go-round. His black jeans
and tan boots looked crisp and new, and his cable-knit beige
sweater clung to his firm torso, emphasising the broad shoulders
that had once been there for Cassie to lean on, cry into, to
kiss... No, she couldn't go back down that rabbit hole. She must
focus. This was too important.

Waiting for him to catch her eye, she lifted a hand. He
spotted her and smiled, waving back as Cassie pointed ahead of
her to the doughnut van, but rather than see her signal, Grant
was now staring at Marina. He had stopped pacing, his eyes
seeming to bore into the side of Marina's face, as his jaw
twitched in the tell-tale manner that Cassie knew so well.

'Let's join the queue.' Cassie eased Marina forward. 'It
won't take long.'

Grant was hesitating by the merry-go-round; his hands
going in and out of his pockets as he seemed to be waiting for
Cassie to give him permission to approach. A sudden flash of
sympathy at his obvious nervousness made her beckon to him,
the need to get this over with overtaking her own nerves.

Grant walked slowly towards them, just as the person in
front of them moved away and Marina stepped up to the van.

'Two jam doughnuts, and an apple cinnamon one, please.'
Cassie smiled at the young man inside the van, a shock of
carrot-red hair sticking straight up, above piercing blue eyes.

'Righto.' He nodded, then placed the three warm doughnuts in a paper bag. As he leaned out of the hatch and handed

the bag to an eager Marina, Cassie felt Grant move in next to her. She caught a whiff of the sandalwood soap he favoured, the memories it evoked plucking at her heart in perfect time with the chiming music coming from the merry-go-round opposite.

Cassie took Marina's free hand and they all moved away from the van in unison, a threesome, deeply connected and yet strangers, in so many ways. The irony of the situation struck Cassie as she eased Marina onto a low bench and then sat beside her. Grant followed suit and sat on Marina's opposite side – the child seemingly still oblivious to his presence.

'Marina, sweetheart, this is Grant. The special friend I told you about.' Cassie helped Marina get her doughnut out of the bag as the little girl glanced fleetingly over her shoulder at Grant, then back to her prize. 'Can you say hello?'

Marina took a giant bite of doughnut, sending a glob of crimson jam spurting out onto her jeans. ''Ello.' She spoke through a gooey mouthful; her eyes glued to the merry-go-round ahead.

'Ick, what a mess.' Cassie rummaged in her bag for a tissue, or a wet wipe, only to see Grant reach over and scoop the jam up on his thumb, then pop it into his mouth. Cassie was startled by the intimacy of his action and looked over at him, her eyes wide.

Just as she was about to speak, Marina chuckled. 'That's my jam.' She turned and looked up at Grant, and then it happened.

Time slowed to a crawl as Marina held her doughnut up, suspended in front of her, and scrutinised Grant's face. Cassie tried not to squirm, as she wanted to shift to be able to see Marina's expression, but the body language alone was eloquent. There was definite recognition there, that the child felt but probably couldn't understand, and as Grant smiled warmly at Marina, Cassie exhaled. She was torn between relief and an odd kind of jealousy at the palpable connection she was witnessing, her own journey with Marina having started out much less easily.

'Yes, but it was good jam going to waste.' He gave an exaggerated grin. 'You can have some of mine, if you like?' He held his hands out expectantly. 'If I had a doughnut, that is.'

Cassie lifted the bag and handed it to him. 'Sorry. We did get you one.' She watched as he took the bag, pulled out the doughnut and looked down at Marina, who was still transfixed.

'Let's see who can take the biggest bite.' He waggled his doughnut. 'Ready, steady, go.' He stuffed half of it in his mouth as a bubble of jam oozed out on one side. Marina took a second, then copied him, another line of jam trickling down her chin.

As Cassie watched, her jealousy gradually melting into the beginnings of thankfulness, Grant and Marina locked eyes and then laughed, the same gentle hiccup followed by a little snort, and Marina's eyes widened at the sound.

'You laugh funny.' She eyed him, her cheeks pulsing as she finished her mouthful.

'So do you.' Grant licked the jam from his cheek and then glanced over at Cassie. For a second, she thought she saw his eyes fill, then he grinned again, shoved the last bite into his mouth and rubbed his sugary fingers down his thighs. Seeing it, Marina lifted her sticky hands up, then mimicked his action, leaving a glossy white streak down each leg. Then, she reached over and brushed some sugar from Grant's knee, her little hand working determinedly as Grant smiled at her, his eyes now visibly full.

'What a mucky pair.' Cassie choked out a laugh, determined to keep the energy positive, despite her sudden, overwhelming fear that this intrinsic connection between Marina and her father might ease Cassie out of Marina's heart. Then, shaking off her childish insecurity, she tutted and pointed at the carousel. 'Come on, let's get on and have a ride.'

. . .

Grant held one of Marina's hands and Cassie the other as they walked four steps, then swung her high into the air ahead of them. Marina laughed heartily and Cassie registered that this was the first time she'd heard such unbridled joy in the child since they'd met.

'Up you go.' Grant laughed, the familiar sound taking Cassie back in time.

'Wheeeee.' Marina was panting softly, her eyes alight and her hair flying behind her as they lowered her to the ground again.

'OK, last time.' Cassie puffed. 'Ready?'

Marina nodded, looking back and forth between Cassie and Grant, then she launched herself forward, tugging on their arms. 'Come on.' She squealed. 'Again.'

Grant glanced over and caught Cassie's eye and mouthed 'Thank you.'

She held his gaze and nodded, a surprising flicker of affection for him making her snap her eyes back to the path ahead.

Ten minutes later, they were walking across the gardens, back towards the bus stop. Cassie was next to Grant, and Marina was on his opposite side, holding his hand. The bond had been created, which filled Cassie with hope, that the palpable connection between father and daughter would continue to strengthen.

28

Twelve days later, as the evening sky turned to an inky black outside the loft, Cassie was packing for Lewis. The exploratory surgery was behind her, but the results were still pending. The waiting was the hardest part, her emotions taking anxious dips and then soaring with optimism as she visualised only the positive outcomes that were possible, and she was thankful that she had planned this trip, which would be a welcome distraction.

Sadie had tried to persuade her to stay at home after the surgery, so that she could look after her, but Cassie had refused, saying that she had promised Marina, and that she was looking forward to getting out of the city for a few days.

They had seen Grant twice more, meeting for a walk around Stockbridge and then at a park with a swing set that Marina had loved. Each time, things had gone well, and Cassie was delighted at the ease with which Marina had accepted Grant, and her comfort around him.

Now, Marina was hovering in the doorway watching as Cassie piled the clothes she was taking with her onto the bed. Marina was in her butterfly-covered pyjamas, a dark line above her upper lip where she'd just drained a glass of chocolate milk, and her mane of hair in a sagging ponytail. 'Can we bring Raffy?' She tucked the giraffe higher under her armpit and moved further into the room.

'Of course. Raffy is family. We'd never leave him behind.' Cassie unzipped her giant holdall and began stuffing clothes inside. As she said the word family, she felt a tugging at her centre. Her family had been brutally diminished by the loss of her father, and sister – a snatching away of two of the people who meant the most to her in the world – and the reality of that was still hard to accept. What she wanted more than anything, for Marina, was not to feel this way. Never to feel adrift, or lonely, and as Cassie lifted a couple of sweaters and crammed them into the bag, an idea bloomed.

Grant was Marina's family, and while they hadn't told her yet that he was her father, there was no denying her comfort around him. He was a natural. At ease – not pushing Marina but responding to her cues and signals as if he'd been parenting her for years. While it was still difficult for Cassie to be around him, residual hurt and mistrust making her want to keep him at arm's-length, she was relieved beyond measure at the way he had embraced his daughter, and as Cassie's idea began to take root, she shoved another sweater into the bag and turned to Marina. 'Come here, little one.'

Marina crossed the space between them and leaned against Cassie's side, the faint smell of chocolate coming with her.

'How would you like Grant to come to Lewis with us?' She lifted the heavy ponytail from Marina's back and twisted it around her fingers.

Marina looked up, her eyes meeting Cassie's. 'To come to my house?' Her expression was hard to read, her eyes clear, and yet there was no smile.

'Yes, to stay with us for a couple of days.' Cassie tucked a stray tendril behind Marina's ear. 'Only if you want, though.'

Marina cuddled Raffy closer to her chest, excitedly. 'OK.'

She gave a single nod, then stuck her thumb in her mouth. 'He's really nice,' she mumbled around her thumb.

Amused by the ease with which this decision had been taken, Cassie hugged her niece to her side. 'OK. Good. It will be fun.' Cassie smiled brightly, a flash of concern at what she'd just done making her pause. Was she ready to be around Grant for a couple of days? Meeting in the park was one thing but being at the cottage would mean they were together, basically in isolation. As she hesitated for a moment, wondering if she could get out of this now, she looked at Marina's contented expression and the answer was clear. 'Shall we phone him and see if he wants to come, then?'

Marina nodded. 'Can I talk to him?' She still spoke around her thumb, a smile bracketing the little digit.

Cassie nodded, Marina's desire to talk to her father endearing, and a sign of her growing confidence, which felt wonderful to witness. 'Of course you can. Come on, let's get the phone.'

Grant had been floored by the invitation, had said he'd need an hour or so to see if he could arrange cover at the clinic, and that he would call them back. Meanwhile, Cassie tried to help Marina pack. She was excitedly piling what she wanted to take with her on the floor of her room. 'And *Green Eggs*, and my rain boots, and my unicorn jumper.' Her eyes were aglow, her excitement contagious – seeping into Cassie like a warm tide. 'How long until we go?' Marina tossed another T-shirt onto the pile.

'Tomorrow. We're flying early in the morning.' Cassie laughed softly as she gathered several of the items from the floor and began to fold and put them into a second holdall. 'We'll leave here after breakfast, and we'll be at the cottage at lunchtime.' She grabbed several pairs of socks and pants from the little chest of drawers under the window and added them to the bag. As she leaned down, her stomach knotted in pain, making her gasp. The surgery had left her with three small incisions on her abdomen, each with a tiny butterfly plaster on it, but this pain had been deep inside – nothing to do with the wounds. As she started to hum tunelessly, hoping to camouflage the sound she'd made, Marina looked up from her task, her eyes lingering on Cassie's face.

'Aunty Cassie?'

'Yes, love.' Cassie straightened up, afraid Marina had noticed her gasp.

'Do you like Grant?' She tipped her head to the side, like a curious puppy.

Cassie's eyebrows jumped. 'Yes, I do.' She nodded, then pushed a couple of T-shirts into the bag, hoping she'd sounded convincing. The innocent question, while disarming, felt somewhat loaded – its true punch still to come.

'He's kind.' Marina blinked several times, then, as Cassie held her breath, the moment passed as Marina dived onto the bed and swung her legs out. 'Tomorrow.' She smiled to herself. 'Going home tomorrow.'

Cassie sighed, relief at being spared the inquisition for now making her feel lighter as she pictured them back on Lewis, in the stunning spot overlooking the water.

The drive to the cottage felt so different this time that Cassie had been quiet, focusing on the scenery and letting Marina chatter to Grant.

'The birds are better here. Look.' She pointed at a large flock of sea birds, rising from a lush field to their left. 'And the sea is warm like my bath. The milk is yummier, too.' She made a little smacking sound with her lips, which made both Grant and Cassie laugh. 'It tastes like ice cream.'

Grant twisted around and squeezed her knee. 'So that's why you always want to add chocolate to your milk in Edinburgh?' He snorted softly. 'Hmmm, are you a budding chef, or just a cheeky monkey?' He laughed again as Marina joined him, their voices melding into a joyful sound that brought a grateful smile to Cassie's face, as she focused ahead.

Grant brought something unique out in the child – reaching her on a different level than Cassie had been able to – and hearing the animated little voice coming from the back seat served as confirmation that, despite her trepidation at having him come here with them, it had been the right decision to invite him.

Cassie navigated her way across the island, crossing the small bridge over the river, tracing the rugged coastline as they headed west. As she watched the gilded, mid-October light bouncing off the moors, she thought about the cottage. There were a few things that, having had some distance and time to let Isla's death permeate, she thought she would like to take back to Edinburgh.

In the studio, sitting on the workbench, there had been two unfinished pieces of sculpture that Cassie had briefly noticed. Too overwhelmed at the time to linger in the room, she'd closed the door and left them in the dark. One of the works was a park bench, with a single figure sitting on it. The figure had a narrow back, long waved hair in a messy knot at the top of the head, a blanket with deep folds draped around the shoulders, and the feet were indistinct from the ground, looking as if the figure was emerging straight from the rock below. From behind, it seemed like the person was staring out to sea, but what had struck Cassie the most was the slope of the back, as if it were weighted under a burden so cumbersome that sitting up straight was an impossibility. It had reminded her of Isla, and the way life weighed on her, and now that the finality of her sister's heartbreaking death had become Cassie's new reality, she wanted to take the piece of art – keep Isla close and remember all the good times they'd shared before betrayal or forgiveness had become part of their story.

Behind her, Marina was staring out of the window, her face glowing and her eyes darting from one side of the car to the other. 'This is the way home.' She chimed. 'The sea is over there.' She pointed to her right. 'My house is there.' Now she pointed dead ahead, her mouth fluttering around a smile as she nodded to herself.

'I can't wait to see it.' Grant twisted around and gave her a thumbs up. 'If it's still sunny when we get there, will you show me your beach?' He glanced over at Cassie, who kept her eyes on the road.

'Uh-huh.' Marina nodded. 'We can make a castle.' She reached over and patted the back of Grant's seat. 'Aunty Cassie made a mermaid last time.' She grinned, her joy at being here almost palpable.

'Sounds like a good plan.' Grant turned back to face the road, his arm lingering on the back of Cassie's seat. 'Your Aunt Cassie is really good at things like that. At a lot of things.' He spoke to the windscreen, but his words were for Cassie, and she heard the compliment there. Slightly unnerved by the gesture, a sort of verbal olive branch, she just nodded.

'And your mummy was so good at making beautiful things, too.' She looked at Marina in the rear-view mirror, Cassie's decision to keep mentioning Isla, keep her present for her daughter, feeling right.

'She was good at drawing, and stories and soup.' Marina's profile was sharp against the light behind her, her nose aquiline and her lips full.

As Cassie waited for more, or a sense of sadness or pain to follow the statement, to her relief she saw only calm in the little girl's countenance. Glancing over at Grant, Cassie caught him staring at her. 'What?' She lifted her eyebrows.

'Nothing.' He shook his head, his eyes crinkling at the edges as they slipped back to the road.

By the time they'd arrived at the cottage, the sky had darkened, and the heavens had opened, big fat raindrops peppering the patio as they'd all huddled together at the front door while Cassie unlocked it.

Once inside, Marina had dumped her wet coat on the sofa and rushed down the hall to her bedroom, Raffy's head bouncing along the floor behind her. Cassie had picked up the soggy coat, hung it up and then given Grant a quick tour.

While Marina had crawled under her covers with Raffy, singing along to a CD of *The Little Mermaid* that Cassie had put on for her, Cassie had taken Grant out to Isla's studio. He'd been as amazed as Cassie when she'd first seen the evidence of her sister's talent, and now she and Grant were talking in hushed voices, a sense of reverence feeling appropriate, given the circumstances of them both now standing in this space.

'My God, this is utterly beautiful.' Grant stood by the unfinished figure on the bench, his eyes wide as he ran a finger over the corner of the work. 'I had no idea she was this gifted.'

He glanced over at Cassie, who'd been looking inside the kiln, surprised to see something at the very bottom. She reached in and pulled out a small figurine of a child with a sand bucket in one hand, and a long-stemmed flower in the other. She wore a knee-length floaty dress, the incredible movement depicted in the skirt beckoning to Cassie's fingertips, and the flower looked like a gerbera daisy, the heavy head dangling at the child's shin.

'Gosh, I nearly missed this one.' She held up the exquisite piece of art, and Grant moved to her side. 'It's Marina. Look at the shape of the face. That little tilt of her head.' Cassie blew a layer of dust off the figure and held it up higher. 'How was it possible that I didn't know my sister was capable of this? Of creating this kind of beauty?' She felt her throat knotting as Grant gently took the sculpture from her hand.

'It's not hard to miss things about the people we love. Sometimes we're just too close to gain an accurate perspective.' He scanned the figurine and then her face. 'But it takes effort, and serious planning for a person to hide themselves this concertedly, Cass. So don't blame yourself too much.' He smiled kindly at her. 'Isla had her reasons. She was an enigma, that's for sure.' His words settled on Cassie, and she wanted to let them soothe her, but her sense that she'd failed her sister wouldn't quite allow that.

They lingered in the studio for a few more minutes, then, taking the small sculpture with them, they went back inside to start cooking dinner.

Grant was standing at the window, taking in the view. The storm over, the sky had cleared, and a breathtaking sunset was painting the sky above the bay with swathes of crimson, tangerine, and mauve. The water was still and glassy – the sky mirrored on its surface. 'This place is stunning.' He shook his head. 'I can see why she loved it here.' He turned to face Cassie, who was blowing up an air mattress for him, her thigh burning from using the little foot pump.

'Yes, me too. It wouldn't take much to fall in love with it.' She kept her eyes on her feet, afraid to meet his gaze. Grant had been careful not to crowd her, hanging back and giving her space to operate around the house, but she'd sensed his desire to constantly be in the same room as more than him simply being polite. She might have allowed him back into her life for Marina's sake, and all evidence so far pointed to him having good intentions in that regard, but Cassie's heart was still profoundly bruised by what he, and Isla, had done. With the best will in the world, it would take more than a confession, a delayed apology and a handful of visits to get past that – even for Marina's sake.

29

Marina had asked if Grant could sleep in her room, but even before Cassie could protest, he had grimaced comically. 'I'll sleep out in the living room where I won't disturb anyone. Trust me, Marina. You'll be glad I did because I snort and whistle like a big fat steam train.' He'd grimaced, making Marina giggle.

Cassie was grateful that he'd handled the situation so gracefully, and after a light dinner they'd all played a game of snap at the dining table, then she'd put Marina to bed.

At Marina's request, Grant had read her a story and Cassie had been secretly pleased that Marina had chosen something other than *Green Eggs and Ham*, that having become a nighttime ritual between them that Cassie treasured. She had left them to their story, cleaned up the kitchen and settled on the sofa with her book, when Grant emerged.

'Can I sit with you for a while?' He hovered near the window. 'Unless I'm disturbing you.' He pointed at her book.

'No, it's fine.' She closed the book and set it on the side table, her stomach flipping at being alone with him. 'Would you like a drink?'

'I'd love one.' He nodded.

A few moments later, each with a brandy in a rustic, pottery mug, they sat at opposite ends of the sofa and talked quietly, sharing more of what had happened to them both over the past six years. She told him all about building the business, about her father's death and meeting Stuart – and, of course, the shock of Isla disappearing and how it had affected them – never mind discovering she had a niece. Sharing these life-altering events was making her feel vulnerable – as if she was letting him in more than she was ready to – but, surprisingly, something inside kept her talking.

Grant listened, silently sipping his brandy, and letting her talk, his eyes darting from her face to the window and back, as if checking in with the horizon was keeping him grounded amidst her revelations.

As their conversation flowed, suddenly craving some reassurance, Cassie was tempted to tell him about the exploratory surgery and the likely diagnosis she was facing. But, deep down, she knew that there was no point in speculating until she had the results and knew what lay ahead, so, reluctant to taint the welcome peace of the moment, she held back. Besides, he was still on the outer edge of her trust zone, and as disturbing images of him and Isla together flashed behind her eyes again, she decided to keep at least some of the armour that had been there ever since he'd shattered her heart locked in place.

When it came to his turn to talk, Grant told her that he had never married but had been in a long-term relationship with an ICU nurse that had ended the previous year. Wanting a fresh start, he'd considered moving to London to work at Great Ormond Street Hospital when a colleague had offered him a partnership in his Stockbridge practice, which meant that Grant could also consult at the Royal Hospital for Children and Young People. He'd bought a terraced house in Stockbridge and, also in the time that had passed, his father had died of a coronary. His mother was now living in Brighton, close to his sister, and he had a niece and a nephew, both under six.

As Cassie listened, she tried to picture Marina as part of a family like that, with cousins, and another grandmother, and while it felt oddly removed from Cassie's own life, the notion that Marina belonged in that picture was undeniably comforting.

They talked for an hour and a half, then the subject of when to tell Marina that Grant was her father came up. Grant was restrained and respectful, deferring to her judgement. 'So, how do we do this?' He got up and poured them a second brandy. 'I mean, how do you think it's best to handle it?' He flopped onto the opposite end of the sofa, the faint smell of sandalwood wafting across the space between them. The memories it sparked, of her tucking her face into his neck, when he was fresh from the shower, sent a surprising shockwave through her that made Cassie draw her feet away from his.

'We do it gently, perhaps take her outside somewhere, make sure she's as relaxed as possible, then we tell her the truth.' Cassie shrugged. 'She already adores you, so I can't imagine she'll be anything other than happy.' She eyed him. 'She might be confused at first, and have questions, so you'll have to be prepared.'

Grant nodded. 'Yes, I'm sure she will.' He paused. 'How do you tell a five-year-old that you're her father but had no idea she existed until a few weeks ago, and then make that digestible?' He frowned. 'I don't want to cause her any more pain.'

Feeling the genuine nature of his words, Cassie shook her head. 'Neither do I, but I think it's important that she knows the truth so that she can build honest bonds with you.' Cassie nodded to herself, the tiny nugget of fear at being supplanted in Marina's affections surfacing again, despite her effort to quash it.

They agreed that, if the weather was cooperating, going on a picnic the next day would be a good idea, and would provide them with the neutral, congenial environment they wanted, to break the news to Marina. With that settled, they got up, washed their glasses, and said goodnight, Cassie keeping her distance as Grant moved around her in the kitchen. Despite their easy conversation, and her surprising decision to open up to him, she was not ready for a friendly hug, or worse, a brush of those lips against her cheek.

The midday sun was bright in an almost clear sky as Cassie prepared the picnic lunch. Marina was sitting at the island colouring and Grant was standing out on the patio, his hands on his hips as he took in the view of the beach. Seeing him there, perhaps in the exact spot that Isla had stood every morning, was surreal and yet, as Cassie packed the last of the sandwiches into a basket, she felt that he looked like he entirely belonged. She'd shared Isla's sanctuary with him, so now it wasn't private to Cassie and Marina anymore, and the feeling was slightly unsettling. Even so, Cassie was sure she'd done the right thing, for Marina.

Rather than go down to Uig Sands, directly below the cottage, Cassie had suggested they take the ten-minute walk west, to Carnish Beach. There was a footpath that Cassie had discovered early one morning on her previous visit that cut through the low hills, passing a pretty stone barn and farmhouse. The path wound through a field with sheep dotted across it and then dropped down directly to the beach.

Carnish Beach was an idyllic arc of white sand, enclosed on two sides by impressive grass-covered headlands. Vibrant green slopes spilled down on both sides, ending in low ridges of rock that seemed to crumble away into the crystal-clear, turquoise water. Sitting on the beach, with her back to the cottage, Cassie had seen the most stunning, undisturbed view of the North

Atlantic, that had brought her to tears, and now, rather than protect it from him, she found that she wanted to share that with Grant.

Now, as he stretched out on the patio, his arms going up above his head and his shirt separating from the top of his jeans, exposing a strip of pale skin, Cassie swallowed and turned to Marina. 'Right, are you ready to go?'

Marina looked startled, then swung around on the stool, her eyes going to the window. 'Where's Grant?' She slid off the seat and padded across the room.

'He's outside already. We're the slowcoaches.' Cassie smiled at her niece. 'Do you need the loo before we go?'

Marina shook her head. 'Nope.'

'Good. Then let's go before the sun disappears again.' She lifted the woven basket and held her hand out to Marina. 'Have you got your bucket and spade?'

Marina pointed to the patio. 'It's outside.'

'Great, then we're off.' Cassie pulled the door behind them and looked at Grant. 'Ready?'

'Yep, ready and waiting.' He gave a mock bow. 'And hungry.' He leaned down and gently poked Marina's arm. 'You better not eat all the sandwiches.'

She hesitated, then seeing his face, she smiled shyly. 'I only like the banana ones.' She slid her free hand into his. 'You can have the fishy ones.'

Cassie laughed softly, once again, the child's refreshing candour calming Cassie's residual nerves at spending the day ahead with Grant, and at the news they had to share with Marina. 'You mean tuna?' She jogged the basket higher up her forearm.

'They taste like the water.' Marina nodded ahead of them as they turned left at the curve of the hill and walked towards the footpath. 'All salty, and smooshy.'

Cassie nodded towards the start of the footpath as Grant

looked over at her and smiled. 'That's a very good description, Marina.' His eyes held Cassie's for a moment too long, then, sensing her discomfort, he looked away.

Ten minutes later, having passed the farm, and counted eleven sheep scattered across the lush pasture, they reached the end of the path, Carnish Beach lying directly ahead. The early-afternoon light was bouncing off the white of the sand, making the water a surreal shade of turquoise, once again bringing to mind the beaches of the Caribbean, as Cassie let go of Marina's hand and led the way. There was a spot she had in mind at the left side of the bay, close to the foot of the headland, offering protection from the breeze that was rolling in from the ocean. 'Let's set up over here.' She walked on ahead, leaving Grant and Marina to follow, their two voices melded into a gentle harmony as the wind whipped Cassie's hair across her face.

She could hear seabirds above, their familiar conversation filling the air as they circled before a dive into the lukewarm water. She took a deep breath, letting the clean, briny air fill her lungs, then, reaching the spot she wanted, set the basket down and pulled a long, striped blanket out and flicked it into the wind.

'This is amazing.' Grant was behind her, his hands on his hips, as Marina plopped onto the sand and began pulling off her socks and shoes. Her jeans and floral hoodie were bright against the paleness of the sand as Cassie knelt on the blanket and began to set the lunch out on a series of paper plates.

'Come and have some lunch before you paddle, little one. Then we'll build a giant sandcastle.' She gestured towards the food. 'Better be quick or Grant will clean us out.' She smiled as Marina looked over, then stood up and made her way to the blanket.

Grant sat on Marina's opposite side, kicked his shoes off, rolled his jeans up several times and dug his bare feet into the sand. 'I can't remember the last time I sat on a beach.' He accepted the sandwich Cassie offered him. 'It's so peaceful.' He waved the triangle of bread at the view, the blue of the sky deepening as it dipped towards the horizon, and the curved headlands on either side seeming to hug them inside the sanctuary of the bay. 'Why would you ever leave a place like this?' His eyes darted to Cassie, a momentary flash of concern there that she caught, but decided not to delve into.

'It is special, that's for sure.' She nodded, then took a bite of sandwich, watching as Marina bit the end off of a carrot stick, and then brushed the remainder against her leg to get rid of some grains of sand the breeze had carried into their circle.

'Mummy made us a tent here.' Marina pointed over her shoulder to where the grass of the slope behind them met the sand. 'We had a fire and had marshmallows.' She nodded to herself, then popped the rest of the carrot into her mouth.

Grant stared at her profile for a few moments, his eyes glittering, then he looked ahead again.

'That sounds like fun.' Cassie reached over and gently rubbed Marina's back. 'Maybe we can do that tomorrow?'

Marina nodded. 'OK. Will you be here tomorrow?' She turned and directed her question at Grant, her eyes giant blue pools of hope.

Cassie's heart buckled as she watched Grant set his sandwich down and wipe his mouth with his palm. 'Yes, I'll still be here. If it's OK with your Aunt Cassie.' He paused. 'And you, m'lady.' He gave Marina a comical smile.

'It's OK.' She nodded, so matter-of-fact that both Cassie and Grant laughed, creating a gentle, joyful harmony that instantly filled Cassie with joy – then a sense of loss at what might have been.

Sensing that the moment was now, she nodded at Grant, her eyes saying everything. Sitting up straighter, he lifted his hand, palm up, as if giving her the floor. Cassie took a deep breath and leaned back on her hands, stretching her bare feet out beyond the blanket, her heels connecting with the cool sand.

'Marina, Grant and I have to tell you something.' Seeing Marina's eyebrows gather, Cassie rethought her approach. This little girl had had enough bad news for a lifetime, so positioning this next piece of information positively was crucial. 'It's good, and happy news, and we think you're going to like it.' She sat up and brushed the sand from her palms. Marina twisted around on the blanket, half a sandwich with a large bite out of it suspended in front of her middle. Her gaze swung back and forth between Cassie and Grant, as Cassie found a smile. 'You know how I told you that Grant was a special friend?' She watched as Marina nodded slowly, letting the sandwich drop to her knee. 'Well, he's more than that, Marina.' Cassie reached out and lifted Marina's free hand from the blanket wrapping the cool little fingers in hers. 'Sweetheart, Grant is your daddy.' The words out, Cassie felt the air leaving her as if she had run a mile. Her eyes were glued to Marina's face, whose mouth had gone slack as she started at Grant. 'Do you understand, little one?'

Marina took what seemed like several minutes to process what she'd been told, then she dropped the sandwich onto a plate, brushed her hands together purposefully and tipped her head to the side.

'Marina, darling, you can ask us anything you like. Tell us what you feel like inside here...' Cassie patted her own fluttering chest. 'Grant and I love you so very much. We want you to—'

To Cassie's surprise, Marina carefully stood up.

Grant had crossed his legs under him and was swaying from side to side slightly, as if unsure where the inevitable hit would come from. His eyes were wide as Marina stepped over Cassie's legs and settled herself in front of him, mimicking his pose.

'Do you want to ask me something, Marina?' Grant's voice

was soft. 'You're a very special little girl, and I'm so happy and proud to be your daddy.' He held a hand out to her.

As Cassie held still, afraid to move and disrupt this seminal moment, seconds slid by in which Marina stared at Grant, scanning his features as if she was seeing him, truly seeing him, for the first time. Then she leaned forward, her index finger going to the cleft in his chin as she gently pressed her fingertip against his skin. 'Why were you away for so long?' She sat back, her narrow brow creasing as Cassie's heart threatened to implode. 'I missed you a lot.' She lunged forward, wrapped her arms around his neck and let her cheek rest on his shoulder.

Grant swallowed hard, gently easing her onto his knee. 'I missed you too, Marina.' He folded her into his arms. 'I really missed you.'

Cassie left Marina and Grant and took a walk along the shore. The tepid water splashed against her ankles and her eyes were stinging as she turned back to see them sitting opposite one another on the blanket, their backs curved like matching half-moons, and their heads inclined towards each other.

Marina's reaction had been utterly heartbreaking, as if she'd been waiting for the entirety of her short little life for Grant to come back from wherever he'd gone. Seeing how he'd responded to her had been everything Cassie could have hoped for, and as one critical piece of her fractured life slid into place, now Cassie needed to find out what was going on inside her body, and what that meant for them all.

30

The following week, after a restful stay on Lewis, the first three days having Grant there going better than she'd expected, and then the remaining days blissful, alone with Marina, Cassie was at the studio. She was working on the initial designs for a new range of pewter necklaces with matching bangles, called the Oceans collection. She was deep in thought, sketching the outline of a necklace, with a coral-like edge to the links, when her phone startled her. Seeing Doctor Carnegie's number, her pulse quickened, but scanning the studio, she saw that Syd was hunched over his design board with his back to her office, listening to music on his headphones, and that Hector had still not come back from lunch. Relieved, Cassie dropped her pen and picked up the phone. 'Hello?'

'Cassie, it's Graham Carnegie.' His voice was level, giving nothing away. 'How are you feeling?'

She nodded to herself, counting back the days since she'd had a severe bout of pain and vomiting in the night, right after they'd got back from Lewis. 'Not too bad, thanks.' She visualised him smiling, then delivering his good news, letting the hard knot of tension in her chest finally unravel.

'The results are in, and I'm afraid it's not great news.'

Her stomach flipped. 'Oh, OK,' she whispered. 'Just tell me.'

'The mass in your gall bladder is malignant, Cassie, and it looks as if the cancer might have spread to the lymph nodes.' He paused. 'You'll need to have your gall bladder removed, and then a course of chemotherapy to follow.'

Cassie clamped her eyes shut, images of ugly scars, her hunched over the toilet, and chunks of fiery red hair coming out in her hands, sucking the air from her. Then she pictured Marina, the heart-shaped face crumpled in pain and the dark-rimmed eyes full of tears when Cassie had just begun to see joy in them again, and anger took the place of fear. No. This was not her life. This was not going to happen.

'Cassie, are you all right?' Doctor Carnegie's voice was loaded with concern.

'I'm here.' She opened her eyes to see Syd standing in the doorway of her office, a deep frown puckering his brow. 'Hang on, Doc?' She cleared her throat, her tongue feeling dry and spongy. Seeing her face, Syd mouthed 'sorry', backed out of her office and gently pulled the glass door closed. 'OK, sorry. I can talk now.' She sat back in the chair, her entire body feeling leaden. 'So, surgery will be when?'

'As soon as possible. Then we'll start chemo as soon as you're strong enough. We need to hit this head on, Cassie. Get you back on your feet and focusing on the future.' His voice cracked around the last word, sending a new shard of fear through her. Did she have a future to focus on?

As Doctor Carnegie continued to talk, explaining the process, and telling her everything she'd need to do to prepare for surgery, and what to expect afterwards, she let her mind float away from what she was hearing. She pictured herself on Carnish Beach with Marina, building sandcastles, and them paddling in the warm water of Uig Bay. She saw them lying in bed reading *Green Eggs and Ham,* walking in Princes Gardens, and eating warm doughnuts, then riding on the merry-go-round. Then, she saw them with Grant, Marina walking between them as they swung her high up into the air, and Cassie knew, without a shadow of a doubt, that she would do everything she could to beat this. Having found Marina, Cassie couldn't contemplate letting go, or having the child grow up without her. She wanted to be present for all the seminal moments in Marina's life – school drama, her first love, perhaps seeing her off to university or college, her first day at her first serious job, then, one day, helping her choose her wedding dress. All these precious moments melted together to form a picture of a life, so deeply entwined with Cassie's happiness now, that the idea of missing any of it was unthinkable.

Whatever else happened, it was critical that, from now on, Grant was part of Marina's life, too. But even though Cassie was feeling easier around him, even opening up to him a bit more, her instinct was still to hide her illness from him. She knew she wouldn't be able to, for long. It was likely that, even with Sadie stepping in here and there, Cassie was going to need him to help with Marina while she recovered, and that would eventually call for full disclosure, something that felt distinctly uncomfortable to Cassie. But this wasn't just about her anymore.

'What's the prognosis, Doc?' She forced some power into her voice as she leaned forward on her elbows, her forehead dropping into her hand.

'It appears to be advanced, Cassie. The surgery and chemo combination will give you the best chance, but we won't know the full extent of things until...' His voice faded.

'I understand.' She forced a swallow. 'Until they've got in there and dug around more, so to speak.' She laughed – a forced, brittle sound.

'Pretty much.' He sighed. 'I know this is a lot to take in, especially after the last few months you've had, but you and I don't mince our words, Cassie. So, I won't lie. While it's not a great scenario, we have a plan.'

Cassie eyed the door where Syd was still hovering outside, pretending to check his phone. 'Doc, I have to go. Can you please send me an email or a letter with whatever you need me to do next? I'm going to need some time to get everything sorted out for Marina, and work.'

'Absolutely. I'll get my assistant Christina to send you all the details. She'll also give you the consulting oncologist's information, and we'll start the ball rolling on getting a date for surgery at the cancer centre.'

Cassie tried to picture the next few months of her life being taken over by hospitals, well-meaning people in white coats invading her body, her personal space, being connected to IV drips and monitors, and the prospect filled her with dread.

'Thanks, Doc.' She stood up, adrenaline sending a trail of tingles running down each leg as she leaned forward against the desk.

'Cassie, I'm sorry it's not better news, but we'll do everything we can.' His voice was stronger now. 'You're not alone.'

Cassie gave a half-smile. 'I know.' She walked around the desk and let her hand settle on the door handle. Her eyes met Syd's, his questioning and full of concern, and she felt the remaining strength she'd just mustered begin to wane. 'Talk soon, then.' She tugged on the handle, the door feeling insanely heavy as she pulled it open.

'Call me any time if you have questions. Bye for now, Cassie.'

As she slid the phone into her back pocket, her breathing now ragged, she stumbled through the door and into Syd's open arms, instantly feeling his strength surround her. The smell of coffee lingered on his shirt as he pulled her into his chest, his giant palm pressing into her back as she began to cry.

'I've got you, darling girl. Just try to breathe,' he whispered. 'I've got you.'

Syd refilled her mug with tea and added some milk before passing it back to her. They were sitting on the floor in the kitchen area, where, a few minutes earlier, Cassie had slowly slid down the wall and drawn her knees into her chest. 'So, you're going to tell Grant, right?' Syd was eyeing her, his mug suspended in front of his mouth.

'I think I'll have to, but not right away.' She sipped some tea, noticing the unaccustomed sweetness. 'Ugh, this is gross.' She grimaced, leaning back against the wall and balancing the mug on her thigh.

'Sugar for shock. My mama swore by it.' He scowled at her. 'Just drink it.'

She rolled her eyes and took another sip. 'Seriously, this will make me barf.'

'Oh, for God's sake.' He heaved himself up from the floor, took her cup and threw the contents down the drain and poured her a fresh cup from the pot. Handing it to her, he tutted, 'You're such a prima donna.'

She laughed softly, her stomach tensing in pain as she watched him sit back opposite her, his impossibly long legs sticking straight out in front of him in a childlike pose.

'Why aren't you going to tell him now?' Syd frowned.

'Because he's just beginning to form a bond with Marina, a sweet, natural connection. If I tell him now, it might taint that – perhaps make him feel he's got to rush things, you know.' She shrugged.

'I'm sorry, but that's crap.' Syd shook his head. 'You need his support now. Not later.'

Cassie stared into her cup. 'That may be, but it's my decision.' She met his gaze again. 'I know what I'm doing, Syd. And besides, I'm still working through stuff where Grant's concerned. We are beginning to mend fences, but there's still a long way to go before I'll fully trust him again.' The stubborn images of Grant and Isla together surfaced again as she shook her head. 'He's trying, Syd, I'll give him that. But I'm still in self-protect mode at the moment – and even more so where Marina is concerned. I'm OK with him getting more involved with her, but as for me...'

'You are the most stubborn person I've ever met, man.'

'True.' She nodded, balancing the mug on her knee. 'But I'll tell him when the time is right. I promise.' She felt the heat of the mug seeping through her jeans, the warmth comforting against her chilled skin.

'Good.' He nodded. 'And I am here for whatever you need. I'll cover for you at work, of course. Now that things have settled down a bit, it's not a problem. You can still sketch in your hospital bed, so don't think you're going to get away with anything.' He grinned. 'I can help with Marina, too.' He hesitated. 'And, Cassie?'

'What?' She saw the fullness of his eyes. 'Don't you dare cry, Sydney. I mean it.' She wagged a finger at him, trying to smile as a new rush of fear threatened to choke her.

'I was just going to say that if anyone can do this, you can.' His voice shook. 'Sorry. I'm just a crybaby.' He gave a strangled laugh and swiped his nose with the back of his hand.

'I love you. You know that, right?' She shunted along the wall, careful not to spill her tea, then moved in next to him, taking his free hand in hers. 'If you're here with me, my chances are increased by a hundred per cent.'

He squeezed her hand. 'God help cancer, that's all I can say.' He leaned his cheek on top of her head. 'That nasty weasel doesn't stand a chance against my best friend.'

. . .

Grant had returned her call just as she was putting Marina to bed, and Cassie had said she'd call him back, again, once Marina was asleep. Half an hour later, standing at the living-room window, watching the sparkling lights of the boats out on the water below, she'd waited for him to answer.

'Hey. Your message worried me.' There had been genuine concern in his voice. 'Is everything OK?'

'Marina is fine, don't worry.'

He'd audibly exhaled. 'Good. And are you OK?'

She'd taken a moment to gather herself, then she'd said, 'Yes, but can we get together tomorrow?'

It had only been a second or two before he'd simply said, 'Where and when?'

The following day, while Marina was at school, Cassie had dashed home for a lunch break. She and Grant were now sitting in her living room, the windows propped open, and the brine of the sea mixed with roasting coffee floating in on the cool breeze. A distant foghorn moaned as Cassie handed Grant a mug of tea.

He was pale and slightly drawn, as if he'd not slept well. His clothes looked rumpled, and she noticed the dark shadow on his cheeks and chin. 'Did you not go home last night?' She sat on the sofa, facing the window, and curled her legs under her.

Grant sat opposite her in the armchair. 'No. I had a patient who... He was six and, well, let's just say it was grim.' He nodded sadly. 'I stayed with him until his parents could get back from Glasgow.' He sipped some tea. 'Don't suppose you have a dram I can toss in here, do you?' He gave a dry laugh. 'Yesterday wasn't a great day, or night, to be honest.' His eyes were hooded as he scanned her face, then seeming to register that he needed to focus, he sat up straighter. 'So, what's going on? Have I screwed something up already?' His smile was anxious, and Cassie could see the effort behind it, and it touched her.

'No. Nothing like that.' She shook her head. 'I just want to talk to you about Marina, and you two spending more time together.' Her nerves began to spike at the next step she was taking, letting him in even closer, so she took a gulp of tea, hoping the heat would ease her taut throat.

'Oh right.' His relief was almost palpable. 'That'd be great. What did you have in mind?'

'I was thinking that you could start this weekend. Maybe take her out on your own, have some one-on-one time.' She worked to keep her voice light – the thought of not having Marina with her, already painful. 'Then we could make it a regular thing, and once you're both comfortable, perhaps she could come and stay with you now and then.' Her pulse was ticking as she watched his reaction.

'Are you sure you'd be OK with that?' His eyebrows jumped.

Even as he said it, her mother's words came back to her in a rush – *try to forgive them. Marina deserves a loving family.* Separating the hurtful things he'd done to her from his role as Marina's father would not be easy, but Cassie knew that he shouldn't have to ask permission to spend time with his daughter. It was time to try to trust him again, let his actions speak for his intentions, regardless of how challenging that still felt.

'Grant, you're her dad. Of course, I'm OK with it.' The obvious joy that flooded his face was once again touching. 'It's time she got you to herself a bit.'

'I've got three, decent-sized spare rooms. The biggest one is currently a pseudo gym, and dumping ground, so I'll spend some time sorting it out and make it nice for her.' He paused. 'Thank you, Cassie. I know this must be hard for you.' He smiled at her. 'You're doing an incredible job with Marina, you know.'

Cassie heard the genuine nature of his compliment, and a tiny sliver of the stubborn reserve inside her slid away. 'Thanks, but she's pretty easy to be around.' She drained her mug and stood up. With a date for surgery coming soon, she needed to focus on practicalities and get things in place, so she turned to face him. 'Do you think you could start on the room this weekend?'

He followed her into the kitchen. 'Um, yeah. Probably.' He hovered behind her as she put her cup in the sink. 'It just needs a good clean, and then I'll get some new sheets, and some toys, et cetera.' As he watched her pass him and walk into the hall, his brow creased. 'Is there anything wrong, Cass?'

Feeling suddenly transparent, as if he could see straight through her skin, muscles, and sinew, spying the tumour that was invading her, she shook her head, a little too emphatically. 'Not at all. I'm just a bit tired, so I'd appreciate the help, and honestly, the occasional night to myself.' She shrugged, hoping she'd sounded believable.

'Well, in that case, I'm happy to help.' He lifted his jacket from the coat stand. 'I'll get to work on the room and then you can come and see it if you like. Give it your seal of approval.' He smiled at her. 'I think you'll like my place. It's one of those Georgian terraced houses in Stockbridge, off Glenogle Road. It's not huge, but it's full of light, and it even has a wee garden out the back. I'd love to have you over.' He nodded. 'Both of you.'

Cassie held the door open for him, her determination to keep her secret beginning to waver. It would be so easy to crumble, right at this moment. Tell him what was really going on, fall into his arms and ask for his help, but she wasn't ready for that. She would face this next step alone, and if things continued to go smoothly with him and Marina, then, at some point, she'd decide whether to trust him with her truth.

31

Surgery had been scheduled for three weeks out, on the fourteenth of November, which meant that Cassie and Marina had been able to enjoy more regular get-togethers with Grant, and more Sunday visits to Sadie. Cassie had been determined to make the time as fun and engaging for Marina as she could, and so far, it had been going well.

This being their last Sunday visit before surgery the next day, when they got to Sadie's house, Marina was quieter than usual, as if picking up on the nervous energy that Cassie was battling to keep at bay.

Sadie looked bright-eyed, her voice slightly brittle, as she repeatedly hugged Cassie, her arms lingering around her daughter's waist – her message of love, and support, making Cassie's eyes prickle with grateful tears. Telling her mother about her prognosis had been an emotionally charged conversation, and ever since, Cassie had been slightly nervous to be around her in person, in case either or both of them melted into tears.

Now, as Sadie busied herself in the kitchen, serving up their lunch, she turned to Marina. 'So, darling, how is school? Have you made any special friends?'

To Cassie's surprise, along with a flare of shame that she had stopped asking Marina this question, Marina nodded. 'Yes, Polly. She's got blonde hair, and she likes cats, and swimming like I do.' She'd smiled. 'She has two mummies.'

Earlier that week, the school counsellor had told Cassie that Marina was responding more in class and being slightly more social, even venturing out to the playground during breaks, but this major new development was a joy to hear. 'That's great, sweetheart.' Cassie beamed at her, setting Marina's lunch in front of her. 'Maybe Polly can come over to play sometime?' She sat opposite Marina and locked eyes with her mother, who nodded approvingly.

'OK.' Marina shrugged, then lifted her fork and began to eat. That Marina was finally making friends was the gift that Cassie needed right now. Anything that gave her hope that her niece might begin to feel that Edinburgh was her home glittered like gold.

Cassie had arranged for her mother to come and stay at the loft with Marina for the one night that Cassie would be in the hospital. Until Grant had finished the work on Marina's room, and proved that he could cope with her staying overnight, this had felt like the right choice. But despite the growing bond between Sadie and Marina, and the obvious joy the child brought her mother, Cassie was still nervous to overwhelm Sadie, too soon. 'Are you sure it's OK, Mum?'

'We'll be fine, Cassie. Marina and I will bake, watch telly, and read together.' She smiled encouragingly. 'Don't worry about us. Just focus on getting through the surgery, and back home.'

Cassie nodded gratefully, her mother's face a picture of comfort – just what Cassie needed right now.

· · ·

Doctor Carnegie had told Cassie that she'd need around a week to recover, at which point they'd assess her readiness for the chemotherapy to begin. Cassie was generally able to keep her nerves at bay and remain pragmatic about the surgery itself, but when it came to the chemo, there her courage wavered. Her primary concern, aside from coping with daily trips to the clinic and likely feeling ghastly for a few weeks, was her ability to hide what was happening from Marina. The thought of scaring the child or, worse still, making her feel insecure again when she just seemed to be finding her feet in her new life had kept Cassie awake at night to the point that she had developed dark circles under her eyes.

Now, the night before surgery, Cassie sat cross-legged on the bath mat while Marina shoved a little yellow duck around in the bath, cutting a path through the sea of bubbles. Cassie had left it to the last minute to tell Marina that she was going to be away for the night, and now that the time had come, Cassie's stomach was knotted tightly.

Marina's cheeks were crimson, her hair bundled on top of her head and kept in place by a thick band. Her lustrous eyelashes were damp and clumped together, forming tiny spikes, and she was humming something that Cassie didn't recognise.

Cassie leaned back against the wall and kept her voice steady and as casual as she could. 'Marina, I'm going to be away tomorrow night. I have a work meeting, and it's too far to drive there and back, so I'm going to stay the night there, then come home the next day.' She eyed Marina, who stopped playing with the duck and frowned. 'It's just one night, and Granny Sadie is going to come and stay here with you. You two will have fun, watching TV and reading stories, and she said you can bake something together. Then, she'll take you to school the next day, and I'll be right here when Granny brings you home in the afternoon. OK?' She swallowed nervously, hoping that she hadn't given Marina too much information all at once.

Marina lifted the duck out of the water and set it on the corner of the bath. 'But why can't I come with you?' She pouted. 'I'll be good.'

Cassie hated having to lie to this amazing little human, but there was no other way to protect Marina from what was happening. 'It's for work, sweetheart. So, I can't take you with me, I'm afraid.' She smiled. 'There would be nothing for you to do there, and you shouldn't miss school, anyway. Polly will wonder where you are.' Cassie grabbed the side of the bath and pulled herself up. 'It'll go really fast, and before you know it, I'll be back. I promise.' She carved a cross on her chest.

Marina frowned. 'I don't want you to go.' Her chin began to tremble. 'I want you to stay here.'

Cassie reached down and took one of Marina's sudsy hands in hers. 'I know you do, little one, but sometimes I have to do grown-up, work things. I will miss you loads, but then we'll go on some new adventures when I get home. OK?' She rubbed her thumb across the back of Marina's hand, feeling the tiny bones, so vulnerable and yet incredibly resilient.

'Can Daddy come and stay?' Marina lifted her chin abruptly, as if the idea had just come to her.

Her eyes prickling at the first time she'd heard Marina refer to Grant this way, Cassie turned and dragged a towel from the heated rail on the wall. 'Not this time. But maybe he can the next time.' She held the towel out and Marina stood up, letting Cassie wrap her in the soft cotton and lift her out of the bath. 'Right, let's get your PJs on and then we'll have some hot choco-late before bed.'

'Then we'll read *Green Eggs and Ham*.' Marina wrapped her arms around Cassie's neck, bringing the warm, soapy smell of the bathwater with her.

'Of course. Like we do every night.' Cassie negotiated her way into Marina's bedroom.

'When you're not here, Granny can read me Paddington.' She leaned back from Cassie's arm's, Marina's eyes clear and sending a message that Cassie was so touched by, and grateful for, that her legs threatened to buckle.

'Granny can read whatever you want, sweetheart. But I do love when we read that one together.' She sat Marina on the bed and unwrapped the towel, rubbed her dry, then reached for the pyjamas under the pillow.

'Then, I want Paddington.' Marina nodded decisively, her little hands tugging the pyjama bottoms on as Cassie turned to look out of the window, her blurred vision filtering out the edges of the evening skyline.

The following evening, Cassie's surgery was over, and she was lying in the dimly lit hospital room, staring out at a gloomy sky. It had been raining since she'd been moved back to her room from recovery and now, with a cup of tea and a slice of dry toast next to her, she shifted stiffly up in the bed. Her stomach ached, a dull, thudding pain that seemed to follow her pulse, and as she lifted the teacup, her hands trembling, she checked the time on her phone and saw that it was 9.15 p.m.

When she'd woken up an hour or so ago, she'd called her mother right away, her tongue thick and her head still groggy. She'd said she was fine, through surgery and would phone her the next day when she was ready to be picked up. Sadie had reported that all was well at home, and that Marina was glued to the TV, watching *The Little Mermaid*. Relieved, and too tired to tell her mother that she'd let Marina stay up too late, Cassie had quickly fallen asleep again.

Now, as she sipped some of the lukewarm tea that a sweet-faced nurse had brought her, she let her mind wander to the upcoming weeks. She had no idea how she would navigate her recovery, then chemo for a month, while trying to work and take care of Marina, even with her mother's help, and for the first time since she'd found out about the cancer, Cassie allowed herself to give in to feeling utterly overwhelmed.

As she closed her eyes, tears forced their way out in waves, leaving damp tracks on her cheeks, then trickling under her chin and plopping onto the hospital gown she wore. It was all too much, and for once, just this one time, she needed to let herself grieve. She cried for herself, for her father, for Isla, her mother, and for Marina. For all the hurt in the world, and then for the shadows of things that she feared might be coming, until finally her throat felt ripped raw, and she had no tears left.

Just as she felt sleep tugging at her again, her phone rang, making her jump. She saw Sadie's number, and as she answered it, her hands shook to the point where she nearly dropped the phone.

'Hi, Mum.' Her voice was ragged, and anxiety instantly gripped her, as she heard crying in the background. The unmistakable sound of Marina's sobs speared right through Cassie's centre. 'What's going on?' She sat up, a grip of pain in her middle making her gasp.

'I'm sorry, love. I didn't want to bother you, but she's inconsolable.' Sadie sounded anxious. 'Everything was fine, then she went to bed and fell right to sleep. An hour later, she came running into the lounge crying. When I asked what was wrong, she said that she had dreamed that you died, like her mummy, and nothing I say seems to convince her otherwise.' She paused. 'Marina, it's OK, sweetie. I'm talking to your Aunt Cassie now.' Sadie spoke gently, her voice almost drowned out by the mournful sound of Marina crying. 'Come on, come and speak to her.'

Cassie shook the hair from her eyes and pulled her shoulders back. 'Put her on, Mum.' She instantly heard watery sniffs.

'Marina, it's me, Aunt Cassie. I'm here, little one. I'm right here.'

'I want you to come home.' Marina wailed. 'I need you to read *Green Eggs and Ham.*'

Consumed with wanting that too – more than oxygen – Cassie pressed her eyes shut and took a second before saying, 'I can't come back until tomorrow, sweetheart. I'm so, so sorry. But Granny is there to take care of you and if you go to sleep like a good girl, I will be there when you get home from school tomorrow – like I promised. I will never break my promises to you, Marina.' Cassie swallowed hard. 'I will be home tomorrow. So when you go to bed now, look at the lovely statue of you and your mummy that's next to you. She will watch over you too, until I get back. You're safe with Granny, Marina. Everything is going to be all right.' She fell back against the bank of pillows, drained and suddenly freezing cold.

'Noooo. You need to come now. I want my mummy. I want...' Marina's voice rose as her panic began to seep through the phone.

'Marina, can you put Granny back on the phone please?' Cassie swallowed. 'Let me talk to Granny Sadie.' She spoke louder, unsure whether Marina had heard her.

Sadie came back on. 'Sorry, love. I just wasn't sure what to do for the best.' She was beginning to sound desperate, and as Cassie let her head fall back against the frame of the bed, she closed her eyes, the solution materialising, and yet not something she wanted to accept. What she was considering felt like yet another giant leap of faith, and yet there was no alternative.

'I'll call Grant and ask him to come over.' She shook her head, her mass of hair tangling at the back of her neck. 'I'll phone him now.'

. . .

'Where are you, Cassie?' Grant sounded tired. 'Is anything wrong?'

Cassie didn't know where to start, but there was no time to waste on apologies, or lengthy explanations. Marina was in crisis, and this was the only solution, so Cassie began to talk.

A few moments later, there was no judgement, or awkward questions, Grant simply said, 'I'll be at the loft in fifteen minutes. Tell your mum to put on *Frozen Two* and make her some hot milk.'

Tears were streaming down Cassie's face as she nodded, silently.

'And Cassie, I'll pick you up tomorrow. No arguments. Text me the time you're being released, and then you and I need to talk.'

She nodded again, her voice held hostage by a surge of relief so strong that it stole her breath.

'Try to get some rest and I'll see you tomorrow.' He didn't seem to expect her to speak, and that, in this moment, was exactly what Cassie needed.

32

The following day, Cassie had been released at noon, and half an hour later, when she walked out of the clinic, Grant was waiting for her. He had brought coffee and a blanket, which oddly, despite it being a mild day, Cassie instantly wanted. So, as he gently helped her into the car, she wrapped the soft wool around her legs.

'Right. Home.' His face was drawn, his eyes flicking from her profile to the road as he pulled out of the car park.

His silence felt weighted with expectation, and Cassie knew she owed him a proper explanation. She took a deep breath and focused ahead, as seeing his face would make this harder. 'Grant, I need to say something.'

'OK.' He looked over at her briefly.

'I'm sorry you had to find out what was happening to me this way. I was planning on telling you, but not until I knew more. Once I knew what the next stage was going to be like.' She swallowed. 'I don't know what to expect, so...' She gulped.

He nodded, the muscle in his jaw twitching. 'You could have asked me, Cassie. I see cancer patients every day. I just wish you'd trusted me with this.' He paused. 'You don't need to do any of this alone.'

Cassie shoved the hair away from her face and turned to look at him. Trusting him was the piece that she was still struggling with, but he'd stepped in when she and Marina had needed him, and that counted for a lot. His knuckles were white around the steering wheel and his shoulders looked taut as he shifted in the seat.

'Thank you, for last night, Grant. I really appreciate you jumping in like that. I don't know what I would have done if you hadn't helped us out.'

'Of course I would help. I will always be there for Marina, and for you, Cassie, if you'll let me.'

She acknowledged both the truth of his words and their hidden message, and as she took in his sharp profile, the heavy brow, the wide jaw, the capable hands, she simply nodded as her mother's words filtered through her mind again. *Try to forgive him, Cassie... Life leaves no room for regrets... All we can do is focus on the future.* Sadie was right, and all Cassie could focus on for now was Marina, and how she could protect her from what was to come.

'Presumably Marina has no idea what's going on?'

Cassie sucked in a breath. He still had the knack of getting inside her head, even after all these years. 'No, she doesn't.'

'These next few weeks are going to be hard. I won't lie. They're going to take a toll on you, and you're going to need someone around.' He paused. 'I've also seen the effects of hiding this stuff from children, and it's not pretty. Marina is bright and intuitive, and you'll need to be honest with her.'

'It's too much, Grant. She'll not cope.' Cassie shook her head. 'She'd been through so much already.'

He pulled up at a traffic light and looked over at her. 'I know she has, but think how much worse it will be if you wait...' He caught himself, his cheeks colouring slightly as he looked ahead again. 'I know it's not my business, Cassie, but I really think that a tailored truth that she can take in, understand, is better than a lie.'

Cassie bit down on her lower lip as she considered how on earth she could present the truth in any way that would not rip the ground from under her niece. Ground that was still somewhat unstable. As she pictured the scene, frustration surged up inside her. 'What the hell do I say, Grant. So, Marina, I have a tiny little bit of cancer, but not to worry, it'll all come out in the wash.' She sighed. 'She's five years old and has just lost her mother.' She looked away from him and stared out of her window, blind to the steady stream of traffic around them. 'All I want to do is keep her safe and shield her from all this.' She swept a hand down her body.

'There are ways to prepare her. We have counsellors who can help, too. She lives with you, Cass. She'll know something's wrong.' He sounded anxious, but Cassie was unable to assuage his concerns, her own growing to such a magnitude that she felt crushed beneath them.

'Just leave it for now, Grant. I'll give it some thought,' she whispered. 'Can we please just go home?'

Grant straightened his arms, pushing himself back in the seat, then pulled away from the lights. 'I want to talk to you about that, too. I've been thinking about this a lot since last night, and I think you should move in with me for a few weeks.'

She swung her head around, her jaw slackening. 'What?' This was the last thing she'd been expecting.

'I mean it, Cass. Just think about it, please. My place is more than big enough, and I can help with Marina. I'll take some time off. God knows I have it coming.' He looked left and stopped at a pedestrian crossing, then pulled ahead again. 'You'll need help with chemo, at the clinic and at home. I can take on the school runs and keep Marina occupied to give you the time to rest.' Seeing a space ahead, he edged the car to the side of the road and switched off the engine. 'Please, Cassie. Let me do this for you, and for her. It's little enough considering everything that's happened.'

His eyes were full, his earnest tone shaking Cassie out of her momentary state of shock as she considered what he'd said. Would it be so bad to accept his help for a while? To let him see her truly vulnerable – literally at her worst. Could she do this and keep her heart safe, because despite the tiny seeds of trust beginning to sprout, being around him was still hard. Her sense of him wanting more from her had initially been disturbing, but as she thought about his continued efforts to repair things between them, and to build a relationship with his daughter, Cassie was startled that, for a split second, she wondered if she might want more, too. Rocked by the notion that she'd let herself think that way, she shook her head.

The practicality and pros of his suggestion were being swamped by the list of cons that were still swirling in her mind, but right now, Cassie needed someone to support her, and Marina, and it was too much to ask of her mother, alone.

Taking a few moments to let her decision percolate, she caught him scanning her face, his mouth in an anxious line. 'If we do this, it would only be for a few weeks. Until I'm through chemo.' She dropped her chin, her eyes locked on his. 'And my mum will want to help, too, so I'll need to talk it over with her first.'

'Absolutely.' His face brightened. 'You make the rules.'

Cassie's anxiety was beginning to wane, and the sense that she'd shed an invisible weight from her shoulders made her exhale. 'OK, then. I'll give it some thought and let you know in a day or so. OK? And I'd insist on paying some rent, and I'd buy all the food and stuff. We wouldn't freeload.' Her eyebrows lifted.

'No way on the rent, but I'll give you the food thing.' He

smiled at her. 'I'm a crap cook, so you'll have to help me out with that.'

'I remember.' She laughed softly, picturing a shared student kitchen with few utensils and some mismatched dishes. 'That's fine.'

She watched as he turned the engine on and eased back out into the lane. He had the hint of a smile tugging at his mouth that transported her into the past again – memories of him lying and looking at her when she woke up, or him smiling that way when she would get animated about something she was working on. In her heart, she knew that he was a good man, despite all that had transpired, and now, dulling her pain over his role in her betrayal was a growing sense of gratitude.

'Thank you. Grant,' she whispered. 'This offer means a lot.'

Grant had taken her upstairs to the loft and made her a cup of tea and some scrambled eggs on toast before he left. Cassie had then spent the afternoon on the sofa scanning emails. She had warned her mother, when she brought Marina home from school, not to let Marina dive on her, Cassie's stomach being extremely tender and bloated. The surgeon had told her it would take a week or so for her to fully recuperate, and she was surprised by how drained she felt after a short car ride and a couple of hours of work.

Just as she closed the laptop, she heard the door open, and then Marina came running towards her. Unsure how best to protect herself, Cassie grabbed a cushion and laid it across her lap, then opened her arms to the little girl.

'You're home.' Marina dumped her backpack on the floor and fiercely hugged Cassie's neck.

'Just as promised.' The feel of Marina's arms around her lifted Cassie's spirit as she inhaled the school smell – a mixture of dust, crayons, and fruit juice. 'How was school today?' She eased Marina back a little and patted the sofa next to her.

Marina sat down, her little fingers twining through Cassie's. 'OK. Polly and I made hand paintings.' She held her free palm up. 'Mine is green.'

Sadie closed the front door and came into the living room. 'Hello, my love.' She smiled at her daughter. 'How are you feeling?' Her eyes were full of concern as she leaned down and gently kissed Cassie's forehead.

Cassie hugged her mother's neck, then leaned back. 'I'm fine.' She then mouthed, above Marina's head, 'Just a bit sore.'

Sadie nodded, then, seeing her empty plate on the coffee table, lifted it and took it into the kitchen. 'Want a quick cuppa?' she called over her shoulder.

'Please.' Cassie dragged Marina's backpack closer to her feet and opened it. 'Is your print in here?'

Marina nodded, then dropped onto her knees and dug into the bag. Pulling out a slightly crumpled piece of art paper, she smoothed it against her stomach and then handed it to Cassie. 'I gave it eyes.' She pointed to the palm of the small handprint, where two blue circles transformed the hand into a face, with thick spikes of hair reminiscent of the football character Wilson, in *Castaway*.

Cassie held the print up and nodded approvingly. 'I think it's absolutely brilliant. We should get a nice frame for it and put in on the wall.' She smiled at Marina, who nodded, then slipped her thumb into her mouth. 'Are you hungry?'

'Nuh-uh.' Marina shook her head. 'I ate my lunch.' She mumbled around her thumb, which Cassie reached out and gently removed from her mouth.

'What did you have?'

'A cheese sandwich, apple and a juice box.' Marina's eyes were fixed on Cassie's.

'Yum.' Cassie smiled. 'Want some yogurt to keep you going until dinner time?'

Marina nodded, getting up nimbly from the floor and taking the handprint from Cassie. 'I'll put it in my room.' She held the paper against her and smoothed it again. 'Is Daddy coming today?'

'Not today, sweetheart. He'll come over tomorrow, and maybe he can take you to school. Would you like that?' Cassie asked hesitantly, unsure what reaction she'd get to this new arrangement she'd made with Grant. They'd decided to wait a week or so to tell Marina about possibly moving in with him, not wanting to pile too many changes on the child too soon, but in the meantime, he'd insisted on taking on the school runs to allow Cassie to fully rest.

To her relief, Marina smiled. 'Will he come for breakfast?' Her eyes were alight. 'Granny showed me how to make toast with jam.' She beamed. 'I made soldiers.'

'Clever you.' Cassie laughed. 'Then perhaps you can make some for me, tomorrow?'

Marina trotted away towards her room as Sadie walked back in carrying a steaming mug which she set on the coffee table in front of Cassie.

'Are you really OK, love?' She folded her arms across her middle and stood with her legs wide apart, as if positioning her tiny frame between Cassie and an approaching enemy.

The irony of that struck Cassie as she patted the air. 'I'm fine. Honestly.' She shrugged, her conversation with Grant flashing back to her. She needed to know what her mother thought about his suggestion before she could trust herself to make a final decision. 'Can I ask your advice about something, Mum?'

Sadie stepped back, her brow knitting. 'Of course.'

'Grant wants us to move in there for a while, just until my

chemo is over. I know it's going to be rough on me, but I'm not sure if it's the right thing to do.'

Sadie's frown lifted as her eyebrows knitted together, then she tipped her head to the side as she considered what Cassie had said. 'Well, if he's offering to step up, perhaps you should let him.' She shrugged. 'I'm a bit surprised, if I'm honest, but I can see why he'd suggest it. He is an expert in what you're going through, after all.'

Cassie let her mother's words circle for a second or two, conflicted between wanting to agree and still questioning Grant's ability to come through for them. 'But can I really trust him, Mum? He hasn't exactly got the best track record as far as I'm concerned. What if he flakes out on me again – because if he does, this time it will be on both me and Marina?'

Sadie nodded, then walked over and perched on the opposite end of the sofa. 'Time has moved on, Cassie, and he seems to have grown. You both have.' She gave a half-smile. 'I wanted to take care of you myself, but he might have a point about what's best for Marina. She needs stability more than anything else and having her father around could make all the difference to her coping with you being unwell.'

Cassie eyed her mother, seeing the clarity behind Sadie's eyes, the lack of doubt that in turn seeped into Cassie's troubled heart. 'As long as you don't think it's a mistake.'

Sadie shook her head. 'No, love. I don't. But it's totally up to you.'

Ten minutes later, Sadie paced over to the window and looked down at the water. 'Do you need anything before I go?' Her pale blue trousers and light floral shirt feeling too summery for the brisk day that had greeted Cassie outside the cancer centre.

'No. But thank you. And thanks a million for everything

you've done.' She pointed at the armchair opposite her. 'Aren't you going to stay a bit longer?'

'I think I should get off home, and let you and Marina settle back in, but can I hug you properly first?' She held her arms out. 'I'll be gentle.'

Cassie put the cushion aside and pushed herself up gingerly. 'I love you, Mum.'

Sadie held her close, her mother's arms gently circling her back. 'You're my sweet girl, and I am so proud of you,' she whispered. 'Feel these arms around you. Do you feel them? I will hold you up, Cassie. For too long now you've been taking care of me. Worrying about me. Changing your life to accommodate my inability to get over losing your dad. Well, that ends now. You need me and that's my job. I am your mother.'

Cassie melted into Sadie's arms, all Cassie's bravery and determination to stay strong disintegrating. 'Oh, Mum. I'm so scared.'

Sadie's grip tightened around Cassie's back. 'I know, and I'm not letting you go. Not now. Not ever.'

Cassie's throat knotted. 'Believe me. I'm not going anywhere if I can help it.' As she said it, she hoped with all her heart that the universe was hearing her.

33

By the end of November, a cold front had brought the beginning of winter rushing in, the Water of Leith turning a murky grey and the skies above it loaded with ominous rain. Even the sandstone warehouses across the water from the loft seemed to lose their honey-coloured warmth in the cold, silvery light.

Five days after her surgery, Cassie was feeling much stronger and had been back at the studio in the mornings, working on the Oceans collection. Syd had been delighted to have her back, and Hector had strutted around playing the bagpipes, making her laugh and press her palm into her stomach, which was still tender.

Her pain had been hovering around a two on the scale, which to Cassie was a welcome reprieve, and after the first few days at home, she'd even begun sleeping better, sometimes not waking until the alarm rang at 6.30 a.m.

Grant had been true to his word, taking Marina to school and bringing her home, even though Cassie had told him she was fine to do it, but each morning when he arrived at the loft, Marina would dash into his arms and then chatter happily as he put her coat on and led her to the door. It was obvious that she loved this new routine and so Cassie had gracefully relinquished the duty to Grant, even though it left her with a pang of sadness to do so.

When they'd told Marina the previous day that they'd be moving into Grant's house for a while, she'd seemed delighted. 'Will I have a bedroom for me?' She'd been sitting on the floor in the living room, twisting a puzzle piece around, then trying to fit it into the wrong spot.

'Yes, you will.' Grant had nodded. 'I've painted it specially, and there's a surprise waiting for you. And one for your Aunt Cassie, too.' He'd winked as Cassie had met his gaze, her eyebrows lifting.

'Oh really? And what kind of surprise would that be?' She'd smiled at the mock offence on his face.

'Nope. Not a chance. You will both have to wait and see.' He'd sat on the floor next to Marina, picked up a puzzle piece and handed it to her. 'Start with the corners, sweetheart. It makes it easier.'

The only downside to the whole conversation had then been telling Marina that Cassie was poorly and would have to take some medicine that might make her feel bad, so she'd need them both to take care of her for a while. Marina had listened intently, then her lower lip had begun to tremble, her eyes filling with concern. 'Why are you ill?'

Cassie had drawn her into her arms and spoken softly, close to her ear. 'It's going to be all right, and you and your daddy will help me get well.' Feeling Marina's anxiety permeating her own aching heart, Cassie had looked up at Grant, who'd been nodding approvingly. 'It'll just be for a while, and Granny and Uncle Syd will come and see us all the time, and we'll be able to play in the garden over there, too.' Her voice had become ragged at this point and seeing her struggle, Grant had stepped in.

'I'm excited that you're coming to stay. It's going to be really great, Marina. You'll see.' He'd knelt in front of her. 'Your Aunt Cassie will keep us both in line.' He'd nudged Marina playfully. 'But you and I will keep *her* in line, too. OK, partner?'

Marina had taken a few moments to consider what they'd said, then asked, 'Will my room have the sea outside?'

'No, sweetheart. Daddy lives in Stockbridge, so there's no sea, but the river is nearby that we can walk to, and there are ducks that we can feed, and lots of other things to do.' Cassie had lifted Marina's heavy ponytail and draped it over one shoulder. 'Everything will be fine, little one. Trust me.' Cassie had sucked in her bottom lip, the sense that she was asking too much of the child, and possibly making promises that, through no fault of her own, she might not be able to keep, overwhelming.

Despite her remaining trepidation at the decision to stay with Grant, Cassie had to admit that there was a sense both of relief and anticipation about it, and as she let herself relax into that, the easier she seemed to breathe.

Having Grant checking on her had become a comfortable part of her day. She would anticipate his arrival – tidying up the kitchen, then going into the bathroom to check her hair, sometimes swiping on a little nude lipstick and pinching her cheekbones to brighten her pale complexion.

Today was Saturday, and they were going to his house to see it before moving there the next day, after their lunch with Sadie. Cassie's chemotherapy would begin on the coming Monday and Grant wanted them settled in before that happened.

She had suggested that Grant join them at Sadie's, and he'd seemed keen to go. Having them reacquainted felt like another piece of the puzzle that would be put back in place, and having her mother coming to see them regularly, at his home, would mean that Marina didn't miss out on her time with her grandmother, which was invaluable. Her bond with Sadie was deepening by the day, with phone calls, and video chats each bedtime, and it gave Cassie such joy to see it blossom that much of her concern over the future would filter away with Marina's giggles, and her mother's warm laughter. Both sounds were panaceas that eased the flicker of fear inhabiting Cassie's heart about her prognosis.

Now, Marina was on the sofa watching *Sesame Street* on the laptop as Cassie checked her reflection in the hall mirror. Her eyes were less sunken than they'd been recently, and she had a little colour in her cheeks. Her pastel-blue sweater made her eyes look a deeper green than usual, and her hair was behaving for once, deep waves of red framing her face. As she took in her features, once again seeing Isla staring back, it was as if Cassie could suddenly see inside herself. She saw flesh, bones and a network of muscles and ligaments. She saw blood coursing through veins and arteries. She saw her heart, contracting with every beat as her pulse thumped softly inside her head. Buried deep beneath the architecture of her being, an alien had been evicted, and while that was liberating, Cassie couldn't help but wonder whether it had left a trail – a line of breadcrumbs that would attract its kin to inhabit her again. The sudden morbidity of her thoughts made her shake her head, lift her chin and fix her gaze on her own eyes. If the only way to eradicate that trail was to essentially poison the well with chemo, then she'd handle that, whatever it brought with it, and left in its wake. She knew that she could do it, for Marina.

The doorbell startled Cassie, so she took a second, then turned her back on the mirror, went into the hall and opened the door. 'Hey.' She smiled at Grant. 'We're ready to go.'

'Great stuff.' He laid a hand on Cassie's shoulder and dropped a light kiss on her cheek. She caught the soapy scent of sandalwood and felt his warm breath against her skin. Momentarily frozen, this being the first time he'd made this kind of affectionate contact, she swallowed – embarrassed that she wasn't sure how it made her feel.

Saving her from the awkward silence, Grant turned to Marina.

'Right, Miss Marina. Close the laptop up and let's get your coat on.'

Cassie snapped herself back to the moment, spun around and began busying herself with locating coats and gloves, finding the new scarf she'd bought for Marina, with tiny bumblebees all over it, and helping her pull on her favourite wellies.

With the child finally wrapped up warm, and Cassie wearing her toffee-coloured wool coat and her jeans tucked into long leather boots, she lifted her keys from the hall table. 'Lead the way.' She smiled nervously at Grant, seeing anticipation rippling through his entire body, in the way he stood, poised at the door, as if ready to push away from running blocks before a sprint.

'Right. Let's go.' He held the door open for Marina, who slid her hand into Cassie's as they walked to the top of the stairs.

As Grant came up next to them, Marina held her free hand out to Grant. 'Come on, Daddy, slowcoach.' She gave a cheeky little smile.

Grant laughed. 'I'll show you slowcoach.' He swept her off her feet and tossed her over his shoulder like a bag of coal, her long hair hanging in a wavy curtain down his back.

Caught off guard, Cassie laughed heartily as Marina squealed, 'Put me down.' Her giggles increasing in volume, her small hands pattering on Grant's lower back. 'Daddy, you're so silly.'

He turned to face Cassie, his eyes alight. 'If you weren't post-op, you wouldn't be safe either.'

'I don't think so.' Cassie lifted an eyebrow. 'I'd like to see you try.' A wave of joy filled her chest, making her blink several times.

Grant's eyebrows jumped as he jostled the still wriggling

child, setting her carefully back on the ground. 'Is that a challenge, Miss Hunter?' He grinned now, the trademark cleft deepening as he focused on Cassie's eyes.

'Not at all.' Her face felt suddenly warm as she flapped her hand at him. 'Come on, or we'll still be faffing around here at dinner time.' As her heart skipped, and she swiped the hair nervously away from her face, Cassie avoided his eyes as she led Marina down the stairs. How was it that after everything that had happened between them, he could still affect her this way?

Grant's house was a pleasant surprise. Not because it was sparkling clean and tidy, because even in his dingy student accommodation he'd been a neat freak, but because it felt so homey. Coming from her fairly spartan loft, Grant's sunny living room, with its shiny elm floors and high panelled ceiling, felt cosy, and welcoming. The two large bay windows overlooking the street gave the room such character that Cassie suddenly missed that in her own place.

Aside from its distinct architectural features, where his house differed the most from hers was how it was decorated. He had an eclectic mixture of old and new furniture that worked so well together that Cassie took a moment to scan the various items, trying to figure out what it was that made them seem so at home next to each other. The long, light-grey sectional sofa screamed modern, and was most probably, by the look of it, a recent purchase, while across the room an old, red leather wingchair, with a cracked, buttoned back and dark, mahogany legs looked perfect next to the sleek, marble-fronted fireplace and the chrome and glass-topped coffee table. A sisal rug pulled it all together and the fireplace had an old wood-burning stove in it that grounded the whole room.

On the wall behind the sleek wood dining table, hanging between the two bays, was a large, frameless oil painting. It was a dramatic view across an angry sea to what Cassie believed to be the Isle of Skye, the familiar peaks of the Cuillins spearing into an amber-tinged sky. As she turned to ask him if she was right, she saw him helping Marina out of her coat. 'This place is gorgeous, Grant.' She tugged her own coat off and looked around for where to hang it.

'Thanks.' He smiled, 'Let's do the tour first, then we can have a drink and a bite to eat, if you like.' He turned and hung Marina's little red coat in a slim cupboard next to the front door, then took Cassie's from her hand and hung it too. 'Follow me, ladies. The kitchen is this way.'

Marina was quiet, but seemed intrigued, sticking close to Cassie's side as they walked through the bright, open-plan kitchen filled with white cabinets and a large farmhouse sink. It overlooked a long, narrow garden with a circular patio at the end, next to a slightly ramshackle shed.

Grant led them into a back hall, where a wide staircase wound up and around the corner to a first-floor landing. They followed close behind him, both looking at the series of water-coloured prints of dogs, hounds mostly, that lined the staircase wall. 'These are my boys.' He pointed at the first print. 'That's Brutus, Marina. He's the boss-dog.' He turned to smile at Marina, who stared up at the large, liver and white hound. Cassie had never thought of him as a dog lover, so this new aspect to his personality was intriguing. Grant then pointed ahead at another, narrower staircase. 'Let's keep going up.'

They climbed the second flight of stairs that opened onto a bright hallway with one stripped pine door on the left.

'This is your room, Marina.' Grant's eyes were sparkling. 'I hope you like it.' He opened the door and swept a hand in front of him. 'In you go and tell me what you think.'

Marina walked in, stopped stock-still and gasped, her hands clamping over her mouth. The room had a pitched ceiling on

one side, with a large skylight in it, and at the back a long
picture window overlooking the garden.

'Fairies.' She spun around and looked at Cassie, then Grant,
then back at the ceiling, and the wall behind the single bed tucked
under the picture window, where three stuffed pigs were lined up
against the pillows. Behind the bed, against the creamy background of the walls, was a broad wallpaper border running from
the door to the picture window. It was of a woodland scene, with
tiny rabbits chewing lettuce leaves, field mice in sun hats, frogs
sitting on glistening lotus leaves and several pairs of doves perched
in the tall trees above. There were little pools of water, one with a
giant koi sticking its smiling face out, next to clusters of yellow
daisies with their petals facing up towards the rays of sunshine
spiking down from an azure sky. Right in the middle of the wall
was a group of fairies, each dressed in a pastel-coloured outfit and
sitting on top of a giant toadstool, their frothy wings sparkling as
the southerly light bounced off the tiny specks of glitter that decorated them. 'I have fairies again,' Marina squealed, and then
launched herself at Grant. 'Thank you, Daddy.' Her expression
was so filled with joy that Cassie moved quickly into the room,
turning away, and looking down at the garden as she blinked
repeatedly through the happy tears that wanted to come.

'This is so lovely, Grant. Just perfect,' she whispered, as he
moved up next to her.

'I saw her room on Lewis, and I wanted her to feel at home.'
He gently bumped Cassie's shoulder with his bicep, the firm
muscle seeming to bounce off her prickling skin.

'You nailed it.' She turned to look at him. 'Thank you.'

Behind them, Marina was now standing on the bed,
touching the decorative border, her eyes wide as she made little
bouncing movements – gradually jumping a little higher each
time.

'Be careful, now.' Cassie moved over to the side of the bed.

'Don't jump too high, OK?' She held a protective hand behind Marina, who was oblivious, her smile wide, and the tip of her tongue now poking out between her pearly teeth. 'It's beautiful, isn't it, sweetheart?'

'Like at my house.' Marina jumped a few more times, gradually slowing down. 'I love it.'

Moments later, with Marina still up in her room, Cassie and Grant were back down on the first floor, standing in another sunny bedroom. Once again, the wide window overlooked the back garden, and long, ivory-coloured curtains tipped the pale wood floor. The queen-sized bed was draped with a gauzy net, gathered on a large ring that was suspended over the centre of the bed. The duvet was a deep cream colour with trails of pale pink hydrangeas seeming to sprout from the end of the bed, weaving their way up towards the giant pillows that were stacked two deep on each side. There was a small desk and chair in one corner next to a tiled fireplace and in the other corner was an old-fashioned pedestal sink, with a fluffy white towel draped over an antique rail on the wall. 'You're just across the hall from me.' Grant gestured towards the door. 'Close but not too close, hopefully.' He grimaced.

As she scanned the serene space, Cassie's eye was instantly drawn to the bedside table, where a framed photo sat next to a pretty, vintage lamp and a vase full of buttery roses. Making her way around the bed, the photo came into view, and her hand flew to her mouth. It was of her and Isla, standing in a garden with their cheeks pressed together, wide smiles and each holding up a tall glass with a green drink in it, topped with a tiny pink umbrella.

Cassie's eyes filled as she lifted the photo and ran her finger over the outline of Isla's cheek. Afraid her voice might fail her, she blew out a long breath. 'This was at our engagement party.' She glanced over at Grant.

'Yep. In that square foot of garden at Andrew's godawful flat, above the pub in Haymarket.' He laughed softly. 'Good times, eh?'

Cassie nodded, her throat knotting as she remembered Grant's long-time flatmate at university – a fellow medical student who drank like a fish, swore like a trooper and called her Casablanca – much to her annoyance. 'Yes, good times, indeed.' They'd all been so carefree and happy, back then, unaware of all the challenges that awaited them.

34

They'd been living with Grant for nearly three weeks, and the cold of December had begun in earnest, when Cassie had hit her lowest ebb. The chemo was tough, taking hours each session, and then leaving her weak and nauseated. Grant had done a miraculous job of shielding Marina from the worst of it, and Cassie's gratitude towards him was growing by the day.

He had taken Cassie to and from the cancer centre for all her appointments and had helped her cope at home, suggesting a specific anti-nausea pill that he used with his own patients, which had helped her significantly. He'd held her hair while she crouched over the toilet, stroking her back until she had emptied herself, then he would strip her bed and put clean sheets on it while she showered. To her embarrassment, he'd even leave her clean laundry piled on the end of her bed – her underwear neatly folded into little squares that made her smile nervously as she tucked them away in the drawer.

He'd welcomed Sadie's frequent visits, taking long walks to allow them to have time alone together, which Cassie greatly appreciated. He'd also entertained Marina when Cassie was working at the desk in her room, or resting, and he kept the child from worrying about her aunt's absences from their excursions by telling Marina that Cassie wanted them to have a special father–daughter picnic or walk in the park. So far, Marina had seemed to accept his explanations.

To supplement the hearty dishes and fresh baking that Sadie would bring for them, Grant had even been cooking some light, healthy meals, trying to get Cassie to eat, but the flesh had melted from her bones and most of her clothes now hung on her. She was perpetually cold, so he would stoke the fire in her room every afternoon when they got home from the clinic, and pile extra blankets on her while she was napping. His kindness was a refreshing part of her day that Cassie was focusing on, more and more, as her overall ease around him grew.

Cassie tried each day to be up and showered, with a little make-up on to disguise her pallor, by the time Marina got home from school, and most days she managed it. Only twice in the last week or so had she been too weak to come downstairs, and both times Marina had gone up and sat on the floor in Cassie's room, telling her about what had happened at school and showing Cassie her drawings or the new list of spellings that they were working on.

Today, Cassie had been trembling ever since she'd got home from the clinic and just now, when she'd run her hands through her hair, the first hanks of long red strands had come away in her fingers. Sad resignation held her still as she stared at her reflection in the mirror above the sink in her room, and she hardly recognised herself. For once, Isla's face did not come to her, just the shadow of her own – drawn, dark-eyed and sunken-cheeked – a look that gave her a worrying glance into the future.

As Cassie gathered the long strands from the sink and rolled them into a ball between her palms, for the first time in weeks, she allowed herself to fully confront the what ifs of her situation. What if she didn't come back from this? What if they didn't get it all? What if she was a ticking time bomb, just weeks, days or even hours from the next cancer cells showing themselves? What if this cruel disease got the better of her and left Sadie and Marina adrift? Tossing the hair in the waste basket next to the sink, she blinked her vision clear. No. She wouldn't go there. If there was one thing she was, it was determined, and she'd not lie down and give in. She'd fight for her life, for her mother and her niece, and now, after the events of recent weeks, for Grant, too. They all deserved her best and she'd give it to them – come what may.

As she turned her back on the mirror, hearing activity downstairs, Cassie pulled a long scarf from the drawer next to her and tied it loosely around her hair at the back of her neck. She pinched her cheeks roughly, then pressed her shoulders back, feeling the muscles of her upper back pulling.

She'd chosen a loose sweatshirt to hide her thinness, over baggy track bottoms that she held up with a narrow belt. With her feet shoved in her fluffy slippers, she took a steadying breath, then made her way out into the hall and went carefully down the stairs.

In the kitchen, Marina was sitting at the breakfast bar with a biscuit and a glass of milk in front of her, her face flushed and her backpack abandoned behind her stool. Grant had his back to the door and neither of them had heard Cassie come into the room. As she hesitated in the doorway, Marina took a sip of milk, set her glass down and said, 'Daddy, is Aunty Cassie your best friend?'

Cassie was startled by the unexpected, gauche question, taking several steps back and leaning against the banister, out of sight.

'I think she is, yes.' Grant replied. 'We've known each other a long time – me, your Aunt Cassie and your mummy.'

'You were all friends together then?'

Cassie's hand hovered over her mouth, puzzled by this line of questioning. Where was this coming from and what was Marina trying to figure out?

'Yes, I knew them both at the same time. We were all friends.'

Cassie frowned, curious what was coming next.

'I like Anabelle at school, but Polly is my favourite.'

'That's nice, sweetheart. I loved both your Aunt Cassie and your mummy, very much.' He paused, the sound of running water punctuating his sentence. 'Sometimes things change between grown-ups, over time, Marina, but you'll understand that more when you're a bigger girl.'

'Was Mummy sad that Aunty Cassie was your best friend?' Marina seemed determined to dig into this and, hearing that, Cassie felt slightly panicked. Was Grant trapped? Would he tell Marina that he and Cassie had once been engaged? If he did, how on earth would he explain what went wrong, and how Isla ended up being her mother? As the potential tangents for this conversation began to swirl around her, Cassie sat on the bottom step and let her head rest in her palms. Forcing her breathing to slow down, she was struck by a surprising realisation that brought her back up straight. Grant could handle this, and she needed to trust that. The man she'd seen recently, the one who had stepped in, cared for her and his child so willingly, would not let either of them down. Moreover, she was now convinced that he would never do anything to hurt or confuse Marina, and that knowledge was a welcome gift.

'Your mummy and I were special friends, almost like family, but Aunty Cassie and I had a different kind of friendship. One that was super important to us both. We loved each other very much, and both of us loved your mummy, too. So, I don't think your mummy minded that Aunt Cassie was my favourite.' He spoke gently, behind his voice, the sounds of him moving around the kitchen. 'Just like Anabelle is your friend, but she knows that Polly is your *best* friend.'

'OK.' Marina sighed. 'I miss Mummy. She felt so cosy when she hugged me.' For a moment, Cassie felt desolate, until Marina added, 'Aunty Cassie loves me the same as Mummy. I love her a big lot.'

Cassie pressed her palm to her mouth, feeling a rush of uplifting happiness so intense that it made her sway.

'She does love you very much, Marina. We're both lucky to have her in our lives, aren't we?'

'Uh-huh.' Marina chimed. 'I'm going to go and see her.'

Cassie heard the scrape of the stool against the wood floor, so heaved herself up from the stair and smoothed her palms over her hair just as Marina darted into the hall. 'Hello, little one.' Cassie found a bright smile. 'How was school today?' She held onto the banister, then slowly stepped down onto the floor.

'I had lots of lessons, then me and Polly played with chalk on the ground outside.' Marina beamed, then tipped her head to the side as a tiny frown split her forehead. 'Aunty Cassie?'

'Yes, sweetheart.'

'You are Daddy's best friend, and mine too. Even better than Polly.' She held a hand out to Cassie and let it linger in the air.

Her entire body tingling with joy, Cassie took the little hand in hers. 'That's the most wonderful thing you could ever tell me.' She nodded. 'You two are my best friends, too.' She cupped Marina's cheek, their eyes locking as Marina lifted Cassie's hand to her lips and gently kissed the back of it, the gesture so sweet that Cassie gasped.

'I like when you are with me.' Marina held her gaze, as if wanting to make sure her message had been received. 'I like being with you and Daddy. I love you, Aunty Cassie, and Mummy too.'

Cassie counted her rapid heartbeats and willed herself

not to cry at this first declaration of love – to fold at the knees and smother the little girl, cover her eyelids with kisses and beg her never to give up on that love. This bond, this deep connection, would keep Cassie anchored and ready to face anything in order to stay. But that wasn't fully within her control, and the realisation snatched at her throat. Irrespective of her determination, or sheer will to beat this cancer and live a long and happy life, as Marina's legal guardian she had a responsibility to ensure that Marina was taken care of, whatever happened. While there was so much out of Cassie's control, she could still do something about that, even though the thought of not being the one to care for Marina was unbearable to consider.

With Marina's words, and Cassie's consequent revelation spinning inside her head, she had hardly slept. By 4 a.m., bone-sore and tired of staring at the ceiling, she crept downstairs to get some orange juice. Too tired to find a glass, she stood inside the floodlight of the open fridge and sipped from the bottle until she heard rustling behind her. Startled, she swung around to see Grant standing there, his pyjama bottoms pooled around his bare feet and his University of Edinburgh T-shirt drooping below his waistband. 'Busted.' He laughed softly.

'God, sorry.' Cassie put the top back on the juice and returned it to the fridge. 'I used to give you hell for doing that.' She smiled at him – embarrassed. 'If you can't beat them...' She shrugged, suddenly conscious of wearing only a long T-shirt that barely covered her behind. Grabbing a dishcloth, she held it in front of her. 'Can't sleep either?'

'Nope.' Grant moved past her, filled a glass from the tap, then drained it as she slipped behind the breakfast bar.

'Actually, this is good because I need to talk to you about something.' She slid onto one of the high stools. This moment had presented itself at just the right time, and she would make the most of it – before she changed her mind.

'Oh, yes?' He leaned back against the sink. 'What's up?'

Cassie took in the gentle, dark-rimmed eyes – duplicates of Marina's – and suddenly, her decision felt utterly appropriate. 'I want to put some things in place.' She halted at the shock that clouded his face. 'Hey, don't look like that. I've no intention of popping my clogs any time soon.' She laughed softly. 'Just hear me out.'

Grant frowned, then moved over and sat opposite her. 'OK. Tell me.'

'Marina is so happy around you, it's like she's come back to life. I know she loves me, and that means everything to me, but there's an intrinsic bond between you two. It's palpable when you're together.' She paused. 'So, I want to name you as Marina's legal guardian, in the event of my death.' She swallowed, the word tasting as sour as it was frightening. 'Just in that event, then there will be no issues with her ongoing care or custody.' She nodded decisively. 'Is that OK with you?'

Grant wiped his hand over his mouth and placed his palms on the bar. 'Yes, it's perfectly all right. Perfectly. But, Cass, there's no reason to assume that you're not going to get through this.' He frowned as he leaned forward on his elbows. 'I've seen patients come back from situations that looked hopeless, and that's not where you are.'

Cassie nodded. 'I know that, and believe me, I've got every reason in the world to stick around.' She met his eyes, hers prickling with unshed tears. 'Think of this as housekeeping if you like.' She smiled at him. 'Ducks in a row, and all that.'

He nodded, then raked his hands through his hair. 'As long as that's all it is.'

'It is, I promise.' On an impulse, and without overthinking it, she reached across the bar, her fingers extended. 'Trust me.'

He took her hand, his long fingers cool in her palm. 'I do,

Cassie. I'm just so grateful that you're starting to trust *me*, again.' His eyes were glittering. 'I won't let you down.' He squeezed her hand.

'I know, Grant.' She scanned his face, and deep inside, warming her heart was the knowledge that finally she believed him, and she hadn't needed him to even say it.

35

The following day, Cassie stood at Grant's kitchen window, her phone pressed to her ear. Heather, Ian Bannister's assistant, had sounded pleased to hear from her and had gone to find him.

Having had the conversation with Grant, the time was right to put what they'd discussed in place, and as she waited for Ian to come on the line, Cassie ran through a mental list of everything she had to do for the remainder of the week.

Her fourth week of chemo was underway, after which she would get a break for a few weeks, to let her body recover. Then, more tests would reveal what the next steps were – her future now an unnervingly blank page, waiting for its contents to materialise.

While at the clinic, hooked up to the IV, she had been sketching the final designs for the Oceans collection. It comprised five sets of matching bracelets and necklaces, all reflecting elements found in the ocean. There was the Reef, the Shore, the Wave, the Shell and the Anemone, each set echoing the shape and form of its namesake.

As Cassie had grown increasingly weak after therapy, Syd had been coming to see her at Grant's house every few days to pick up her sketches, then taking them back to the studio and rendering them into the CAD programme. 'These are perfection, man' His eyes had glowed. 'Maybe your best yet.'

Now, the designs were complete and soon it would be time to begin producing the first round of samples – a stage of the process that Cassie always looked forward to. Seeing her inspiration take on form, holding a new piece of jewellery in her hands and feeling the weight and balance of it, the smooth and textured surfaces and each precise curve and angle, never failed to thrill her.

While she'd been working on the collection at the clinic, Cassie had also been working on a side project up in her bedroom, with the tools and materials that Syd had brought her. Marina's birthday was coming up in a few days and as a special surprise, Cassie had been making her a silver bracelet. It had a double row of tiny hearts, each looped through the next one and the one above and was held closed by a padlock-shaped clasp inset with a small, blue tanzanite. Tanzanite was Marina's birthstone, and Cassie knew that they were known for helping raise self-confidence and consciousness, and enhancing creativity. It was believed that these stunning stones possessed the power to convert negative energy into positive and represent new beginnings. All these qualities either already existed within Marina, or Cassie wanted them to always surround her niece, so the significance of the stone was perfect. As she pictured the almost-complete bracelet, Ian Bannister's voice tugged her back to the moment.

'Cassie, great to hear from you. How are you?'

'Hi, Ian. I'm fine.' The lie came so easily that she stopped herself abruptly. 'Actually, that's not entirely true – that's why I'm calling.' She turned her back to the window and began to talk.

A few minutes later, Ian spoke quietly. 'Cassie, I don't know what to say. I'm just so sorry that you're going through this.'

Cassie nodded, his sympathy touching and yet threatening to unseat her. 'Thanks, Ian. Life is a bitch sometimes, but I'll get through it.' She closed her eyes at the worn cliché and then turned back to face the garden, where a robin was preening itself on top of the fence at the right of the garden. The rhythmic and repetitive motion of the bird's tiny head was calming in its simplicity. 'I just want to get things in place.'

'We can absolutely get that process underway. I'll just need some info from Grant. Copies of the paternity test would be helpful, and then we can get started.'

Cassie felt relief flood through her. 'Thanks, Ian. As I said to Grant, I'm not planning on shuffling off any time soon, but it needs to be set up should things change.' *Things* such as her body's cellular make-up and her ability to fight off future invaders, should the worst happen.

'Right, of course.' He sounded more matter-of-fact now. 'Can I contact Grant directly?'

'Yes, absolutely. He's waiting to hear from you. I'll email you all his details.'

'Good. Then all we'll need is for you both to review and sign everything. I'm thinking we can have the paperwork ready in a few days.'

'That's great. We're coming to Lewis for a long weekend, for Marina's birthday, so we can pop in in person.' She pictured standing in his office in Stornoway, this time with Grant next to her, and despite the nature of the meeting, she smiled. 'It'll be good for you to meet him, Ian. As Marina's father, he's obviously going to feature in all aspects of her life, from now on.' She pressed her bony hips against the sink, letting the significance of what she'd said percolate. After all these months, all of the hurt and recriminations, she and Grant had finally found a new equilibrium. Telling Ian that Grant would be a permanent fixture in Marina's life was true, and the thought brought with it a deep sense of peace. As she let that peace wash through her, feeling it filling up tiny gaps of hurt and worry she'd been harbouring, she realised that peace was the thing that had been missing the most for her, ever since Isla had disappeared, six years ago.

That evening, Cassie had been feeling well enough to bath Marina, and read her *Green Eggs and Ham*, and while Cassie had been upstairs, Grant had made her an omelette and some toast. When she'd come downstairs, he'd set the plate in front of her. 'I'll go up and kiss her goodnight, and I want to see a clean plate when I come back down.' He'd made a face that had made her laugh. 'No joke.' He'd dipped his chin. 'If you lose any more weight, you'll slip through the bloody iron grates out in the street.' He jabbed a thumb over his shoulder, then left the room.

She'd done her best to eat the warm, fluffy eggs, the toast more than she could stomach, but fifteen minutes later, she had to admit she felt better. Now, Grant was sitting across the room, staring at her, his mouth twitching with something unsaid. Recognising the signs, Cassie laid her open book across her thigh and raised her eyebrows. 'What is it? You're like a kid with a big, fat secret.' She pressed her lips together, comically. 'Spit it out.'

His face instantly relaxed. 'You know me so well, it's spooky.'

She laughed softly. 'I've had the same thought, more than once.' She closed the book and put it on the coffee table, then sat back, lifted her feet and crossed them on the glass tabletop. Seeing him baulk, she tutted, savouring the return of their teasing banter – something she's always enjoyed in the past. 'God, sorry, Mr MacFussy.' She plopped her feet back on the floor. 'Better?'

Grant widened his eyes. 'Yes, actually.'

'So, what's going on?'

He leaned forward, his elbows on his knees, his expression full of excitement. 'I wanted to ask you both to stay a little longer. Your treatment's over in a day or so and we have the trip to Lewis coming up, so why leave before we go? You can stay here, finish Marina's bracelet and get some strength back. The trip will be a good opportunity to rest, too. Then, when we get back, if you want to go...' He let the sentence trail.

Cassie was frowning, trying to see to the bottom of this request, and, taking her by surprise, what she thought she saw there sparked irritation. 'Is it because you don't think I'm going to get better? That I'm going to need you to nursemaid me forever? Or that I'm not going to be able to take care of Marina?' She shook her head. 'Is that what you're thinking, Grant?' Her voice shook. 'Because that could be a little insulting.'

To her shock, his eyes filled as he stood up and crossed the room. 'You couldn't be more wrong.' He sat next to her and took her hand, her fingers icy in his warm palm. 'What I'm thinking is that we've wasted so much time, Cass. Years of not talking. Being angry over things that didn't matter, that we couldn't change about each other, or that belonged in the past. I've realised over these past weeks, and seeing you with Marina, that I still... I mean, I never stopped...' His voice faded as he massaged the back of her hand with his thumb.

Cassie's pulse began to race. Was he serious? Did he still love her? And if so, if that was what he was saying, did she want that?

His glistening eyes locked on hers. 'If you still have any feelings for me, tell me now. And, if so, let's make up for all that lost time, Cass.' His mouth lifted at the edges. 'I predict that you'll be around for a long time to bug the hell out of me, and I wouldn't want it any other way.' He paused as she blinked several times, unable to form a word. 'I want us to be together not because I want to baby you, or wash and fold your damn smalls, but because there's never been anyone but you, Cassie.'

His voice was thick with emotion. 'I want you and Marina in my life. It's as simple as that.'

Cassie's mouth drained of moisture as she scanned his face. This face, that she had loved so much, that had only become more handsome with the years, and that had represented all that had been good in her life for a while, was seared on her heart. As she thought about going back to the loft, to the airy home that had felt so right to her for years, a rush of loneliness flooded through her. She didn't want to go back there, and not because she'd grown tired of the décor, but because Grant wouldn't be there every day, and the realisation was so liberating that she felt as if she might float up from the sofa and hit the ceiling, like a balloon. She had no room left for anger or loneliness, no time for grudges, or any more things to be left unsaid. She wanted to forget the past, forgive him, and Isla, make the best life she could. So, all she had to say now was yes.

'Cassie?' He stroked her cheek with his fingertip. 'What's going on in that head?' His eyes were warm, tiny creases at the edges giving him away.

Cassie covered his hand with her free one and took a deep breath. It was now or never. 'Are you sure this is what you want, because if we do this, there's no going back. We can't do that to Marina.' She shook her head. 'So, are you sure?'

He held her gaze, then spoke softly. 'I know what *I* want. What I'm asking is, do you want the same thing?'

Her chest was aching with the sense that her heart might explode, so she exhaled slowly and fixed her eyes on his. This was really happening. 'Yes, Grant. I do.'

He leaned in, hesitated for a moment, then kissed her, his tongue tentatively touching hers. As Cassie opened herself up to the kiss, wrapping her arms around his neck and drawing him closer, she knew she had come home, at last.

36

Five days later, the cottage was chilly when they arrived, and Cassie immediately turned up the heating, then unpacked the food they'd bought at the local shop, while Grant laid a fire in the grate.

Filled with renewed positivity, after their conversation at home, Cassie had been focusing on the future – a brighter picture than she could have imagined just a handful of months ago. She'd been feeling tired but nonetheless, energised, and now, being back on Lewis was feeding into that, keeping her spirits high.

Rather than run straight to her room this time, Marina was sitting on the sofa watching Grant, Raffy tucked under her arm and her thumb in her mouth.

The flight had been bumpy and while Cassie had fought to hide her nerves, Grant had kept Marina occupied with a puzzle on his iPad. They'd picked up a hired car in Stornoway and, this time, Grant had driven across the island, giving Cassie the opportunity to soak in the landscape. As they'd cut through the gentle hills and verdant farmland, followed the river, and crossed the narrow bridges, with each curve of the road, Cassie understood Isla's love for this place more and more. There was a mystical quality to the light – glowing as if a golden filter had been placed over the landscape – that evoked calm – something that Cassie craved. That gentle sensation rising inside her, and mentally replaying the night she'd spent with Grant, after their kiss, she had eventually fallen asleep, just minutes before they'd reached the cottage.

Now, with the early-afternoon light beginning to wane, typical for late December in the Outer Hebrides, Cassie decided to light some candles. While Grant sat next to Marina and they began looking through her colouring book, Cassie raked through the kitchen drawers searching for a lighter. At the back of the obligatory messy drawer that every kitchen requires, she found an old Bic lighter and a box of birthday candles. Holding them in the palm of her hand, Cassie smiled. 'Thanks, sis. I'm going to bake her a cake tonight, after she's gone to bed, then surprise her with it in the morning.' She lifted her chin and whispered to the ceiling, 'I adore her, Isla, and so does Grant. You'll never have to worry about her being cared for and loved.' She closed her eyes. 'I miss you so much. We all do.'

Grant circled her waist from behind, startling her.

'God.' She yelped. 'You scared the doo-dah out of me.' She turned to face him, planting a kiss on his smile. 'Where's Marina?'

'Gone to play in her room.' He looked at the ceiling. 'Did you tell Isla I said hello?'

'In a way.' Cassie leaned her cheek on his chest, catching the fresh, laundry scent of his T-shirt. 'This feels right, doesn't it?' She could feel Grant nodding.

'It does. You and me. Us and Marina. This place.' He leaned back as she straightened up. 'I think I could grow to seriously love this house.' His eyes drifted to the window, a brisk wind buffeting the tall gorse along the ridge behind the beach.

'I know. Me too.' She nodded, a thought that she'd been

playing with privately now seeming ripe to share. 'I was planning on selling it and putting the money into Marina's trust
fund, but what if I kept it until she's twenty-one, and she can
make her own decision what to do, then? That way, we could
bring her here whenever we can manage it. Let her stay
connected to the home she loves so much.' Cassie moved to the
window and stared out at the water below, row after row of
white peaks curling away towards the now magenta horizon.

'I think that's a good plan. She doesn't exactly need the
money, and the place she was born is irreplaceable. All her
memories of Isla are rooted here.' He pressed both palms down
towards the floor.

'Precisely.' Cassie smiled at him, feeling her renewed love
for him growing, and as it continued to bloom, so her bruised
heart healed a little more.

'While we're on the subject...' He beckoned to her, and they
walked to the sofa, hand in hand.

The fire had taken hold, long orange flames licking up the
network of logs in the grate as they began to crackle, and a delicious smoky smell filling the room that sparked a rush of childhood memories. Whenever she'd been ill, Cassie would sit on
the floor by the fire in their house in Dunkeld, a cup of chicken
soup in her hand, her face turning scarlet from getting as close
as she could before her mother would scold her and tell her to
move back a bit, in case any sparks made it around the guard.

'Cass?' Grant's voice tugged her back to the moment.

'Sorry. Just wandering down memory lane.' She smiled at
him, then shifted closer, linking her fingers through his. 'What's
on your mind?'

'This is just an idea, so don't feel bullied or pressured, OK?'

'OK.' She nodded. 'Not being bullied. Got it.' She
suppressed a smile as he waved her sarcasm away.

'So, I was thinking that we should consider where we're
going to live. I mean, your place is great, but if we're going to

make a permanent home for Marina, for us as a family, my house probably makes more sense.' His eyebrows lifted in question. 'What do you think?'

Cassie stared at him. A family. That was what they were and hearing him say it just confirmed how much she had been wanting this, hoping for it, and not even knowing she missed it. They were the family that Marina deserved and with that came the potential for so much joy and love that Cassie's eyes filled.

'We haven't really talked about living together permanently, Grant, but now that we are...' She watched him seem to hold his breath. 'I think it's perfect.'

'Really?' He beamed. 'No what ifs, or reservations?' He eyed her.

'Honestly?' She sucked in her bottom lip.

'Always.'

'Then, no. None.' She shrugged. 'Unbelievable, right?' She laughed, a lightness filling her chest.

'All right then.' He held his hand out. 'We're doing this.'

She took his hand, his skin warm under her fingertips. 'I think, if we don't end up killing each other that is, I'll sell the loft in the spring. It's served its purpose, and it doesn't feel like home anymore.' She paused. 'I hope another move won't upset Marina, though. She's doing so much better these days.' She dropped his hand and slid under his arm, draping it across her chest and reconnecting their fingers.

'I don't think it will. She seems happy at the house, and if we are together, she'll be fine.'

Just as Cassie was picturing them all, sitting in his cosy living room, playing snap, or watching TV, a hole began to appear in the perfect picture, and she sighed. As she began to nibble at the cuticle around the thumb of her free hand, Grant stroked the hair away from her neck and kissed it, his lips dry and warm, sending sparks across her skin.

'I have one more suggestion. Again, just food for thought.'

He paused as Cassie dropped her hand back into her lap and waited for him to continue. 'If we're going to be a family, then we should truly be a family, so what about asking your mum to come and live with us, too?'

Cassie sat up and swung around to face him, her heart racing. He'd done it again. Got inside her head. 'What?'

He looked a little anxious. 'We could give Sadie the room you've been using. Turn it into a nice space for her. She can have the bathroom in the hall, as we'll use my en suite.' He paused. 'Marina will be snug as a bug up in her fairy den, as she calls it.' He shrugged. 'I know I'm probably rushing things, Cass, but I just want us to get on with the rest of our lives. Having her gran there all the time could help root Marina even more, make her feel totally secure.' He swallowed nervously as Cassie lunged forward, circling his neck with her arms and burying her face in his shoulder. He patted her back softly. 'So, that's a yes, then?' She felt the ripples of his gentle laughter under her ribcage.

'Oh my God, yes. If Mum agrees, of course, that would be perfect.' Her voice was muffled as the tears began to course down her cheeks, dampening the neck of his T-shirt. 'Thank you.' She was being given a second chance at love and now all she needed was good news from Doctor Carnegie, after the next round of tests to come after Christmas. More than anything, she needed to hear the priceless word, remission, to underline this second chance at life.

Grant had been determined to take Marina out to the beach to fly a kite, before it got dark, so when she had come out of her room, the three of them had wrapped up warmly and walked down onto the sand. Now, Grant was unravelling the long string on the kite, a huge purple butterfly, with colourful tassels hanging from the tail. 'So, you unwind it slowly, then we'll run along the beach until the wind grabs it and we'll let the string unravel more to let the kite get up into the air. OK?' He was on one knee, his dark jacket zipped up high under his chin and his eyes were soft, brimming with affection, as Marina nodded.

'Can I hold it?' She reached for the spindle.

'Yes, you can. Once we get it up in the air.' He moved a strand of hair that blew across her face. 'Shall we give it a go?'

Cassie smiled and nodded when Marina glanced over at her. 'Off you two go. I'll stay here and film you on my phone.' Cassie fished her phone out of her pocket, proud of the spontaneous excuse to avoid running in the sand. Despite feeling her strength beginning to return, thanks to Grant's gentle care, she was certainly not able to run yet. 'OK. One, two, three, go!' she shouted into the quickening wind as Grant and Marina took off across the beach, Grant timing his steps to allow Marina to keep up as the butterfly took to the sky, diving down, then swooping upwards as the kite began to climb. Marina was squealing and Grant laughing as they stopped running and he showed her how to release more string, their heads together as he knelt at Marina's side. Seeing them side by side, their bodies bending in towards one another, filled Cassie with such contentment that she tipped her head back and whispered to the sky, 'That's my family.'

Cassie held the phone steady, filming them, until the wind whipped a sheet of hair across her face. As she tried to gather it with her free hand, she felt a handful of strands separate from her scalp, with zero resistance. She hesitated for a second, seeing the red threads wrapped around her fingers, then she flicked the long tresses into the wind.

Returning her focus to Grant and Marina, she stuck her chin out and sighed. Her hair would grow back, and hopefully her life would go on, and if it did – now it would be even richer, thanks to the two precious people ahead of her on the beach.

37

'Birthday cake for breakfast?' Marina's eyes were huge as she darted into the kitchen, hugging Raffy's floppy neck, her strawberry-covered pyjamas drooping around her narrow hips. 'Daddy said it was OK.'

Cassie laughed. 'Yes, little one. Only on your birthday, cake for breakfast is OK.' Cassie lifted the banana loaf that she'd baked and covered with a lemony butter icing. She wasn't much of a baker, but she was proud of the slightly uneven loaf, and when she'd pulled it out of the oven at 10 p.m. the night before, Grant had told her it was perfection. She'd snapped a picture of it and texted it to her mother, and Sadie had replied, *Well, look at you! Mary Berry eat your heart out*

While he had gone to wake Marina up, Cassie had stuck six of the little candles she'd found in the cake and lit a sparkler which she'd added just as Marina appeared, followed by Grant.

'Whoa, look at that.' He grinned. 'Spectacular.'

'Happy birthday, sweetheart.' Cassie carried the cake over to the dining table, where she'd laid three places and added pretty napkins.

Grant had been up early and lit the fire, and as the three of them sat at the dining table, two wrapped presents next to Marina's place, she shoved Raffy behind her back and clasped her hands together under her chin, the sparkler reflected in the sky-blue of her eyes.

'Right, cake first, then presents. Ready?' Cassie eyed Grant, who nodded, then they both began to sing 'Happy Birthday'.

Marina's face glowed as she stared at the sparkler, seeming to be mesmerised by the tiny arcs of light, and as soon as it fizzled out, she pointed at the candles. 'Can I blow?'

'Of course.' Cassie pushed the cake a little closer to her niece. 'And don't forget to make a wish.'

'What will I wish for?' Marina looked surprised.

'Anything you want, sweetheart, but you mustn't tell us what it is, or it won't come true.' Cassie recited exactly what her mother had told her, every year, a sweet reminder of Sadie's gentle love that made Cassie smile. In just a few days, Cassie would go back to see her mother, and with Grant at her side, they'd talk about her moving in with them. Cassie wasn't sure exactly how Sadie would react, but Cassie wanted her little family around her now. She hoped that Sadie would agree, the opportunity to spend more time with Marina a delightful incentive.

Marina's cheeks puffed out as she leaned over and blew with all her might, the candles sputtering, then going out.

'Well done.' Cassie smiled.

Marina joined in when they started to clap, her eyes flitting between Cassie and Grant, and her whole face taken over by a smile so beautiful that Cassie's heart felt full to bursting.

'Who wants cake?' She removed the candles, as Grant lifted one of the plates from the table.

'Me,' he and Marina chimed in perfect unison, Marina's hand going up as it might in class at school. 'A big piece,' she added.

As they sat in their pyjamas, eating cake, and drinking tea, and juice, rain battering the windows and running in thick rivulets down the glass, Cassie let herself imagine Isla sitting with them, watching her daughter turn six. Cassie wondered how many changes Isla would see in the little girl. If she'd feel that Cassie was doing a good job caring for Marina, easing her through her grief and into her new life in Edinburgh. As Cassie took a mouthful of cake, the lemon icing leaving a pleasant tang on her tongue, she sent a silent wish of her own out into the ether.

Ten minutes later, Marina was tearing into the gift that Grant had carefully wrapped the night before. As the paper floated to the floor and she grabbed the box, she squealed. 'Thanks.' Then she lifted the box and shook it. 'What is it?'

Grant laughed, reaching over and helping her open the box. 'It's a Stamp A Scene kit.' He locked eyes with Cassie, who was smiling as she cleared the table. 'See all these different wooden stamps? You use the ink pads inside and then you can design a garden, with all these flowers, and the creatures who come to play there.' He pointed at the lid, which was beautifully illus-trated with four elegant fairies, a path of fairy dust, the sun and moon, a pond covered in glossy lily pads, a colourful bird and various other woodland creatures.

'Where will I make it?' She was lifting the stamps out and setting them on the table.

'We'll use a big piece of plain paper and then you can put the stamps wherever you like.' He nodded as Cassie came back to the table. 'Maybe we can help you with the first one, then you can make as many as you want.'

Cassie sat down and pulled a fresh mug of tea towards her. She was dying to give Marina her present, but at the same time didn't want to detract from the fun that the child was already having.

As Cassie sipped her tea, watching Marina examining each stamp, then carefully placing them back in the box, Grant caught her eye. Turning to Marina, he said, 'OK, kiddo. How about you open your present from Aunty Cassie now?'

'OK.' Marina scanned the table, spotting the little box wrapped in silver tissue paper, with a silky yellow ribbon tied around it.

Cassie smiled her thanks to Grant, for his sensitivity, and slid the box across the table to Marina. 'Happy birthday, my love.'

Marina shoved her mane of hair over her shoulder and then let her fingers rest on the bow for a moment. Cassie caught a flash of sadness in the dark-rimmed eyes, and then Marina said softly, 'Yellow is my mummy's favourite colour.'

Cassie nodded, marvelling at the depth of emotional intelligence that her niece was already capable of. The appropriateness of Isla being remembered, right at this special moment, was both heartbreaking and perfect. 'Yes, I know, sweetheart. She loved daffodils and goldfinches and always hogged the yellow fruit pastilles.'

Nodding, Marina's eyes cleared, and she tugged the ribbon off, ripped the tissue away and lifted the lid of the box.

Cassie had covered the bracelet with a layer of the packing foam they used on all their pieces of jewellery, but seeing Marina's puzzled frown, Cassie realised that she needed to explain. 'Lift that up, and your present is underneath.' She pointed at the foam, nodding encouragingly.

Marina pulled the foam away and gasped. 'Hearts.' She looked over at Cassie, her eyes alight.

'Yes. I made it specially.' Cassie walked around the table and crouched at Marina's side. 'Shall I put it on for you?' She lifted the bracelet from the pad and let it dangle in front of Marina.

'What's that?' Marina pointed at the tanzanite in the clasp. 'Is it a diamond?' Her eyes were wide with wonder.

'It's called a tanzanite, and comes all the way from Tanzania, in East Africa.' Cassie wrapped the bracelet around Marina's wrist and closed the little padlock clasp. 'It's a special stone that people who were born in December wear.'

Marina held her arm out, staring at the bracelet. 'It's pretty.' She waggled her wrist back and forth. 'It's like a grown-up's.'

Cassie stood up and dropped a kiss on the top of Marina's head, glancing over at Grant, who was hugging his coffee mug to his chest, before she went on. 'Yes, it is. Because you're getting to be a big girl now, and if we always make sure the clasp is closed properly, and you only wear it on special occasions, you won't lose it.'

Marina nodded. 'Can I wear it to Polly's party?' She tipped her head to the side as if considering her next statement.

Taken aback at the mention of a party she knew nothing about, Cassie nodded, then mouthed 'what the heck' to Grant, who shrugged. 'Absolutely. When is Polly's party?' Cassie asked.

'Her birthday is near Christmas, and she says Santa comes.' Marina nodded to herself as Cassie let the significance of what she was hearing permeate. That Marina wanted to go to a party felt momentous, a giant leap forward in her healing, and as Cassie swallowed over a nut of gratitude, Grant read her expression like a book and smiled.

'Can I make one for Polly?' Marina shook her wrist again.

Cassie cleared her throat. 'Of course. When we go home to Edinburgh, we'll go into the studio, and Uncle Syd can help us, too.'

Marina nodded enthusiastically. 'Can he come for tea again?' She fingered the bracelet, her lips pursing as she twisted it around her wrist, and then she slid off the chair. 'He's so funny.'

'Sure, he can come.' Grant reached for Marina and drew her onto his knee. 'We'll have another birthday party when we get home, and Granny Sadie, Syd, Hector and Polly can all come.'

Cassie raised her eyebrows. 'Well, guess who can make the cake for that one?' She moved behind Grant's chair and playfully clasped her fingers around his neck.

'No problem. I'm a dab hand at cake.' He laughed. 'Not.'

By noon, the rain had still not stopped, and they had moved into the living room, where Marina knelt at the coffee table happily stamping random figures on the piece of art paper Cassie had given her.

Cassie was sitting on the rug, with her back to the fire, and Grant was facing the window, swiping through the news on his phone. Sighing contentedly, she leaned forward, her elbows on her knees, and let the warmth of the fire reach a little lower down her back. The heat was soothing and as she closed her eyes, hearing only the soft thump of the stamps, and the tick of the clock on the mantel, she let the peace of the moment seep into her. In three more days, she would speak to Doctor Carnegie, and find out what came next, but for now, this perfect moment was all she wanted to focus on.

She had planned a simple dinner that evening and then, after Marina was in bed, a quiet night for her and Grant, and as she pictured them sitting together, having been in their pyjamas for the entire day, something she'd never allowed herself to do before, she laughed softly. With everything that had happened, and the way her life had changed so dramatically, in a matter of months, this simple act of self-indulgent relaxation seemed like growth, and she liked the way that made her feel.

38

Grant had read to Marina while Cassie tidied the kitchen and poured brandy into the two glasses that she'd brought with her, this time. As he came back into the living room, she lit the large white cathedral candle that sat on the coffee table, then curled up on the sofa.

Grant put two more logs on the fire, accepted the brandy she held out to him, then settled next to her. 'I think she had a good birthday.' He tapped his glass gently against Cassie's. 'Well done, Aunty Cassie.'

Cassie lay her hand on his thigh. 'Well done, us. But I must admit, I cracked it with the cake, surprisingly.' She chuckled.

Grant pulled her closer into his side and kissed her temple. 'Nothing you do surprises me, anymore.' She felt the prickle of his unshaved cheek against hers.

Cassie enjoyed the burn of the brandy as she held some on her tongue, then, as she shifted to lay her head on his shoulder, a twist of hair floated down onto her lap. Gathering it up, she sighed. 'Will you still fancy me when I'm bald?'

Grant hadn't noticed what had happened, but now he looked at her balled-up fist. 'Of course. Bald. Fat. Skinny. Sick.

Grumpy. There's nothing that you can do, or be, that will scare me away, Cassie. You're stuck with me.'

She closed her eyes and breathed deeply, the woodsmoke tangy and warm inside her nose. 'Ditto.' She nodded against his shoulder. 'Stuck like glue.' As she said what she and Isla had used to say to one another, an image of her sister's face floated into Cassie's mind – Isla's tentative smile, so often hiding something painful. 'Do you think we let Isla down, Grant?' She straightened up, feeling him tensing next to her.

'*I* did, certainly.' He leaned forward and put his glass on the table. 'I never forgave myself for basically taking advantage of her that night. Using her like a Band-Aid on my self-pity.' He shook his head sadly. 'I was a selfish sod, but how do *you* feel you let her down?'

'I didn't understand how much pain she was in. I would get impatient with her and tell her to get a grip, when inside she was crumbling.' She paused. 'I was her sister. Her twin. I should have known what was really going on. Been more sensitive. Compassionate.' Her throat began to tighten as he circled her shoulders with his arm and pulled her back into his side.

'You're being too hard on yourself, Cassie. You were a child, too.' He swept the hair from her forehead with his finger. 'We were all so young.'

Cassie wished his reassurance was enough to wash away the guilt that still plagued her, but as she felt its familiar tug, she knew she had to do more than let herself off the hook, that easily. 'What if we did something to honour her? Something that would help others who struggle the way she did.' She turned to face Grant. 'We could set up a foundation for mental health, in her name, here on Lewis.' The idea was taking flight, even as she gave it life. 'If she'd had more support right here, in the place she felt the safest, maybe...' She gulped, still unable to shake the thought that rather than the pull of an undercurrent, perhaps a toxic mix of guilt and regret had caused Isla to walk into the sea that day. 'We need to do more than just remember her, and care for her daughter, Grant. We both owe her more.'

Grant scanned her face, his mouth rippling as he considered what she'd said. Then, he took her hand. 'I think that would be a perfect way to honour her.' He stroked her palm. 'Maybe Ian Bannister can help us figure out how to set it up?'

Cassie got up and stood with her back to the fire, a bubble of excitement making her face tingle. 'Yes, I'm sure he could point us in the right direction.'

Grant stood and joined her at the fire, his arm circling her waist. 'Let's phone him tomorrow.'

It was as if a light had turned on inside her, casting its gilded beams into the darkest parts of her heart – its warmth healing the cracks it found. They would do this for Isla – create the legacy that she had been denied. There was no way to go back, with any part of life, but there were ways to move forward that now, finally, felt right.

As Cassie felt Grant's arm around her, the beat of his heart at her side, she knew that there was nothing she couldn't take on, and that feeling was as precious to her as her new little family had become. She would not let them down. She'd be the partner, mother, daughter and friend they needed, and deserved, and no one and nothing, not even cancer, would get in her way.

She turned to face Grant, her eyes glittering. 'I love you, Grant.' She held his face between her palms. 'So much.' She rose onto tiptoe and kissed him, tasting the brandy on his tongue.

'I love you, too.' He looked mildly surprised at her sudden declaration, but joy took over as he pulled her closer and kissed her again.

As they stood in the firelight, listening to the gentle tick of the clock and the soft hiss of the glowing embers, Cassie heard a shuffling from across the room. Turning around, she saw

Marina coming towards them, her hair matted behind her head as she ground a fist into her eye. 'Can't you sleep, little one?' Cassie beckoned to Marina, who squeezed in between them.

'I was dreaming about Mummy. She was on the beach with us.' There was a tinge of sadness in her voice, but not the crippling grief that Cassie had heard five months ago, when she'd first been here on Lewis with her niece.

'That's lovely.' Cassie cupped Marina's chin in her palm, as Grant put his arm around Marina, closing the circle. 'What were we doing?' Cassie asked.

Marina took a second, then lifted her chin. 'Flying the kite.' She blinked, then dropped her head, pressing her forehead into Cassie's middle.

Cassie's eyes snapped to Grant's, as he smiled sadly back at her. 'Well, maybe we can fly it tomorrow, if the rain goes off?' Cassie said.

Grant nodded as Marina leaned back from them, a tiny smile curving her lips.

'Can we always fly it when we come here?' She yawned, her thumb going into her mouth.

Cassie gripped the back of Grant's arm, taking a moment to reply. 'Yes, we'll always fly it, and each time we do, we'll think about your mummy being here with us, running along the beach and watching it soar.' Cassie made a swooping motion with her free hand. 'She'll always be with us, Marina. Always loved, and never forgotten.' She tucked a long strand of hair behind Marina's ear. 'Now, I think it's time you went back to bed.' She stepped away from the fire, her hand held out.

Marina slid her fingers into Cassie's, then she found Grant's hand, too.

'Can we all read *Green Eggs* together?' Marina looked up at them, an expression of pure innocence and anticipation that tugged directly at Cassie's heart.

'Yes, we can read it together.' Cassie smiled at her niece.

Above Marina's head, Grant's eyes were gently asking if this was OK.

Seeing the tentative expression and feeling the depth of his caring surround them all, Cassie nodded. 'We'll read it together, every night from now on.'

'When we're in our house in Edinburgh, too?' Marina tugged their hands, leading them towards the hall. Her referral to *our house* caught Cassie slightly off guard, but that Marina was obviously referring to Grant's place was yet another gift that Cassie had not been expecting.

'Yes, there too.' She nodded, seeing Grant blot his eyes on the sleeve of his T-shirt.

As she helped Marina back into bed, handing *Green Eggs and Ham* to Grant, who was sitting at the end of the bed, Cassie smiled. 'You start, and I'll finish.'

His eyebrows lifted. 'Are you sure?' He took the book from her and looked down at it, then back at her face.

'Yes, I've never been surer of anything, in my life.' She nodded, the knowledge that she entirely believed that, with every piece of her heart, everything she needed.

EPILOGUE
ONE YEAR LATER

Grant wiped Sadie's glasses with a soft cloth and handed them back to her. 'Ready?'

She inspected them, then slipped them on, her red-rimmed eyes darting to the door where Marina was standing, looking out at Uig Bay. 'Not really.' Sadie shook her head, her lip trembling.

Grant sighed, picked up the two identical boxes from the dining table and tucked them into his pockets. 'We'll do it together.' He held his arm out to Sadie, who hooked hers around it, her bony fingers gripping him through his thick jacket.

Marina was standing still, her back to them, as Grant approached.

'Ready, sweetheart?' He laid his hand on her shoulder, seeing the kite dangling at her leg.

'Yes,' she whispered, then looked up at him.

Grant looked down into duplicates of his own eyes. 'You look nice.' Marina wore a bright blue sweater over her jeans, then a multicoloured, striped scarf that he'd tied in a loose knot at her throat. Her red coat was getting too small for her now, but she loved it, so Grant had let her keep it, especially for today.

The wind was gusting across the patio as they made their way carefully down to the beach. The sky was clear, aside from a few fluffy clouds that masked the weak December sun, and the brine of the sea floated across the sand, bringing with it so many memories that Grant had to halt a moment, to steady himself.

As they reached the sand and began walking towards the water, Sadie dropped his arm and edged ahead with Marina, and seeing their backs moving away from him, his thumb instantly went to his wedding ring, gently turning it around his finger. He was still not used to wearing it, but now he pictured it acting like a lightning rod, drawing all the pain from his heart down through his fingertips and out into the breeze.

Marina turned to face him, the kite moulding itself to her middle, pressed in by the gusts of wind that were now buffeting the beach. 'Here?'

Grant nodded. 'Looks good to me.' He walked over to them, seeing Sadie surreptitiously wiping her nose, then stuffing the tissue into her pocket. 'Right. Shall we get this baby up in the air?' He gently took the kite from Marina and unravelled some of the string. 'Ready to run?'

Marina nodded, her bottom lip trembling.

'OK, Granny Sadie, watch this.' He smiled at his daughter. 'Ready, steady, go.' As they ran along the shoreline, the kite instantly being pulled up into the wind, Grant watched Marina, her eyes on the butterfly above them and her mouth slightly open. As the kite lifted, dipped again, then cut straight up into the sky, they stopped running, and both staring upwards, he handed the spindle to Marina. 'Here, you can do this now.'

She glanced over at him, her eyes full of tears, as she took the spindle and carefully let out more string. 'It's really high.' She tipped her head back. 'Wow.' Her voice was tugged away on the breeze.

Grant stayed close to her side but gave her enough space to

lose herself in what she was doing, the only gift he could give her today that might ease her suffering. As for his own, he knew of nothing that would help, and for now, that was OK. He needed to feel it, to breathe through it, because if he didn't, he might not find his way out the other side.

Sadie was standing a few feet away, and when Marina turned to see if her grandmother was watching, Sadie waved. 'Well done, pet.' She gave Marina a thumbs up. 'Keep going.'

Grant smiled gratefully at his mother-in-law, his heart breaking for all the loss that she had endured – more than any person should have to face. That they were living as a family now was a saving grace, and every day Grant acknowledged the rightness of the decision he and Cassie had made, more than a year ago.

As the kite began to sink, the wings bending upwards as it floated down to the sand, Grant put his hand in his pocket, his fingers finding the edge of one of the boxes. The next step would be the hardest part of this day, and as he pulled the box out, he looked down at it, his vision blurring.

On the lid written in thick black pen, in Cassie's distinctive hand, was the name Isla Jane Hunter, the H leaning forward, as if into the wind. Holding the box close to his chest, he pulled out the second one and closed his eyes for a second before looking at the lid. Here he saw his own handwriting, the words Cassie Isabelle Henderson, and the date, 28 November.

As his chest ached so much that he took a step backwards, Sadie moved in next to him, her hand on his shoulder. 'All right, son. Let's do it now.' She sniffed, but Grant heard the strength in her voice, something he had not expected, and yet, thinking about his wife, and how she had coped with the last, challenging months of her life, he should not have been surprised.

He held Sadie's gaze for a moment, then nodded. 'Right.'

Together with Marina, they walked to the water's edge and, crouching down, with his back to the wind, Grant handed Isla's ashes to Sadie. They'd talked this through, and Sadie had wanted to scatter them, saying that Grant should do the same for Cassie, and as he watched, Sadie held the box in her palm, lifted it to her lips and kissed the lid, then carefully took the top off.

Marina was at Grant's side, her hand in his, as they watched Sadie turn the box upside down, a cloud of ash being lifted into the wind, just as the clouds moved away and the sun lit the beach, highlighting the pristine white of the sand. 'Rest easy, my love,' Sadie called into the wind. 'You will always be loved.'

Grant wiped his eyes with his thumb, and did the same for Marina, then let out a juddering sigh, before he knelt down and eased the lid off the other box. He looked at the soft grey grains inside and clenched his teeth. This was not how he'd remember Cassie, or how he'd have wanted to say his last goodbye, but this had been her wish and he would honour that.

Taking a breath, he turned the box upside down and stood up as the grey cloud was lifted by the wind, rising like a flock of birds before scattering into thousands of tiny dots that disappeared into the sky. 'I'll always love you, Cass.' His voice gave way as he dropped his chin to his chest.

Next to him, Marina was crying, fat tears gliding down her cheeks. 'I want Mummy, and Aunty Cassie.' She sobbed. 'I'm so sad, I want to go home.'

Seeing the agony on her young face, his own pain had to be muted, for now, so he gathered himself and drew her into his side. 'I know, love. Me too. Come on. Let's walk a little.' He took her hand, then beckoned to Sadie, who slowly joined them. 'You know that I love you, and that you will never be alone, Marina. We will always miss and love your mummy and Aunty Cassie and we'll never forget them. But we are a family now.' He looked over at Sadie, who was wiping her cheeks with her palm. 'And we'll take care of each other, forever.' He squeezed Marina's hand.

'Promise?' Her breath hitched.

'Promise.' He nodded. 'And remember what Aunt Cassie always said about promises?'

Marina swallowed, then whispered, 'We never break them, no matter what.'

'Exactly.' He found a smile. 'So, every time we come here, we'll fly the kite and think of them both, and that way they'll stay with us always.'

Sadie patted his arm. 'You're a good man, Grant.' She gave him a watery smile. 'I'm grateful that Cassie had you in her life.'

Unable to speak, Grant took a moment, then whispered, 'I was the lucky one, Sadie.'

A LETTER FROM ALISON

Dear reader,

My heartfelt thanks for reading *The Child Between Us*. I hope you enjoyed it. If you would like to keep up to date with all my latest releases, just sign up at the following link. Your email address will never be shared, and you can unsubscribe at any time.

www.bookouture.com/alison-ragsdale

This idea for this story came from the experiences of two mothers I know and love, and whose strength has been an inspiration to me for much of my life. It was also inspired by my remarkable sisters. The bond that we have goes beyond genetics and runs deeper than friendship, too. I am so fortunate to have two best friends in my sisters, and I'm thankful for them every single day.

While Cassie and Isla's story is about betrayal, the gravity of secrets, and their consequences, it is also a tale of love and forgiveness that explores the deeply woven bonds of family and siblings.

Thanks again for choosing to read *The Child Between Us*. If you enjoyed it, it would mean the world if you would take a moment to write a review. They are a great way to introduce new readers to my books, so I'd be truly grateful.

I love to hear from my readers, and you can connect with

me through my Facebook author page, Instagram, Twitter, Goodreads, or my website. I look forward to hearing from you.

Thanks again for reading.

All the best,

Alison Ragsdale

www.alisonragsdale.com

facebook.com/authoralisonragsdale

twitter.com/AlisonRagsdale

instagram.com/alisonragsdalewrites

ACKNOWLEDGEMENTS

Thank you to my wonderful publisher, Bookouture. They are a dream team of consummate professionals, and I'm privileged to work with them. Special thanks to my editor, Kelsie, for her support, and expertise, and for working patiently with me to get deep inside these characters' heads and share their stories.

Thanks also to Ruth T, Natasha, Lauren, Kim, Noelle, Peta, Mandy, Jade, Anne, and everyone who helped this story make its way into the world. I am so grateful to be working with you all.

I was fortunate to have Heather Glen, an expert in Scottish family law, to consult on the legal aspects of this story. Thank you for taking the time in your busy schedule to make sure that I didn't put my foot in my mouth. Also, thanks a million to Jennifer McCulloch, for her invaluable input on the Scottish school system and support resources.

As always, a special thank you to Lesley and Carly, my sisters, and my rocks. Your opinions mean the world to me.

Thank you also to all the family, friends, readers, reviewers, book bloggers, my Highlanders Club members and ARC crew who unfailingly support me and my books. You are my book-family, and you make my writing life better, just by being part of it.

Finally, to my husband. Thank you for being my first reader, gentlest critic, and my staunchest supporter. I wouldn't want to do this without you.

Made in the USA
Las Vegas, NV
17 October 2022

57548650R00184